INTERRUPTIONS

INTERRUPTIONS

LOVE, CHAOS & REVOLUTION IN IRAN

A NOVEL BY
MASSUD ALEMI

IBEX PUBLISHERS,
BETHESDA, MARYLAND

Interruptions: Love, Chaos & Revolution in Iran
A Novel by Massud Alemi

Copyright © 2008 Massud Alemi

Cover illustration taken from a photograph of Evin Prison in Tehran.
Photograph of author by Jeff Lautenberger.

All rights reserved. No part of this book may be reproduced or retransmitted in any manner whatsoever except in the form of a review, without permission from the publisher.

Manufactured in the United States of America

The paper used in this book meets the minimum requirements of the American National Standard for Information Services—Permanence of Paper for Printed Library Materials, ANSI Z39.48–1984

Ibex Publishers strives to create books which are complete and free of errors as possible. Please help us with future editions by reporting any errors or suggestions for improvement to the address below or: corrections@ibexpub.com

Ibex Publishers, Inc.
Post Office Box 30087
Bethesda, Maryland 20824
Telephone: 301–718–8188
Facsimile: 301–907–8707
www.ibexpublishers.com

Library of Congress Cataloging-in-Publication Data

Alemi, Massud.
 Interruptions : love, chaos and revolution in Iran : a novel / by Massud Alemi.
     p. cm.
 ISBN-13:   978-1-58814-049-4 (hardcover : alk. paper)
 ISBN-10:   1-58814-049-0 (hardcover : alk. paper)
 1. Iran—History--Revolution, 1979—Fiction.   I. Title.
 PS3601.L3535I58 2008
 813'.6—dc22   2007027575

To my parents,
who gave a great deal and not merely life.

in·ter·rupt (in't• rupt'), *v. t.* **1.** to cause or make a break in the continuity or uniformity of (a course, process, condition, etc.). **2.** to break off or cause to cease, as in the middle of something. **3.** to stop (a person) in the midst of doing or saying something, esp. by an interjected remark. **4.** to cause a break or discontinuance; interfere with action or speech.

ONE

Farzin Rouhani would remember the last day of spring 1981 as the first time reality warped. He would recall that Tehran's air was so hot and immobile a dropped feather fell like a rock. By then he had developed the habit of going over to see Bijan in his apartment halfway across town. Farzin had the route memorized by then. Turn the corner from Vali-e Asr onto Shaheed Beheshti Avenue, and he would be but five blocks away from wicked bliss. Only on June 20, 1981, the baking street indulged more people than usual, and the sun staked sharp streaks of pain into his skull. The heat was treacherous, dry, and scorching. Shaheed Beheshti lay barren and treeless, while buildings shimmered in the heat rising off the softening asphalt, stamped by tire tracks every which way.

Just before Farzin decided to leap over the open curbside gutter, a youthful swarm of men and women, numbering in the thousands, came into his full view. They had sprung up from nowhere, like mushrooms after warm summer rains. Holding placards and banners, women chanted slogans while around them patrols of stone-faced youths with armbands formed a human chain. Farzin shielded his eyes with his hand in an army salutation, frozen in time. At the outer edges they held hands, determined as organized workers at a May Day parade. It was a juvenile crowd, restive and militant. *The Counterrevolution?*

Backing off, Farzin waited for a gap in the long procession, but there was no end to it. With every fresh surge there was a man or a woman leading the chant, "Censorship, oppression, freedom...."

Then, out of the blue, a mob of bearded motorcyclists, dressed in black, appeared from the opposite end of the street, their engines at full throttle. They bore green banners, a sure sign of the Hezbollah, the uncompromising arm of the Revolutionary Forces, wailing a chant over and over again, "Only one party—of Allah; only one leader—Ruhollah." The bearded men were intent and purposeful as they moved, in unison, like a black mass, swinging chains and clubs. No sooner had they arrived than the harrowing screams began. As Farzin watched, the black mass dealt with the unarmed demonstrators, now to the right, now to the left, like a giant bulldozer, never looking back.

An edge of terror in the air made Farzin's scalp crawl. Vanguards of the cyclists chased the crowd, which at this point pushed toward the pavement, thrusting Farzin backward until he felt the coarseness of the wall behind him. At the center of the roaring mob was a middle-aged man, who sat on the back of a Yamaha with one hand around the driver's waist and one hand holding a powerful megaphone. In the middle of gas fumes and the whacking of clubs against softer heads he loudly and unapologetically urged the cyclists on, saying, "Hypocrites are doomed; Islam is victorious." His followers repeated after him, "Hypocrites are doomed … Islam is victorious."

Avoiding the cyclists, Farzin lingered on the perimeter of the swarm, attempting to wade through. He had left home early to drown himself in Bijan's understanding embrace. And he was now only five blocks away—just five blocks, and if he could bypass this drama, he could be there in no time at all. He felt the dampness of his palms and rubbed them on the sides of his pants.

The circle closed in. A fully bearded cyclist in army fatigues dismounted. Though he was clad in army green, his wispy bangs hinted this was no soldier. Farzin watched him lock up his bike and stand with his feet apart, a hand in his pocket. Directly across from him, a man was standing just as confidently on the other side of the street. They could almost have been twins: same boots, same bangs, and the same focused look in their eyes. Both appeared to be searching for someone.

Farzin turned around, debating the wisdom of even attempting to cross the street at this point. Perhaps he could find a different way, or chart a different route, to Bijan's house. The trouble he had to go through. *Of course Bijan was worth it.* This mess would give them something to discuss later. He looked back but the man was no longer there, although his bike was. Farzin was anxious and suspicious as he stepped into the street. At that same moment, he felt hands touching his waist and upper torso from behind. It was the kind of touching that people might do when passing each other in a crowd—only more intimately. Rough but trained, the hands vanished just as quickly as they had appeared. Farzin wondered if someone was checking him for weapons—*but why?* The cyclists were still chanting, "Get lost, bastard hypocrites. Enough …. Enough whoring for the West!" They threatened, "Go home, or we'll do to you what will make the birds weep!"

Momentarily, Farzin caught sight of a cyclist who disembarked from his vehicle to pick up a brick from the gutter. His intention was all too obvious. Within seconds the brick was airborne. Soon, others followed. Flying bricks slowly twisted and turned as though self propelled. Occasionally they were accompanied by rocks that flew high and far into the march. Farzin pulled back, not knowing which way to turn. But even at the perimeter, there was no safety. Fists and feet danced in a hysterical flurry and, in response to them, clubs rose and plunged with merciless whacks. The human chain finally broke. There was a pattern to the Hezbollahi club-wielders' attack like the dance of bees—an unmediated, impulsive animal reaction to an irritant. The march coiled upon itself like a cobra; the rhymed chants merged into a timorous bellow, as the floating anxiety peaked; thumping footsteps joined the cries and shouts.

The motorcycles' parade ended in a full-throttle fury of fumes. Abandoning their vehicles, bikers gathered double file on the skin of the march, and cut across the crowd, still shouting belligerent slogans. "When my leader commands," they roared, "blood I will shed."

Bijan still on his mind, Farzin cursed his entanglement in this mess. Meanwhile, war clubs clattered on the roofs and sides of parked cars and slammed against soft flesh. It was beginning to seem impossible to cross through the mayhem. The bearded man in army fatigues had managed to cut through to the other side, though. Farzin watched him playing with a toothpick in his mouth, leaning sideways against a yellow phone booth. *How had he crossed the street?* As the bedlam neared a crescendo, Farzin found himself in the middle of the demonstration, at the heart of the action. Air and the sky, all became one angry song. Now the marchers began to form demands, broken and rhythmic, "Oppression, tyranny ... People, you must rise ... Rise." This was Tehran at daggers drawn. Even in the days of the revolution, Farzin had not been this fearful; there had been some order to it, then. You could part with the demonstration and go home anytime you fancied.

A single gunshot rang out, then another, reverberating against the buildings. The demonstrators held on steadfastly as a barrage of shooting began in a wild cacophony. Farzin found himself being hustled along by the throng as it swayed this way and that. It became impossible to differentiate the Hezbollah members from the marchers, motorcycles from knives and chains, smoke from dust, clubs from kicks, and blood from sweat.

It was at this precise moment when, for the first time, Farzin had the odd and inexplicable sensation of the world turning syrupy and slow flowing. To be sure it was to repeat itself twice more, but June 20 was the first time reality had warped in no uncertain terms, time slowed to a crawl, and nothing happening made any sense. As he looked about, people were still marching but took their steps gingerly, their dancelike effort now an exercise in vanity. Even the cyclists, their bloodshot eyes radiating hatred, raised their fists as if under water. Silent fury oozed from them.

Pamphlets blanketed the asphalt. A swish of a shining blade slashed the heat. Farzin caught only a glimpse of steel before it buried itself in a woman's chest, slowly, ever so slowly, slitting her body open right before his eyes. He looked at himself to inspect his own reaction and noticed his body exhibiting the same languor as its surroundings. He returned his attention to the young woman. The vertical wound administered with the skill of a butcher was on display in vivid detail, but caught as he was in the slowness, he could not escape the imposing dynamics of the world around him. He followed the hand holding the switchblade; it belonged to a boy with the silky beginnings of sideburns, looking horrified and nearly as baffled as his victim. Blood soaked the woman's clothes and stained the pamphlets strewn about her. Farzin stood less than eight feet away and could see beyond the fat of her bosom, the red of muscles, and the white of her ribs. He was so close he could smell the blood gushing to the beat of her pulse. Two steps and he could touch her. Instead, he stared at her trembling figure, which seemed at first glance resisting the temptation to fall. Marchers noticed but kept their distance, carrying on the struggle. The young woman certainly understood that—she would have done the same. Wavering, she raised her hands and held her fingers outward to display her chest spewing, as if her lodged spirit were struggling furiously to be set free. "Look at me! Be warned that only blood will nourish the struggle." And they understood.

There was a sudden and reverent silence in the street now. It was as if people were watching an asteroid or a car crash—an incredible event over which they had no control. The only reaction worthy of the incident seemed to be to clear away, leaving her standing in the middle of a circle. She closed her eyes on her stunned peers, as if to focus on an internal tug of war. An irrepressible fright released itself into the noon swelter, percolating to the edges of the march. Farzin's eyes were fixed on the deep cut in her chest. She took one step his way, half-stumbling, half-resisting, and he saw her chalk-white face twitching with pain and her right hand, stained crimson, trembling as she tried to cover her wound. Then, just as she slumped to the ground like a bundle of newspapers, Farzin, quite inadvertently, reached out and grabbed her sweat-drenched head, preventing it from crashing onto the bone-dry asphalt.

The young woman's fall marked the end of the dreamy sequence of events. The world sped up to its normal velocity and the noises were heard again at the chaotic levels of moments ago. Farzin noticed all the eyes staring at him, holding in his hands the drenched head of the assaulted woman. He slowly laid it down and backed away a step as he rose to his feet. He felt as though he had awakened from a deep slumber. The woman's body jerked once, but her eyes were closed. The cyclists had started again behind the gathered crowd.

Out of the ensuing devastation a skinny youth with a long neck, a bulging Adam's apple, and an armband came forth and examined the young woman like a doctor. He produced a checkered cloth from his backpack. Hastily he wrapped her in the sheet, first the legs, then the chest and head. Her eyes moved under half-closed lids. Gathering her in his arms, like a groom carrying his bride on their nuptial evening, the skinny fellow disappeared as Farzin watched—a fait accompli; she had played her part, now was offstage.

In a fleeting second, as he gained his full composure, strong grips tightened around Farzin's arms and wrists. He felt the poking of a hard object in his back and a sinking in his heart. An imperious voice warned him against the very thought of fighting back. Not that he would have, otherwise.

Two

After the downfall of the monarchy, there came to power a cluster of oblivious nationalists who, in cahoots with cruel mullahs, submitted to a backward theocracy. Their submission was hesitant at first but gained heart as they went along. They were aided in this by the hooligan *lutis*[*] who put the fear of God in the populace. Tehran, that old sprawling maze of hot streets bathed in smog and abused by bad drivers, metamorphosed into an exhibition of fanatic fervor. The fast-moving events leading up to the demise of the monarchy had peaked in a head-spinning, collective euphoria for most West-leaning professionals. A handful of intellectuals, who had not bought into the whole charade, were just as happy to see the aged repressive order crumble, though they were wary of the unfolding of a new one. At this point in the sham, however, the challenge of political instability had worn off. Now the unpredictable air of the revolution's first year was supplanted by inevitable violence that spilled into the streets.

It was the uncertainty of those days in 1981 that made every scene and gesture so memorable. Colleges and universities were shut down as part of a plan to fight foreign influence, irresponsible behavior, and immoral thoughts. With nowhere to go, college students were shepherded into K–12 schools to replace the expelled "reactionary" teachers, who, in the grim years of monarchy, had been "poisoning the minds of the youth."

A thin film of dust covered the furniture in Professor Rezaii's office on the shut-down campus of Tehran University, where a group of recruits briefly met, fulfilling their training requirements

---

[*] *Lutis* are street toughs associated with the bazaar and the mosque.

to substitute for ousted teachers. Everything in the room was either gray or brown and smelled of mothballs. As in cramped and musty secondhand bookstores, a fine dust had become part of things. It settled on wooden chairs with faux-leather upholstery, on books and stationery, and sank into the folds of the only window's faded curtains.

Young and eager to accomplish their mission, four men and seven women took their seats. The women, in loose-fitting headscarves, had bright faces, lightly made up. The men were all too serious, with shirt buttons fastened up to the collar.

The professor's spiritless demeanor betrayed his indifference toward the project. All the same, it was in that professor's seminar that Farzin Rouhani felt a certain warm sensation when another young man brushed his thigh against him. He had always felt a curious attraction toward athletic men his own age. Farzin liked their sweaty brows and straight backs, strong shoulders and biceps; cocksure and virile men, they were often boisterous and crass. But this fellow was quiet, and Farzin found him a distraction. His name was Bijan, and he was obviously self-assured and observant, with slanted eyes that seemed to be holding the world in derision. Farzin was emboldened by the sudden dynamism developing between them, sensing a positive and yet subtle reciprocity.

In time Farzin learned where Bijan lived and one balmy morning found himself standing outside his apartment. Butterflies danced in his stomach as he pressed the doorbell. The pretext of his visit was to go over their text and training manual, which was accomplished rather quickly. Afterward they sat around smoking cigarettes, discussing the postrevolutionary arts. From the beginning, Farzin found his host unpredictable and full of energy. As it turned out, the attraction was mutual. Thinking back on that day, Farzin could not recall the exact sequence of the give-and-take, fleeting glances, hand gestures, shifting bodies, the dizzying waft of mint breath, clammy hands, and the pressure of lips. What he would later remember was the intensity of his desire and the daring of the moment. Yes, the daring of the moment, if nothing else. Bijan personified the fluidity of that unspeakable passion that pulled at and gratified all senses. He was a mysterious world unto himself, the quick wit, cataclysmic neurosis, the hastening of the muscular slope of the lower back, the pungent smell of yearning. The men managed to pass several secretive hours together with hardly a conversation between them, a feat that was to repeat itself over and over that spring.

Three

Farzin Rouhani was now in control of his senses, more or less. As he tried to explain that there had been a mistake, his pulse began to hammer.

"Are you kidding?" he said defensively. "I'm not in with this crowd." And he heard, "Sure you're not." Frustrated, he protested mildly but said nothing about his pending appointment with Bijan, who was waiting for him at that very instant.

His bearded captors seemed to sense his reluctance to go along with them and congratulated themselves for having caught a "fat one."

"Who're you calling a fat one, me?" Farzin said incredulously. *A mortal of so little consequence in the world who's got nothing to do with this thronging craze, an organism totally on its own? Therefore, since it doesn't matter what I do or believe, I never mingle with it, hardly, hardly ever. Me, who in the last few minutes drew the necessary lessons from having witnessed the knifing of a woman without getting disturbed much, after all, she being a human being whose breast had pumped out blood thinner than the crawling liquid in the gutter?*

"Now, move," they said. "We'll have time to talk later."

"But wait a minute," Farzin said. "This must be a joke; either that, or you are dead mistaken, or both, because I'm not the fellow you're looking for."

"Oh, you're not, are you?" one of the men replied.

"No, I'm not. What do I have in common with these punks? Tell me. Look, where is my banner, or the knot in my brow, where, where? Does it seem like I sympathize with a soul in this crowd, any one of whom has come here to yell and shout and go back home beaten to the bones, tired, sore-throated, sore-footed, knifed, and clubbed? Who are you calling a fat one? Who?"

His nervous ramblings were cut short as the men hurried Farzin to a side street, and a waiting black Mercedes-Benz, and shoved him inside. The revolutionary triplets followed him in, one in front, two in the back—one on each side of their captive. All hope to see Bijan evaporated as Farzin began to realize that he was being taken somewhere. He wondered how the day could get worse.

FOUR

As the car found its way out of the furor, Farzin weighed his options. There must have been some sort of logic to it all. They could not just pick up pedestrians haphazardly, at least not without accounting for their actions. So, there was a chance that it would all be cleared up and in the end they would apologize for troubling him. *And even if they did not admit to their mistake, it would still be all right, as long as they let me go.*

A shortwave radio crackled as the car steered away from the marchers. The driver turned the dials some but then shut it off with a grunt. Here and there the Guardians of the Islamic Revolution, the main component of the Revolutionary Forces, were rushing in the opposite direction. They made way for the car as it found its way into the traffic. Past Enqelab Avenue, cars huddled together; there was no trace of the protest march. The agent sitting to Farzin's right let out a loud belch and the sticky stench of decay and onion.

"Put your hands together," he commanded.

As Farzin pressed his palms in a Buddhist salute, the man slapped handcuffs on him, and his partner pulled a thick black cloth over Farzin's head. Farzin got but a waft of their offensive sweaty odors. It seemed that sweat and dirt were in style in those days of extreme inelegance.

It was a silent ride. For an hour the car wove impatiently through traffic. Farzin tried to make out the sounds of the street. Twice the car stopped; each time the driver got out for a few minutes, then came back, and the ride resumed. From the sound of it, they were heading in a southerly direction, toward the sordid shantytowns outside the city limits. They passed forsaken, half-constructed buildings and unattended development projects, many of which had been abandoned in fear of the revolution—relics of a past so readily lost in memories. Daylight was weakening.

The car came to its final halt in a dusty alley, and strong hands hauled the suspect out. Urgent questions tumbled upon each other in a flurry. Things needed to be sorted out, secrets divulged.

The questions flew at Farzin. "Quickly, your position and responsibilities, in detail."

"How many cadres under you?"

"Where's your safehouse?"

"Quickly, quickly. Who's your contact?"

"Names. We want names."

"Where and when is the next march taking place?"

"Guns …. What about guns? How many, and where are they stored?"

Five

It had cooled a tad; a gentle breeze chilled Farzin's skin. The musty blindfold was finally taken off. Amid shanties and abandoned makeshift huts, with no one in sight, Farzin Rouhani made up his mind to cooperate with his captors; whatever it was they wanted to know. *What secret codes are they speaking of? What do they mean by "position"?* Considering the nature of his dalliance with Bijan, words could play a tricky part. They wanted him to name persons unknown to him.

"But, please, I'm a teacher," he said. "I teach history."

One of the men, the one with bad breath, mumbled something to challenge the relevance of Farzin's occupation to his counterrevolutionary activities.

"Excuse me? What does *that* have to do with anything? The fact, gentlemen, remains that I am a teacher."

"And what business might a teacher have with the counterrevolutionary marchers, huh?" Stink Mouth replied.

All right, might have easily given in to certain "positions," but obviously they are referring to something else. Keep focused.

The men talked among themselves, but Farzin could not hear what they were saying. From the moment he was arrested, during the entire ride, and now in this dusty alley, they had been addressing him in the formal you, *shoma*, as opposed to the informal *to*, but there was a bitter sarcasm in their voices, which was meant to imply that none of his answers were believed. The Persian language is a lush province where a lot can be conveyed by the deliberate use of the wrong tone. Now it was time to make a jaunt across. They circled around Farzin, and one of them punched him in the stomach. As Farzin grimaced, another one reached over and unlocked the cuffs. The driver and one of the agents held Farzin upright, while the second agent punched him in the stomach. Doubled over in pain, Farzin was kicked in his chin and sent sprawling backward. Stink Mouth leaned on the car and looked toward the fast-descending sun.

The captive kneeled, coughing. He wished somehow to communicate with his captors. *Gentlemen, I gather material only from books, not from the streets. I teach history to four classes, fifty-five students per, and dissect dynasties, their foreign wars and internal feuds; I draw timetables and review battlefield strategies. Fifty-five sets of eyes and ears per classroom.*

His bruised lips felt numb; he sighed. The men must have concluded he was resisting them, because they started all over again. One dealt him a terrific blow to the head, and another slammed him in the chest, and this continued, one blow succeeding another. Their voices meshed and blended, until Farzin could no longer tell what they were saying. A ringing began to echo in his head, and a knot of pain made itself present in the pit of his stomach. A warm stream trickled down the corner of his mouth, painting his jaw on its way down his collar. When he bowed his head to save it from iron heels, little coins of blood, one here and one there, fell to the ground as if there were holes in his pockets. Then the assailants stopped.

All that was left was the ringing in his ear and the pain in his bones. Complete silence opened like a wound and there was that smell of putrid onion again. It was totally quiet, and it was soft where he landed. It felt like he was lying on a soft cloud, and there was his grim mother coming down an endless staircase, one step at a time.

Six

"You're not a teacher anymore, *yauroo*."[*] A voice echoed in Farzin's head. "Hear that?" Thus, Farzin Rouhani was summarily relieved of his job, so the burden of assaulting a teacher was lifted from the conscience of the Revolutionary Forces.

The voice assumed his victim could still hear. "The Central Committee will handle your case." A large shadow bent over to emphasize these words. "Yeah, the brothers there know how to deal with rats like you." Voices and grunts came from afar. They sounded to agree, and were congratulating each other. The handcuffs and the blindfold were put on again.

Stink Mouth picked him up and threw him into the back of the car, on the floor in the tight space between the front and back seats. He sat in the front. Two of the overcoat-wearing officers left on foot, and the dusty black car took off.

It was dark out, and the windows were down. Warm wind blew in, bringing the unconscious man to awareness. He managed to wiggle his blindfold up by pressing his head against the seat and pushing downward. Peeking from under the cloth, he was able to see a tiny portion of the starry sky. Floating in it was the moon, a reminder of the real world outside the car. He felt himself fainting.

Recovering his senses, Farzin gained his bearings. He found himself crouching on the floor, pain in his bones. The car cruised uptown along ubiquitous poplar and plane trees, through quiet, indifferent streets. The full moon gleamed, a drop of blood in the black ink of the sky. Up a little ramp, and they were in Yousefabad,

---

[*] *Yauroo* is a very colloquial manner of referring to another person.

a middle-class neighborhood in northern Tehran. The car swerved and pulled up to the curb at the corner of the square, in front of the Central Committee, a solemn division of the Revolutionary Forces. The barking of stray dogs echoed in nearby alleys. A guard stood casually by the entrance to the building, a cigarette between his fingers, exhaling a plume of smoke through his nose. Except for the yapping and howling of Yousefabadi curs, the night was quiet.

Inside the building it was brightly lit; aged paint was chipping off the walls. There were no administrators in sight. Dilapidated wooden furniture was scattered about the lobby, begging to be discarded. Stink Mouth directed Farzin to the duty officer's booth.

"Got you a fat one, here," Stink Mouth said. "We picked him up in the march. Busy little buggers running all over the place. You should've seen it."

The night officer seemed interested in a crust of dried blood on Farzin's forehead as it glimmered under the white light.

"Like I said, they were all over the place. Got a strong hunch he's one of the ringleaders. He hasn't come clean, though," Stink Mouth continued.

Having hastily inspected Farzin's injuries, the night officer jotted down some notes in his book, signed it, tore off the top sheet, and handed it to Stink Mouth.

"That's all, Brother," said the night officer. "Have a good night's sleep."

"After today," replied Stink Mouth, "I'll sleep like a donkey. Good night."

The night officer removed Farzin's blindfold, causing him to squint in the bright light.

"Come with me," he said.

He led his prisoner down narrow stairs to a water closet. Unlike the rest of the building, the stairway was dimly lit. Graffiti covered the damp cement walls, which were swollen and blooming with mold toward the bottom. A long tin sink at one corner clung to the wall precariously with a few bolts. The night officer instructed Farzin to clean himself up, and to drink some of the water while he was at it; it was going to be a long time before he got another drink. Farzin gulped a few mouthfuls and his jailer reached over and shut off the tap—long before he had his fill. When they emerged from the urinal, the night officer showed him to his three by six foot cell. He took off Farzin's cuffs and slammed the steel door as he left. His feet echoed down the bright hall as Farzin looked about the tiny cell with its well-worn filthy mattress. *So, it has come to this!*

As the initial shock of events waned, hunger began to pinch Farzin's stomach. He tried to think about the conversation that had taken place between Stink Mouth and the night officer. When an ache began in his head, he lay back and contemplated his surroundings. His eyes fell on a nail-carved figure of a reclining nude on the opposite wall. This Venus had a small head, protruding bust, diminutive hands, elephantine thighs, and the most prominent of genitals. He stared at it for a long time. The figurine presented itself as something more than a five-minute job done by a ruffian out of boredom. To Farzin, the passion that had driven the nail into the wall evoked a humiliated, repressed desire, human and wretched. It symbolized the clinging of a heterosexual man to the last residues of hope. He paused on that thought. Then he wondered what would symbolize his urge to live. What was the index of his passion to go on?

SEVEN

The door took its time to open. For a moment Farzin was unsure of his whereabouts. A guard stood waiting in the hall, indifferent and serious.

"Quickly, get up and come with me," he said.

Farzin put his hand on the back of his head and suppressed the pain. Memories of the day before rushed in as the guard held up the handcuffs and motioned for Farzin to hold up his wrists. Once the cuffs were in place, the guard cocked his head for Farzin to leave the cell.

They entered a minimally furnished office: a metal desk, a small wooden table with bowed legs, and a bench that wobbled when Farzin sat on it. Stink Mouth was already there. A framed picture of the ubiquitous Imam Khomeini, the lightning rod of the Revolutionary Forces, scowled from the wall. The guard left without a word and closed the door behind him.

"My name is Hamid," said Stink Mouth as he faced Farzin. "I'll be conducting some routine questions, and you will answer me, truthfully, to the best of your knowledge. If you cooperate, I'll guarantee you a fair trial; if you don't, God only knows what— It'll be out of my hands. Understand? The choice is yours."

Farzin understood. He was going to cooperate with Brother Hamid; no reason not to. *Who in his right mind wants yesterday to repeat itself?* He nodded.

"Good. Looks like we are off to a good start," said Brother Hamid. "Now, let's begin with your name and address."

Farzin spelled out his last name and his street address. Brother Hamid took notes on an official form. He gave the impression he had done this hundreds of times before, had every move down to an art, every question memorized. He fired off another question, while still writing the answer to a previous one.

"Are you or your father by any chance a member of the clerical society?"

"No."

"Then your claim to the Rouhani name is false, is it not?" Literally, the word rouhani means spiritual or sacred. In the Shiite vernacular, it is a euphemism for the cleric. A mullah is a *rouhani*. Seeing the confusion on Farzin's face, Brother Hamid rephrased his question.

"What is so sacred about you and your family that you can lay claim to such a divine name? What gives you the right to call yourself Rouhani?"

Ever so determined to oblige, Farzin said simply, "It's my name; that's what I've always been—a Rouhani. Farzin Rouhani. And my father is Nozar Rouhani, and his father was Emaud Rouhani."

Brother Hamid followed up with yet another seemingly irrelevant question. "Was he a clergyman?"

"It's just a name for heaven's sake," said Farzin. A swift backhander knocked him off the bench.

"That's to help you see the seriousness of your situation. Now, are you a Rouhani?" Farzin sat up, fighting back tears. His head felt like it was about to explode from inside.

"Yes, that's my name. No, that's not my profession."

"I don't see why you're bickering with me," said Brother Hamid. "To say that you're not a cleric, and that your father and grandfather weren't clerics either, doesn't tell us anything about who or what they were, does it? Do you agree with me, Brother Farzin?"

"I didn't understand a word of what you said, Brother Hamid."

As opposed to the leftist activists, who referred to each other as "comrade," devout Moslem revolutionaries in the underground movement against the Shah took to calling each other "brother" or "sister" to stress their separateness from those infidels. Then, with the victory of their revolution, the term found universal use just as "comrade" would have, had the revolution been won by the left.

"Don't play with me," Brother Hamid asserted. "Or I'll do to you what will make you sorry for the rest of your fucking existence." Getting up from the floor and seating himself back on the bench, Farzin decided to be more careful. His interrogator seemed to be jumpy about a great many things.

Brother Hamid looked young, about twenty-five or -six. He was fine vindication for those who believe that a physique announces the man. His face, with its stubby nose and rounded chin covered by a bosky black beard, was flattened into the shape of a round, imperfectly decorated birthday cake. A young man of ungovernable tempers, he had set out to correct all the wrongs of the world but now was finding the burden of his duty too much.

"Are you or were you one of the organizers of yesterday's march?"

"No," came the emphatic answer. "Where did you get that idea?"

"Not sure," replied Brother Hamid. "Call it an educated guess," he said casually, as if amusing himself.

Educated guess, he called it, but he also made sure that his prisoner understood there was a good amount of secret intelligence behind the allegations. As in, "We know much more than we let on, but for security purposes we are only going to show you the tip of the iceberg." Farzin knew better and would not be intimidated. He had already come across the insight that without their cause, the likes of Brother Hamid were nothing, useless creatures in the horrifying abyss of life.

As Brother Hamid rose from his chair to pace the length of the room, his hands behind his back, Farzin noticed for the first time that he dragged a leg behind; he was lame.

"I'm innocent," Farzin said.

"Why are you here, then?"

Farzin composed himself before saying, "I was hoping you might like to tell me that." Before Farzin finished his sentence, a fist landed on his left cheek, knocking him to the floor for the second time.

"I'm telling you that you're guilty as sin and a liar." Brother Hamid's uncommon stamina and confidence were awesome. "What were you doing yesterday at the demonstration? Tell me the name of your connection. What were your plans and responsibilities?"

My plans and responsibilities?

"I had no plans and no responsibilities. I was just walking down the street, minding my own business. Look.... With all due respect, you gentlemen have really botched this up. You've got the wrong guy." *So, it's come to this! I'm now begging.* "Last night I thought about this whole thing. I'm not going to hold it against anyone. Just let me go home, and we'll forget it, huh?"

Brother Hamid turned to Farzin and slowly walked up to him, exhaling his putrid breath. His brown eyes were bloodshot.

"Look," he said. "I'm going to repeat myself one more time. Normally I don't do this. Give me the names of your collaborators. Can't you see that you're finished?"

Without another question Farzin was thrown back in his cell, his head throbbing with pain. Obviously, things were not going well. The same pattern of questioning continued for three more days. On every one of those occasions a sharp pain in his temples preceded the actual blows delivered to his head and back. On the fourth day, Brother Hamid stopped by to check on him.

"Hey," he said casually, as if to a friend. "What're you doing?" He was being loud while grabbing Farzin's neck and pointing at his Seiko. Farzin felt his headache coming back, thought he was going to be hit again. "*Besmellah**, baba; it's prayer time," Brother Hamid said, rushing his prisoner out the door, as though it would irritate God if they were the least bit tardy for prayers. "Hurry; hurry."

Praying was the highest form of worship, Brother Hamid preached. It was an exercise, too, the bending of the joints and all. Bending down from the waist, stretching the back and leg muscles; squatting on the floor toward Mecca, which not only stretched the ankle muscles, but also eased the flow of blood to the brain for clear thinking. In addition to his passionate attachment to this belief, Brother Hamid liked to think that modern science approved of it, too. Like a second opinion that happens to confirm the first one, it consoled his mind.

"If you had started to say your prayers earlier in life," he now said to Farzin, "like you were supposed to, you wouldn't have ended up here in the first place." This was so clear to him that Brother Hamid saw no need to wait for Farzin's reaction. His one endearing quality was that he was willing to give you a break. Stern in his judgment, he would not shut the door in your face entirely either. "It's not too late, you know. God is forgiving."

They went together down the dimly lit flight of stairs into the windowless basement and the mildewed reek of the washroom. Farzin turned the stiff tap, and water exploded with fury against the metal basin as he held out his hands. The cool spray felt good on his skin. He proceeded to perform ablutions under Brother Hamid's scrutinizing gaze. Meanwhile, Brother Hamid's voice

---

* "In the name of God."

filtered through the musky air. "I don't have to emphasize the depth of the trouble you're in," he said. "Simply put, participating in antigovernment rallies is a serious crime. Your single option is to cooperate, or else."

There was no arguing with Brother Hamid. Frustrating to Farzin was that there was no way to prove to him that he was innocent. After prayers and breakfast, they made their way back to the office to continue with the cross-examination. Farzin held his head in anticipation of more blows, but there were none coming today. This time the nature of the interrogation had altered; it was now decidedly more conversational. Brother Hamid seemed particularly gabby as he made a point about the revolution. "All those nights I guarded the streets," he said in a monotone, "until two, three, and even four in the morning—where were you?" Briskly pacing up and down, Brother Hamid was declaring the revolution his personal achievement. "It's our revolution because we gave the martyrs, and we paid the price. But you don't care about that. What do you care about—anything?" he said accusingly.

Not particularly wanting to cause waves, Farzin kept his response perfectly level.

"Were you ever shot?" he asked.

"Of course I was shot," said Brother Hamid, ever so ready for a chance to tell his story, to prove he owned the revolution. He pulled down his khakis to show Farzin a scar running north-south on his lap.

"Listen to me," Brother Hamid said, after a moment of reflection. "I use a direct method of questioning prisoners; if they cooperate, they will get my respect. However, if they don't …. Well, you don't want to know how bad it can get."

Farzin was amused, as amused as one could be under the circumstances. Brother Hamid went on "I often let them tell me what they want to tell me first, and then direct them to where I think the lead is. Why don't you take this pen and pad and organize your thoughts?" He produced a white notepad from the desk drawer and put it in front of Farzin. "Don't say anything now, just take it and think about it." Brother Hamid added he was doubtful that Farzin would come clean about his role in the protest march, but despite all that he was giving him a chance. His faith demanded that he try to remain objective.

Little did he know what idea had suddenly occurred to Farzin.

Eight

Brother Hamid had rarely found time to reflect on the events that had propelled him to his current position. He owed much of his reality to the revolution and its ubiquitous leader. Without the revolution, he would have been what destiny had mapped out for him, a high-school-diploma-holding drifter, stuck behind the gates of higher education, perhaps finding a low-ranking job at the bazaar, courtesy of his father's friends. But the Imam had called on him to overthrow the usurpers and Koranic evildoers. He and a few lutis in the neighborhood had planned their derring-do a week before they set out to do it. No one knew where the actual secret police headquarters (SAVAK) was located? But it had not been a well-kept secret either, for word got to them: Saltanatabad, a northern Tehrani neighborhood where women from well-to-do families roamed the streets without covering their auburn hair. It was a fortress. The thought of what they planned to do was daunting but they had the force of Allah on their side, and the whole country seemed to be rooting for them.

They had three rifles total and a couple of revolvers. Through a murky web of like-minded activists, Hamid was put in touch with an army draftee who had sent word that he could get into an actual army tank and drive it through the walls, if necessary. Unimaginable, but Brother Hamid believed him. The bastard was going to steal a tank, as if it would be parked in the street. Brother Hamid's collaborators said the guy was crazy, plain and simple. The army draftee told them, "Don't worry about it; put it out of your mind." But, of course, they hadn't. Hamid finally decided, "We'll do it, no matter what."

So that night they waited until it got dark. They divided into two groups. The first group was going to attack the front of the building, while the second group was going to the back. Brother Hamid and his closest buddy were in the first group. They were supposed to wait until the second group was ready on the other side, and they were supposed to let them know when. It was overcast that night and, with power outages, it was hard to see much. Brother Hamid would never know the exact sequence of events from then on but something odd threw off the plans, because before it was time, he heard gunshots and screams of "Allah-o Akbar." Brother Hamid's team didn't wait any longer, and they fired at what seemed to be the watch guards, and the watch guards fired back. They were at it for a few minutes, when out of nowhere Brother Hamid heard noises, and next thing he knew, at the preplanned hour, a tank appeared from the shadowy end of the street and ran into the wall of the compound, making a hole. Brother Hamid could not believe his eyes, but the army draftee had come through. Behind the tank there were hundreds of people with shovels and sticks and bricks, anything they could get their hands on for the sake of their faith. Naturally, Brother Hamid's team did not waste any time and went in, where bullets were raining on them, whizzing in the dark. There was a white fog everywhere and terrific bangs of guns.

The crowd followed them in, crawling through the hole the tank had made in the wall, with bullets flashing in the dark, drawing red luminous lines in the air over their heads. Men who were so daring or stupid—depending on your outlook—could easily have had their heads blown off and their hearts pierced by the red meteors. And a few of them did. That was when Brother Hamid felt a sting in his leg and, at first, did not think much of it. It felt like a bee sting; then a peculiar cold invaded his bones. But there was no time to stop. His buddy yelled at him; Brother Hamid thought it was out of excitement, to charge him on. Or he was going to say something, perhaps tell Brother Hamid that he had been shot. When his buddy finished yelling, a sniper took his arm right off. And he was still standing. Then Brother Hamid saw what was going on. He had wanted to get to the offices, where the soldiers and snipers had taken cover, to get his hands on the assailants. But all around him were these people who were following him, and they were getting hit left and right, fountains bursting from their limbs, the blood spattering on their faces and getting into their eyes. And they kept at it. If this were someone else's narrative, Brother Hamid would dismiss it right off the bat as the imaginings of someone whose objectivity should be doubted. As someone who was in the middle of the mayhem, he saw it with his own eyes, and he believed in the power of his faith. He believed it on empirical grounds: they were not falling. He saw a man who was shot in the face and was still alive. He was covered with blood, and he was still shooting at the second floor. If there was hell on earth, Brother Hamid saw it that night. People getting shot and refusing to die. That was something he would remember for the rest of his life.

Finally, they prevailed and went in. What looked awesome from outside held very little inside. Once he went into the second-floor offices, over the dead bodies of the soldiers, he did not see much, except guns and ammo. Brother Hamid had fancied that was where they tortured prisoners, but little more than arms and logistics were kept in Saltanatabad. So, the participants in that fateful raid walked out with Uzis and hand grenades. Of Brother Hamid's original collaborators, eight of them were wounded and, of those, half finally died. Had he gotten his wound a little higher and to the right, he would be pushing up daisies now. But that never concerned him—"If you want the wild monkey, you have to climb the tree." What bothered Brother Hamid was that punks like Farzin Rouhani, who had no idea what had transpired since the nation's awakening, dared to send their fists into the air against the regime that he had given his blood to found. Brother Hamid would be willing to bet none of Farzin's friends who were marching the other day had participated in the revolution against the Shah as eagerly.

Nine

Back in his closet-sized cell, Farzin held the notepad in his hands. His eyes drifted from the paper to the engraving on the wall. The question about what symbolized his urge to go on came back to him. If his predicament was going to be a test of his will to live, what would be the measure of his success? Simply enduring the hardship of solitary confinement for a crime he did not commit, or trying to get out of this trap by any means he could muster? Memories rushed to his head, the present abrading the past, folding into it, taking the shape of a dream. The way Bijan's broad forehead sloped down to meet a largish Roman nose, his lips intimate and full. The kisses so rich and satisfying, Farzin now recalled their flavor and texture. Kisses as prelude to drowning in the proceedings of the tongue, the insinuating, exploring tongue, prying. And the hands, with those long, bony fingers clasping his and guiding them to places out of the way. Leading them to his body, prodding him to enfold and caress. The arch of the lower back, the softness of the skin there, its dampness, all coming back to him now. In retrospect, Farzin's attraction toward Bijan seemed a witch's spell. In the days since his arrest, he often wondered whether he would ever get over him. On occasion, he had been terrified by his obsession. On occasion, he had been delirious. In the end, the spell had proven stronger than any of his qualms. If it were not for fear of getting into hotter water, Farzin would have begun his report by writing about where he had been heading on the day of the march.

The first sentences he wrote were self incriminating. *Isn't Brother Hamid looking for a name and an address? Oh, Bijan, what am I doing here? Dear Bijan, this isn't meant to be.* And when his pen came to a halt, he scratched over the writing. After a moment, he tore up the page into the tiniest pieces.

Hardly an hour had gone by when the sound of footsteps stopped outside his cell door. He heard the sound of keys jingling and the door swinging open. Farzin looked up to see Brother Hamid's thickness blocking its frame. He shot a vexed look at Farzin. His was the unsympathetic face of a man for whom life had fractionated itself effortlessly, things being either immediately good and sacred or forever bad and disposable. With his index finger he motioned for Farzin to put down the notepad and follow him.

Back in Brother Hamid's office, Farzin could not help but notice the jailer's restlessness, his shirt damp with sweat and his mind obviously preoccupied.

"We're backed up way over our heads in here," he began. "In a couple of days you're going to be sent to the Office to Combat Vices. You'll be there until you decide to cooperate with us ... That is, *if* you decide to." Brother Hamid paused, as if to examine the effect his news was having on the prisoner. He even made a gesture with his hand for Farzin to say something, or exhibit a sign of incomprehension, but though the prisoner appeared to understand what he was told, he had no clear reaction to it. A mixed look of dismay and worry flushed Farzin's face. Finally he opened his mouth.

"What do you want from me?"

Brother Hamid replied with a question of his own as he resumed his walking about the room. "What part of cooperation is hard to understand?"

There was no answer as Farzin looked puzzled.

"Give me details, details, details," Brother Hamid said through clenched teeth. His meticulously trimmed beard and mustache dripped with beads of onion-infused perspiration. "Details are what we want. Facts, with the names of places and people involved, etcetera, etcetera. We want everything you know. We already know a great deal about you and your activities. You may think we don't." He stopped to throw a look at the smiling Farzin.

He resumed his pace.

"Smile all you want," Brother Hamid continued, "but I'll tell you one thing. You're lucky we didn't find any weapons on you, or else I would've personally taken you to Evin." He paused again, as if to stress his point. Evin, the notorious prison for political prisoners, loomed large in the psyche of every Iranian. Political prisoners were tortured and shot there.

Brother Hamid began in a milder tone, "Got one piece of advice, though. Don't try to weasel out of this because, honestly, we're giving you a chance to redeem yourself, to spare your life, if that means anything to you at all."

Brother Hamid looked at his watch impatiently. In his quest, he tolerated nothing short of pure facts. He did not have patience for absurd stories. To him, the world was no less than a chaotic zoo in which everybody was lost. The Imam, the guiding spirit of the Revolutionary Forces, had come at last to sort things out and seat everybody and everything in its proper place. "And don't you try any fancy stories, either," he was saying now, "or you'll be sorry you were born. I'll make no more of you than cat does of mouse, you hear?" Brother Hamid was face-to-face with Farzin, their noses almost touching as he railed at him, spraying his face with spittle and sweat. "Or, I'll do to you what will make the flying birds weep."

Silently, Farzin admitted defeat. The man wanted answers .... If so, that would be what he damn well was going to get. Brother Hamid stepped back and dropped into his chair.

"I'm warning you," Farzin finally said, looking straight into Brother Hamid's eyes. "I'll talk all you want and then some. I'll tell you about strange gardens and cruel conquerors; I'll tell you the Secrets of Survival and the names of far-away places you've never heard. I'll tell you so many details that you'll curse your nosy self to death." *Here's the battleground, step in if you dare.*

Brother Hamid started to say something, but this time Farzin raised his palm and closed his eyes in mock obedience. The interrogator's interest was renewed, as if God had answered his prayers. He picked up a notepad and began scribbling on it. He bit his tongue between his lips and wrote in large, unsophisticated letters.

"So," he inquired, "the insurrection started from a place far away from here? Instigated by a foreign agent?"

"Damkan is a spot on the map," Farzin said. "And the passenger trains stop there."

"Tell me more; who is your contact, etcetera, etcetera?"

"What contact? My whole family has roots there. My father, for example, was a judge."

Brother Hamid lifted an eyebrow and prodded, "So, the insurgents have hands in high places! What is your father's name?"

"My father's name is Nozar Rouhani, the descendant of the great Mullah Abbas. None of the Rouhani women, I might add, had any character except … never mind. Come closer," Farzin instructed his jailer. He found a new assertiveness in himself. He repeated, "Come closer, I mean it."

Brother Hamid leaned forward on the desk, cocked his head, and offered an ear.

Once upon a time, or should I say suspended in time, just outside Damkan, under the dome of a pistachio tree, sat an emaciated cleric whose beard and gaze hung intently down on a book. With an immense turban the color of night and eyes circled with carbon, he was a conspicuous figure, not only respected but feared.

The cause of fear surrounding the prescient sage was the overwhelming idea that he somehow possessed a secret magic under his tremendous headgear. The magus, in his declining years, was known to all as the great Mullah Abbas.

TEN

"Not so fast," said Brother Hamid. "Slow down, so I can keep up."

Satisfaction glowed on Farzin's face as Brother Hamid's tone lost its sarcasm and became ... accommodating. "Would you care for a glass of water?" he said to his prisoner. "Some tea, perhaps, sugar cubes on the side?"

Farzin ignored the question; sinking into a dreamy haze, his mind summoned the great Mullah Abbas, with his large piercing eyes, reclining under a gargantuan pistachio tree. Brother Hamid was oblivious. "Shall I get you a cushion for your back, baba?"

Sitting there under the weight of a family tree as heavy as history itself, on a broken-legged wooden bench, Farzin Rouhani began to give an honest account of the life of a character who had shaped his fate. Stories flew out of his mouth, his hands, his eyes. Names came and went in a flash, personages and props whizzed by at dizzying speed.

His jailer, who had begun recording his tales, grew tired and finally his hand stopped on the pad. "One moment here," said Brother Hamid. "I can't keep up with this. Besides, what are you talking about? Slow down; give me a break." He rubbed his fingers, mulling over an idea. "Here," he finally offered. "Take this paper and knock yourself out. Don't let me interrupt you, all right, Brother?"

Thus the seed of a full collaboration, not totally satisfactory to either party, was planted in the hopes of a future tree. Farzin began immediately. But it was not an easy task with Brother Hamid looking over Farzin's shoulder, breathing death-breath down his neck. After a while they were forced to modify the terms of their agreement somewhat. Toward evening, Brother Hamid escorted his prisoner back to the cement suite, leaving him there with more paper than before.

The grand man of God had a family of ten who lived in the boondocks of Damkan, near the antiquated Silk Road to China. They lived in a mud cabin on such a vast piece of land that it would have taken a whole day for a pair of feet to go from one end to the other. According to the whitebeards and coffeehouse celebrities, Mullah Abbas had always been there. They said it had been so long that they could not bring to mind whether he had purchased or simply taken over the lot of land on which he had built his home, and around which a thick, high clay wall had been erected. The five-sided cabin had a wooden door, a woodstove, and four windows: one facing south and one facing west, a third one letting in the morning sun, the fourth gaping at Polaris.

The mullah had devoted his whole life to the principle that the Holy Book contained everything one needed to know, including all laws of nature and society, and his regime among the believers had become one of total submission. The credulous multitude, impressed by the sight of him and imposed on by the claims to supernatural power, paid him willing homage, year in and year out. This could have had something to do with that secret he had hidden under his headdress. It was said he was the discoverer and sole possessor of the elixir of immortality and ultimate wisdom: the Secrets of Survival.

Eleven

The sound of heavy footsteps in the hall and the key turning in the door brought Farzin's back to the present. The door opened; Brother Hamid appeared somewhat disheveled and perturbed. "Getting fancy on me, eh?" Patience, as Farzin had learned, was not Brother Hamid's forte.

"Putting me on, are you?" he said, glaring at Farzin.

Farzin threw up his hands. "I'm just warming up; this is only the start."

Brother Hamid's accusing glare ricocheted off the walls like a bullet. "You good-for-nothing cheat; who do you think you're dealing with—a five-year-old? What nonsense is this? I want to know the answer to a specific question, and you're talking voodoo."

"I know I've been sidetracking," said Farzin, good-naturedly "but this is where the story begins."

"Damn right you've been sidetracking. Cut the crap, I tell you."

"But you've got to bear with me," asserted Farzin evenly.

"Shut up! If you don't get to the point, you're going to end up in Evin faster than you can blink. Hear me?"

What to do? Evin was fearsome for its fingernail-pulling devices. They administered electrical currents to one's testicles. Farzin did not want to end up there at all, but he was considering something else.

It did not matter if Brother Hamid liked it or not, Farzin had things to record, anecdotes to relate, and a secret to decode. He had stories to weave and traditions to sift through, if he was going to explain why he was in the streets, despite a government ban, on June 20, 1981. It was going to get more complicated still.

Mullah Abbas always wore a dark robe and bore a massive turban. His nocturnal meditating was a long-standing habit. He drifted into a delirium reciting his magical verses. During these episodes, his face was a wild visage, all bones and eyes, with a broad nose and knotty brows, a wide prominent forehead, and a large mouth with taupe lips that constantly mumbled verses from the Holy Book. When he came out of his trance, his wife, Golsha Khanoum, would fix him a tray of his favorite meal of goat cheese, bread, yogurt, boiled fava beans and mint, or yogurt and cucumber, according to the season. An unchanging feature of the tray was an enamel bowl of water in which pistachio kernels floated on the surface. Engaged as she was with house chores and raising children, she would then leave him to his repose under the pistachio tree, a thing that was to him of great worship.

Sitting with his legs well tucked under his thin body, Mullah Abbas prayed with conviction and humbleness, regarding himself simply as another particle of creation, an inconsequential, perishable being whose only task was to pay homage to the Lord of the universe. He used his prayer beads until his fingers were enervated and aching, moving the precious stones along the string that connected them, like a line of pedigree. Thus, he lavished on God the attention he could not give his eight offspring. Often, at the peak of his prayers his large eyes would swell with passion, as though a fever had seized him, and Mullah Abbas would weep and moan and carry on all through the night.

Twelve

But truly, what did Brother Hamid know? This could have been the most telling story in the whole world, yet he would not have known the difference. He stormed into Farzin's cell first thing in the morning, clutching a sheet of paper in his fist. He shouted, "I don't believe it." And when Farzin asked him why not, he responded by saying, "Because I don't."

"Tell me why you don't," insisted Farzin.

"Because I wasn't born yesterday," Brother Hamid said as he threw the sheet of paper in a corner.

"All right, as you say," Farzin conceded.

"You're wasting my time," Brother Hamid continued. "I have no use for fiction."

Farzin remained silent, averting his eyes. Brother Hamid was now standing in the hallway, about to shut the door, when he paused and asked, "What was wrong with your ancestor? Was he a loony?"

Farzin felt the color rise in his face. "Look," he replied. "If I wanted to lie, I'd elaborate on those stories of the saints who regularly visit the 'soldiers of Islam' at the war front, all right?"

The war with Iraq was in its second year. The Iraqis had not yet captured Khorramshahr, but they were close to it. The Basiji youth, the apples of Imam's eyes—not to mention the sacrosanct pillars of the Revolutionary Forces—were volunteering themselves, in waves, to go over the minefields and get themselves blown to pieces to make the path for tanks and heavy artillery. They did this wearing little plastic keys around their scrawny necks. Everyone had heard all that bunk about the plastic keys to heaven. The Basiji youth were given to understand that upon death they would go straight to heaven, no questions asked. Everyone had also heard the stories of regular visits to the makeshift hospitals by one particular saint, who made midnight appearances mounted on a white horse, offering his canteen to the wounded soldiers of Islam.

In retelling these reports, Farzin had struck a nerve. Brother Hamid did not stand a chance. He shut the door and left in a huff.

When Mullah Abbas became advanced in age, it was natural for him to take on an apprentice. The boy's name was Bahraum; a youth of twenty-two, he was keen on knowing everything there was to know about the Secrets of Survival. Carving a nook for himself beside the elderly man, he took to caring for the cleric like a son, minding his steps so as not to interrupt the old man too often, especially when he was in the midst of his reveries. However, Bahraum occasionally stopped by the lofty tree and politely put forward his queries, products of his inquisitive mind. As long as he could remember, he had been searching for the key to the ultimate question, the answer that would eliminate all questions forever. His curiosity knew no boundaries. Every time the sage illumined a fragment of existence, his disciple would fall to the ground, take the grand man's hand, and press it against his lips.

Thirteen

The year 1729 came to be known as the year when the horses perspired blood. The clatter of galloping hooves dominated the deserts of central Persia. In Damkan, the silhouette of Ashraf Khan's army loomed in the blazing vista. Soon, horsemen spread across town, along with the clang of armor, cries of the brave, shrieks of the wounded. Distant voices were heard crying, "Damkan's burning! Damkan's burning!" Ashraf Khan, the shepherd who called himself king, at the head of five thousand sheepherders, conquered the town and left a heap of rubble. The air reeked with the stench of decay. Corpses lay in the alleys under the sun, half-hidden by the buzzing feast of flies—a shifting black veil darkening the sky over the dead. The dizzying sound of tiny wings reverberated against earthen walls, and caws of crows drawn to the inflated rotting corpses stitched the air. They landed forlornly on rooftops and looked on, or took off and dissolved into the grayness of sky.

The mosque, Tarikhaneh, was raided on a hot summer day. Dismembered limbs piled near its bloodstained entrance; a raven on a low, straight-winged cruise, from a spiraled minaret with eighty-six steps to the window with a broken latch, flapped once, then abruptly landed on a severed human head. Worshippers, slightly raised by bloat, stretched lifeless in the open space used for praying. The floor, never before carpeted by anything but a soft and even dust, was soaked in blood.

Ashraf Khan had a square face, pointed brows, a sharp-pronged mustache, and the look of a man forever consumed with vengeance. He was concerned that an old man and his family had survived the massacre. They had been spared, and that was unacceptable. A man was a man, no matter how advanced in years. Ashraf Khan made ready to pay a visit to Mullah Abbas's orchard. He sent his tents, camels, soldiers, and retainers ahead. "I shall squeeze the old monkey's neck with my own hands," he was overheard saying to his adjutant, the ruthless Sirdar Khan, who did not think the venture worth the effort.

"An old geezer," reasoned Sirdar Khan, "living among fruit trees with his family and a devoted student; a crazy bunch, really. He talks to himself and sometimes to his cane, that sort. Not worth the effort."

Nevertheless, the horizon was aflame when five thousand warriors came storming over the plains. Drums and horns and the hammering of hooves stirred the sleepy silence of Mullah Abbas's arborous grounds. As the commotion ceased, Ashraf rose on his saddle, turned this way and that, squinted at the trails of the brown wall on both sides of the orchard. Looking across the field, he gave a nod to Sirdar Khan.

They entered silently through the gate and saw in a sedentary position the mullah under the arching pistachio tree, its many branches sinking backward into the sky. With discipline, swords dangling from their sides, they kept in step on the rough terrain until all five thousand of them were enclosed by the orchard walls. Calmly watching their orderly invasion, the ancient mullah did not move. He remained on his cushion, with an astrolabe by his side made of twelve plates of polished silver for the twelve months of the year. He had been studying the invading army, the strange creatures with cruel eyes. There were so many of them, looking so alike, and a peculiar, disciplined evil emanated from their flawless ranks.

Bahraum had stepped out on the porch. That early in the morning the young scholar's behavior was noteworthy. As Golsha Khanoum steered a couple of her children, who had walked out half asleep, back into the house, the mullah's wily disciple had a sense that a confrontation with Ashraf Khan had become unavoidable. If Mullah Abbas was to unleash his powers to defeat the occupiers, Bahraum was going to be there to witness firsthand the power of the Secrets of Survival, and perhaps even to learn some of its key detonators. So close was he to sinking his teeth into the magic, he could taste it. He stood beside his mentor, shadowing his cool, detached appearance, as if the trespassing army bore no consequence to him at all.

Ashraf Khan recognized the book the mullah held in his lap. Despite the reports he had received, the cleric did not seem so crazy. He had expected to see him quaking on his knees, begging for mercy, but the aging mullah showed no such signs of weakness. The khan, who sat well on his stallion, dismounted with deliberation and strutted forward with the assured steps of a conqueror. He walked a few paces, stopped short, and as if he had forgotten something, returned to his horse. The animal displayed a beautiful Bokhara saddle made of fine leather. From its saddlebags he pulled out a thick leather-bound volume of the Koran, its front cover adorned with gold calligraphy. He walked back to the mullah and held it up in plain view.

"Men of God," he said firmly, "normally do away with false pride." Ashraf still had not abandoned the expectation of meeting a meek surrender. "*Ohoy*, is it that the grand Agha does not see us fit for a proper reception?"

Bahraum stirred in his place. He wanted to say something, to defend his teacher, but he too remained mute, as though the mullah's serenity had silenced him. "We cannot fight him," Mullah Abbas had told his disciple the previous night. "So, perform *Taqieh*,* while displaying reverence. Our day will come. To hide the truth is the ultimate art of a Moslem. Your God and mine is an avenger who in time will set things right."

---

* Proscribed in the Koran, *Taqieh* is the art of hiding one's true intention in the face of adversity.

Ashraf, glowering at the intransigent mullah, sent these words barreling out of his mouth: "*Ohoy*, I am here to salvage the faith from the tyranny of your ilk. The people on this land have shamed our beloved Prophet. That's why God has sent me on a mission to cleanse the earth of hypocrites." He pointed to his forces lined behind him. "My men are soldiers of the Prophet," he declared. Feeling exceptionally powerful, he was in no haste to finish this matter.

Perhaps because Mullah Abbas had a dignity that could not be ignored, he had to be humiliated. "*Ohoy*, you seem too hard-headed for an old man. I shall shed your blood and kill your sons to terminate your line." Again, not a word came out of the mullah. Ashraf paced the ground, to and fro. Who was this callous man who flouted him as if he were a lowly thief, neither worthy of an answer nor of an insult? Somehow, despite his nature, Ashraf Khan decided not to let the mullah control his temper. "*Ohoy*, show me a miracle to spare your life. They say you're a man of God. Well then, get down to it with your magic. You have until tomorrow to pull off your best work, or your humble shelter goes up in smoke." He pointed skyward as his face opened into a snide smile.

Fourteen

Six days and eleven hours passed before Farzin Rouhani saw sunlight again. After a cursory breakfast of bread and feta, he was swept into a patrol car and told to keep his mouth shut. Everything seemed the same as the day of his arrest, except that his eyes were not covered. And he knew beforehand where they were taking him: the Office to Combat Vices, one of the many headquarters of the Revolutionary Forces. An armed guard sat beside the driver, staring straight ahead for the entire ride.

It was hot and dry; few signs of the June 20th march survived in the streets: a burned tire in the gutter, half-torn posters hanging from walls, dangling in a gentle breeze. *What happened to all the clamor and noise, the cries for human freedom and justice?* He leaned his head toward the window and allowed the breeze to comb his hair backward. In the street, orange taxicabs competed with each other for daily bread, and motorcycles zoomed in and out of traffic at hurricane speeds. They cut in front of the cabs, and the cabbies blasted them with their horns. The air reverberated with the earsplitting sounds of engines and horns as people went about business as usual. A dark blue and grayish cloud of gas fumes, spat out by transit buses, hovered above the traffic.

It was not long before they stopped in front of the Palace. The staunch aloofness of life had lent a cheerless quality to the magnificent neoclassic structure. Immersed in a dark nimbus that inspired curiosity, the structure with its yard spanned a whole city block. People were crowding its huge portals. Farther down, more people squatted by the wall, hands over foreheads to block out the sun. Three guards holding automatic rifles, the barrels pointing earthward, stood on both sides of the gate. Two of them watched the street like statues, the third paced slowly about.

The home of the Office to Combat Vices was a tidy construction of windows, lemon bricks, limestone, and Tabrizi marble, arranged in a symmetrical facade. A relic of the olden gentry, it now stood for the virtue-prescribing and vice-prohibiting edict of the faith. Built twenty years earlier, the marbled edifice had once been in mint condition in well-to-do northern Tehran. As the city grew, the mansion slid southward, coming to rest just slightly north of center. Now standing amidst a crowded neighborhood, it was mute testimony to the affluence of the vanquished or otherwise migrated nobility.

The patrol car parked in front of the Office to Combat Vices, and Farzin was led out. A group of farmworkers, carrying envelopes and stamped papers, surrounded the entrance. Without having secured an appointment, they were trying to bargain their way in, with no success. As Brother Hamid led his prisoner by the arm through the main entrance, Farzin could feel the contempt directed toward him—like that provoked by one entering a much-coveted nightclub out of turn.

The entrance—a postrevolutionary affixation to the Palace—was entirely of steel, thick and heavy. On the other side of the gate, a tiled yard greeted them, an ancient willow bent over in submission in one corner, almost touching the earth. From the adjacent garden, dusty medlar boughs intruded over the wall. Outlandish for a revolutionary cause, the edifice backed into walled sylvan acreage where huge trees with nightingale nests on their higher boughs, presided with nostalgic elegance. There were gaily colored flowers everywhere. As they walked in, Brother Hamid led Farzin through a door to the right, where they were met with a patrician aroma that, lingering from the past, gave an impression of unusual tranquility. They passed two muscular guards wearing bulky beards and holding AK-47 rifles. Doors to enter, doors to exit, and doors in between chambers.

The hall immediately beyond the entrance was spacious, covered in a wan yellow marble in the layered way of the European neo-classic design, with a two-story foyer and ornate pilasters. The ceiling in the foyer met the walls in crown moldings. There was a spiral stairway that made heads dizzy and stomachs flop. Winding round the stairs, the balustrades were as thick as a man's torso. A couple of guards were standing by the entrance, next to an antique wooden desk with a large notebook on it, monitoring the flow of traffic. AK-47 rifles hung casually from their shoulders like cameras on tourists. The guards logged the names of visitors and the new detainees, made them stamp their fingerprints below their names if they were going in, and put a check mark in the next column as they left the building. Farzin signed his name below the last line. The guard opened an ink pad and helped him stamp his forefinger; neither one spoke a word. Farzin felt he had entered a bizarre realm in which people communicated through means other than speech: a hand told him to walk, and he obeyed; another hand pointed the way, and Brother Hamid conducted Farzin through the doors. They now entered the main hall.

Once they were in, Brother Hamid temporarily seemed to have forgotten his mission. He looked around and let out a breath of raw onion.

"Been here lots of times," he assured Farzin, his eyes devouring the surroundings. "Can never get enough of it."

At the far corner of the main hall, a wide flight of stairs dropped from the second floor. "Every time I walk through here," he confided in Farzin, "I get tongue-tied." A guard directed them to the second floor. Farzin looked around, the last residues of hope evaporating. He held on to Brother Hamid's arm, not wanting to let go of the only person he knew in this place. Brother Hamid sat on the bottom step of the stairs and said, "It's goodbye for now, *yauroo*, but you'll see me again, I promise you that."

Farzin wondered what to do. How could Brother Hamid let go of him when he had just begun to open his family vaults? He relayed that much to Brother Hamid, who retorted in return, "*Ohoy*, what about it? Just keep on writing your report and be factual. I'll come back to look at it when I can." He fumbled for a pack of cigarettes from his breast pocket, took one and put it between his lips, and offered one to Farzin. They shared a smoke and eyed each other.

"I'm still your interrogating officer," Brother Hamid said through tight lips, hardly holding on to the freshly lit cigarette. "And I'm still counting on your cooperation. I tried, but couldn't get out of it. So I'm telling you, if you do cooperate, it'll be easier on both of us."

Farzin took the caveat lightly and said nothing. He shook his head in sheepish obedience, as Brother Hamid went on. "You'll get a few years and, God willing, you'll get out. Now, write what's relevant: names, places, dates, etcetera, as much as you can remember. Above all, write what you were doing in the streets on the day of the march."

Brother Hamid was in a hurry; the driver was waiting for him in the car. Farzin had the length of a cigarette to say anything while his captor sat on the steps, stating, "What you've given us so far is absolute garbage. Who gives a damn about your great-grandfather?"

Farzin felt the need to correct, "Great, great *great*-grandfather."

"Still," came the reply, "who gives a pistachio about him? Forget it. What we want to know are your connections, in the *now*, a record of your underground activities from the beginning to present."

"First of all, *I* give a damn about him," Farzin shot back, emboldened as they were not alone. He would not get beaten in public. "Secondly, it's *all* relevant. Can't you see that?"

Brother Hamid was at the end of his cigarette. "No, I can't. I've had enough of your horse manure.... What the hell is the matter with you? You soft brained or something? Just write down the facts about *your* life. What *you* did, what *you* saw. I want to know whom *you* saw, whom *you* talked to, etcetera, etcetera." He rose to his feet. "These folks here aren't as patient as I've been." Farzin took a drag, still listening. "These folks don't like being taken for a ride. And let me tell you something else: they have ways of making you talk."

Farzin was finished with his cigarette. "Haven't I been doing just that?"

Brother Hamid didn't respond as he led the prisoner to the second floor, where the warden awaited them. Brother Hamid signed the required forms and turned over the detainee. Then he turned his back on Farzin and disappeared down the steps. The din in the hall downstairs seemed to be getting louder.

Fifteen

There were about a hundred inmates in three smoke-filled rooms, connected by a shared hall. Two of the rooms were average sized; the one in the middle was more spacious, about fifteen by eighteen feet, with a barred window that looked out onto the yard through the leaves of a plane tree.

A pile of shoes in the hall, before it branched into the three rooms, foretold of the natural disarray ahead. Farzin obediently took off his shoes and left them at the margin of the heap by the door. The rooms were disgraced by a collective human buzz and the acrid odor of dirty socks. Out of the corner of his eyes, Farzin regarded the inmates and felt their quizzical stares. Being in the company of society's rejects perturbed him—*It could only be a prank of fate.*

A cursory survey of the three rooms, a servant's residence in the Palace's former life, revealed persistent neglect; they had seen better times. Farzin walked into the windowed room, also the most crowded. Men of various ages squatted everywhere, by the walls and in the middle; some were pacing. Everyone noticed Farzin's entrance; he could tell by the way they averted their eyes. He found a place by the wall and sat down next to a couple of chatting inmates. Holding his head between his hands, he stared at the pattern of the carpet.

It was not long before he became bored with nothing to do. Conversation should have been effortless; it was the only thing that had not been taken away, but for some reason everyone seemed to be avoiding him. He did not know how to change that, or what was the appropriate behavior to adopt. He did not want to seem vulnerable. He had heard stories about prison violence and rape and was determined not to become a victim. He knew how to fight back, but he felt trouble could be avoided if he just acted in milieu. Finally, he decided to keep to himself and not seem bored. *If someone initiates talk, then I'll be responsive.*

Several times on that first day Farzin caught himself staring at some anonymous feet and at the moth-eaten carpet as he sat on the floor. He pulled a pen and a piece of paper out of his pocket. The air was pungent with sweat and thick with injured pride. It was cluttered on top of that, and it was noisy and distressing, quite unsuitable for gathering his thoughts. A horrendous task with all those people around and he had to do it. The floor turned out to be an uncomfortable place, so he rose to his feet again and paced the middle of the room. Moments later, he headed for the toilet.

One bathroom served all the inmates. A cheap cake of soap, cracked and dingy, sat innocuously on the elevated corner of the basin. The shower rod was pulled out of the wall and hung loose by one end, kept in place by two rusted screws. The latrines stank, the wall mirror was broken, the lightbulb was out, and the tub was black with mildew. A leaky faucet had left a brownish streak in the sink, and a broken exhaust fan blocked any fresh air from coming in through the small window.

Farzin went straight to the tub and sat on its edge. Soon, there was a rapping noise on the door. He opened it—*nobody, a prank.* He came out sullenly and found his niche in a corner of the room, opposite the window. He began to scribble his thoughts.

It is said that the next day something odd happened. All night Mullah Abbas was there, right under their noses, but come dawn he was gone, out of sight, and that scared the dungarees off the Afghan guards who were keeping an eye on him. What terrified them most was the inexplicable shape they saw in his place under the tree. There was a hole in the air in the shape of the mullah's outline, as though his body had turned into a *translucent object made of dense air; as if he had left his shell there as a clue. For that day and the next four, he was to be found inside, sitting on a dhurrie*[*] *in the middle of his pentagonal home, his feet tucked under his body. When Ashraf and Sirdar Khan walked into the house, they found the room pitch black, all curtains drawn.* "Show us your miracle, old man," *said Ashraf.* "Or prepare to die."

---

[*] Dhurries are inexpensive rectangular cotton floor coverings.

Sixteen

The great man did not take his eyes off the book, just quietly raised his right arm. Then, as Bahraum pushed aside the northern curtain, the most amazing thing happened. Outside, it was hot, but now the trees were green with leaves, loaded with luscious fruits, and mellifluous brooks meandered among banks of flowers. Hot gusts blew easterly, but did not last long, and alternated with cooler breezes from the west. The clicking and trilling of nightingales on tree branches was unending. Ashraf squinted in disbelief at this transformed desert landscape; he was speechless and slightly perturbed.

Next day the opposite curtain was pushed aside; the entire vista lay spread out through the southern window. Icicles hung from the roof and tree branches alike. A strong, frigid air rushed in; a windstorm picked up from the wasteland. Brittle snowflakes, swirling in the brilliant sun, crystallized on the tips of tree branches. Suspicious of trickery at work in the snow business, Sirdar Khan stuck his head out the window, only to find the plains deep under a thick mantle of frosting. From the branches of snow-covered trees that bore ripe apples and pears just the day before, stalactites hung in their slow earthward descent.

On the third day, the western window was opened to a vernal landscape and a full range of orchard sounds: the melodious song of whippoorwills, the long shrieks of the crows, and the gentle murmur of crystal streams. There were sparrows jumping from branch to branch, emitting endless jolly tunes. Hordes of quadrupeds roamed the fields as far as the eyes could see, and clouds of bustling birds made rounds. Swarmed by industrious bees and hoopoes leaping and hopping on the grass, the orchard was in full bloom; wildflowers on the ground painted a thousand dazzling, delicate hues. Fritillaries, gentians, primroses, convolvuluses, chrysanthemums, heliotropes, jonquils, narcissuses, hyacinths, and mallows colored horizon to horizon.

On the fourth day, autumn appeared through the eastern window, with yellowed leaves falling and the wind sweeping sand under a gray sky. By now, Mullah Abbas's stare had rested on the leader of the occupying force and his adjutant, freezing them with awe. My God! Which of them did not feel his flesh creep? After the show of the curtain on the fourth day, Mullah Abbas held his volume of the Koran in one hand, in the other his beads that now beamed a peculiar opalescent hue.

"You have been given what you asked for, and I wish to go no further," he said, his voice deep and somber. With every change of season, he had eyed them with a victorious grin while horror grew on their faces. "Seize the day, and take your men and leave, for your dagger holds no terrors for me. My hell, and that of my land, is in this life." He then began reciting from the Holy Book.

Ashraf spoke to no one for hours. Fear trickled into the troops, and rumor passed that the Khan had been frightened by the old man's mumbo jumbo. Of course, nothing could have been further from the truth. Quite the contrary, Ashraf Khan was not fearful of Mullah Abbas, but he had taken a hard blow to his pride. He took the mullah's magic as a calculated ruse to humiliate him before his men. A rabid urge for revenge shook his very foundation, as a result of which Golsha Khanoum and her eight offspring were hauled into the yard.

No sooner had the children been rounded up near the overwhelming, indifferent pistachio tree than Sirdar Khan approached them, drawing blade out of its scabbard and wielding it in the air. Without notice he grabbed the eldest son by the arm and forced him to kneel, pressing his head down against a fallen tree limb. He glanced at a bemused Ashraf Khan with eyes half closed in orgasmic delirium and, without warning, the smallest clue, or the slightest twitch of a muscle, wham! Off was the child's head. He struck with such speed that only a flash was seen of the blade. The head rolled off the log onto the ground as a violent quake seized the boy's body.

Golsha Khanoum's cry rose to the sky, wandered among the trees, while the great, silent Mullah Abbas looked at the scene of his son's beheading with the indifferent, opaque eyes of a pious man. In his vengeful grief, his face was that of a jaguar swept by a rare moment of indecision. Then, a scornful frown darkened his forehead as he heard the arrogant voice of the Khan. "Your life is spared, old man; so we have decided." What was he saying? That he was resolved to keep his promise? At the expense of the children? Allah, what shame and who's ever heard? The cruel man went on. "What do you say now, Agha? Where is your God, eh? Will He interfere with the fate I dreamed up for you?" Stung with such cruelty, Bahraum could hold out no longer. Pain gripped his heart in its clutches, and tears surfaced in his eyes.

"What is it going to be now?" Bahraum is reported to have asked. "What does fate hold?"

"Accept defeat," is all the grand man said in the urgency of the moment. Then he once more fell silent while Golsha's wailing and weeping filled the orchard air. Her children were soon rounded up, as she held tight to her youngest one. Her husband of so many years had never seemed so faint; she felt a pang of terror as loneliness crept beneath her skin. She stared at him while he mumbled the holy verses, his lips barely moving under the wool of his face, as a result of which the air began to congeal, and everyone present found it hard to breathe. The wind of good omen, *bastami*, had begun to flutter down Mount Damauvand. First it rushed as a soft breeze, then it picked up speed, became stronger. Before Ashraf could count to three, a tremendous roar came down over his head and went rolling across the horizon. The orchard sank in a frightening dusk as dark, menacing clouds piled up in the southern sky, one on top of the other.

Immune to the violent gales blowing from the mountains, the mascaraed mullah made no effort to keep the sacred book from soaring away. Thus holy sheets joined the desert sand and momentarily ascended high into the sky. While he still gazed upward and lifted his hands, a cloud hurried across the heavens, and from its depth came a growling thunder. The great destroying rage of Mullah Abbas had been unleashed.

Seized by panic, Sirdar Khan ran to the queue of children standing on the portico. He paused for a moment to catch his breath and then, without rhyme or reason, began slicing through them, left and right. When Golsha Khanoum threw herself in front of her children to shield them with her body, a swift strike opened her belly to the wind. Blood sprayed in the air, painted the wall. There was a confusion of noises, the neighing of horses, human cries, and the heavy roar of the wind reverberating against the mountain. The whole orchard raved with sounds—the creaking of the trees, the shouting of the troops. A wall of solid ubiquitous wind battered the soldiers and their horses. The dust that blinded the animals and men alike was as cruel as the rage of Sirdar Khan, whose blade had slain all but one of Mullah Abbas's children.

Seventeen

When Farzin took his pen off the paper, he noticed a few inmates had gathered around him, looking over his shoulder. As if encouraged by him noticing them, they now seated themselves beside him and asked what he was doing so quietly and diligently. Was he writing a letter to his fiancée? Farzin had only been among them for half a day and they were already advising him on how to write to a woman to ensure her fidelity. Aside from the petty nuisances, such as sharp smells and prying characters, being in jail would become somewhat less intolerable by afternoon.

As the day wore on, his cellmates' curiosity waned. Once they understood the purpose of his endless struggle with pen and paper, they lost all interest in his report, and left him alone at last. *Why the sudden aversion?* The weight of his loneliness imploded inside, and doubts invaded him. Perhaps, he had been left alone because he did not fit into their world: he was too quiet, reserved, and even standoffish; his alleged crime, a political one, was incongruous to the rest.

By the morning of the next day, Farzin fell into the groove of his new environment, making efforts to establish good relations with the inmates. Spared their prying and their demographic inquisitiveness, he could now focus on writing his report. He would be able to write without stopping for breath until sundown and afterwards for as long as the light lasted.

He wrote avidly, round-the-clock, which presented a different problem: the notepad Brother Hamid had given him was now filled and paper was scarce. Determined not to hinder his flow, he began to write on anything he could find. Some of the inmates were helpful to his mission and passed on scraps that came their way: dismantled cigarette packs, the inside of the silver foil from a biscuit box, and brown paper bags.

Brother Hamid had promised to send more notebooks but they had not yet arrived. Farzin decided he would put in a formal request for paper when he had an audience with one of the judges. For the time being, he wrote in minuscule letters, jostling them just so to make the most of whatever paper came his way. He wrote in the morning and in the afternoon in between the mandatory group prayers. He wrote while on the toilet, or in the queue waiting for breakfast, lunch, and dinner. He wrote in the middle of the night, while most everyone went to sleep, in the light of the streetlamp, filtered through the plane tree outside the window, casting perpendicular rays into the room. He wrote like a madman, as though his life depended on it. He wrote because his life *did* depend on it.

Let's not beat around the bush. In order for Farzin Rouhani to be, a miracle had to have ensued. Whether a miracle or a heroic deed, Golsha Khanoum pulled off the most astonishing of feats. Suppressing her pain, she grabbed her youngest child in feverish despair, crawling indoors. Her gallant act went unnoticed by the occupying troops, who were now caught in the middle of a whirlwind. The cacophony was complete and the troops would seek refuge in vain. As soon as the wind caught their tails, it knocked them off their feet and hurled them north south east west until they were, finally, sucked into the sky. Line by line they disappeared, flapping their arms, their strange noises swallowed by the vacuum of the desert. Though unprepared for this mayhem of revenge, Lord Ashraf was quick enough to hop on his horse, gather as many of his men as he could, and make leave of the orchard as fast as a fox-chased rabbit.

Bastami yanked the last remaining invaders up into the air and flung them against the flat boulders of the mountain, until there was no sign of them in the orchard or on the surrounding plains.

Not long after the massacre, the returning villagers found the orchard in quiet disarray. Golsha Khanoum was inside with her youngest, under a sheepskin blanket, the child fighting suffocation under the weight of his dead mother. Mullah Abbas was softly weeping over his fallen children. There was no trace of Bahraum, and the lonesome abode of the vengeful mullah stood silent witness. Earthquakes would crack its walls and, in time, the roof would come down, creaking and crashing. Its ruins would remain over months, years, centuries to become a refuge to roaming jackals. Children would be told to clear away from it, and passersby would throw rocks at it as a payment for their sins.

Over the following years, Mullah Abbas advanced the cause of stoicism on long moonless nights, accompanied by the lonely call of the owls, and never again invoked his powers. And the gift slowly trickled out of him, never to be fully retrieved.

Eighteen

Farzin embraced the urge to sound out his stories with his fellow inmates, but to his dismay they failed to grasp the magnitude of what he was telling them; anything outside their immediate surroundings was too complex a thing to fathom. Except for a peculiar character, who expressed some vague interest.

"Mohammad is my name, knife fighting is my game," the man introduced himself. He was a native of Tabriz. Thick brown hair, graying temples, and a droopy walrus mustache set him apart from the rest. Green eyes returned to his square face the calmness and sensibility of which the creases on his forehead robbed him. His down-to-earth manners made his bookish speech stand out, peppering it with a touch of sarcasm. A tattoo, a large pale blue anchor, on the back of his right hand indicated that he had seen long jail terms, in places with names that Farzin could barely recognize: Ghezel Hessaur, Kelaurdasht and Ghal-eh. He also mentioned Evin, the notorious prison for political activists before and after the revolution. Sitting there on the floor, drinking tea, holding a cigarette between his yellowed fingers, he reminded Farzin of the handsome man on the back cover of an American magazine, the Marlboro Man.

One could see he was bored out of his mind, like a tethered ape, and too intelligent for his own good. Farzin gave him three sheets, smudged and wrinkled. In silence, Mohammad read and returned the sheets, flattened. "Thank you for indulging me," he said, sounding genuinely grateful.

Mohammad was a walking paradox, Farzin began to divine. Taller than average, he did not appear so because of a slight hunch. He was plainspoken but spoke perfect Persian with somewhat of an archaic purity, the mark of a nonnative speaker. Had one paid close attention, one could hear the not-so-distant music of his Turkish mother-tongue in his speech—the call of the homeland. An irreverent smile played at a corner of his mouth, especially when he commented on religion, which was quite frequently. Having observed him in conversations with others, Farzin also discovered that all talks with Mohammad somehow turned to religion in the end, and one could always count on him to come up with unfavorable conclusions. Unfavorable to religion, that is.

Presently, Mohammad began to tell Farzin how he had ended up in the Palace. One Thursday night under a blue moon, drunk as a skunk on bootlegged *arak*, he had stabbed two louts with his pocketknife. The details of the assault he could hardly remember. Even though he spared both their lives, they wanted to see him fried, or at the very least suffering a modicum of torture at the hands of the Islamic police.

He had to teach them a lesson. The hoodlums claimed they had barely survived his attack, but that was not why he was in the Office to Combat Vices. The accusation had nothing to do with the knife fight but with the fact that he had committed a vice: he had been drunk when the fight broke out. *That* was the beef.

"Even if I hadn't knifed those bastards, they still would've put me in here." He had on a wrinkled shirt, once white, now brown around the collar and cuffs. His right sleeve, rolled up above the elbow, kept sliding down; every now and then he pushed it back up. "But I'm a sinner, I am," he went on. His gift of blab was boundless, saving even the most mundane chatter from extinction. "My vice is drinking .... I admit it, your honor .... Will I ever give it up?" He lowered the corners of his mouth. In Mohammad, all the photogenic features of the Marlboro Man and a certain Persian mythical hero, Rostam, were smoothly blended. An aura of intense reality moved with him—he who fell within it felt its energy. He had all this without the benefit of magnificent horses trotting behind him in a cloud of dust. Nonetheless, he was in poor health and often coughed for hours at night while most everyone else was asleep.

"I used to drink nothing but the best," he said. "Jack Daniels, Hennessy, Johnny Walker, but nowadays, I tell you, I have lowered my standard." Farzin believed him. Mohammad's square face wore a focused expression that immediately engendered trust. He had a way with words. Jokingly, he bragged about having started the revolution almost single-handedly, complained about having gotten nothing in return. The mullahs, he claimed, rewarded him by throwing him in the slammer. That strain of reasoning was familiar to Farzin. It was the quintessential Persian gripe about the betrayal of destiny. "If a thousand pussies fall from the sky," he said, "not one will land on my cock. But if two cocks fall from that very same sky, they'll get into a fight over which one gets to go up my ass first." Not exactly what you'd call a glass-is-half-full kind of guy.

Then he was off on another track. He maneuvered between stories with such lucidity, one could easily get lost for hours. It was a conceivable ploy in a place where time seemed to have stopped.

Having spent three weeks in the Office to Combat Vices, the Marlboro Man was familiar with the prison's hierarchical administration. From the inner struggle among the four mullahs at the top, over total control of the affairs, to radical methods used to extract confessions, ironically dubbed the Test of Innocence, administered by a spiteful prosecutor named Brother Daudyaur, Mohammad was the most informed inmate in the Palace. Those who knew how to approach him, would come away with many of the latest, with a side order of humor to boot.

Nineteen

First the blankets were shaken out, then the sheets. No trace of pillows anywhere. Piled up in neat squares, blankets covered a good portion of the wall and, when sitting next to them on the floor, you could lean your back against them. Mohammad showed Farzin how the beds were unfolded at night, then refolded and put aside in the morning. Each room had a stack of its own. He also showed Farzin his private stash of cigarettes and copperware. Touring the bathroom, he stuck his hand behind a loose tile and produced a solid bar of soap—"in case of shortage." Pointing at the window, he said that prison was a microcosm of the real world. "Really not much different," he said, pontifically. "The same laws of physics and gravity govern both; perhaps there are more freaks and nitwits in the prison per capita. More clowns, that's for sure, but essentially the same. I've been in longer than I've been out." He said this as calmly as though reflecting on a distant past too vague to remember. He was, of course, referring to being "in" prison, but his reference unconsciously made its mark with Farzin on a different plane. Farzin wondered if he could say that about himself. He swiftly drew parallels with himself being in the euphemistic closet, and whether he would ever be able to "come out."

Farzin's report had been put off long enough. He was feeling the need to get back to it. But a new thought had piqued the Marlboro Man's interest.

"I'm curious to know where you screwed up," he asked.

Farzin was caught off guard. "Pardon me?"

"I mean, what are you here for, baba?" He repeated his perfunctory question. Farzin hesitated, out of an ingrained respect for his elders. Then he told about his assigned task: reporting the true account of his life in exchange for his life. He was feeling relieved to have come clean to a friend. But it was somehow important that Mohammad didn't get the wrong idea. "I didn't turn a hair during the whole beating and arrest," Farzin informed his new friend. But Mohammad, an unsentimental man, burst into a peal of laughter.

"You, my friend," he said, "have been taken. Yours is a no-win situation." He grinned, showing a row of golden teeth. His unabashed revelry in Farzin's dilemma was vexing, but Farzin knew Mohammad had a good heart and a rare honesty. Farzin could not hold that against the man, but at the same time he decided it was time to strike back.

He turned to his friend and said, "You don't impress me as a Marxist or a Moslem." Laughter waned.

"I believe in God, I do," responded Mohammad. "The Koran I have read cover-to-cover. It told me not to give up on anybody, and that it is possible to become the ideal man in this world. Marx satisfied my longing for the extreme and the absolute. It was as if I had to have this enormous scope before I acquired specificity and became myself. But if you ask me what's my religion, I'll tell you: the religion of laughter. I believe in the religion of laughter." He went into his garrulous mode again. "For years I wanted the Shah physically dead without having a good personal reason." Mohammad pointed at his head and went on. "Then I realized, it's here you must kill the Shah and the Imam. Yes, we wouldn't have been licked had we laughed a bit more. Had we stuck to the Shah and laughed at the grim face of our religion, we wouldn't be here today." Mohammad seemed to be turning sour now, and resignation crept into his voice. "Our sin of not laughing enough is going to be held over our heads till kingdom come…. But what's the point?"

Not directly challenging him, Farzin feigned boredom. "If you believe in God," he said matter-of-factly, "what's with complaining?"

Mohammad furrowed his eyebrows. "God's job, my friend, is to dispose of all things kindly, to put religion into man's head by reason, not by force." Farzin gave him a skeptic's smile, which went ignored. "Threatening a man by force to accept a religion is to put fear in his heart by force, terror rather than religion. You see, baba?"

Farzin's thoughts were not at all collected. He had to get back to his neglected report. Swiftly excusing himself, he strode across the room and picked up his pen and paper.

Presently, Farzin was wrestling with a question of perspective. Sifting through memories, he recalled a few of his father's friends and coworkers who, when Farzin was growing up, told him stories about his father, Nozar Rouhani. At picnics and family gatherings, sometimes these men would join the Rouhanis with families of their own, and in the idyllic afternoons, after all the food was consumed and all the games were played, they would gather the children around to tell these stories of great luck and chivalry. It would make them feel good about themselves, and about being with Nozar Rouhani, who was the closest person they knew to a national hero.

Twenty

The unremitting, oozing heat killed appetites. Cursory lunch was consumed in apathy. Afterward, hands and mouths sought cigarettes, and the tea maker began his ritual boiling of water. Once it was ready, Mohammad gently placed a glass of pale tea on the floor before Farzin. An oily opalescence swirled on its hot surface, and it smelled of tuna. Mohammad joked about its pallor. "Guard-alert tea," he described it, "pale as donkey's piss." He took a swig of his own and set to smoking a butt he had found in the ashtray. Then, as if just remembering, he pointed to a fellow sitting nearby with a group of inmates. "You see that *prince* over there?" he said, pointing with his eyebrows. "Believe it or not, he's an architect." He raised his voice and continued, "An *artist*, for crying out loud, and yet, he's here with the rest of us." Farzin took in the man's profile. The architect had a long face, a tall and bony structure. The back of his head trimmed square. There was something about him, a calmness and, at the same time, a foreboding that was appealing.

"Jamal's his name," Mohammad said, "the maker of the tea and a true ladies' man." To emphasize what he meant, Mohammad gave a certain intonation to the following words, "You could say he's an *admirer* of women." Having overheard his name, Jamal turned his head and nodded. An Oriental sore stained his right cheek.

"Piss on admiring," Jamal contested, in jest. "It's more like an addiction." Around him, others were giving out audible sighs and snickers. *Grown men giggling like schoolgirls at the mention of the other sex.*

Jamal was a lively entertainer, Farzin learned soon enough. A winsome man, he sported a dark, tiny mustache and a charming, albeit yellow, smile. He took a drag of his cigarette and acknowledged the intro by saying, "Wish they'd realize the sacrifices I make to get in their drawers." He shook his head and continued, "This is not my first time in here, but damn it, I'll do it again. Because it's nature's will, or we wouldn't be slaves to our dicks." He turned to Farzin and said, "Want to see the lash marks I've gotten so far?" Without waiting for a response, Jamal pulled down his pants, showing calves covered with welts and black streaks. In describing the origins of the red and black markings on his legs, he talked with his hands and maintained an aloof posture.

Farzin had noticed him before, always wearing a dirty shirt with a pack of filterless Oshno cigarettes sticking out of its breast pocket. When he grinned, his skin wrinkled around his mouth and his yellowed, diastematic teeth with rounded corners showed through his lips. Smoking was Jamal's trademark, his second addiction and the source of his nickname. He was known for lighting each cigarette with the butt of the previous one, nostrils perennially at work like a chimney. Lifting his shirt, he now turned away from Farzin and displayed red and white lines crisscrossing his blistered back.

Mohammad shook his head disapprovingly. "The son of a bitch is proud of it," he said. "There is no redemption for you, my friend." They both laughed as if it was an old joke between them from way back when. Chimney turned to Farzin.

"Come on, I'll show you how to make tea, and you can ask me anything you want. Hope to make a good tea master out of you ....There aren't very many of us around, you know." Farzin would agree. In jail, tea makers were in constant demand.

Jamal said it was a sensitive position to be in, being in charge of the tea. One got to decide when and how much tea to make. One also got to choose who drank first, who drank last. One got to assign tasks to others, to wash the few available glasses, or to fill the sugar container, which was the sorriest looking thing Farzin had ever seen. It was handcrafted out of a piece of thin cloth tucked in the drawer part of a large matchstick box. Nevertheless, being in charge of something in that tight-knit community was a weapon to use against one's enemies and a way to reward friends. "Got to be fair, though," cautioned Jamal, the smoking tea maker. "Can't abuse your position too often, or you'll cause a riot."

Brewing tea in jail was an art in need of skill. Farzin watched as Chimney plugged two partially exposed wires into the wall socket. The other ends of the wires went through a coil and attached to two tin lids that acted as electrodes. It looked like the lids had come from tuna cans. Hence the tuna smell.

"Never mind the taste," Chimney said. "The real downside of it is that you get hooked. It's the price you pay for power, you see. The first day on the job I was drinking with the guys, one glass in the morning and one after each meal. After a while you get spoiled, start making tea in the middle of morning, in the afternoon, in the middle of night. You get a funny taste in your mouth. You have to drink more."

At forty-five Jamal was a traditional architect, with an emphasis on traditional. He had never gone to a vocational institute, had not even finished high school. Having learned his trade in his own vital, hands-on style, he was a natural. When starting as an apprentice to a professional architect, he had pulled up his sleeves and dug in, lied to his employers at times, saying he knew more than he did.

"Here, look over my shoulder," he now said to Farzin. "Keep a close watch in case the wires get prankish." There was always a chance of a loose connection, or of wet wires pulling a funny number on the operator.

"That happens often enough, you know," he explained to Farzin, who seemed unsure about whether Jamal was serious. Chimney had one of those harmonious Persian souls, so rare these days; a candid sense of humor that enabled him to tell the most outrageous lie with the straightest face. He also laughed a lot, big hearty guffaws as well as quiet, disturbing titters. He would burst into laughter after each admission of guilt.

"I've been up twice, down once," he said nonchalantly. "Down" was the common reference to the basement of the Palace, where Brother Daudyaur was said to work his miracles with the inmates. "Up" meant the third floor, where the accused were tried, and where a point was repeatedly made: that this was the virtual end of things. The grimness of the experience would make you wish you had died. The entire process, though, looked well thought out, even legal and normal. Yet, there were no defense attorneys present. The judge, the jury, and the prosecutor were all one and the same, God's revengeful agent, working for the divine under simplistic terms.

So now, what did Chimney have to say for himself? To get down to it, being married had not stopped him from falling for his landlord's ravishing young wife, whose eyebrows joined in the way characteristic of Middle Eastern women. He said he fell for her thin waist, and Farzin rolled his eyes. Oh and her name; her name was softer than a rose petal at dawn, more yielding than the last rays of a dying sun, a zephyrean music that invoked heaven's envy. Mauhrou. Ahhh! She spent many mornings on her veranda, doing her chores. She sifted batches of rice and prepared fresh herbs, or simply lay down in sun-soaking idleness.

Twice a week around noon, she bathed her four-year-old stepdaughter, Fereshteh, in a plastic tub and let the child play in the water. How many days had Jamal missed work standing, in drooling paroxysms of desire, on the flat roof overlooking them, worshipping the recumbent statue of that beauty? Hours would pass as he peered over her with a bulge in his pants. It was like a sleep that left him exhausted and unsatisfied. Sometimes he would release himself to the dream induced by her sight. Sometimes he would surprise his wife with undue affection, conceived by the sight of Mauhrou's curves. Later, he would be back on the roof once again, like a dog after a bone.

She moved about in her silent, looming way and occasionally caught sight of his bobbing head on the terrace, watching her with his feverish eyes, his lewd contemplation. Mauhrou would then make a show of her disgust by spitting and by calling on the names of Imams aloud.

Although his unannounced hobby made her ill at ease, she did not speak to her husband about it, hoping, perhaps, that Jamal would grow weary of her and disappear in the face of contempt. A complying virgin on her wedding night, she was not raised to flaunt her desirability. Likewise, complaining to her husband would not have appealed to her, either. So, what to do? She left him to be punished by God is what she did. That disembodied being up there somewhere who would punish the evildoers and evil thinkers. Jamal would pay for his sins on doomsday, she might have assured herself. Meanwhile, she avoided his stares, rushing through her daily, repetitive chores.

A curious view: with him observing her, things seemed to be getting done a heck of a lot quicker. Conversely, when he was not there, and how could he have known, she found her days unnaturally slow. She would throw a glance skyward and be relieved. But in that relief, also, was an element of boredom. Her days became long and tedious, and the scorching heat made her thirsty. She would lie down and stare at the walls, thinking she would have finished her chores by noon had he been watching her.

Twenty-One

Something about the summer casts aside inhibitions. Jamal knew why. He had a theory for that. If spring is responsible for love, summer unleashes lust. And so it was on one of these sultry summer afternoons that Jamal set out to consummate his undying desire. That particular day, with his wife out visiting her father at the hospital, Jamal was all alone. He noticed Mauhrou was nowhere in sight, which set melancholy in his heart like cold, black cement. Determined to own the beauty who had so pained his soul, and working on the assumption that the heat might have driven her into the basement, he tiptoed his way down the stairs, to where he suspected she would be taking her siesta.

Descending the steps, trembling, he muttered what little Jalaluddin Rumi he had committed to memory. *What atom is there that danceth not with abandon in thy praise?* The long and winding stairs were hot as he began his journey but lost their heat as he sank farther into the bosom of earth, each step cooler than the last. He felt them with the skin of his bare feet, a chill working its way up his spine to seize him. He did not know if it was from the falling temperature or the courage of his deed. Was she asleep, or was she disturbed, as he was, by impure thoughts? *What if she was asleep? More important, what if she was not? What then?*

Farzin was absorbed by the narrative, but for different reasons than the teller intended. He saw Jamal in his bold campaign to conquer a woman and began to view Jamal's prey as the other, who was at that moment absent to tell her side. Farzin put himself in her chador and tried to imagine what she saw. Just as Jamal's feet were about to touch the floor of the basement she sprung up, hearing the beat of his heart. Their eyes met and locked. The air teemed with dampness and her smell—torrid attar that set his manhood astir, while neither one spoke a word. Staring at her scared-gazelle eyes, he drifted toward her, a vessel in search of friendly shores to dock. Though the little thing wrapped herself in her chador to avoid the unavoidable, he kept closing in, a faint smile on his mischievous lips. When it became absolutely impossible to disregard his intention, she whispered a soft "Hello."

Her timid whisper sent a different message than intended, though. She was terrified. Her heart wanted to leap out of her throat. *What's he doing down in the basement? Has he lost his mind, the pitiful, miserable man?* Naturally, she did not want her stepdaughter, asleep nearby, to awaken. The "hello" was an acknowledgment that meant, "now you can return to whatever hole you crawled out of," which went unheeded by Jamal in his one-track-minded haste. The semidarkness of the basement had made him blind to the body of the sleeping child, and he mistook Mauhrou's whispering as a further sign of her willingness to indulge him.

He touched her foot and rubbed it gently. She hesitated amid scents, sheets, and temptations. With a tremor, he captured her hand, touching her silk skin and inching his fingers upward to the fleshy arm ....

And so it went. One minute he looked sheepish and tame, the next, she was sparring to push him away. But he pounced on her, gaining by the minute, until she softened, her bones melting in the delicious stupor of surrender.

The listener who was Farzin, this moment, could neither forgive Jamal for his transgression nor condemn him. He decided just to follow the events as they tumbled from Jamal's tongue. After Jamal vowed that whatever followed would remain a holy secret in the safe of his heart, she let him have his way on the condition there was to be no kissing. Jamal agreed to the terms readily as he touched her under the skirt with a trembling hand.

Of course, Chimney would have his young listener believe that when his hand touched her skin, her eyes shut and her lips emitted a soft sigh, but who could vouch for that? He was both the narrator and protagonist of the story, the only source of its verification, his own witness. *Do not all victors rewrite history to their own advantage? Do not claims of happiness and prosperity bestow themselves afterward on conquered lands?* Farzin was none too convinced by such self-congratulation. He would neither believe him nor call into question his claims, especially now that Chimney was about to admit he had been electrified to discover she had waxed the mysterious regions of her body. Her damp, willing skin there was like something out of a dream.

A passionate lover given to romantic scenes and dramatic gestures, Jamal had professed he would kill himself for her if necessary. He recalled that he had even said to her, "I will offer my worthless ass to the altar of your charm, my dear." In the struggle that had been going on, the air had assumed a pulsing rhythm, which then peaked, leveled, and subsided.

Then groins met for the second time in a harmonious dance of hips grinding against each other and departing, deliberately slow moving. She clung to him, exhaling her basil breath into his hard-shut eyes, digging her nails into his back. And the third, sweaty time; he was attending what must have been the inexpressibly enthralling business for the third time, when little Fereshteh was stirred awake by insuppressible amorous exclamations in the vicinity. Her almond eyes wide and wondering, she raised an interesting and valid inquiry, "What is the purpose of this?" And that was how the most naive of questions, the most serious of all, a truly simple one, came to demand an answer. Her animated voice hung in the dark with that quintessential question, and what followed can best be described as sheer pandemonium.

The unlikely lovers should not have been surprised, though, since the little angel had inherited that figure of speech from none other than her father. The question, which was now frozen in the silence of that basement, was part of a universally inoffensive language that the hadji often used as a tool of his trade. But a sinner needed no proof of his own sin. What to do? Without the benefit of a satisfactory third resolution, Jamal withdrew himself and jumped to his feet. Not uttering a word, he ran to his flat upstairs more rapidly than he thought he was physically able, cranking his body's rusty hinges, even banging his knee against the door, but too fearful to feel any pain.

Afterward, the ultimate question simply lived out its course: What is the purpose of this?

Of course the hadji would find out what had transpired that afternoon upon coming home at the end of a particularly distressing day. Haunted by the idea of his wife's defilement, he stormed to his tenant's apartment like a madman. Hiding inside, Jamal heard the ferocious knock but refused to open the door. *Can anyone blame him?* Nevertheless, the cuckolded husband continued banging on it until it finally flung open. And just as soon, he rushed to his tormentor, fist in the air, and struck him hard on the nose. Jamal stepped back, tottering, and collapsed. He lay supine, face to the ceiling, his cap rolling to one side. Now that Jamal was down, the hadji went on beating him with no less fervor, screaming the Fereshteh question: "WHAT-IS-THE-PURPOSE-OF-THIS?" After that, all hell broke loose.

A mellow being, the hadji was calm and collected in most circumstances. Therefore, even he would have trouble accounting for the source of this sudden surge of violence. It was as though a weakening sense of inadequacy and humiliation had brought the good fellow to the brink of madness. In the realm of grave sins to be punished, how could a calamity such as this be let to slip by? It was as if his whole existence urged him to do something, even though it seemed the way he was handling himself was simply against his grain.

He had just arrived home from work in anticipation of a restful evening. He had imagined his wife helping him take off his jacket, as she normally did, taking his tired feet in her caressing hands, rubbing them until he felt rejuvenated, as she did every day. But now, the pain in his heart had elbowed aside the pain in his feet. What gave him the strength to assert himself so, a sixty-three-year-old man at that? There was nothing in the air or in the water, rest assured. Rather, it might have been the voice in his head that kept repeating "A thing like this cannot slide by."

That's one thing Farzin could never understand about the straight man's world: that to be a man, one must act like a man, in hopes that the very act would bring back the essence of manhood. The cuckolded husband would do anything to defend his *namoose,* as though his powers of recuperation verged on the supernatural.

Namoose, in the Iranian untranslatable sense, is a sacred concept in every straight man's subconscious; not defending it when disrespected is a sign of cowardice. It's not quite honor in the Western sense but an integrated part of the much too complicated area of sexual politics; an idea in the vicinity of what constitutes femaleness in the eyes of a man, having to do with ownership of women's genitalia.

An assertion: it does not necessarily have to be the genitals of one's wife; it could very well be those of one's unmarried sister, mother, servant, lover, a friend's sister, or whoever else happens to be in the affected field that one's namoose has come to constitute. All in all, a man is mandated by the unwritten codes of the society to defend not only his own namoose, but also (in cases of emergency) his brother's, his friend's. Failure to do so, regardless of the reason, brings shame to a man and his family, his brother, friends, and so on.

When the neighbors gathered in the house, on the stairs and in the alley, they were whispering in each other's ear, or mumbling to themselves, "What's the purpose of what?" There were fists and kicks pelting Jamal's head and stomach while, in the street and over the stairs, onlookers were still wondering, "What's the purpose of that?"

Then someone divined the meaning of the hadji's query and shouted back, "What's the purpose of *this*?" and people all over around understood the meaning of the Fereshteh question. They began to whisper to each other or to mumble to themselves, "Ha! That's the purpose of that! Now we see." Jamal had raised his hands over his face, a sharp pain rising in his skull, when the brothers of a nearby Committee, a subsidiary of the Revolutionary Forces, parted the crowd of onlookers and pulled him away. The brothers wore guns at the waist and carried rifles, using them to shove the crowd of susurrous neighbors back. A Jeep was parked around the corner. Jamal was dragged to it through the patches of accusing spectators. The brothers threw him in the back seat and assured all concerned that the bystanders should all be heading home now, because everything was, truly, under control.

But before the Committee brothers came to the rescue, other things were being said in the green flashes of spite, which this pen shies away from repeating; things so extreme that they put the gathered ensemble of neighbors to shame. They turned red in the face, and sweat ran from their temples. That was the first time Jamal did not respond to insults that were aimed at the female members of *his* family. He had caused so much pain. His opprobrious conduct had brought shame in catastrophic proportions to the hadji's household, as a consequence of which the hadji could, by God's law, take his life and only then live honorably thereafter. Because namoose is the most sacred territory of a straight man's existence—his very manhood—a territory onto which trespassing is absolutely forbidden. Only blood could wash away the stain on his honor, restoring his shaken manhood. Blood clarifies the nature of namoose: it exudes a certain aura of incontestable authority. Chimney was to pay for befouling another man's possession, destroying his existential balance forever. The hadji, most certainly, would have liked to kill him but he did not. Chimney had the neighbors and the timely arrival of the Committee to thank for that.

So much he had paid for his brief amorous encounter with his landlord's wife, and so much more he was yet to pay.

Twenty-Two

Four times, the muezzin intones the name of the Lord, "Allah-o Akbar." First, it's a short declaratory strike, precise: God's great. The second time, it's reaffirmation of His greatness: *God* is great. It is He, who is also the Creator, who is great. By the third time, you already know God is great, and you wait to hear just how great. The fourth time, Allah is great like nothing is great; an immense greatness, all-else-is-nothing greatness, nothing-exists-but-his-greatness greatness. It's a long, two-syllable word: Al-laaah.

Allah is most great, Allah is most great; I bear witness there is no god but Allah. I bear witness Mohammad is Allah's messenger.

The inmates awoke lazily, eyes opening and arms stretching, not wishing to get up just yet. The muezzin's solemn voice burst into the twilight of the otherwise silent morning. It came sharp, embellished, tremulous. With a high and clear note, it summoned the faithful to rise and pray. *Come to prayer. Come to prayer. Come to success. God is most great. There is no god but God.*

The inmates had lain sideways on the floor like books on a packed bookshelf—one arm under their trunk going numb, the other on the hip. Some began lighting cigarettes while still in horizontal repose. The muezzin continued with staunch commitment as three inmates emerged from under the sheets: a skinny old gentleman with silver hair and two peasants in baggy clothes. They drew long, body-stretching breaths, folded their blankets, and placed them by the wall under the tacked-up photograph. They were dancers moving to a silent tune in the dim of dawn. Their slow, quiet movements suggested a conspiratorial hope. Cigarette smoke filled the air in layers of blue.

The silver-haired gentleman had been charged with adultery. The word was he had jumped in the sack with his sister-in-law. Quickly repenting when brought to the Office to Combat Vices, he'd seemed genuinely sorry for his misdeed, at such an advanced age. The odds, too, were in his favor. His wife had been dead for five years now, which made him a widower, a more justifiable category for adultery, as regarded his punishment, than had she been alive. Moreover, he was much too frail to bear a hundred lashes. The divine justice, therefore, had allowed him to purchase out 82 percent of his sentence and receive the remainder in three installments. Which he did, and now he was allowed to walk home a free man.

The peasants, though, were not as lucky. They were young and muscular Kurds from a border village in the west. The Moral Squad, a recently established subdivision of the Revolutionary Forces, had found them, drunk out of their minds, squatting by a wall on the sidewalk. There was the suspicion they might be sympathizers of the Kurdish rebels. The poor slobs had traveled to Tehran to buy agricultural hardware. Their sole purpose had been to find the best bargain when, out of the blue, someone in front of a farm-machine dealer offered them a bottle of black-market *arak sagi*,[*] which they ended up drinking on empty stomachs, right there in the street with pedestrians looking on. The crowd Farzin had seen by the entrance of the Palace on his arrival could have been the family members of the young Kurds, who had all the odds stacked against them. It was said they had taken their hundred without even a peep.

The door finally opened when everyone got out of bed and formed a line to use the bathroom. The threesome were escorted out, while a fresh group of sinful souls entered. There were six of them: four in army uniforms sporting potbellies, the other two in

---

[*] Literally, "dog's sweat;" Iranian variant of a Mediterranian liquor much in the vain of Greek Ouzo or Turkish Raki, but without anise.

well-worn jackets and with nicotine-stained fingers. It turned out they were low-ranking government employees, one wearing glasses, the other a broad mustache. A curious air hung over the newcomers as they walked into the windowed room and stood around the window.

"I don't drink," offered the bespectacled government employee. "Never have. Food poisoning's what it was." He shifted foot to foot, then began to pace back and forth. His friend, the mustached one, sat down on the floor close to Farzin and ignored the inmates gathering around them. He grabbed a cigarette from his pocket.

"Am a Moslem myself," he said to Farzin. "Never have abandoned my prayers. I don't belong here." Farzin regarded him with interest as the other lit his cigarette.

"There's this revolutionary Brother who accused me of something," the mustached one offered, "but you know, he's very young. I think to myself, what does he know, you know?" Though his nails were bitten down to the quick, he preached with a translucent arrogance. A thought flashed through Farzin's mind about the mustached one's remark: even in the jails of our land everyone clung to a pure version of the faith. No one ever questioned its boisterous claims, rather, one tried to adapt oneself to its rigid rules. This quaint animal lived off the worst of our fears. *It is something we do to ourselves.*

"What in the devil are you doing in here then?" Jamal interrupted the mustached one.

"A mistake, brother," his reply came matter-of-factly. "Just a simple blunder. As soon as the misunderstandings clear away, I'll be out." It was obvious he was perturbed by Jamal's inquisitiveness.

"And what kind of blunder is that, brother?" Jamal was not letting go. When Mohammad held out an interjecting hand, relief came to the mustached government employee.

"Let me clear up something, baba," said Mohammad. "Everybody here is a victim of either his belly or underbelly." A small crowd, slowly gathering around Mohammad, nodded. He looked the poor fellow square in the eye. The low-ranking government employee looked peeved but kept quiet.

"Then quit your excuses," Mohammad continued. "You've had your drink, and I say more power to you. But don't pretend you didn't do it. Don't lecture us about blunders and whatnot, because you are convincing no one here. Save the crap for the suckers upstairs." A hush fell on the newly arrived inmates as Mohammad continued.

"Take me, for example. I take full responsibility for my drinking. It's about the sanest thing you could do in a country gone mad. And this *baba* here, Mister Jamal Memarchi, fucks anything that moves on this earth, and believe me he's paid his dues. But you don't see us whimpering about. The moment we get out, we'll do it again. I promise you that. You know why? Because life's a grab bag. Go see for yourself."

He was not addressing the government employee now, just ruminating to himself out loud. The other fellow found himself in a vast audience that was dead quiet.

"The problem with us is we're always looking for scapegoats. The way is not to bow, but to stick your finger up society's ass and say, fuck you, society. Fuck you, because you have no business locking me up, that's what you have to say."

Having wrapped up his monologue, Mohammad lit a smoke while Jamal pulled out his tea-making paraphernalia. Breakfast would not be ready until after the morning prayers, but Jamal was holding a tray out to the new inmates.

"For our guests at the Hotel Palace," he said.

After a little while, Mohammad drew closer, shook their hands, and began the inevitable process of making them feel at ease. No matter how brutal the fight, he always ended it like a gentleman. Farzin overheard snippets of pleasantries they were exchanging.

"His Fucking Grace is so out of it he spells cunt with a K," Mohammad said about one of the judges. "And we, dear gentlemen, are required to sit before them, cross-legged, and lips zipped up." A gale of laughter swept over the circle. Then, Jamal stole the show from him and galvanized them all with the promise of something new. He retold the story of the hadji's wife with complete sound effects and histrionics. This time, though, he allowed the ending, which was a rarity: she had died on the way to the hospital from head injuries; her pretty face smashed with a broomstick, those beautiful eyes blackened by her heartbroken husband. Jamal, saddened by her death, said it would be only fair if he took on his share of the blame. He already had, he said. He turned to show his bare back, bearing long bruises from here to there and blisters. A blunt, too facile, smile appeared awkwardly on the corner of the bespectacled fellow's mouth.

Farzin had been thinking that Jamal enjoyed the attention his lash marks got him. With the pride of a wounded soldier, he was now discoursing on the details of the workings of a whip. A good whip, fellows, has slanting teeth. When it goes up, they open like a shark's mouth, and when it comes down, they close, biting off the skin, the flesh. His arms flying in the air, now up, now coming down, demonstrated the workings of an imaginary whip. The whole room was watching Jamal, whose predilection for chasing female bipeds now seemed larger than life. At the least it prepared his audience to expect the worst for themselves. Their eyes gleaming with respect, they watched Chimney, savoring every gesture and word of a man who had seen it all, done it all, and lived through it all. If they followed the Marlboro Man for his seniority and wit, it was Jamal from whom they drew their aspirations.

An imperious, baritone voice came rumbling over the speakers. "Brothers should get on with their ablutions. Get ready for the prayers; God willing, they will be accepted."

As a routine, Mohammad unleashed his humor. "Forget about these corrupted souls, will you? By Allah, they don't deserve the Almighty's mercy .... Best is to leave them alone, because they've never prayed in their lives. *Ohoy*, the truth is they don't know the first thing about praying."

Then, a coarse and abrupt voice came over the system. It named ten prisoners to get ready to go "up." Mohammad was included. Farzin bit his lips and listened carefully; there was no mention of him. Mohammad put his hand on Farzin's shoulder.

"Patience, my friend. Your turn will come, too."

Meanwhile, the inmates stood in rows of six or seven, facing southwest. Mohammad put on his socks in preparation for meeting the judge. "Pray, my ass, you ninnies," he addressed his fellow inmates. "I know what's going on in your chalk-filled heads." Putting on his shoes, he continued, "Look at you sons of bitches; so holy I want to throw up." Shaking his head remorselessly, waiting for the door to open, he cast his eyes about the room.

"You should all be shot for your hypocrisy, no doubt." He gave the clear impression that even if he had not been on his way "up" to see the Agha, he would not have been standing to pray like the rest of them. He seemed to be the only one who could shirk the prayers, flout every rule, the entire system, and get away with it. That was what made him the ultimate antithesis to the administration of the Office to Combat Vices.

Farzin was heartened by Mohammad's defiant gestures but did not find the courage to follow him as far. He rationalized his conformity by reminding himself that, after all, the charges brought against him were far more serious than those Mohammad faced. Farzin wondered whether courageous heroes and remorseless criminals were not alike in at least one respect: fearlessness.

The summoned ten took off with a big fuss. The door closed behind them. The droning of prayers filled the rooms, eyes fixed on the carpet, lips moving silently. Afterward, breakfast rolled in, and an hour later Farzin found himself crouching against the wall, trying to put his pen on a crinkled piece of paper. But he could not drive out of his mind the thought of his friend, who would soon be facing the revolutionary justice. He had heard the judge's name from Mohammad, and something told him that the encounter would not have a good ending.

Twenty-Three

Agha Shirazi's revolutionary credentials were impeccable. During the reign of the first Pahlavi king, when it was decided the clergy was an impediment to progress, all across Persia the mullahs were hunted down and beaten like stray dogs. A handful of young and ambitious mullahs put up resistance, though, Agha Shirazi among them. A relative unknown in the clergy hierarchy, he exhibited such courage and defiance against the dictator that the men of cloth had no choice but to take notice.

In Persia in the 1920s, as midnight leaflets spread dissension, islands of malcontent sprouted up in the ocean of modernity and progress that was sweeping the land. That's how Agha Shirazi went from being an agitator cleric to an underground organizer. More than that, he became an icon in the struggle. Long before Khomeini appeared on the scene, mainly in defiance to the second Pahlavi, the pamphlets and propaganda that came out of the religious underground resistance against the monarchy were mostly issued by Agha Shirazi. There were always a few scribes around him who would jot down his pronouncements, to be distributed among the believers.

The best year in Agha Shirazi's memory was the one after the Sipah-Saulaur Mosque was rebuilt with the money sent from the Najaf scholars in Iraq. The young Shirazi had visited the mosque when it was brand new and had caused quite a scene. The day was a memorable one in which he faced arrogance, and the showdown took the breath out of his companions. He and his scribes had gone to the mosque to pray on the same day the monarch had descended to inspect the new construction. The rebel mullah and his friends were attending to their ablutions by the fountain pool in the mosque's courtyard when the Imperial Guards came and ordered them to clear the way for the Commander in Chief. Imagine that!

You're splashing your face with water, then all of a sudden you raise your head and see a dark figure, twice your stooped height, and clad in a fearsome uniform, who orders you, "Clear the yard for the Shah."

Understandably, everyone present vanished into the basement of the mosque. From their hiding place, though, they peeked through a tiny window that opened to the courtyard. And what did they see in their horror that fixed them in their spot, glued to that tiny bit of an opening? They saw the young mullah still bending over the pool, taking his time dabbing his forehead with his wet hand in ablution. They saw him proceed to do the same to his feet, first the right foot, then the left one, as if nothing were going on around him that demanded his instant attention. He had not moved a centimeter from his spot since that fearsome soldier had raised his voice. Then, they saw him sitting at the edge of the pool, wiping his face with a small checkered towel. They saw the guard's scowling, red face and heard him snarl, "*Ohoy* there, mullah, pack your things and disappear, now."

"Hmmf!" The young mullah kept on with his task, slowly put on his socks, first the right one, then the left, and said not a word.

"Hey, *yauroo baba*, you deaf?" said the soldier. "Didn't you hear me, mullah?" From where the scribes were, they saw the other soldiers closing in on their friend, this man of God, and they saw something else, the power of his conviction.

Now there were four or five soldiers huddling over the unheeding mullah, who was obviously ignoring them for whatever they took themselves to be. They said to him, "Have you taken leave of your senses? Stop this nonsense and clear away, quick. The Shah is passing through the mosque, you know. So beat it, or you'll be locked up."

When they had made up their minds to remove Shirazi, the door to the courtyard opened and hey presto, the cape-wearing monarch entered the scene in a starched, olive-drab uniform and shiny black boots. He cast a look about the yard with those eyes of his that were known to have been able to drill a hole in one's head. Recently he had emerged triumphant from a campaign against a warlord in the southern part of the country. He wielded power without abandon or mercy. When he walked in and saw his soldiers about to lay their hands on this godly cleric, he ordered them to halt. His roar echoed in the courtyard as if an irate lion had just stepped through the door.

The great Reza Khan, formerly known as Reza Maxim for his habit of wearing a cape, approached the mullah and asked him what was going on. "I am an insignificant creature of the Lord," the young Shirazi replied. "I happened to be performing my duties to God, which I consider of utmost importance. Your servants wish to remove me so that I am not a thorn in your lordship's eyes. But I shall not stop my prayers for you or anyone else, no matter how many tin medals are mounted on your chest." Those were the exact terms he used in describing the Shah's adornments: "Tin medals."

The company in the basement supposed that would be the end of Shirazi, as they knew him. No small offense to have ridiculed the dictator, but what did they happen to see next from their hiding place? They saw Reza Khan throw back his head in a body-shaking laughter. Without another word, he left the young cleric to his ablutions.

From then, Agha Shirazi's ascension in the ranks of the Shiite clergy was a straight line to the top.

Twenty-Four

The ward was quiet, an engine out of gas. A drowsy stupor had fallen over the inmates. Some were leaning back against the wall, catching a nap. Smoke thickened near the ceiling. From where Farzin was sitting by the stack of blankets he could see Jamal's back, arms moving as he conversed with his new friends, the army officers. Robust and manly, they were in their mid-forties to fifties with heavy eyelids and dark crescents under their eyes. Their puckered uniforms drenched in sweat, their shame somewhat evaporated, they were talking freely with Jamal. The rest of the inmates were watching from a distance, waiting for Mohammad to return. Farzin had no interest in hearing about Jamal's sexual adventures again. One glance the other way; there was the bathroom door, the small hallway, the door to the outside world. The sun rushed to recede below the western horizon. Holding a stack of papers on his knee, Farzin pressed his pen down gently; it raced hurriedly across the thick, brown paper.

The idea had come to him to show Brother Hamid the true power of the Secrets of Survival. Brother Hamid had reservations about Farzin's account from the beginning, always accusing him of lying, maintaining that these stories had nothing to do with Farzin's case. Farzin felt that if he could show his jailers the real power of the Secrets of Survival, he could then begin to relate to them one of the biggest stories of all time. The only problem now was the issue of how to begin. What would be his angle, the right point of view to choose, in telling his father's story in order to keep intact its veracity? Who among his father's friends told the story better than the others? Farzin had to think hard now and remember. This was the time to remember.

Good old Mr. Manuchehr Partow would have you believe the whole Russian encounter came about so dangerously, recklessly, it could only have been attributed to Nozar Rouhani's obdurate personality. If Mr. Partow could rely on history, the Russians had always been irascible players in the Iranian political scene, more so than ever now that they were equipped with a mesmerizing ideology. Had not they already brought the Sa'id cabinet to its knees and pressured the prime minister to resign? Little did Mr. Partow expect this descendant of Mullah Abbas to stand up to them as though the mighty Russians were a mere band of thugs.

Twenty-Five

In 1940, Mr. Manuchehr Partow had been in the district attorney's office for over five years. He had worked side by side with half a dozen district attorneys who served in the town of Khameneh, but he did not have as clear a memory of any of them as he did of Mr. Nozar Rouhani. Their relationship started in the cold climate of their shared office, where two antique desks and a small kerosene-fueled Aladdin heater were the furnishings. He remembered the new district attorney as a stocky man in his mid-twenties, with a limp in his left leg that was equally as significant as his simple minded idealism.

There was no justice to it; even though Mr. Partow was the older of the two (by eight years), and had a longer service record, Mr. Rouhani was appointed to lead the DA's office due to some freakish decision by the newfound bureaucracy. His university credentials no doubt had something to do with it; they had given him a jump start unavailable to Mr. Partow's generation. For this, Mr. Partow silently envied his supervisor. After all, Mr. Partow did have seniority. But he also believed in the system with his whole being and did not complain when the orders came. There must have been a good reason for Mr. Rouhani's good fortune. Not just educated but dedicated he was, and brilliant and serious. Furthermore, for motives unknown to Mr. Partow, it seemed Mr. Rouhani was unable to see things in any light other than the civil code he had embraced so guilelessly. For that, if not for any other reason, Mr. Manuchehr Partow came to love and respect Mr. Nozar Rouhani.

The noisiest-ever commotion in town occurred two weeks after Mr. Nozar Rouhani had settled into his new position. Seven truck drivers had gotten into a knife brawl over a woman of questionable repute. It seemed they had not been able to peacefully decide who amongst them should go with her first. Blades shone in the moonlight, and anger ripped the placid air. A few drops of blood, and the police had put them all under arrest. Paper dossiers piled up and telephone calls flooded the DA's office, most notably the one from the police chief.

It was a frigid morning when the telephone rang. Mr. Partow immediately recognized the high-pitched voice of the corpulent police chief.

"The Russian commandant is here," he said quickly, "with five armed guards." His voice was a note higher than usual and he wanted a decision. Mr. Partow passed the receiver to his boss.

"What does he want?" Mr. Rouhani said as he took the receiver.

The commandant did not care about why the police had booked those hoodlums. He just expected the district attorney to release them, immediately, so they could take their cargo up north to the war front.

"Bullshit."

Mr. Partow, who was politically inclined and followed the news religiously, made a note to himself that Mr. Rouhani might not be familiar with the implications of the political treaty that had been signed in the capital. He might not have thought of the consequences of what he was now saying to the police chief.

"You know the law," Mr. Rouhani was saying. "What're you ringing me for?"

"If you would please run it by me, once," the police chief said, "it might help me to remember."

"I can't release anyone without the court's order." Mr. Rouhani hung up before the chief could say anything else.

Butler Mamdali was a bent man in declining years with tattooed arms and chest, who fired up the kerosene heater first thing in the morning, every day, and prepared steaming tumblers of tea for his superiors. This morning he had brought Mr. Rouhani his tumbler, full just as he liked it, not too strong, with two sugar lumps beside it on the saucer. The kettle, set on the Aladdin, billowed a steady steam into the room. Mr. Rouhani had started the day as usual, relaxed. After the phone conversation with the police chief, he and Mr. Partow had engaged in a small exchange that was indicative of their relationship. Mr. Partow had been the initiator of the exchange.

"I think the Russians will insist on the truckers' release," Mr. Partow had said. He had said it casually, just to ease the rising tension. At that point, he might have said anything, but it so happened that that particular thought was on his mind, and he said it, no regrets. He watched as Mr. Rouhani tossed his pencil on the ledger in front of him and raised his head with a general's confidence. He nailed his stare on Mr. Partow, whose forehead turned a vivid shade of red.

"What sovereign country are you living in, Mr. Partow?" When he heard no reply to his question, he went on. "Allow me to remind you that I work for the Ministry of Justice. That makes me a servant of this government and this nation. And my job, as a servant of this nation, is to defend its sovereignty at all cost. If you would like to continue working for this government, I suggest you assume the same position." He directed his cold stare down at his desk, indicating the end of the conversation.

Half an hour later, the firm bootsteps of the Russian commandant were heard climbing up the humble stairwell of the district attorney's office. They echoed throughout the dull, antiquated building.

Butler Mamdali opened the door and ushered the commandant into the office, where he clicked his heels and saluted. In the middle of the room stood a baby-faced officer in his early thirties with a walrus mustache, a high pompadour, and the bluest eyes

Nozar Rouhani had ever seen. Anger had painted his clean-shaven face chalk white; the tips of his mustache twitched like a squirrel's tail.

Mr. Partow stood up to acknowledge the Russian but noticed that Mr. Rouhani had not risen from his seat. The Russian took his cue from this, turned to Mr. Rouhani without pretension, and spoke directly at him.

"If you don't release them now," he said, his hand firmly on his pistol, "I will take them by force." His Persian was fluent, and Nozar Rouhani found him intimidating. He looked at the Russian and remained quiet, hands joining each other, fingers locked, his thumbs chasing each other in circles.

"I know why you don't wish to speak to me," the Russian went on. "You lawyers are the same the world over." At this he turned to Mr. Partow and said, "He's not deaf, is he?"

Mr. Partow answered, "For formality's sake—"

"Fuck formality," the commandant snapped back; he left as fast as he had come, and it wasn't long before the telephone rang in the district attorney's office one more time.

"This guy is here again." The police chief was obviously nervous. "He means business."

"No problem," said Nozar Rouhani. "Just write up a process-verbal in two copies and make him sign it. Then let him take the prisoners, and send me a copy as soon as possible."

Hanging up the phone, Mr. Rouhani dropped everything and began to write up a report to his superiors in Tehran. Accompanying the report and the copy of the process-verbal, he sent a letter addressed to the minister:

As a new agent of the Ministry of Justice in Khameneh, I feel increasingly ambivalent as to what our role should be in this God-forsaken town. As is evident in our report, the police arrested a band of criminal elements that had shamelessly disquieted our neighborhoods, but because of a gunslinging Russian commandant, we are unable to prosecute them according to our books. If the Russians can curb our judiciary whenever they want, then what is the purpose of our mission? Would it not be more appropriate if we closed up shop and went home? How to save face? If this servant is worthy of making a suggestion to the honorable minister, he would humbly suggest this story be related to the Russians, via our capable Foreign Ministry, with the intention of committing the Russians to a minimum of diplomatic protocol and respect for our sovereignty so as to prevent such breaches of justice in the future.

Mr. Nozar Rouhani had Mr. Partow type the letter neatly on his fine letterhead. He read it several times to make sure there were no errors, then added "Respectfully Yours," by hand, signed and sealed it, and sent it to Tehran via courier.

Three weeks later, the Russian commandant showed up in the DA's office; his demeanor softer, a faint smile on his lips.

"That report of yours to Tehran," he said. "There must be some misunderstanding." The commandant joined his palms in front of his chest and gave them a shake. "Please understand," he kept saying. "We're on the same side—please."

He waited for Nozar to offer him a seat, to give a cordial sign, a crack, so he could slide in and flatter him. But Nozar remained defiant, did not offer him a seat, nor did he give the officer a chance to charm him with saccharine pleasantries.

"Maybe we didn't do right by you, but we always have respected the local law. And for that reason I'm here to apologize to you and ask you to withdraw your complaint."

Nozar could not hide his surprise; his letter had had some effects. An amused smile spread on his face. For the first time in this ordeal he must have felt powerful enough to sneer at the Russian.

"All right, Monsieur Commandant, I accept your apology."

The commandant extended his hand, which was accepted with reluctance. He said softly, "Would you report to your superiors that everything is forgotten, then? I mean, you know—as a goodwill gesture .... It's not important to me, you see—it's only a formality."

The smile froze on Nozar's face. He leaned over his desk and brought his face close to the Russian.

"FUCK FORMALITY."

The sheer force of Nozar Rouhani's shout seemed to shock the commandant. He turned to Mr. Partow, who also looked wide-eyed, and turned back to Mr. Rouhani. Then his thin lips opened in disbelief and he fell into a burst of wild laughter as he stared at the DA. Mr. Partow kept out of the fray like a child keeping out of adults' affairs.

Mr. Rouhani continued. "From what I've noticed about you, commandant, you're a straightforward man. As a token of appreciation, I will be just as direct with you, because both of us are busy men and I hate to waste your precious time. As far as your formal apology goes, like I said, all's forgotten, and you can count on that. But a formal— that is—retrieval would have to be contingent upon the return of the prisoners who were taken out of our jailhouse. That's all I have to say on this matter, and I wish you a good day."

Stung by the district attorney's sharp tongue, the Russian left without a word. He had never been humiliated by a civilian before, not even in his own country. If it were not for his strict orders to reach a speedy compromise with the mulish district attorney, he would not have even gone so far as to apologize. Personally, he didn't care, but as was explained to him, things had to go silky smooth for a while because there were important oil negotiations being conducted between Comrade Stalin and the Iranian government, and nothing was to be allowed to obstruct them.

Mr. Partow had sensed the Russian's anger at the turn of events. He was fearful of how this game would end. He clearly did not have the stomach for it but secretly admired Mr. Rouhani for his courage. *Where did he find the brass to contradict the Russian?*

That was not the last of the commandant, however. Barely a week had gone by when he was back in the district attorney's office. This time four of the seven drivers were with him, handcuffed and looking puzzled.

"I won't move a centimeter from my seat," said the commandant, "until you, Mr. District Attorney, fulfill your promise."

He looked on as Nozar Rouhani wrote a letter to the ministry. In it he stuck to the facts, reporting that four of the seven wanted individuals were back in city jail, awaiting trial. He signed and sealed a copy for the Russian officer, who folded it and fled out the door.

Still, that was not quite the end of the Russian. His wounded pride would not let him rest until he could savor payback time. A showdown was inevitable.

Twenty-Six

A commotion by the door disturbed the calm. Farzin looked up from his notes. Dinner was on its way. There was no sign of Mohammad, so Jamal, being next in the pecking order, prepared to supervise the giving out of food. Jumping to his feet, he summoned his lieutenants. He delegated authority to whomever popped in his way as he headed to the door. Meanwhile, a gigantic pot of stew rolled in on four wheels.

"*Ohoy*, get on the other side," he said. "Watch out, *yauroo*, it's hot." The predinner hustle and bustle had begun. As he moved about swiftly, Jamal's shouts beat the idle atmosphere. "*Yallah baba*, what to do?" He said "move, move" to idlers. He poked and cajoled and it was very clear this was no time to disobey. "Give a hand here, fellows. Make way, make way." He doled out the silverware and said, "Mind giving us a hand? No stealing." He admonished, "You shit-head, *goh*, I said you, *goh*, get out of my way." Sweat slid down his forehead; he wiped off the running drops with an overused kerchief. "Not you, I'm talking to that jackass …." White plastic sheets of a lunch-spread, *sofreh,* three feet wide, made a square margin on the floor of every room. The water jug, bread, salt and pepper shakers, and spoons sat side by side on it. The inmates not involved with the food distribution sat on both sides of the *sofreh*, engaged in small talk, waiting. Jamal served the steaming meal with a large wooden ladle. Bowls of brownish liquid with yellow islets of potatoes passed hands, dancing their way to the remotest corners of the seemingly endless *sofreh*, landing on the plastic sheet like flying saucers.

Standing near the bathroom door, Farzin watched the action. The speed and organization of the inmate body made ludicrous any hint of spontaneity. He admitted to himself that there were more complex mechanisms at work, efficient in subtle ways. The setting invoked the whole enigma of Persian food being as complicated as the Persian soul. It moved him each time he watched this riveting display of caring and discipline: an intimate cooperative experience not unlike that of a beehive. Farzin had come to know the players and their gesticulations; he could predict every one of their quirks. From spreading the *sofreh* to handing out the utensils; someone here with dishes, someone looking for a place to sit. Saltshakers and bread arranged in a row; *does that indicate something?* Count loves-me, loves-me-not. Spoons crossing the forks; *what story does that tell?* There was going to be a problem? Ho, ho. The fights were all behind and, maybe, some would be ahead. But for the time being, let's break the bread, toss it in the bowl, and let it soak up the gravy. Farzin had replayed this scene in his mind over and over. It was as though a hidden thread connected each fellow inmate to the ringmaster, Jamal. All seemed content with their duties, convinced that what they were doing was essential.

Twenty-Seven

Dinner was Abgousht, a stew of meat, potatoes, onions, split peas, and dried Omani lemons. But surprise, no surprise, there was no meat in today's Abgousht, only peas and potatoes floating in the thin gravy. How do you explain the absence of meat in a dish that is named after meat? It's like making pomegranate paste without pomegranate. "We share our food with the guards," explained Jamal to the army officers. "They take the meat, we take the rest; poor sons of bitches."

In the midst of dinner the door opened and in walked Mohammad, slumped and pissed, a butt drooping at the corner of his mouth. He looked at the spread with disinterest, even derision, and everyone thought he no longer found it appetizing to eat with them. Perhaps he was being let go and he'd returned to gather his things. Nevertheless, a place opened for him to sit as a sign of respect, and when he ignored the invitation no one seemed rebuffed. It was expected.

"Not hungry," said he. Mumbling to himself, he went straight to a corner by the wall and squatted. "A motherfucking mullah acting as the judge?" he was heard cursing under his breath. "Whose idea was it in the first place?" He put out his cigarette and pushed the corners of his thick mustache between his beefy lips, chewing them with intent. An inquiring silence poised itself in the air.

Dinner over, the inmates gathered in the room with the window to play games and tell jokes. Farzin, Jamal, and a few others gathered around the Marlboro Man to find out how his hearing went. They prodded him to recount everything from the moment he had walked out the door. That was the easy part. Six of the summoned inmates headed downstairs to the basement. Two guards in front and two in the back led them in single file. Soon they disappeared behind the imposing columns. The remaining four went for their respective hearings, an armed guard assigned to escort each upstairs. Golden rays slanted through windows. Boots marching echoed in the empty halls.

Twenty-Eight

A young, dark-skinned guard with glaring eyes and a thin feathery beard, laboring under his machine gun, beckoned Mohammad to follow him. Mohammad obeyed, suppressing the embarrassment of having to follow a child a quarter his age. Silently they went through the hallway with Mohammad throwing glances about and behind, inspecting the corridors, evaluating the possibility of a breakout. They were soon standing outside the Agha's office.

When the revolutionary forces had taken over the Palace, Ayatollah Shirazi's office was handpicked in the newest wing of the Palace in a suite complete with a large bathroom, a sauna, and a whirlpool for six. A sign of the revolutionary times, this last item was covered with a plastic sheet. At the beginning, the problem had been the ornate decorations. Thus the door's golden knob had turned to brass, and the walls rid themselves of superfluous pictures. Perished were all ungodly references. Removed were the armchairs and sofas and expensive lamps with fringed shades. A tape of Koran recitations played nonstop somewhere in the vicinity. The place now spoke of God and piety and prayers.

The fur-faced child-guard stuck his head in the door and out. He explained that the Ayatollah was busy right this minute. "Let's fill out some forms."

So down the stairs they went to the filing office and got busy with the forms. They checked back twice more; the Agha was still unavailable.

Noontime. Lunch was in full swing with the low-ranking brothers in the kitchen, which was in an entirely different wing of the building. Greasy pots and pans hung from even greasier walls. The grill was piping hot, as was the oven, a cook busy with each. The brothers sat on long benches and ignored Mohammad. The bread made a round, torn to pieces by rough hands. They ate and left their plates in the sink, even though there was no one to wash them yet. It turned out that everything was washed once a day, at nighttime, when the cleaning crew came late from another job. A good look at the place, and thoughts of escape occurred to Mohammad. The building appeared less of a fortification now that he had had a chance to see more of it. There were only a dozen guards. *Nothing to it.*

The Agha was finally ready to see Mohammad at two o'clock, and not a minute earlier. No sooner had Mohammad walked in the door then it shut behind him. In the back of the room, a stooped, bearded figure in a long caftan sat cross-legged on the floor behind a small table. A pair of rimless spectacles hung down at the wings of his eagle nose, while a second pair peeked from his breast pocket. He was framed by two huge windows. The Agha's turban lay unwound next to him. A white lace cap resting on a hairless head signaled distinction and taste. In addition to the books on the table, there were three other piles around him on the floor. And nearby, on the carpet, stood a cut-glass Fatah Ali Shahi waterpipe with a beaded, translucent maroon bowl that made gurgling sounds every time the Agha put his mouth to the end of a hose attached to its hand-carved stem.

The ayatollah had been regarding a slim folder which consisted of a few pages of notes in longhand, wrapped in dog-eared brown covers. It was obvious that his eminence had just stepped out of a bath. Leaning back on a couple of cushions comfortably placed on the floor, he seemed out of breath, a rosary in his frail hand keeping count of the hushed holy verses emitting from his lips, through white coarse hairs. Gently caressing the beads with his freckled fingers, he smelled as if he had been soaking in rose water. He seemed well served and well fed. A framed photograph of the republic's founder, the soul and spark of the Revolutionary

Forces, scowled down at Mohammad from the wall. The smell of freshly washed carpet lingered in the air, mixed with the attar of henna and the sweet floral aroma emanating from the Agha's threadbare, yet clean, clothing.

Mohammad waited to be acknowledged with the sheer confidence of a man certain of his innocence. Only, he had no inkling his wait would be in vain.

Twenty-Nine

Agha Shirazi's lips moved ever so slightly as he silently read Mohammad's file. Without raising his head or uttering a syllable, the Agha motioned for Mohammad to step forward. Round and round, a fly buzzed in the air above the senior cleric's head and finally bumped into the window. Three candles and a tulip lamp, perfumed with musk and ambergris, looked out of place on the shelf between the windows. Standing amongst all that piety, Mohammad felt the itch for tobacco rise in his throat but decided against it. The craving remained within him, suppressed like a genie in a bottle.

Occasionally, the ayatollah wrote something in the margin of the folder or remorsefully shook his head. The irritable silence poured in from the walls, and Mohammad found the utter stillness of things unbearable. He hoped the grand Agha would soon speak to him and, one way or another, get it over with. The Agha, however, took his sweet time perusing the file, and the silence stretched. In all his prison experiences, Mohammad had rarely felt so helpless, rarely imagined a day that he would be so much at the mercy of another man, much less a character so despised and feared. The full impact of this realization blanketed his entire being.

Standing idle at the center of the room, Mohammad studied the flowery pattern on the carpet. It was a deep red, paisley work of Kaushaun, with all the exuberant secondary colors for which Persian carpets are famous: pistachio green, brown, light earthy pink. It was a plump cushion of a texture, tight knots. He traced the floral patterns that converged in the middle, forming a red circle. Suddenly, he felt the room move about him. He rubbed his eyes and recalled thoughts of escape he had entertained earlier. *A man could easily fit in one of those stewpots on ball bearings. That would be the way to get to the kitchen. What then? How to get out of the kitchen and into the street?*

The door behind him opened and shut; a veiled woman quietly entered the room. Agha Shirazi raised his head from the folder. His searching glance passed Mohammad as if he did not exist. Then the same hand that had instructed Mohammad to approach the center of the room invited the woman to come nearer—a vague, fragile dance of the wrist, come, come. Throwing the file on the table, he looked at the woman from above his glasses and ordered Mohammad to leave the room for now, "and wait outside until you're called."

Confused and angry, Mohammad backed away in the direction of the door. His frustration did not stop him from noticing the woman, who had a small build. She held her chador tight around her face. As Mohammad approached the door, she moved out of his way, and he noticed a few ginger hairs that sprung out of a mole on her right cheek. She stole a glance at him as he opened the door to exit.

Fur-face had been leaning against the wall. He didn't ask what had happened or why Mohammad was out so soon. They waited together. The halls were not air-conditioned, but a current blew, once in a while, a breeze of warm air. Mohammad felt the growing weight of his eyelids. He sat down with his back to the wall and stretched his legs. He was tired, but the thought of Agha Shirazi and the woman having sexual congress on the other side of the wall intrigued him. He smiled meekly at the notion.

After a few minutes of sitting outside the ayatollah's office with Fur-face watching him, Mohammad found himself in a reclining position despite the hardness of the floor. And it was sleep that crept in and washed over him. Woken an hour later, he saw Fur-face, who was crouching over him, as if examining his dreams. Then he struggled to stand up. The door to Agha Shirazi's room opened and shut quickly as Mohammad rose to his feet. The silhouetted figure of the woman, fixing her chador outside the door, caught his eye. In her struggle to tidy herself, she showed a glimpse of her face and neck, not entirely unwillingly. Mohammad took it in, the flash of skin, and stared at her, leaving no doubt he was doing so, yet she did not seem rushed or even embarrassed. She was so smooth she was a treat, almost a work of art. She then secured her chador and disappeared down the marble spiral staircase.

That was a summary of Mohammad's day. He stamped out his cigarette in the matchbox ashtray and rose to his feet.

Thirty

Mohammad got up to introduce a new game he wanted to play. "It's called the Islamic Justice Game," he said, pacing up and down self-absorbedly. Did anyone know what Islamic justice was? Certainly they did, but a positive answer was not enough.

"Listen up, brothers," said Mohammad, mimicking the guards' vernacular, dragging his syllables. "Calm down and listen up. Take the cotton balls out of your ears and put them in your mouths." All eyes were on him now, conversations cut off or dissolved into whispers as he raised his right arm to quiet an imaginary audience stretched beyond the walls.

"In the name of Allah, the Compassionate, the Merciful," he began. "Hail to the great leader of the Revolution, and salute to the martyr-rearing nation of Islam, and hail and glory to the infidelity-fighting soldiers of Islam, who are battling against the Eastern and Western arrogance, and so forth, led by the world-predator America, and so forth, and its Zionist agents and so forth." Here he paused to suppress a chuckle. "We are now in the court of Islam, and as you know everybody must remain silent throughout the proceedings." Raising his index finger, he continued. "One peep out of anyone, and I shall have his *doo-dool* cut off and fed to the dogs." A gale of laughter erupted. Mohammad pointed at the only fellow who was still laughing after everyone else had stopped, a naughty smile playing at the corner of his mouth. "You, Brother, come forward .... Why don't *you* stand on trial before this dear crowd?"

All heads turned toward a dimpled, scrawny, and somewhat languorous youth with the gleaming, expectant eyes of a child. He sprang to his feet with a perkiness suggesting he might be one dome short of a full minaret.

Loony Enayat was one of those unsuspecting human specimens who adapts easily to any situation. He had been in the Office to Combat Vices longer than anyone else—eight, nine, ten months? Loony Enayat would not mind being here for the rest of his life, Jamal had once said, a sentiment commonly shared by all, and especially corroborated by Mohammad.

Presently, Mohammad put his hand on Loony Enayat's shoulder. "This man you see before your eyes," he said, "has had a rough past. His sister was arrested around Saint Davood's shrine this winter past, for soliciting customers. Himself? He's been a poor beggar since he learned to walk."

With that introduction, Enayat came to life. "Go on," said Mohammad kindly. "Care to say something?"

"The finest beggar in Shah Abdul Azim," said Enayat—the town located south of Tehran with the shrine of Saint Abdul Azim being the tomb site of Imam Reza's brother. Loony Enayat just had to make certain the history was not trampled upon by their ignorance.

The misplaced pride with which he corrected Mohammad drew a laugh and amused Mohammad. He patted Enayat on the back.

"Very impressive," Mohammad emphasized, smiling a mocking smile that mirrored itself on the lips of his audience. "Why don't you display your art, friend? Come on, just for us."

Momentarily, Loony Enayat dropped to the floor and with a twist of his arm and wrist affected a handicap hard to disbelieve. Meanwhile, his tongue stuck out, and his head cocked sideways, shaking violently. Enayat's hoax produced another laugh, and Farzin thought he saw an odd spark of joy in his eyes. *Perhaps it reminds him of the good old days, when his job was to offer peace of mind.*

People fall for that. The petite bourgeoisie hopes God, in return, will take note of their generosity and keep illness and misfortune at bay.

The illegitimate child of a merchant and his mute housemaid, Enayat had found himself on the streets of southern Tehran after the merchant's wife kicked him and his mother out of his house. The boy was five then. It took his mother quite a while to find and marry someone, a beggar, and a while longer before they moved to a raggedy shack by the railroads. It was not much but it was enough to huddle in with his mother and provide his first memories of her kindness before going out with the other boys from similar shacks to make mischief. There, at least, they had a roof over their heads, if you could call it that. It was made of cardboard; tin sheets for roofing, which was fine, unless it rained.

His stepfather, the finest beggar of the batch, was a kind man who took Enayat under his wing and taught him all the tricks of the trade; he was good at shoving alms bowls at fancy women. He and his stepfather stayed out late together, making money and having a grand time, while his mother worked as a housemaid for the well-to-do. Together they were building something for themselves. His mother even became pregnant again. Her belly came up like a balloon. Nine months and nine days later, she gave birth to a baby girl, and all was truly well. That is, until one day his stepfather left the house and was strangled to death by another beggar in a turf war. And that was the end of Enayat's training. From then he was obligated to earn a living on his own. All was not so well after that in the household of three, without a man.

With the death of his stepfather, the nine-year-old Enayat became the chief breadwinner of the family, which was hard on the little man, especially after his mother became sick and could not find work as easily. This went on for years while he worked hard and made enough to keep his sister off the streets. When his mother died, it became harder to keep the adolescent girl in line. Nothing could stop her from breaking away. No sooner had the government taken their mother away to bury her, than the girl had embarked upon a career of amatory adventure that would lead her down the path to the Office to Combat Vices.

Mohammad pulled at Enayat's sleeve and ordered him to get up; what did he think this was, the holy scene of the saint or something? Then he turned to the new inmates. "Never mind him, gentlemen; got a loose screw in his head. Takes pride in the trouble he went through honing his craft, he does. All day long he talks about the fine points of his craft, whether it's a new scam he's come up with, a catchphrase, or a funny story about something or another that happened either to him or to an associate of his."

Mohammad paused to clear his throat. "Enayat's so dedicated to his profession," he went on, "that before going to sleep at night, he mumbles, 'the most successful beggar.'" With this he smacked the beggar at the back of his neck.

The sight of Enayat being hit by Mohammad was received with delight. He hopped comically up and down, pleading incoherently. Farzin watched the scene from a corner and reached a conclusion of his own. Enayat was harmless and innocent, a child in the body of a grown man. The way he shook his shaven head, tilting it to one side then to the other with his mouth open and his tongue lolling out, *no way that he could be a menace*. And yet the show was going on.

"So, tell us, brother," Mohammad said snidely, "how did you happen to end up in this joint?" All eyes were on Enayat with elaborate interest, waiting for a stupid remark for explanation. The misfit himself took note of his predicament, biting at a cuticle, looking vacuously about the room. He blinked his light brown eyes rapidly in expectation of the coming hour and moved his other hand helplessly before him. Suddenly, apropos to nothing at all, Mohammad came up behind him, slapped the back of his neck, and sent the startled beggar dashing headfirst for the floor.

This drew another round of hilarity. Some laughed with closed mouths, striving to keep a straight face.

"Asked you a simple question, you *jakash*, pimp. Why can't you just answer it?" It was impossible to tell whether Enayat was hurt more from the physical assault or from being laughed at. Leaping to his feet, he clumsily threw a punch at Mohammad, which was ducked. Again, a gale of laughter went up in the air.

Something was beginning to bother Farzin; he was finding less amusement and more humiliation as the scene turned against Loony Enayat. He wanted to interfere with the circus. Once or twice, when Mohammad raised his arm to suggest he was about to attack, Enayat protested with a voice like a squeaky kazoo.

"Don't hit me. Please don't. Why do you hit me? Why? Don't you know if you hit a descendant of the Prophet, you'll go to hell? Don't you?"

Although there was a certain amount of fear in his voice, Loony Enayat made warning signals in the air with his forefinger. And Farzin had a second revelation. He began to doubt Enayat's sincerity in his contempt for Mohammad. Might all have been a hoax; Enayat merely playing along.

"Loony Enayat! Sing for us," someone trumpeted from a corner. Mohammad seconded the idea.

"Sing or stand trial," he said.

Enayat obeyed. Sitting upright like a desperate rat, he folded his legs underneath his body. He raised his right arm slowly, holding his hand behind his ear in the way of Persian passion-play singers. Then a feeble voice as pathetic as it was peevish began to drip from his mouth.

"Yaur ... Friend ... My old-time lover."

To top it off, he closed his eyes to emphasize the lyrics and invoke sympathy, but in lieu of empathy he conveyed wretchedness. Farzin felt there was nothing sadder in the world than seeing

Enayat shake his head slowly right and left as he vented. Sporadic laughter erupted and lingered in the background. Could hardly be called singing, the pathetic act he had embarked upon. His voice was an insult to music and poetry all at once, and his audience, understandably, grew loud and boisterous.

"Yaur ... Friend ... My old-time lover."

But then something else happened. Out of this mess a wailing emerged that demanded sympathy. All jeering stopped; even Mohammad listened with a certain amount of interest. He stared at Enayat and waited until he finished. Then, with one hand under his chin and a gesture half real and half put on, he ordered the poor beggar to get up.

"No! That won't do, I'm afraid," Mohammad said. "You're going to be prosecuted." At this, Jamal and two of his cronies approached the poor bastard. They stood before the audience unfolding a bedsheet, stretched to resemble a white wall behind him. Meanwhile, Jamal spread another sheet on the floor and guided Enayat to stand on it. Now, with the two fellows on either side of him, looking like Revolutionary Guards holding two corners of a white banner, and a third one squatting down behind all them, Mohammad started the procedure.

"In the name of the Almighty, tell us, to what do we owe your filthy presence here?" Winking at the bemused audience, Mohammad made circles around his ear with his forefinger. Enayat squinted, apparently sensing trouble, but went along and began telling his story of how one day he vanished, like smoke rising up into the sky.

After his sister had been arrested by the vigilante Moral Squad, a small independent outfit in the vast ocean of Revolutionary Forces, Enayat wandered the streets for days. He did not know where to begin to look for her, until somebody suggested the Office to Combat Vices, since she had been arrested for prostitution. The man did not guarantee she would be found there, but his suggestion was better than doing nothing. So, there he was at the Office to Combat Vices one bright morning, describing what his sister looked like to the guards. He told them that she was a young woman with long black hair, kind of short, with a large mole on her right cheek and a terrible lisp. The brothers asked him to fill out a form and make an official request. The petition should bear his signature, they said, and a recent photo of the missing person would be helpful; if a veiled photo was not available, any old one would do. That was when Enayat came out candidly saying that he neither read nor wrote and that he had no fixed address. They grew wide-eyed, the brothers did, and probed further: how come? They asked where he lived and what his line of work was. And he made a clean breast of it: the prostitution, the begging business, the whole sappy, long story.

"The most successful beggar in the whole Shah Abdul Azim," he had said. Not very wise of him to tell everything, he understood; it was all in the past and he could not change that now. They sent him away with a guard, and from what he imagined, since then nobody had heard from the crippled beggar in Shah Abdul Azim.

"Overnight he vanished off the face of the earth." Mohammad stepped forward. "You see, brothers," he said mockingly, pointing at Enayat, "this is a true criminal, the most dangerous of them all." Again laughter interrupted the proceedings of Mohammad's court, and this time he did not make a motion to calm it. He just stood there with folded arms, his tongue between his teeth. After a long pause, he read the verdict from an imaginary notepad.

"Guilty," he said.

No sooner had the words come out of his mouth than Jamal yanked the sheet from under the beggar, sending the poor fellow tripping over the inmate squatting behind him. Laughter shook the walls. Some of the audience held their stomachs and rolled on the floor or leaned on the shoulders of those sitting next to them. The rest slapped their knees or howled with abandon. Sitting up, a disturbed Enayat stared at his tormenters, a narrow stream of blood painting his upper lip. His face burning, he turned around and gaped at Mohammad, who lent him a handkerchief.

Enayat opened his mouth to say something, but no sound came out. Perhaps he wanted to protest and to say this was not what he had in mind, that he did not want to be tried in this way. Not a word, though. So he went to his corner and folded up, holding the stained handkerchief to his nose. He jiggled his knee and kept up his rocking, back and forth, back and forth. Later, he quietly crawled under his blanket, looking defeated.

This was the end of the game, for no one else volunteered to be put on trial in Mohammad's Islamic court. The assembly scattered; little groups of four or five formed to smoke and tell tales of past loves. One more day in Farzin Rouhani's life had given way to night. He hugged his knees and glanced out the window. A moonless sky, in all its reverence, displayed a few stars and patches of clouds that would amount to nothing. Beds were being spread here and there. Lights would go out soon. He felt lonely, without a friend. He began to regard Mohammad with different eyes, seeing the weak man he was, the cruelty that was in him.

Clear across the room, Mohammad discussed his day with the army officers and Jamal. Tugging at his cigarette hungrily, he turned his head to one side and blew smoke over his shoulder. What had happened after Mohammad left Shirazi's office? Had the chadori woman, who had flashed a healthy neck and outlines of healthy breasts at him, become intimate with the Agha in the biblical sense?

"But where there is an erection, there is a way," said Mohammad. "They could have temporarily wedded, you know."

Farzin squatted down in a corner of the room with a stack of paper and his well-worn pen.

A few months after the commandant's humiliating defeat at the hands of the young district attorney, and his hasty departure from the office, the Russian garrison threw a party and invited the local worthies and magnates to celebrate the victory of Stalingrad. The invitation that arrived at the district attorney's office was adorned with gold lettering and fancy calligraphy, to fit both the merry occasion and the position of the addressed. It said the following: "The Victory of Stalingrad, as the turning point of the war, has created a tide of optimism around the world. It has prompted the workers and well-wishers of the Allies to celebrate the victory of the civilized world over the perpetrators and blood-sucking warmongers of Berlin-Rome. We, the army of the proletariat, will honor your presence at the third anniversary of this great victory."

With not much happening in the small town by way of entertainment, Mr. Partow and his boss decided to attend.

The lights began to go out. Everyone was in bed, almost everyone. Farzin was used to their snoring. From where he sat, near the window, he stared outside. Even the streetlamp was out now. It was a moonless pitch-dark summer sky: still, icily indifferent, untouchable.

Thirty-One

The anniversary party to celebrate the victory of Stalingrad was held at the Russian armory. The mud-brick building with its ventilation tower, a keepsake from 19th-Century Persian architecture, was bathed in the dying afternoon sun. When Mr. Partow arrived in the company of Mr. Rouhani, the Russians were already working toward a state of mindless inebriation. There were shouts and hoots and the stamping feet of swaying officers around and above and under the square tables that had been arranged in meticulous order but were now in complete disarray. A group of six was dancing to the music of their comrades' whistles and rhythmic applause. A giant flag of the Soviet Union adorned the opposite wall, under the depiction of a solemn Stalin with his great broom of a mustache. For security purposes there were a dozen *saldats* outside guarding the place, ammunition belts strapped diagonally across their torsos, their eyes shining with pride. There were also six or eight armed soldiers inside, watching their superiors make complete asses of themselves.

Upon seeing the crowd of tilting rowdy men, Mr. Rouhani hesitated to enter. If it had not been for Mr. Partow's reassurances that they were there in an official capacity and not for personal pleasure, he would have returned the same way in which he had come. As they entered the armory, having flashed their invites, a well-spoken saldat ushered them into a back room where their host, the commandant, sat comfortably with a group of local dignitaries and military notables around a long and wide table, which was covered with plates of French and Russian dishes, all colorful and steaming. There was *duck à l'orange*, golden crusted soufflés, racks of roast lamb with fresh mint sauce, a huge tureen of bouillabaisse, trays of melon-orange smoked salmon and crystal bowls of pickled carrots, green and black olives, burgundy beets, and tiny pearl onions that glistened like jewels in their sour brine.

The rosy-cheeked commandant seemed amiable, smoking a fat cigar, a snake of apple peel coiled in his plate. He half rose from his seat to introduce his newly arrived VIPs to the ones already present. The garbling in his speech and the slight rocking of his body as he held his cigar at chest level did not escape Mr. Rouhani. He was offered a seat across from the Russian, which he took with great hesitation.

By training, Nozar Rouhani would not step over boundaries he imagined between himself and the commandant. He saw himself as the proud representative of his occupied land, facing the occupier, and did not extend his hand to acknowledge his drunken host.

The commandant was lucid, without any trace of his former anxiety, but was conscious of himself in terms of how he was perceived as an agent of a military might. He tapped the ash from his cigar in a maneuver of classic elegance and doubled his efforts to focus his attention on the district attorney. Words became jumbled in his head, and he found the nuanced language of his host country increasingly elusive.

Halfway through the evening, the commandant raised his glass and, speaking directly to his adversary, expressed his extreme good fortune to be hosting this congregation. Glasses full to the brim with vodka rose in the air and were poured down the throats of hefty men. The only glass that remained unmoved on the table was that of Nozar, who was busy chewing a mouthful rather than following Monsieur Tavarish's lead in drinking.

"I must apologize, Mr. Rouhani," the Russian blurted half drunkenly, expelling a plume of smoke. "I'll have the butler shot at dawn."

The guests turned to Mr. Rouhani and saw that the glass sitting before him was empty. They heard the shaken voice of their host bawling out one of the attendants for having neglected the venerable district attorney, then fell silent as the attendant explained to his master that the venerable district attorney was not slighted but had declined to have the vodka poured into his glass. The guests took note of the district attorney sitting casually in his place, slightly leaning forward, not making much of the whispered commotion. Their bloodshot eyes dilated, they cast their eyes on their dinner plates.

"Does the venerable district attorney deem us unworthy to drink with?" the commandant asked. The bringa-linga of the toasting glasses of a moment ago gave way to the occasional tttling-tttling of silverware against china. Those of the local luminaries who knew the district attorney's character, including Mr. Partow, dreaded his response. The one thought that undoubtedly passed through everyone's mind was that it had been an utter mistake inviting Mr. Rouhani. They all waited for their night to be ruined by a careless remark and silently prayed.

"Mr. Commandant, as well as the gentlemen present here," the district attorney proclaimed, "should know that since my late teens I've lived with a terrible illness, for which a cure has yet to be found. The doctors, not myself, have prohibited me from drinking. I ask for your forgiveness."

With this he poured water for himself, picked up the glass, and drank it. The question on everyone's mind at this point was, Did his answer satisfy the host?

The commandant felt the heat rising from the ground.

"Illness or no illness," charged the commandant, "a man in the company of men doesn't refuse to drink with them. That's the way things are in my country." His voice was so loud it could be heard in the adjacent hall, where joyous shouts and stamping were still in full swing.

"When doctors forbid a man from drinking alcohol," the district attorney answered, "a man listens to them. That's how things are in *my* country."

The local dignitaries who, in the past, had to deal with the stubborn district attorney were not surprised that the dinner party was about to turn into a brawl. What took them aback was what the commandant did next, which was to peel off his uniform as they held their breath. Now, this was a rare oddity from a disciplined army officer. Nevertheless the commandant took off his jacket and shirt to show the horrified congregation five bullet wounds on his stomach and back.

"I've seen seven battles in my life; went on twenty-five missions and was injured three times, but never did I dodge my responsibilities to my fellow men. No illness or wound is strong enough to make me act like a woman."

It became obvious to all present that the district attorney was beginning to feel uncomfortable. More obvious was that he had been baited into this confrontation by his rival, who was carrying an ancient gripe. The first guest to consider this possibility, excluding the district attorney himself, was, of course, Mr. Partow, who regarded the scene with mixed emotions. On the one hand, it was refreshing to see someone rubbing the arrogant district attorney's nose in the dirt, teaching him a lesson. On the other, the national pride that Mr. Partow subscribed to in abundance made him side candidly with his boss. He knew from past experience that either Mr. Rouhani would not be able to hold his tongue and would insult the commandant's immense pride, which would probably prolong their animosity, or he would figure it was beneath him to dignify the Russian with an answer and walk out, which would be interpreted as a victory by the Russian. Mr. Partow favored the second option, as it would even out the score. And that, Mr. Partow hoped, would end the rancor. Whatever the outcome of this quarrel, though, Mr. Partow assured himself, he would live to tell a great story. But he was hardly prepared to accept the actual outcome, which was escalating as he made these observations. The third option, unforeseen by Mr. Partow, brewed slowly in Nozar Rouhani's mind.

"Come on, Mr. Rouhani. Are you a girl? Is that why you won't drink with men?"

Some of the guests, who predicted grave outcomes, had already left the table with the excuse of using the facilities. Remaining were but a few of the Russians, Mr. Partow, and Mr. Rouhani, who selected from the fruit bowl a crisp red apple, gave it a cursory examination, and sank his teeth into it to disguise his fury.

Only the crunching sounds of apple crushing angrily under molars could be heard. Presently, the commandant, holding the table to keep steady, asked a second time, "Well, are you?"

That night Mr. Partow saw a different side of Mr. Rouhani's personality and was horrified. He made a mental note to remember what had happened between the district attorney and the commandant, for the outcome of this showdown would determine the future path of his career and that of his boss.

"Yes, I am," came the answer through a full mouth.

Mr. Partow could not believe his ears as Mr. Rouhani stared blankly into the air, chewing his apple and swallowing it with difficulty. In an instant, Nozar had managed to throw a bucket of cold water over the commandant's fire, conclusively extinguishing the evening's battle. The commandant's face deflated into an ashen sack of disbelief as he dropped listlessly to his chair, avoiding stares.

But that was not what finished Mr. Rouhani in Khameneh. There were other powerful players presently at work to undermine the obstinate district attorney.

Thirty-Two

For reasons unknown the streetlamp that on previous nights had shed its beam into the well of the room was out. A slow breeze caressed the tree outside the window, making subtle music. Farzin could not absolve the streetlamp for depriving him of the light he so depended on. An insomniac's midsummer night beneath the darkness was ahead, and there was nothing Farzin could do to keep his mind off his story. In his usual corner by the window, fragmented papers on his lap, he tried to proceed with his yarn, but the going was tough. He looked outside and felt a weird sense that the trees had moved; strange shadows appeared in the yard. The world once again was changing, he knew; he had the same sense before of slowness engulfing his surroundings. He remembered how things that were in motion came to a halt, how what was melting solidified, frozen like a picture, the day the young woman was knifed before him. He remembered how he had extended his arms to catch her head before she fell.

Still, he wrote like a blind man and hoped for the best.

In the year succeeding the end of the big war, Mr. Rouhani found himself at odds with the deputies of Khameneh in the parliament, who had kingly powers over their home base, and who had discovered the young district attorney to be a descendant of the feared Mullah Abbas. Early on, Nozar had good reasons to stay out of politics and politicians' way, but given the necessities of his job, he quite frequently clashed with this or that deputy as he established the authority of the state. Inevitably, he gained a reputation in political and bazaari circles as a nutty zealot, while his star rose within the ranks of the ministry. As the multitude of politicians taking the seat of the Minister of Justice flittered across the political scene,

Nozar Rouhani moved up and became the subject of the praise and adulation of his peers. If they all wished to be on his side, it was because they lacked a side of their own. And truth be told, that's how Nozar Rouhani came to personify the ideals of the Justice Ministry.

Thirty-Three

From the corner of his eye Farzin Rouhani registered a curious stirring in the texture of the night: an apparition, gliding across the darkness, tiptoeing its way, *where to?* Seized by wonder, he peered out the window to examine whether his eyes were playing a hoax. When he turned toward where he thought he had seen the ghostlike movement, it had vanished. *A flight of fancy in the weary hour of midnight?* He blamed himself for letting the creatures of his imagination play tricks on him. A moment later though, he saw the dark shadow again; its scent, diluted by distance, keenly intriguing, was hovering over where Farzin thought Loony Enayat was asleep. The arch of the back, the dark outline of the calves, and the width of the shoulders were familiar. If it were not for fear of reprisals from every corner, Farzin would have called out his name, inviting him to the window for a smoke. He would ask him if he was experiencing the same slowness as he was. Moistening the dry, bony roof of his mouth, he watched in disbelief as the specter slipped under Enayat's covers.

For an instant Farzin thought he saw a violent jerk under the sheets, subdued in silence. What had he just seen? His cognitive faculties refused to process the information his senses had provided. Nailed to the floor by fear and intoxication of the world closing in on him, Farzin found he could not move from his corner to investigate what had become of Loony Enayat, and he wondered about the speed with which he could still think despite the sluggishness of all things physical. The contrast was scary. It gave the reality he could still make out in the dark a dreamlike quality. Things or shadows were still moving under that sheet, far, far away from where he sat, and yet everything was quiet and close. Perhaps his imagination had flimflammed him out of his senses. It would not have changed anything, one way or another. Besides, at this moment, there were silences pouring in from the yard. He turned his head away from the rocking back and forth under Enayat's sheets, and fixed his eyes on the flowerbed down below.

Through the tree branches Farzin saw the mourning jasmine, the angry narcissus, and the timid roses. They seemed to be moving to and fro, left and right, swirling around even. Shadows were everywhere, the accusing shadows, the brave shadows, the shadows of the dead, and the spiritless shadows. Not so loud; walls have mice. Mice have ears. The shadows spoke, in that silent way they speak, of mothers beating their chests, wailing over the corpses of their sons; of teary-eyed men, graying around the temples, carrying the flogged bodies of their daughters; of the wounded backs of the sinners, the long bleeding lines; of the death squads, always an omniscient arm of the Revolutionary Forces, by the empty pool; of the march of the kerchiefed women, in groups of five, or six, or seven, holding their guns like newborn babies. *Where are they going, wind? What are they doing?*

In the fleeting seconds of remembrance, Farzin Rouhani recalled the images of a young woman falling to the ground and shadows moving rhythmically in the dark. He often wondered which vision would last: the defenseless martyr, who knew all too well about falling, or the rabid urge of shadows pursuing forbidden desire. These images played in his mind like old movies, bringing forth emotions more formidable than he could handle. Pressed hard enough, he would admit it happened three times, altogether, in that tumultuous year, when the world lost its velocity and grew languorous, time decelerating as in slow motion. It was in those moments of slowness that reality seemed to defy the physical laws of the universe, yielding itself up for inspection. In time, the music of the leaves would replace the silence, and it would grow and be incessant.

Thirty-Four

Morning broke with the muezzin's call, followed by the droning whispers, the rising cigarette smoke, and the surging of urban melodies. Outside the window, leaves quivered in the early morning zephyr. Soon the loudspeakers would roar, announcing the names of those who were to meet their destiny—the luck of the draw.

A line formed in front of the bathroom. Queuing ahead of Farzin was Loony Enayat, who did not show so much as a glimpse of last night's gloom, the beating he had taken, or the visit by the dark silhouette. Nose twitching, his eyes blank slates, he was jumping up and down, urging the line to go forward, hurry, hurry. Mohammad approached; Loony Enayat greeted him with a casual smile, as if everything was in kilter. Farzin looked at both of them, puzzled. That whole scene where Enayat had been tricked and humiliated in Mohammad's game replayed before his mind's eye. Had it been all in his head?

"I have a great plan," whispered Mohammad in Farzin's ear. "An escape plan."

Then, as though he had read Farzin's mind, he changed his tone.

"Oh! Come on, you. It was only a game; a prank. Don't hold it against me. It was for a higher cause. Besides, look at him, will you? He greets me, don't you see? Don't be the bowl that's hotter than the soup, okay?"

Farzin looked at the back of Enayat's head as he disappeared into the bathroom. He looked back at Mohammad. And he made the connection.

"His nose was bleeding, Mohammad."

"Never mind that," he said. "I've got a plan you'll want to listen to."

Farzin was next in line. Mohammad hurried to tell him about his plan.

"At about six o'clock, dinner rolls in. Correct? By the time the empty stewpot rolls out, it's er ... eight, right? The cleaning crew shows up around what time, they said? I think nine. When I was in the kitchen, yesterday, I checked out the whole place. Once in the kitchen, you can break out through the window. You'd fit fine in the pot, a small guy like you. Just cover it with the lid and hope no one looks inside. Might have to squat tight in there, though. Damn good plan. Give it a shot, or rot in here if you like."

Too many loopholes, Farzin mused. What if one of them lifted the lid to check for leftovers? It could happen. Or what if the cleaning crew was already in the kitchen when the stewpot rolled in? Even a child would laugh at a plan with so many faults, but he kept his objections to himself. If you wanted to disagree with the Marlboro Man, you prepared yourself for a long argument. That early in the morning, Farzin was not in the mood to be trifled with.

"It sounds interesting. We should talk about it more."

Dizzy with sleep, Farzin stepped into the washroom. The sleepless night before had exhausted him, leaving swollen bags under his eyes. The white-tiled walls gave solace to his soul. He remembered how peaceful it was just to sit there sometimes, all by himself, a luxury becoming rarer as the number of inmates soared. There, he felt his eyes warming, his eyelids becoming heavy. He would not fall asleep in there, he told himself, not even for a few minutes .... Then a switch was thrown, and the disembodied voice came over the speakers, the dry, guttural voice of the divinity himself. Farzin listened to the names, not expecting to hear his own but listening anyway. As he heard Jamal's name, a quick panic settled in his heart. He washed his hands, rinsed his face, and stepped out.

Having been called upstairs for the final verdict, Chimney handed the tea-making gear to his young apprentice and said, "It is your ship now!" He went to hug his friends and said farewells to everyone.

"My turn," he joked. "What to do?" Tears welled in his eyes.

Putting on his socks, Mohammad glanced at Farzin and pulled down the corners of his mouth. "It's better to stay alive," he opined, "than to act a hero and end up six feet under. Have no doubt about it, mister."

Farzin cast a puzzled look at Mohammad, whose fingers now ran through his thick oily hair with the dignity of a worldly man. Mohammad had the authority of someone who had lived many lives. Farzin recalled the shadow last night but said nothing of it. What need is there to mention a quirk in the way of the world when it may or may not correct itself. Jamal had put on his shoes, ready to face whatever was waiting for him on the other side. His last words before he took his leave were simple, but everyone struggled to find a deeper meaning to them than was perhaps intended.

"Who knows about tomorrow?"

Farzin repeated the words and bid his friend goodbye.

Jamal was gone all day.

Thirty-Five

One day, a fellow who appeared arrogant to Mr. Partow, clothed in a bazaari merchant's attire, showed up at the district attorney's office in Khameneh. Speaking in a firm voice, somewhat petulant, he questioned Mr. Partow's judgment in a child custody battle. It was the case of a fatherless boy of ten whose mother had been given guardianship, by the district attorney's office, to look after the large estate left to the boy after his father's sudden death. Leaning on Mr. Partow's desk, the man was becoming agitated as he argued that, from a strict Islamic perspective, the child's uncle should have been designated his guardian, and not his mother. He made a fist and pressed his knuckles on the desk. His threatening posture did not go unnoticed. Nozar Rouhani was in the room and, hearing the man's argument, recognized the situation in which Mr. Partow was cornered. He walked out of the room, called on Butler Mamdali, and told him to see the intruder out.

The man would not move a centimeter from where he was. As Butler Mamdali, acting on his boss's orders, proceeded to throw him out of the premises, the man became even more outraged. Meanwhile, Mr. Rouhani's stern voice could be heard above the tussle, stating, "We represent the central government, and a minimum of respect is in order. Secondly, in case you don't know, it is not up to that gentleman to designate the child's guardian. The law clearly states that with the mother living, she is preferred over the uncle to manage a child's business until he comes of age."

The man must have felt he had not been given a chance to challenge those remarks, because he would be heard from again. Outside the building, he stuck his face to the frosted window and yelled back, "Rouhani, you won't last long in this town. You will be gotten rid of."

When the outraged man was gone, Mr. Partow turned to Mr. Rouhani and said, "I know this fellow. He's well connected. He works for Khameneh's deputy in the Majles. They run a racket here, their own little government."

Mr. Rouhani threw a questioning look at Mr. Partow.

"What I'm trying to say is they control the show around here." Mr. Partow's remark was not far off base.

A few days after that incident, the rumor that the city's elected representative in parliament disapproved of the district attorney leaked onto the gossip circuit. Initially, as was his wont, Mr. Rouhani did not pay attention to the rumors, but the daily pressure mounted to the point that even the vagrant children began to harass his wife in the streets, often sending her home crying. Now that hurt Nozar's pride a great deal. He sent a telegram to Tehran, inquiring about the veracity of the rumors. It read: "I began my service in the Ministry of Justice, wishing to do right by my employer and the decent people of this country. If the ministry is considering removing me from my post due to interest groups' pressure, please accept this as my official notice of resignation."

At the other end of the wire, the political appointee of the ministry sensed the urgency of the telegram and conveyed it to his superiors. The story that Khameneh's member of Majles was seeking the replacement of the district attorney burned the air through corridors of the white-marbled Justice Ministry. As any political novice could see, the repercussions of this interaction would be costly for the ministry. Therefore, any action on this matter was advised to be postponed until the rumors had died down.

That's why Nozar's telegram remained unanswered.

Instead, the Chief of Justice told Nozar, in a rushed telephone conversation, that the rumor had no basis in reality. "The ministry stands behind its employees," he said, "and does not intend to bend to political winds."

The lie finally came to a head during Nozar's vacation, when he went to Tehran. Not wasting a day, he shot straight to the personnel office and asked to see his file. In it he found an unsigned letter of transfer to Damkan with a notice of promotion. *Big deal.* Upon close examination he noticed, down at the bottom of the letter, in longhand: "Do not execute." He went back home and took his wife to the movies.

★ ★ ★

"To the movies?" Brother Hamid said. "Why did he do that? Didn't he care about his job?"

"Nozar Rouhani was a big fan of Hollywood," Farzin offered. "Incidentally, that was the first and last time his wife, who was not my mother, set her foot in a movie theater."

"She was not your mother? Was she his first wife? When did he marry your mother?"

"Slow down, Brother Hamid—one at a time."

"And I thought you wanted to get out of here soon."

"I do, but in order to get to my mother, I have to tell you where she came from and how they met and married."

"You're killing me. Then get on with it."

"Ah, yes." Farzin had been waiting for this. Now was the time to introduce her. Yes, definitely. *There* was a story to tell; a dense commingling of passion and will! Hers was a small-town-to-big-city kind of a ride that's the grub of storytellers. And to know her is to know the region she grew up in: Geellon.

Thirty-Six

In the morning, Farzin's name resounded over the intercom. Mohammad cracked a smile. "Hope for the best," he chimed in, "but prepare for the worst." He said this as a matter of fact, no malice in his voice. "And if the judge does not have time to see you," he said, "not to worry. He will, eventually." Everyone was getting ready for the morning prayers as Farzin exited.

A stout guard, with a bushy beard and belly protruding above his belt—coarse hair coming out of every opening in his clothing—showed the way to the Agha's office at the far end of the new wing. Standing before the Agha's office, the guard pointed at the door and stood at a distance. Farzin turned to him, waiting to be told what to do next. The guard nodded his head and shook his knuckles in the air. Farzin faced the door and knocked; muffled voices came from the other side. Finally, the door clicked open, and Brother Hamid, of all people, stood there to greet him. In silence they looked at each other for a moment before Brother Hamid motioned for Farzin to enter.

The Agha sat pontifically at the back of the room behind his short-legged table, covered with files and books. What hit Farzin as he walked in was the smell of an uninhabited room: freshly washed Persian carpet, mothballs, and cardamom. The scent reminded him of old Tehrani homes kept by finicky housewives: clean and sacred, almost godly. He remembered the amount of work his mother devoted to keeping the house clean. It was part of what made her so endearing, but it also gave her a reason to admonish everyone. Memories of the times she was less than loving to him raced through his head as he looked about the room—times when he had deserved his mother's scolding and times when he had not. He felt his knees shaking from anxiety and fear. Obviously, the Agha had been discussing his case with Brother Hamid.

The Agha looked sickly and ashen; his droopy eyes averred to his poor health. Brother Hamid went and sat somewhat lower than the Agha, keeping a poker face, his previous informalities with Farzin a distant memory now. The caw of a wandering crow came through the open window. The sunshine felt light as a feather, the air crisp. Open books on the table, and one on the floor beside Agha Shirazi, created an aura of reverence. Farzin took off his shoes and advanced on the plush carpet until he was at the center of it. There he found himself surrounded by the floral Kashi patterns, kidney red and rich as they come.

The sage pointed to a place in front of the table next to Brother Hamid, and as Farzin descended to the floor, the Agha put on his spectacles. A flyswatter rested by his side. A rosary lay on the short-legged table next to a magnifying glass. He opened a folder and read Farzin's name and address from it in short breathy gasps.

"Yes, that is correct," Farzin said politely—much depended on the impression he made on the frail man, who sounded as ailing as he looked.

"What's in this report file," the Agha mumbled, "what you told Brother Hamid in the Committee—and most of the things you've been writing in your report are irrelevant." He scanned a sheaf of papers in the folder, frowning at the unsteady writing. "Irrelevant," he said, "but intriguing." Words came out of his mouth with great difficulty.

"From what's apparent, you're skillfully evading the truth by alluding to the irrelevant."

"Sir, I *have* spoken the truth." Farzin wanted to explain, but the Agha spared no time.

"Enough already! Eh. This is not going anywhere." After this burst of temper, the Agha softened his voice, seeking to wriggle his way back to reason.

"We talk common sense," the Agha continued, his tone gentle and caring, "because you're a young man with an impressionable mind. Eh, he who has no fear of the other world, and of God's wrath, may be better off in this world, but what comes to him at the end, eh? Is there an end? We, all of us, will have to cross the bridge of the gatherer one day, regardless of belief or disbelief in God. But he who doubts God will not keep his balance and will slip and fall into the eternal fire. Eh, you could buy your sins back and purify yourself, as innocent as a newborn. On the other hand, eh, if you don't cooperate, you leave us no choice. Those who follow the teachings of the Koran know that Islam must apply *Ghessas*." Farzin knew the word. It was the principle behind the eye-for-an-eye edict. He knew it was not only in the Koran but in other monotheistic books as well. In Latin it was referred to as *lex talionis*. The Agha continued, "The corrupter is like a bad apple that must be done away with, lest it contaminate the rest of the bushel."

"I am in complete agreement with the divine law, sir," said Farzin. "And I am glad Your Honor finds something positive in my report." Having said that, Farzin felt incredibly stupid; especially after the Agha's response hit him hard in the face.

"I wouldn't be glad if I were you. There is more to be reported. I imagine you wish to say *more*?"

"I wish to say more?"

"Don't you? To defend yourself. Got anything *more* to say in your own defense?"

"No. No, sir."

"But why? You have been conducting yourself in a positive manner. All you have to do now is to make a clean break with the past and lighten your burden."

"Pardon me, sir," said Farzin. "But I don't understand what you're referring to." Farzin felt Brother Hamid's sideway stares, the air growing thick, sweat rolling down his armpits, dripping.

An amused look appeared in the Agha's watery eyes, and he started to laugh. It was a hearty, condescending laugh Farzin did not dislike, but it rapidly broke into an unstoppable fit of coughing. Suddenly, the old man's chest heaved up and down, up and down, audibly and uncontrollably. His breathing filled the room. It seemed as though he put a great deal of effort into it. Language, Farzin thought, must have been invented by the weak. The old man seemed smaller when he was silent. One minute he was speaking to Farzin, the next, he was roaring with an open palm against his stomach, bellowing like a diesel engine, tears surfacing in his eyes and watering the white jungle beneath. Farzin and Brother Hamid looked at each other in distress as Agha Shirazi held a half-fist in front of his mouth, his eyes bulging with fear. Farzin felt a bit of fear himself; what if the geezer keeled over right then? *What next?*

As he stared at the coughing man, a side door opened and an adolescent boy in loose-fitting clothes rushed in with a glass of water on a silver tray. Brother Hamid took the glass and held it before the Agha, who grabbed his wrist and, while turning blue in the face, started to shake severely; as a result, his spectacles fell into his lap. The boy didn't look up, not once, and vanished as fast as he had appeared, like a meteor. Feeling somehow responsible, Farzin helped Brother Hamid stretch the fragile body of the cleric toward Mecca. Together they loosened the Agha's collar and wetted his forehead. They acted in unison, Brother Hamid cursing under his breath. The cough receded at last, with little gasps for air, but the Agha's eyes remained rolled up under his lids. Irritated, the warden shoved Farzin toward the door.

"For God's sake, come off your high horse," Brother Hamid chided Farzin through clenched teeth. "What're you trying to do, kill the Agha? Where did you get the idea to argue with the man, ha? If he says you have more to say, you've damn well got more to say, period." He had a knot in his brow and his voice was turning hoarse from being agitated and having to suppress it. Before they came to the door, it flung open, and a white-uniformed man rushed in with a black leather bag in his hand. A look in his downcast eyes implied he knew why he was there. Brother Hamid showed him the reclining patient with one hand and pushed Farzin out the door with the other. The plump guard with the bushy beard was waiting for him. At the last minute, before the door closed, Farzin made an effort to defend himself against the indefensible.

"I know what you want, Hamid."

A weary look spread over Brother Hamid. The only thing that prevented him from slamming the door in Farzin's face, perhaps breaking his nose, was Farzin's foot jamming it.

"You want me to confess to something I didn't do and beg forgiveness, don't you? But like I said before, there's nothing to confess. Pull the plugs out of your damn ears."

Thirty-Seven

As he was being carried down the marble stairs by three muscular guards, Farzin could still hear Brother Hamid's voice ringing in his ears. *You've got exactly twenty-four hours. Make it fast and make it good.* When he was thrown back in with the inmates, where everyone plus the whole world hovered over him with curiosity, he repeated those words under his breath. "Twenty-four hours, make it fast and make it good."

Back at the ward, exactly five packs of cigarettes were shoved under his nose at once. Farzin pulled himself together and grabbed them all before the puzzled looks of his mates. He then, without speaking a word, frantically emptied their contents one by one, returning the cigarettes to their owners after collecting the empty packs for himself. Mohammad's voice put everyone at ease. "There, he's got the writing bug up his ass again."

Farzin wished he had asked for paper before the Agha decided to choke on his own spittle. Five packs did not seem much for what he wanted to say, but it had to do for now. *And twenty-four hours?*

Clouds in Geellon in the rainy season echo with thunder like the grumbling belly of a giant. Housemaids dart through red-roofed houses; the sounds of windows slamming shut fill the air. Then the rain pours incessantly, falling like sheets of silver, stitching nights to days, days to nights, a relentless music of downpouring in the rice paddies that lasts throughout duck season. Geellon is generous in its scent of pomegranate in the non-stop autumn rain, as it is in the attar of tea leaves in its vernal air.

In high pastoral fields, the land is segmented by chartreuse walls of bamboo shoots, bundled together with thin metal wire. Cleaving through the waist-high emerald sea of tea bushes, they mark the end of one lot and the beginning of another. A hundred years or so ago, the bamboo walls were so far apart they did not upset the green velvety coherence of the fields. They were there, come summer or winter, as a piece of the scenery, subject to the laws of God and nature, replaced only every great while, in the spring, for instance, when the earth was alive and the air was brisk.

To the east of its silver ribbon, in the middle of absolute, boundless greenery, the sinuous Sefidroud backed to the lush Elburze Mountains. Its water lapped with low sounds by the shore, where clusters of red-slate roofs capped modest homes. Oaks, elms, boxwoods, and walnuts guarded the twisty and narrow cobbled alleys. Chimneys gently spewing columns of smoke and fig boughs dangling over ivy-covered walls marked the path taken by pink-cheeked adolescent girls, balancing goblets of water on their shoulders or washbasins on their heads, walking in twos and threes to and from a nearby spring in the mistlike rain, accompanied by a neighborhood dolt or dog. The outside walls of the huts and shanties were whitened by slaked lime; their roofs of rice-stems or clay slate were the color of goose blood.

All Geelloni townships and cities, even the capital of the province, Rasht, begrudged Lauhijaun its clean streets and air of sophistication. In 1888, when the telegraph came to Geellon, the first two stations were built simultaneously in Lauhijaun and Rasht. The rivalry between the two ancient cities was such that, if Rasht was the capital of the province, then Lauhijaun was the "gem of the whole creation." It was the first city to open a national park, the first to open an all-girls school and the second to pave its main street with cobblestones. A short while later, a cinema house would open there and call itself "Hope."

Thirty-Eight

The vanguard of modernization was Lauhijaun's police commissioner, often seen on Friday evenings with his Tehrani wife holding his arm *à la Parisienne*, traipsing along the main concourse. It had come as a shock to the town when he returned from Tehran with this thin-boned woman, whose ashen face and soft hands quickly gave rise to speculation that she had not worked a day in her life. Bigger surprise yet when she came out in the streets without a chador, which would have started rumors of impropriety had she not been the police commissioner's wife.

The commissioner's sole flaw was that he suffered from a not so common phobic disorder. His nature simply could not bear even the smallest of earth's vibrations or the sky's lightnings. He was a hulking fellow to be sure, with the oily ends of his mustache passing his ears and a hemisphere of a paunch that made him look serious enough to uphold the law. His masculinity screamed through as if he had just strangled a lion with his bare hands. His knees were round and beefy, his fingers stubby. Though not a fanatic by any means, a ring with a small ruby on the middle finger of his left hand spoke coyly of his religious proclivity. He believed in jinns and fairies and the idea of hell and heaven, but he often found regular praying and fasting hard rows to hoe. From his double chin, half the size of a honeydew melon, and lips overwhelmed by two wings of a huge mustache, one could safely assume that there was an intense drinking habit. And if you could look beyond his ears, which were large and deformed, and his uneven teeth, he was testosterone solidified. His bulging eyes betrayed all the raw maleness that seeped from him. They were somewhat unsure and hesitant, the eyes of a man who swigged vodka like water, and cursed at his servants just as easily as he read poetry to his wife or played hide-and-seek with his children.

Far from an insinuation of cowardice, it must be mentioned that the police commissioner's phobic disorder often put him in compromising situations that promoted a personal brand of humor among his servants. On summer afternoons, when the sky belched and grumbled, his maids would find the commissioner under layers of quilts in a corner of the basement, shouting in that charming Geelloni dialect, "Fetch more quilt; fetch more quilt." He was just like that: an unstable hysteric given to dramatic gestures. Afterward, when all was safe, he would emerge from under the bedspread and blankets with great heaves of breath, his shoulders thrown back, sweating, with an unmistakable sense of the relief of a survivor.

The police commissioner was born in the year of the vast fire. Before he could tell his right hand from left, his parents were lost in the cholera epidemic of 1892, in which 12,000 serfs, peasants, and shepherds died. So many died in the rice fields and lowlands that the corpses could not be buried fast enough, a stench of decaying flesh filled the green valleys. Consequently, the child fled to the mountains with his uncle and lived there with the gypsies for two years. In 1895, when the Russians began the construction of the Rasht-Qazvin Roadway, strong-armed men were hired for manual labor, and their families were put to work on menial tasks. Now ten years old, the boy came down from the uplands; he and his uncle were among the first hired. Employed to lay the foundation for the spiraling route, they made a meager living, and for four years the future seemed not so bleak.

Having completed the construction of the road, the Russians began demanding a toll from the peasants, which set off a rebellion in January 1899. The riots spread fast to other segments of the population, taking over the entire region. The construction workers, in solidarity with the peasants, attacked Pakhitonovski

Station and demolished it in two hours flat. Consequently, they all lost their jobs and fell on extremely hard times. To top it all, the Russians, in return for their losses, severely disciplined the rioters by having their leaders flogged in public, as a result of which the boy's uncle bled to death. Who could blame the boy for fleeing, and for subsequently forming a band of guerrillas to fight back?

Although poorly armed, the boy and his cronies attacked the Russian posts off and on, like a pack of hungry hyenas, and harassed their soldiers. Later, much later, his band joined a large brigade under an Armenian guerrilla leader, which became the basis of the Constitutional Army of Geellon. It was the Constitutional Army of Geellon that eventually would attack the capital from the north, to liberate it from the tyranny of Mohammad Ali Shah, the penultimate monarch of the Qaujaur dynasty, and his Russian backers. The Constitutional Army of Geellon banded with other constitutionalists, liberals, and nationalists from the country's south, and formed the Persian National Army, which set upon Tehran from north and south. It was untrue that the royalists took no notice of the National Army approaching, or that they were taken by surprise. On the contrary, they had good intelligence on the National Army advances and situated themselves at strategically crucial points overlooking major roadways. The royalists had sworn to God and motherland and their king to stop the progress of the National Army, but when they saw what a formidable force the adversary had become, they forgot all their pledges and could not clear their trenches fast enough. They fled westward and hid themselves in fortifications such as the Royal Arch, or abandoned their cause altogether and went home.

That, in short, is how the fellow who would occupy the position of Lauhijaun's police commissioner arrived in Tehran as a deputy to the Armenian Monsieur Yeprim, the constitutionalist leader of the Geelloni faction of the Persian National Army. He rode side by side with Yeprim, and became known in the capital's progressive circles as "that gallant young officer accompanying Yeprim Khan." In the company of Monsieur Yeprim he took part in the secret meetings of the constitutionalist, liberal, and nationalist headmen and got to know quite a few of the famous nationalist leaders and patriots. Later on he would meet and shake hands with the charismatic Reza Maxim, who had not yet begun to entertain the high and mighty ambitions of kingship. They would even exchange a note or two, which gave the young man the impression that he had struck up a friendship with that towering officer from the Persian Cossack Brigade.

As happens with the maternally deprived, the gallant young officer, now in his early twenties, was sexually attracted to older dames. He soothed the pain of being an oddball in the kind, motherly embraces of mature females of certain circles. In this wicked city, vast and crowded, many experiences were to be had by the young, if the wherewithal, or rather the ambition, was there. Wealthy widows were more than willing to adapt to the needs of young and lonely officers whose loyalty had, in one way or another, been amply tested.

Having learned to appreciate the inclusion in the aristocratic circles that had shifted their allegiance to the constitutionalist side, the gallant young officer accompanying Yeprim Khan made love to their widows and displayed a flair for the finer things in life. He was invited to banquets, picnics, poker games, diplomatic receptions, great gatherings, also smaller celebrations of poetry and drama where he learned to repeat Tehrani proverbs, in season and out. Turned on to smoking a water pipe, he introduced his friends to *chai*, the token drink of his hometown. Not that the fine gentlemen and ladies of those circles were ignorant of the existence of tea, but it had not occurred to them that Geellon already cultivated the stubby bushes on such a massive scale. To them, tea was an exotic gift, imported by the omnipotent British, who extorted a high price for it. And to think of it, here was the handsome officer, seen in the company of "that Armenian," often quipping that Geellon headed the fight for democracy by producing inexpensive tea for the masses.

A charming fellow, the gallant young officer accompanying Yeprim Khan had the gift of gab and could sustain multiple conversations at the same time. Tehran's high society liked his discursiveness, teased him for his piquant accent. Ladies especially found his humor sharp and innocent, while gentlemen respectfully referred to him as Monsieur Yeprim's comrade in arms.

Thirty-Nine

If Farzin was going to hang out his dirty laundry for Brother Hamid and Agha Shirazi and the whole world, for that matter, to see, he would do it on his own terms. He particularly tried to fend off Mohammad's prying. For some unknown reason, Mohammad had been trying to find out what he was going to do. Simply keeping him off his back sapped a considerable amount of Farzin's energy, for Mohammad's interest was the keenest.

Next day, ten more inmates answered the call, climbed the stairs with a mixture of hope and trepidation, and came back tongue tied and forlorn. Farzin felt a fellowship with them in that they had all been sucked into one giant fallacy—that it would truly make a difference if they were on their best behavior. Of course no one saw through the lie as clearly as the Marlboro Man, who taunted them with abuse every chance he was given. Despite his stern caveat, though, hope was kept alive. What else could be done? What is the point of life if not to believe in some sort of redemption?

Finally, when Farzin broke down under Mohammad's scrutiny and told him about his aborted conversation with the Agha and Brother Hamid's last warning, using his saddest and least colorful tone, Mohammad was irate.

"You have no soul," he said, to Farzin's chagrin. "Your back is broken. You're just going to sit there and write a contrition letter, you fool. I can see you sitting with your damn papers in the dark, giving away all your damn friends and your damn family secrets for a few drops of blood that weren't worth a damn to begin with. Damn you, fucking fool."

"Is that so?" asked Farzin indignantly. "Well, it's so big of you to be so brave and righteous. Why not flaunt it some more. Put all of us to shame, while you're at it. And pull no punches." He felt the rush of blood in his cheeks and the realization that he was totally, utterly helpless. Still, he kept at it.

"It's easy for you to point a finger," said Farzin to his tormentor, "when I'm the one who's got to make sense of it." His eyes welled up. "Have you any idea what I have to do to get out of here? You weren't there, were you, to see that geezer choking on his own saliva. Hamid tried to pin that on me too. 'If you'd cooperated with us,' he says, 'this wouldn't have happened.' What do you care? You're not the one who's going to Evin."

An acerbic smile appeared on Mohammad's face.

"Ah! He's another breed of rat, that Brother Hamid of yours. Why bother with the brother?"

Farzin did not share the view that his warden was of a different breed and fretted very much about what Brother Hamid was capable of doing to him. It was not the first time since his arrest that he was unsure about the near future.

After this brief exchange, they fell into a silent discord. Farzin returned to his cocoon and continued working on his report..

As long as moneyed folks invited Monsieur Yeprim's dashing aide-de-camp to their activities to hear his eloquent speeches on a variety of subjects, he would oblige and would treat everyone to discussions about his favorite subject, tea and its merits. While advancing the cause of revolution in Tehran, he attended those gatherings with an open heart and enjoyed himself to the fullest. It was during one of those parties at the heart of the well to-do that he met and fell in love with a dame from an old-money Tehrani family. Five years his senior, Malek Tauj was in the habit of rubbing the back of her manicured hands when engaged in deep intellectual fantasies or intriguing discussions, which took place a great deal around the future police commissioner. When he wasn't explicating mili-

tary tactics, he would be spotted shedding light on dark corners of history to a handful of widows and spinsters, who gazed admiringly at his luscious lips. But what happened to him after meeting Malek Tauj? Now, his hosts would notice the woman on the verge of spinsterhood following him around, using every occasion to be near him, every excuse to talk to him, and never coming short of subjects for light chatter.

Forty

Brother Hamid met with Farzin once more to evaluate whether he was fit for readmission to Shirazi's chamber. He raved, advised, scolded, patronized, mocked, and sympathized with Farzin. Hamid did not beat him or even slap him across the face as before. Instead, he made Farzin sit on a wooden chair and answer questions "to the best of your knowledge." The shift in his perception of Farzin, at this point, was so drastic that Brother Hamid felt exhausted afterward, rendering his principles greatly compromised.

To his superiors, Brother Hamid would report that further cross-examination of this particular suspect was a futile exercise. "Additional efforts to link Farzin Rouhani to subversive groups," he wrote in one report "will be a waste of time and resources." As far as he knew, such a connection did not exist. He even went so far as putting in a request to be relieved of interrogating the prisoner, because in his eyes Farzin was no longer a suspect. He asked to be assigned to a different case, a real assignment, where he could use his expertise in fighting counterrevolutionaries or even dope pushers and opium smugglers. Brother Hamid would have rather done anything but persecute someone whose forthrightness had begun to crack the fundamentals of his beliefs …. But, as fate would have it, nobody high up seemed to heed his requests. He was reassigned to this particular suspect, the following day. That's when he learned, with his flesh and bones, another one of life's little ironies. Chained to his prisoner, he could go nowhere and do nothing, except gather more biographical information from him. Whether he liked it or not, he was attached to Farzin, just as Farzin's dismal plight had stuck to him like a leech.

Farzin, on the other hand, displayed a cool distance during their interviews. None of the conscience-ridden qualms that gripped Brother Hamid ever visited him. He took his warden's occasional grunts and nods gracefully, with a certain bemused expression, for all that was expected of him was to admit his guilt and put up with Brother Hamid's desperation in the meantime. And since he drew a certain perverted pleasure out of driving his warden up the wall to begin with, answering his questions had become a complex game of give-and-take.

Early on, Farzin realized he had to give in to some of Brother Hamid's milder accusations to keep up the appearance of cooperation. Being locked up in the Office to Combat Vices was far safer than being in Evin, where the real blood-and-flesh counterrevolutionaries were tortured, raped, and maimed on a daily basis—that much he knew—and for that reason alone he could not leave all Brother Hamid's queries unanswered indefinitely. Meanwhile, Farzin considered the following: there were not nearly as many "corrupted and misguided souls" in the Office to Combat Vices as there would be counterrevolutionaries in Evin. And there were even more counterrevolutionaries outside, blowing up office buildings and Friday prayer sermons. Outside, in the open, the indoctrination of society took place at a quicker pace than inside the Office to Combat Vices, certainly among vast sectors of the population. Outside, there were no calls in the morning to go into a closed room to have one's head examined by someone whose own head needed to be examined, a business very much in practice in the Office to Combat Vices. There were no freaks like Brother Hamid, who read obscure books by more obscure authors who could not even write a grammatically correct sentence. Out in the world the revolution would never run out of fuel, for God was on the Imam's side, the masses of citizenry had been told, and God was omnipotent.

Moreover, there was no torment for people outside these walls by rapping the microphone menacingly against the edge of the desk at full volume. The sound of the microphone hitting the desk echoed so loudly in the ward that it made the inmates press their hands to their ears. Sometimes the torture lasted as long as an hour. One way to counter the effect, Farzin was advised early on, was to hold your head under the open faucet in the bathroom. Then there was only the sound of water. Mohammad showed Farzin how, but as there was only one faucet for all one hundred inmates, it couldn't be a practical means of relief. These sessions of cacophony reminded Farzin of Dostoyevsky and his discovery of the pleasures of inflicting "unnecessary cruelty" as a human characteristic. He remembered a small and gruesome, Dostoyevski-esque creature named Foma Opiskin in a story called "The Village of Stiepanchykovo and Her Inhabitants." Foma preyed on his victims, tormenting them to satisfy his sadistic needs. Farzin imagined him sitting on the other side of the walls, tapping and grazing the microphone on the desk edge.

"Fulfilling a human need, I'm sure!" Farzin said sarcastically to Brother Hamid, after complaining about the daily torture routine. Brother Hamid dismissed the charge as a gross exaggeration. Besides, and this was more of an issue for him, "Wasn't Dostoyevsky the fellow who said that Prophet Mohammad, may peace be upon his family, was an epileptic?"

"Don't know. Was he?"

"How would you feel if someone mocked your sense of dignity by saying that your father was a mushbrain and your mother was a whore?"

Farzin was sorry to have mentioned Dostoyevsky's name. He had forgotten that his warden could lose sight of an issue so easily. There was no use in protesting against his lack of sensitivity, either. Farzin had lost this round, and he cursed himself for it.

Fortunately, Brother Hamid did not dally on this for long and started delivering the good news.

"God bless him," he said. "Agha Shirazi's such a forgiving man, he'll see you tomorrow morning."

That night Farzin did not blink. He gathered his stockpile of cigarette foil, bits of biscuit wrappers, and brown paper and asked himself, "Where am I, and into what malicious riot of things am I rushing?" as though he were reciting some magical spell. And a magical spell it was for, lo and behold, myriad images and forbidden truths poured through his pen, scribbled onto sheet upon sheet of scrap paper that minute by minute fell all around him like lethargic butterflies. If there ever was anything impeding Farzin's antlike attempt to recapture his great ancestor's soul, there was no trace of it now. Images came to him, one after the other, like the pictures in a peep-show box.

The dashing officer of the Iranian Constitutional Revolution married the woman of his life on a warm September afternoon. On the eve of their union, the future commissioner wooingly sang a love song to his bride, made love to her three times in a row, and passed out from the intensity of his passion. In the morning they packed for their honeymoon and left for Lauhijaun.

In time he would show her the house in which he was born and cry on her shoulders recalling the death of his parents. In time he would tell her about his plans, which included spreading justice and punishing evildoers. She would become aroused on hearing him talk so passionately and would touch him in the most sensitive of places, bringing him to life, and they would take pleasure in each other all over again. She learned quickly, though, from the frightening experience of their first night, not to allow him to mount her more than twice in a row. Then they would lie naked in each other's arms under the moonlight and engage in lovers' talk until dawn. Falling in love with Lauhijaun over the following week, they decided to make it home. There they would start a family and he would begin his career.

Forty-One

The police commissioner and Malek Tauj differed in so many ways that any rendition of their likes and dislikes would prove downright silly to their mutual friends and acquaintances. It was as though their differences made them even more attractive to each other, fueled by their love. Their appreciation of honesty and simple people, their passion for classical poetry, and their equal disdain for the new "social poetry" furnished the glue that kept them together.

From early on it was common knowledge that she was everything he was not. Born into the bosom of old money, she was raised a prissy virgin with a flair for Victorian values and romanticism. Strong-willed and well versed in world literature, she had the mannerisms of a cultivated maiden and a fair face well known to high society. What did he want from her? What was she to him? She was his token of pride, the healer of his childhood wounds, and the feeder of his conceited obsession. She was his religion and his heresy, his belief in humankind, his enchantress. His vanity was a bottomless pit whose hunger could only be measured against her selfless devotion.

In the balance of things, what the commissioner lacked in character, he tried to compensate for by providing material goods for his wife. He provided her with a big house in Lauhijaun with servants to shop, clean, wash, sew, and run errands. A live-in cook with two helpers, a laundress, an on-call wet nurse, and jewelry—everything she wished for would be at her feet at the snap of her fingers. And if she could not snap her fingers, there was someone to do it for her. He would have given his life, had she asked for it, but that was not what she wanted. What then *did* she want? The answer is as clear today as it was then. She wanted everything and nothing—to be her own self and not an extension of his name and title. She wanted to find her own path and commit her own blunders along the way. She was born to know it, to give it its name, that all-encompassing, translucent thing of which he never quite got a grasp. Freedom was what she wanted. Freedom to choose not to sit at home and raise children (although she did that as well) but to do something for her less fortunate sisters, the lot of womankind.

Educated in French, she was aware of the ways of the world and the struggle of femalekind in the fantastic countries of the West. Not unsurprisingly, she saw herself as a part of that struggle. Her dream was to contribute to the elevation of her sisters through education: to administer an all-girls grammar school in Lauhijaun, the very first, in the style of the all-girls schools founded and governed by the Armenians in Tabriz and by missionaries in other parts of the country. The idea, which completely consumed her, had already found its way into their marital deed. The wonder of it all was that the petulant police commissioner had consented to such demands, which he had never dreamt might one day be put in front of him by the weaker vessel. You would think a man with his past would exert more clout, but not the commissioner. He had a close insight into the female world and was better equipped intellectually to sympathize with the cause of women than were his male contemporaries. He was known to have spewed the notion that there was no way to restrict a woman who had figured out the path to emancipation, just as there was no use trying to liberate a woman who had no idea she was not free. Kismet worked in mysterious ways.

Home was a castle of a house on a tiny street called Sheriff's Alley. A laden sheen of algae and moss coated the walls of the courtyard, endowing it with unbound charm and serenity. And the manor itself was something out of the One Thousand and

One Nights: two stories high with numerous rooms and halls, with windows in perfect geometrical shapes, and the maroon structure a marvel of grace. Its outer walls were damp, covered by velvety moss that afforded it a look of majestic antiquity. The slated roof sloped at a mild angle, except where the attic—designed to store casks of wine, pickled garlic, and preserved vegetables—caused the roof to flatten.

The mansion had a pleasant seat. Everywhere wild greenery sheltered the grounds, except where a narrow strip of earth showed the padded path trampled by the daily traffic of servants between the kitchen and the draw-well, with its winch to hoist water; further off loomed the shadow of the outbuilding across the yard from the manor. The barnlike edifice had gone through many transformations to serve various purposes: a hayloft, a warehouse, a storage area for winter or famine. The enigmatic world of the outbuilding held large barrels of kerosene from Baku, tins full of Caucasian pickles and Bulgarian feta cheese, locked chests with foreign labels, cans of cooking oil from Russia, jars of pickled eggplants, grains and nuts and gunnysacks of rice, firewood, and other household items. Between the two buildings there were fruit trees (fig, quince, and pomegranate) and flowers of every shade of color—hollyhocks, lilies, jasmine, and fritillaries. A full-time gardener was hired to care for the land after Malek Tauj opened her all-girls school halfway across town.

The middle-aged man who once strode in the company of the Armenian Monsieur Yeprim often complained that his house had become a caravansary (parents and people with petitions and affidavits rushed in and out uncontrollably, at all hours of the day), but his grumbling never went far. Truth be known, deep down he was proud of his wife's work and was elated to hear people praise her the way they did. It pleased him when people paid her attention out of respect; it somehow made him feel important and intellectually adequate. His lifemate being the principal of the only all-girls school in Lauhijaun said a mouthful about him in a town whose literate adults could be counted on the fingers of both hands. It showed that he had come a long way from being a street urchin, having prudently capitalized on his merits.

The commissioner could not have been more content with his life. He loved his children to no end, the two boys and his Sophie, a pretty babe five years old. What better reason to adore a woman who had given him such precious gifts? He considered himself lucky, the way a holy man might think himself a chosen creature of the Lord. Springtime, he took his sons stream fishing, or wild-duck hunting, and taught them how to swim and to build a fire outdoors. He went with his wife and little daughter for strolls in the park and returned the folks' acknowledgments by tipping his hat. They were the talk of the town, the commissioner and his Tehrani wife, and he was conscious of it. They strolled among the flowers; he in his bright uniform, she wearing a pince-nez bought from a German optometrist.

His best-loved child was Sophie, the jewel of his eyes. Sharp-tongued, gazelle-eyed, quick-witted, she was his world and his charmer, the calmer of his temper, the very air he breathed. So many days he shirked his duties just to stay home and spend time with her, converse with her in his silly childlike speech. So many hours he spent entertaining her vainest of wishes and demands. The child radiated such innocence and verve, it melted away his worries; the sound of their laughter often transcended the walls, putting the maidservants at ease. For the effect she had on her father, the servants treated little Sophie with extreme affection, each vying with the others to get on her good side. Conversely, the commissioner would storm into a blind rage if any of them neglected the child, punishing them severely when Sophie was unhappy. In those instances, they cleared away, for he would whip the life out of whomever came in sight.

There were good reasons for him to be the happy man that he was. His wealth exceeded half a million in land and tea plantations plus houses and shops, thanks to Malek Tauj's hefty dowry and her wise investments. Bliss glowed on his face on market day when he walked with Malek Tauj through the rows of vendors. Other than his fear of thunderbolts and the bouts with anger that stemmed from an overpowering love for his Sophie, he was a levelheaded man stuck in a repetitive and uneventful career. That is, until one day when the infamous Khalou Gorban strutted into his house with eight dozen or so poorly dressed guerrilla fighters armed with Russian infantry rifles.

Forty-Two

When Malek Tauj came home from school around noon on that bleak day, she found her house in a state of unprecedented bewilderment. A couple of armed men she had never met greeted her politely at the door but would not answer questions regarding their identity. No sooner had she walked into her house than she saw more strange men through the dense fruit trees. Tents were set up near the barn, which now appeared dark and damp, and whole goats were languidly roasting on spits. The sky was heavily overcast and there was terror in the air.

A row of guns propped up by the warehouse wall nauseated her. Malej Tauj felt her stomach muscles stiffening as she grasped that rebel guerrillas had taken hostage of her household and everyone in it. She recalled a recent conversation in which her husband had unexpectedly dropped Khalou Gorban's name, hinting at the possibility that he might be heading toward Lauhijaun. She remembered him saying that the insurgents were chased by government troops presently in Rasht.

Maids had poured into the yard, wailing, terrified, and feeling responsible for letting the rebels through the gates, even though there was nothing they could have done. When their eyes fell upon their matron, they renewed their hollering and hair pulling, upsetting her even though she had resolved to keep herself composed. Oh, how she loathed female meekness! Did they not know that giving in to fickle disposition would only make matters worse, especially under those circumstances? She only wished there was a way to relate that to them without undermining the gravity of their dire predicament.

Where was the master of the house? The housekeepers did not know, sobbing even louder at the mention of his name as though they had witnessed his death in the most gruesome way.

Where was the leader of the intruding thugs? "Out of sight," said the servants. They had not seen him, but the smoke billowing out of the barn and their meaningful stares told her he had set up his headquarters there.

Having ascertained that his fighters, mainly peasants and villagers, initiated no impropriety, Khalou Gorban had disappeared into the barn. The rebels were given strict orders to remain courteous, quiet, and respectful. Unless they kept their hands to themselves and their eyes averted in the presence of women and children, the punishment would be severe. It was clear that they had gone out of their way not to cause panic, save for the very act of entering the premises uninvited. Still, the foolish housekeepers screamed like spoiled children.

Malek Tauj did not remember as clearly as she would have liked whether her husband had planned to stay home all day. That morning her mind had been rushing ahead to the work at school, and she had not paid attention to what he said about where he would be. Instinctively, she feared he would be in some sort of danger. But where could he be now? Presently, she decided to meet with the rebel leader and demand her husband's release. Her march toward the storage building caused a mild commotion among the rebels. She felt their eyes devouring her as she passed by the cook fire and walked to the door of the warehouse, which had been left ajar. Inside the dimly lit barn a half dozen men were sitting on short-legged kettles in a semicircle, facing a bearded man who was bouncing a little bundle on his knees. Malek Tauj froze on the spot. There was Sophie, sitting on the lap of the burly man she recognized as the guerrilla chief, clapping her hands and beaming up at him—such a trusting child she was, the very essence of curiosity—her cheeks rosy from laughter. Sophie was smacking her little hands as Khalou Gorban tapped his foot to the rhythm of a folk song one of his men was singing, the rest of them clapping along. She even slapped him on his massive beard, clap, clap, smack, and seemed to be making a grand time of it. Repeating this again and again, he had fallen into feeble laughter, and when Malek Tauj walked in on them, he was still recuperating.

Khalou Gorban looked every bit as ghoulish as Malek Tauj had imagined from the stories she had heard about him; hairy arms that ended in huge hands, woolly beard, and a thick neck that made him look like a pathetic cretin. He wore a peasant's outfit consisting of a thick bluish shirt, tight pants that barely covered his ankles, and a sheepskin hat that casually rested on his scalp. Others were clad much the same, their shirts almost covering their bellies. They were muscular men with swift movements and dull gazes. Lumpy limbs extended from their disproportionately long trunks, twisting before her eyes, wrapping around stubby necks, and arms meshing together until they could not be told apart. The rhythm of their handclapping filled her head; with each clap there were tens of arms stretching out even further, entangling with one another and coiling into a giant cord-shaped arm that grew teeth and swallowed her tiny babe. Blood filled her eyes; she felt dizzy, but her legs refused to give in. She heard laughter and shouting, felt a dry pain in her throat.

Not until she was back at the house, with Sophie safely by her side, did she realize what she had done. Lost her mind? All Malek Tauj remembered was the child flying in the air, pulled by the arm, the hubbub of voices and the crowding men, as she prodded herself forward by force of will. The sky had turned scarlet, and the trees and the fire, and strange faces, and a hasty phrase, "Let the lady through," stuck in her mind. Next, she was hugging her Sophie in the quasi-safety of her chamber, the little girl regarding her mother with open-eyed wonder.

That afternoon, the commissioner's whereabouts remained a matter of conjecture. A maidservant, a black girl of fourteen, brought a message to her mistress from the guerrilla chief—a request for an interview. She sent the girl back with the message, "I'll be on the terrace."

Waiting for the abhorred rebel leader, Malek Tauj sat on a wooden chair in her schoolmaster's outfit—a chestnut suit buttoned up to the neck, without the benefit of a veil. She was like that, daring in that regard. School principals had that icy facade down cold. She was one of those who believed strength was in character. For men such as Khalou Gorban, devoid of religious fear, an intrepid disposition would prove impenetrable. Securing her shoulder-length gray hair behind, she found her demeanor advantageous in the mirror. Only her eyes betrayed her intent, which she remedied by hiding them behind her pince-nez.

Gorban's footsteps preceded him up the stairs. From her resting position, she cocked her head, listening. Whomp, thunk, whomp, thunk, whomp. Then, sheepishly, he appeared on the terrace with his cap in his hand, greeting Malek Tauj profusely. His massive trunk notwithstanding, he was not nearly as large as myth had led her to believe. As he sat on the floor, at a considerable distance from her, she warned herself about this man who had the simplicity of a shepherd but was indeed a cunning politician. Having thrown him a glance, she turned her face away. For the remainder of the meeting, her eyes radiated a wrath that could have melted stone. More than once, she reminded him that he represented a loathed occupying force. She said, not without reason, that her husband had been a revolutionary himself, fighting for Liberté, Égalité, and Fraternité. She recounted the police commissioner's service as a distinguished member of Yeprim Khan's entourage for a number of years. The commissioner's captors, she said, were a bunch of marauding fools to take him hostage and must release him immediately. Her voice was vibrant and fragile; fire flashed from her pince-nez.

"What do you want with the police commissioner anyway? And when are you going to leave my house and family? Is this a habit of yours to break into decent people's homes and make yourselves comfortable at the expense of your victims' terror? Do you, Mr. Gorban, really think that you and your cronies are going to win people over by such overt acts of aggression?"

She could not have spoken more bluntly.

The Tiger of the Forest, as Khalou Gorban was flatteringly known in certain quarters, endured the barrage of accusative questions without a flinch. He sensed the strength of Malek Tauj's mind in the way she addressed him. He addressed her with *Madam* and *My Dear Lady*, begging and imploring a number of times, yet knew full well he was unable to impress her. She would not be deceived by any show of servitude. Strange that he found himself admiring the lady of the house, even and especially as she was railing at him. Not fooling himself, he understood that under different circumstances she would not have deigned to throw him a glance; he harbored no illusions as to how she would treat him if they were to reverse positions. But now it was he who had the upper hand, even though time was against him. The best of it had to be made while his reign lasted in this town. A practical man, dead set on his agenda, he understood her condition quite well. When he began his response, he was in command of his emotions, unaffected by the bite of her sharp slurs.

"My friends and I mean no harm," said he. No bandits, they would leave the premises when they received the latest report from the western front and a thorough account of government troops. All and all, he did not expect their stay to exceed a fortnight. Speaking of the police commissioner, he added with a pensive voice, "We have no notion of his whereabouts." He waited for her reaction and got a cool, detached silence. She stared at a fig tree in the garden; under the fog of her despair ran a bedrock of pride. With or without the police commissioner, there were three children who needed to be raised.

  Before the meeting, Khalou Gorban had the vague notion that she knew, for her own sake at the very least, the whereabouts of the police commissioner. He would have much preferred dealing with the man of the house, but now a waft of suspicion won him over. Respectfully, he asked her directly if she knew. Was the commissioner ill and hospitalized? Was he hiding himself in a relative's home? Her eyes glittering with tears, Malek Tauj parried Gorban's suggestion. By the time he got to his feet and went back to his people, a mutual mistrust had established itself between the two adversaries.

Forty-Three

"This is telling us nothing," griped the Agha, as soon as Farzin sat before him on the floor the next day. "Absolutely nothing," the old man repeated. His remark upon seeing Farzin was uncharacteristically distraught. When Farzin stepped into his office, the Agha had been shaking the bundle of papers, Farzin's notes, in the air. "What do we care about the Constitutional Revolution? What does it even have to do with your mother, or your ancestors?"

The Agha was going nonstop. "You were told to be candid, to report frankly, and not to beat around the bush." He paused for a moment and contemptuously threw the bundle on his table. The stack of papers slid out of the folder, scattered on the table, and fell to the floor.

"Eh, have mercy on yourself, son," he continued with less anger now. "Isn't it a waste of youth, eh, spending the sweet days of your life in here instead of being with your family? Eh, think about your parents, why don't you? What have they done to deserve this, eh? Think about them ... eh .... We urge you to think about them."

The only additions to Agha Shirazi's room since their last meeting, as Farzin noticed, were a pitcher of water and a glass that sat on his table. Seemed well attended to, Farzin thought. *But somewhat gloomier than on the previous visit when he suddenly hacked and coughed, nearly choking to death.* The vision was interrupted by the Agha's warning.

"Eh, is this stuff relevant?" Agha Shirazi said. "What does Khalou Gorban's story have to do with your mother, huh?"

Farzin had in mind to explain, but the Agha cut him short with a wave of his hand.

"Enough already," the Agha shouted. "This is going nowhere. And so are you, my son. So are you, eh." Farzin was startled by the scolding.

"Eh, you may not be aware, but we met your mother the other day. And must say, she's a fine lady …. Show mercy for her, eh, even if you don't much care about yourself. Think what it'll do to her. There isn't a mother in the world who can bear the torment of her child. Step down from your satanic ivory tower, eh, and speak truthfully …. If you speak now and make a clean breast of it, no harm will come to you." He lifted his glass of water and showed it to Farzin. "Eh, everything crystal clear, so the world can see it, just like this water." He tilted the glass and drank its content. A few drops trickled down his beard; he wiped them off with the back of his hand. Farzin felt his heavy gaze as the sage studied him in perplexed, hostile silence.

FORTY-FOUR

The Agha stuck his hand under his garb once again, bringing it out with a battered wristwatch he kept there in the folds of his mantle. He stole a glance at it now and then.

"That's all the time we have today. Guard will take you back."

"But it's not—"

"You are an incorrigible young man," the Agha snapped back. "Eh, don't know in what language to say it to you. What has this report got to do with the accusations, huh? Don't even want to guess. Eh, wasting our time and your life you are."

"It's relevant; I swear it's relevant. Please, Agha. You're a man of God, I beg for your compassion. You see, I was drifting—"

"Eh, still are, son. Still are. Get to the point already."

"I will, your honor," said Farzin. "And the point is a simple one, anyway. In short, you're at a point where the Rouhanis have asserted themselves, after a long time of compromising family, wealth, everything. Even the secrets were compromised, although Nozar Rouhani salvaged a bit of it through sheer willpower." The Agha remained silent. He made it clear that he was indulging Farzin, even though his patience was thinning.

"Now enters my mother's family," continued Farzin. "At this juncture, the capacity for patience replaces longevity in my family. Please note that this tendency has been greatly helped by political forces along the way. That's why a pragmatic Rouhani every now and then asserts himself in favor of survival."

"Now, you've lost me. Eh, what does *that* have to do with it? Who would be this pragmatic Rouhani, eh, as you call it?"

"That would be me, sir," Farzin said boisterously.

"I see," said the Agha, raising one eyebrow in mock interest. "So you are the pragmatic one, eh?"

"Well, I'm trying to *explain* exactly that. But you're not allowing me to finish. I had to get out of the house." Once again, the Agha raised an eyebrow.

"On the day of the march, you see," Farzin was quick to explain. "I had to get out of the house. I was going to … get fresh air, you see. Watch people."

The Agha raised both eyebrows now and looked at his watch one more time.

"Haven't got time," he said. "Eh, put it down on paper. Will look at it another day." He dropped his eyes again and closed the file.

"Wait, wait, please. I'm using shopping bags and biscuit wrappers. Could you at least—"

The Agha's hand disappeared under his cushion, reappearing with a stack of white sheets. He held it before Farzin.

"Eh, may God forgive all his children."

That night, while the rain poured incessantly, a brown-skinned maid—Sarah was her name—took her madam's hand and led her through the silent halls to the kitchen, a place Malek Tauj had rarely set foot in, a place of pots, pans, and ludicrous servants. At the end of the kitchen, where on the ceiling was an entranceway to the attic, Sarah stopped. Silence of nightfall and her unspoken mystery compelled the matron of the house to also stop. Then, the black girl pointed up at the square trapdoor and whispered, "Mister Commissioner up there. Wait you, I fetch a ladder."

A faint smile appeared on Malek Tauj's lips. She grabbed Sarah's cheeks in her hands and kissed her on the lips as her heartbeat quickened. Quietly, Sarah melted into the pitch-black pantry and came back with a tall ladder on her broad shoulders. She set the ladder up under the trapdoor and, carrying a candlestick and matches, began to climb.

A few steps up and Sarah turned to her mistress, who was standing spellbound at the foot of the ladder.

"What are you waiting for, ma'am?" she said. "He is dying to see you."

Malek Tauj followed the girl up the ladder until they were both swallowed by the hole in the ceiling, where a strong garlic smell hovered in the air. Malek Tauj stared intently into the dark, whispering her husband's name.

Forty-Five

The police commissioner had seen it coming. From the minute his deputies reported the imminent entry of the Reds into town that morning, an ominous vision of the near future, which included him facing the communist firing squad, depressed his being. Entertaining sharp, distressing epiphanies, he was certain Khalou Gorban would come after him first and foremost. The possibility of some old feud existing between the two was strong, although he did not recall anything specific, except that the story of his friendship with Reza Shah, formerly Reza Maxim, was a local epic. The police commissioner himself took such pride in the story, he often badgered his officers with it, commenting on how things had changed, how respect for one's superiors used to mean putting one's life on the line for them. That was his winning ace with which to barter reverence from his men. Not that they lacked in displaying adequate respect toward their commander, rather the police commissioner was a perfectionist who demanded absolute obedience. Now the ghosts of those stories had returned to take their toll.

Times had changed, and the commissioner had seen it coming. Considering the number of policemen under his command and his inability to obstruct Khalou Gorban's advances, he had decided to offer no resistance. "Avoid bloodshed," he ordered his men, and they accepted his words and did not think much of it, or less of him. Although he had told Malek Tauj he would stay home that day, he went down to the station and discharged every officer on duty. He advised them to change into civilian attire and lay low as if a tornado were coming their way. Next, mounting his horse, he sped homeward accompanied by his loyal orderly; he did not even bother to lock up the station. His haste proved wise because a few hours later, as the commissioner and his orderly dismounted halfway home, and drove the horses into the woods, Khalou Gorban cleared the station out: rifles, guns, ammo.

The candle Sarah now held in her hand, the only light he had seen since noon flickered and cast strange shadows on the walls and ceiling as the two women moved forward on their hands and knees. They stopped at arm's length from the commissioner and his valet, whose skin, pale with fear, glowed in the dark. Facing her husband, Malek Tauj noticed that lavender pockets hung under his eyes like a horse's nosebag. If it weren't for his sunless grin discouraging her, she would have touched his temples. The shame of having been forced to hide in the attic lingered in the air, suspended in the space between them. It made him stammer on every other word as he recounted the events of the day. When he got around to telling her how he had slipped into his own house, in the light of day, so that the servants would not detect his presence, Malek Tauj's eyes filled with tears. She kissed his hand and vowed to protect him from the evil eye. When she spoke, his cheeks swelled and his eyes strayed, but the prominent feature of his face remained the dark pouches under his eyes. There and then she worked out a plan to send up food and water for both men, twice daily. It would sustain them, she was confident.

Malek Tauj stepped down the ladder and her heart beat with a renewed love for her husband and a deep hatred for his enemies. Aware of the government troops camping outside Rasht, she decided to dispatch someone for help. Employing a ruse, she'd be able to keep Khalou Gorban until they arrived. *Wouldn't be impossible.* Main thing was to find the right person for the job. But who could undertake this most important of tasks? *Who could travel fifty kilometers on foot and not shirk the job halfway for lack of perseverance or loyalty? Who would be capable of carrying a weight of such magnitude?* Why, that self-effacing creature was standing right before her, and no time to second-guess herself. She had Sarah change her clothes and sent her on her way with a few bills and a hastily written note to none other than the Shah himself. She made sure the girl put the letter away in a safe place under her garments and divvied up the cash to different parts of her clothing.

In the letter addressed to "Dear Shah of Mine," Malek Tauj explained the peril faced by her husband, "the chief commissioner of the Lauhijaun police," who was monitoring the enemy forces. She emphasized the urgency of her plight. She expected nothing short of an immediate explosion of reaction from the Shah. Maybe His Royal Highness himself would come to the rescue and save the nation in the meantime, she hoped. She concluded the letter with the promise of "praise from future generations who will shower the great savior of the motherland." A brisk signature augmented the seriousness of the situation. Sealed and folded, it disappeared between a pair of ripe chocolate breasts.

Sarah, intimate with the dark like a cat, slipped out the door into the starless night. Malek Tauj, in her haste, could not have picked a better messenger, for Sarah knew her way about that area well. Walking a few kilometers along the familiar path to the town center, she then veered off into the woods. At sunrise, no one noticed her absence other than the kitchen staff, who relied on her buckets of water and swift broom. It was then that Malek Tauj unleashed her rarely practiced but eminently feared stare that silenced them all. They were to fetch water themselves and suppress their wonderings. Sarah's name did not come up again until after the trouble was over.

During their nightly visits, Malek Tauj recounted the day's goings-on to her husband, who did not appear affected one way or another. She treated him as though he were on a mission and many lives depended on him. Her early visits at sunrise when she brought him breakfast were short for the risk of being discovered by servants, the spendthrifts of secrets; she would leave the tray and close the opening. But in the evenings their rendezvous mirrored their youthful adventures. Every evening, she would bring a storm lantern along with her and make a quiet but elaborate feast, complete with red wine in crystal glasses and sweet creamy desserts. She would retell the things she had put in that letter to the Shah, listing the ways she was keeping herself and the children occupied during the day, and the lies she had had to come up with to allay Gorban's suspicions. Occasionally, for all she went through, she succeeded in extracting a candid smile from the somber police commissioner, which came to mean a world to her.

Although she was pushing upward of fifty at this time, her body still moved her around as if she were two decades younger. Her single-minded hope was that fresh food would compensate for the commissioner's lack of sun, movement, and freedom; her single-minded goal was keeping him physically alive and alert. For his burden of shame she had no remedy but kind words and the promise of the future.

On their second day in the attic, the police commissioner dismissed his faithful orderly, who left the house at sunset and took the commissioner's secret to his grave. The burden proved to be so weighty that the commissioner's loyal companion could not live with it. That same evening, his wife discovered him, wrist-slit, in the outhouse after his two days' absence. Malek Tauj received that bit of intelligence and successfully kept it from her husband, whose emotional well-being was fast on the decline. The man in the attic never found out about the fate of his underling.

Then dreams supplanted the epiphanies, those otherworldly vapors that seeped through the cracks and cavities of the floor and plagued him like a disease. Dreams of grandeur came and went in the shadow of time, giving way to the vaporous images of his childhood hardships, the tormented faces of his parents, and his toil in the mountains of his adolescence. The police commissioner would journey back to the earlier years of his career and visit his thinner, handsomer self without the blubbery bag under his chin. Dreams of the riots over bread, gunfights along with Monsieur Yeprim against the despotic forces of the court came to him later, dimmed and fogged with a tinge of nostalgia and the attar of Tehrani women who had so readily given themselves to him. And he heard noises, both from inside his mind and out. Awake, memories flitted through his mind of the days when he had been famous for his fearlessness in combat. No less of a man than Monsieur Yeprim himself had praised his courage before the troops and had said, "If the constitutionalists had a hundred soldiers like the police commissioner in their service, the despotic regime would fold in a day."

Happiness revisited.

The commissioner was proud and happy in the days when women overtly admired him and men vied for his friendship. The days he had walked with his head held high and his chest bulging forward like a horny partridge. Turned many a head he did, as he cruised about Tehran's endless streets. The picnics and the parties, complete with mounds of greasy food and jugs of robust wine accompanied by laughter and music and flirtatious chatter.... Ah, yes, dreaming of Malek Tauj, in her pretty scarlet clothes, sporting a white rose in hair that barely reached her shoulders—dreaming of her hands that danced in the light and coyly brushed up against his arm. Nobody, nothing, not even the morning mist, had such a gentle touch. How tremendously lucky to have met and impressed her the way he did. The images of her in various stages of pregnancy, with her hair down or bundled up in the back, flashed through his mind.

Then he would come to and allow the present to fill his pained, confounded mind. He had shrunk, his bones felt hollow and his muscles were weak. His thinning hair and bulky mustache were fast turning white. His breath reeked of carrion, and he could smell the putrid air caged in his chest. The realization of what the sum of his life had amounted to had fast begun to take its toll. In this, Malek Tauj was a helpless witness. All she could do was to keep her children together and hearten her husband to stay sane. The captivity would not last long; she would remind him as well as herself. It was an "arduous phase of a lengthy and heroic struggle, but a phase nevertheless," she would say to him. He would overcome it like so many other battles and trials he had endured. She was confident he not only would come out of this in one piece but would become a wiser and more prized hero. She even resorted to lies, telling him that government help was on the way. "Please, dear," she begged, "just hang in there for the country, for our children, and for me." Untruths and half-lies, as far as she knew, but were they?

She cooked him his favorite dishes lest the cook's curiosity be roused, an excellent excuse to hone her culinary skills. Having the kitchen help stand by for Gorban and his horde of guerrillas—so their bemused expressions would not be in her face—she rolled up her sleeves and put her heart and soul into it. For the police commissioner, whose survival had become her life mission, she dipped her hands in sticky dough, cleaned rice, ground walnuts, chopped parsley and tarragon, and rinsed chickpeas. No easy task for a woman used to being served. And though she tried her hardest, her lack of genuine skills made a mockery of her efforts, at first producing little more than rare charcoal.

Busy with preparations for so many, the cook did not suspect in the beginning but, after a day or two, caught on to this strange behavior. She attributed the trail of dirty pots and plates to Malek Tauj's unstable condition, due to her grief for her husband whom the cook fancied dead.

The cook was not far from truth as far as death was concerned. On evening five of the police commissioner's exile in the attic, Malek Tauj would find his lifeless body. His skin yellowed by sunlessness, he had died that morning amid tears of shame and nostalgia. Clutching at his heart, as a severe wave of hiccups seized him, he had died leaning on a post in a vomiting position, his mouth frothing. He became fixed in her mind for the rest of her life just as she had found him that night, his body poised against the post, mouth agape.

On the other hand, the faithful Sarah walked fifty kilometers to Rasht, sleeping at night under wild blackberry bushes in the company of salient toads, floundering through the candid, nothing-withholding marshes under the stifling sun, emerging, losing her way, and finally arriving at Reza Shah's camp at the fifth sunrise. Having traveled through the jungles and swamps, fighting exhaustion, hunger, fear, and importunate mosquitoes, she found convincing the guards at the camp station an even harder task.

The guards at the government military camp would not let the poor girl in, nor would they carry her message to the commander in chief even though Sarah's face beamed with fury. Her full lips, the corners of which pointed slightly upward, delivered sounds that might as well have been a different language, which made matters worse, for the guards who scarcely understood her dialect to begin with, now lost her completely. When the hope of getting anywhere was lost, fear replaced her desperation, and she decided to make a run for it. She became a fiery ball and dashed through the gates into the compound, but the guards caught her, dragged her back by her braided hair, and made to throw her out of the campsite.

Three officers were at that moment coming out of a nearby tent. They noticed the skirmish and, on the pretense of taking her to the Shah, lured her into the woods behind the tents, where the living daylights were rammed out of her right under the open sky, not five hundred feet from the monarch's tent. Just as the police commissioner suddenly found himself in the fight of his life, his maid was thrown in a tussle of her own under three heartless officers of Reza Shah's northern regiment, the army whose mission was to save the northern provinces from the Reds who had taken hostage the house and its occupants from which the black girl, currently being raped so savagely, had come. And half the garrison, bored from inaction, had encircled the scuffle on the leaf-covered ground, watching Sarah's body giving up the struggle. She could hear their catcalls and hoots encouraging the perpetrators and wondered if she had not been better off in Gorban's captivity ... A sharp pain shot through the commissioner's heart. He clawed his chest and beat on it, but the piercing would not go away ... Sarah, her eyes shut tight, wept silently as her limp body was bruised and battered. With every hand that poked her, she became more frightened, until finally, out of desperation and pain she let out an earsplitting shriek that scared her tormentors off, just as the commissioner said his farewell to the world. His body shuddered for the last time and remained motionless. A foamy stream of saliva rolled off his chin.

Forty-Six

The day had not yet begun when a hand shook Farzin awake.

"Get up, *yallah baba*," Mohammad said.

Farzin leaped out of bed with a yelp. All around the dim room there were hand-made lanterns—candles burning inside cylinders made of waxed paper. He looked about torpidly. Rubbing his eyes, he tried to recall the events of the previous day. His inky fingers ached still. His tired body resisted rising up, but in the end it was hopeless. A number of inmates had come from the other rooms and clustered around the window, peering into the pre-dawn silence. It was impossible to go back to sleep with the throng huddled close by.

Farzin pushed through and reached for the cool iron bars, imitating everyone else's stare out the window. A serene morning it was, the courtyard somber with no colors, no life. The world seemed tamed beneath the ubiquitous grayness that reigned over it. In an hour, light would bring out its colors, and noises would rouse the day. It was that fine hour of the day, that inevitable moment, when the scent of morning overcomes the night.

Farzin remained at the window even though he could not make out a thing beyond the trees; he was glued to it by nothing but the attraction that something must be out there. They all waited there, the wide-eyed jailbirds. Cigarettes gleamed like tiny glow-worms, each casting a faint light on a grim face.

Then from the left of the courtyard there came the sound of marching boots, sustaining itself for a while, and fading into the woods where the empty swimming pool lay behind heavy rosebushes. A hush fell over the block. Farzin pricked up his ears, as he heard Mohammad's lamenting.

"O Lord," Mohammad was saying. "His turn has come." Mohammad's pitch had a strange ring to it for that early in the day. Farzin felt a weakness in his joints, a slight tremor in his knees, a stirring at the base of his stomach. Since the day he joined the ward, he had not felt so out of place. Standing to his right, Mohammad must have felt the same way, quietly dabbing his eyes with the palm of his hand.

"A few more minutes, *baba*," said Mohammad. "That's all it takes." His remark evaporated in a final puff.

"Where are they taking him?" inquired Farzin, hating himself for asking what seemed to others too obvious. Mohammad went on talking to himself.

"A few more minutes, just a few more."

Farzin's straining eyes had begun to moisten when a sudden shriek spread across the yard, and as though hitting an invisible shield, it dropped just outside the window. A divine baritone then echoed against the thick of dawn. The voice shouted an order, while a second voice melodically began reciting verses from the Holy Book. Not a hiss issued from this side of the bars. A chilling fear crept under Farzin's skin. Terror seeped through the pores of dawn and socked him square in the face. He stared at the strange murky gray of the awakening sky. It appeared to him something was nearing from the clouds; he could make nothing of it, for it was too subtle and pale to name. Holding his breath, though, he felt its vulgar density creeping out of the air, coming through the sounds and the heat that filled the breaking morn.

The voice of divinity baritoned again. The recitation had halted. A slow breeze whirred the message through the woods to its captive audience. Ever so eager to decipher the breeze-blown words, Mohammad pressed his large face against the metal bars as if trying to push cold butter through the tines of a fork. Broken sentences reached them by way of the cool air.

"In the name of Allah ... according to His Reverence ... perpetrator of corruption on earth ...."

Silence supervened the voice but not long enough to give anyone on this side of the bars a chance to react, when, out of nowhere, gunshots rang out in a quick yet harmonious succession: TARRA, TARRA, TARRA, from G-3 automatic rifles that were distinctly different from the AK-47. Three separate rounds of resounding shots, fired in the distance where the empty swimming pool lay openmouthed. It was done. Blood had finally baptized the truth. The earth was cleansed of yet another corrupt mortal, a soul at last freed, a wrong set right. The faithful could now sleep a trifle more soundly, their *namoose* protected.

As a result of and in direct proportion to the gunshots, a wail of sorrow rose up from the inmates before all became quiet again.

Street noise began to make itself present—the hubbub of the traffic. Tehran was waking up; the gears had begun to grind, the unsteady walk of a woman in high heels, motorcycles and engines roaring angrily, orange taxicabs screeching to a halt and zooming off in urgency, two-story buses growling in the distance, moving heavily under the weight of the morning rushhour.

Forty-Seven

At eight o'clock, Brother Hamid showed up at the Office to Combat Vices in his off-duty gear: brown slacks and a black long-sleeved shirt, collarbuttons undone. A patch of black hair curled out from his collar, like a dervish in ecstasy, his eyes aimlessly wandering about. His mouth, surprisingly, did not stink. That was the first thing noticeable about him. During the interrogation, Hamid leaned in so close that Farzin could see the white buds of his tongue as he eagerly spewed forth another speech, the details of which Farzin would forget, but the gist of which he would retain.

Weeks had lapsed since the visit with the Agha. Brother Hamid offered beforehand his sympathies for what was going to happen to Farzin. He said he was sorry, with his hands in his pockets. He said he was sorry, even though he did not know what exactly was going to happen next. They were alone in an office, empty except for a couple of chairs and a picture of the Light of Islam. He pulled his hands out of his slacks and made a gesture indicating it was out of his hands. Farzin happened not to think so, but he had to admit Brother Hamid seemed to have done everything in his capacity to prevent this day, or at least to postpone it.

"They're not going to wait another day. Why should they? Have you anything else to add?"

"This place is so dusty," is what Farzin said. "Look at the paint peeling off." Farzin pointed at a corner of the ceiling with his finger.

"Are you nuts or something? I'm telling you, mister, that you're finished, and all you can say is the bloody paint's peeling off?"

"Yeah, right there," Farzin emphasized.

"Screw the paint, will you?"

"But—"

"What have you to show for all the time you've been wasting? Huh? You still think this is a joke? Because if you do, the joke is on you, hear? Soon you'll be going down to the basement, so much is clear, and there's nothing I can do about it." The mere mention of the basement reminded him of the infamous Test of Innocence, whatever that would be, and its administrator, Brother Daudyaur, which caused the hair on Farzin's neck to stand on end. An excruciating pain made itself felt in his temple as he soaked his shirt with a shower of perspiration. He decided to protest.

"That's not fair."

"I know what you mean, but look at you, acting all the time like you've lost your mind .... It won't matter what I think anymore, even though I happen to think you're innocent; it's not enough. You've not been *cooperating* is all."

That was not what Farzin had in mind. "That's not what I meant," he said.

"What then? What's not fair?"

"What's not fair is I'm not finished yet .... You've got me going with this report, and now you're telling me that I have no time to finish what I started? "

"Wise up, brother. You're almost finished. Even your stories can't help you now."

At this Farzin had to let go. Unfolding his arms, he revealed another thick stack of paper. Brother Hamid held out his hand for it. He was an expert by now, this Brother Hamid. One look at the opening remark and he knew what he was dealing with. He smirked.

"If you don't entirely believe it," Farzin said excitedly, defensively, "ask the Agha Shirazi." The Agha being not only a founding member of the Revolutionary Forces but also an admirer of the Lightning Rod of Islam, the Ayatollah Ruhollah Khomeini. Farzin went on. "They are all so cozy in this joint you'd think they cared about the fate of their prisoners. And you. You just picked me up in the street on the same day that an anti-government rally was in full swing, and had no clue what I was doing there or where I was going. Just arrested me and wrongly accused me of subversion. Things that hardly, hardly matter now, because obviously everyone here has already made up his mind about who I am and what I've done or, in this case, what I haven't done." Farzin paused, took a deep breath, and finished his tirade. "How on earth can I prove to you people that I am innocent?"

Brother Hamid held his breath for the answer to the next question.

"Okay, what were you doing and where were you going? Come clean now."

"I was going to my boyfriend's house."

"What did you say?"

"That's right. I have a boyfriend, and I was going to visit him. He lives about five blocks away from where you picked me up. I was going to see him."

"And you've been hiding that all along? That is considered withholding information, punishable by law. I'm simply *shocked* at you."

"Bullshit, Hamid! You would have had me shot if I had told you. Even now I'm not so sure you'd do otherwise."

"Then why sing now?"

"Because you won. You wore me down and I don't want to go on like this anymore. You have defeated me, but now I am glad that you were wrong about me. I am no revolutionary. You and your worldview have put such a terror in me that I wish I were. Thanks to you, I wish I were a subversive. Although by being what I am, I might be, without even intending to be."

"What are you talking about now?"

"I'm talking about all those times that you wanted me to start from the beginning. 'Begin from the beginning,' you said. 'Tell us everything,' you said. And oh, 'Don't leave anything unsaid,' remember? Well, how could I even begin telling you something like that without running the risk of being shot right there and then? And who would have cared? Especially about that."

"So, you are right," agreed Brother Hamid. "I would have probably treated you worse. But at least you wouldn't have been a suspect for treason." He paced the room, thinking. "You would have been treated as the homosexual that you are and not the dissident activist that we thought you were." Brother Hamid touched his beard and looked at the wall. "And, the whole time, who you really were was lost in all this. You became invisible to us. That's a valid point. We made you invisible. We made a liar out of you. We only wanted to hear what we wanted to hear. And that made you invisible. We defeated ourselves." Brother Hamid was lost in his thoughts.

The evidence of Farzin's victory was all over Brother Hamid's face. Farzin regarded his interrogator with an air of superiority now, for he had struck the final blow. He knew that Brother Hamid understood, because Hamid started to shrivel up, like a raisin, brooding quietly.

Farzin sat there beside Brother Hamid and busied himself with rearranging the pages of his report, smoothing the edges on some of the paper, straightening others. At the end of his contemplation, Brother Hamid's eyes sparked back to life. It was as though he had decided he was not confused. Maybe flustered, but not confused anymore. Farzin could see that in the movement of his body, a truck gearing up to move a heavy load. He put himself in Brother

Hamid's shoes to see if there was room for optimism. It was obvious there was no point in holding Farzin prisoner any longer, but to stop the gears of revolutionary justice, it would take a lot more than persuasion. Brother Hamid had a long battle ahead of him.

"Frankly," Brother Hamid said finally. "I've given up on you. You're a lost cause, as a prisoner." He explained that the only thing left for him was to take Farzin back to the block and let him await his fate. *The poor son of a bitch would probably spend the rest of the day getting worked up.*

Personally, Farzin was pleased to finally have a sense of victory. He admitted to himself that something of the Secrets of Survival was at work; now he could hold up a mirror to Brother Hamid's face.

Farzin sat Brother Hamid down like a doctor about to tell a man of his wife's death. He poured a glass of water and reassured his jailer by declaring that he was right, and that the Secrets of Survival had nothing whatsoever to do with anything. He could not afford spending another day disappointing Brother Hamid. There were other idiosyncrasies that needed attention, and he needed to push on to the year 1953 and be done with it.

Forty-Eight

In a large tent, barely half a kilometer away from where Sarah was left to pull herself together, the Shah-in-Shah, in full olive drab uniform and his trademark cape, was poring over incomplete and inaccurate maps with his advisers. A towering statue of asperity, he rarely found his advisers ill informed or incompetent, but when he did, he would question their intentions. Now, the vacuous look in their eyes was most deplorable.

At times like this the Shah would lose his temper all too quickly. From the way His Majesty pounded his fist into his open palm, his advisers were once again privy to the brewing trouble in his pulsing, graying temples. Reza Shah was in the habit of calming himself down by yelling at his subordinates and by beating them, whether majors or foot soldiers; vented his anger in the most unrestrained manner. Presently, he banged on the table covered by erroneous maps, not once, not twice, but until his fist was throbbing and beyond, until he heard what must have sounded like the howling of a jackal. Oblivious to the shameful misdeed of his officers, he raised his piercing eyes and asked a revealing question: "What's the howling?"

The answer, with wild hair and clothes torn, was brought to the door. Dumbfounded by the sight of the young dark-skinned girl, who was hardly able to stand straight, the Shah ushered her in and sat her on a chair. And the girl, not recognizing His Royal Highness, begged him for an audience with the Shah. Her nose bleeding, her hair tossed in a chaotic frenzy of mud and semen. The only other words emitted from her lips were Gorban's name—Khalou Gorban, the one and only—the effect of which was like a snuffer on the flame of the Shah's glabrous head. His frightening brows coalesced in a lasting grimace. Quickly, he sent his orderly to fetch his personal doctor.

Sarah would have mentioned the beast's name sooner had she known the soldiers were so keen on him. Had she known it would fling open the gates or stop the assault on her girlhood, she would have yelled it at the top of her lungs for the world to hear. Now in the presence of the Shah, in soiled clothes and broken spirit, she felt anger rising in her throat; she blinked rapidly. The military man before her noticed her bruised arms and torn garment that spoke their tale of injustice for which he had a keen ear; he made a mental note to investigate the cause of her miserable condition. For now, he wanted to know everything that was there to know about the insurgent whose name had slipped her lips.

"What's your name?"

"Sarah ... My mistress, she sent me to give you this." She let go of the front of her dress, which fell open, revealing a red scratch on her left breast, as the letter, having taken a beating of its own, dropped to the floor. With stammers and stutters, she relayed Malek Tauj's message and wiped her eyes with her dirtied fingers. She watched the military man's face relax and relapse into another scowl, a pensive frown, free of anger.

Afterward she was fed, clothed, and paid handsomely in cash, but she was not told what to do with it.

Both then and later, Reza Shah's decision to advance toward Lauhijaun in pursuit of the rebels was attributed to the military intuition of a genius. For years, textbooks would shove his knack for military matters down schoolchildren's throats as a divine gift. His campaign against Khalou Gorban would become a case study for a somewhat bloated assertion that His Royal Highness, *from the beginning*, knew what he was doing. Excluded all along was Sarah's testimony—not even alluded to, as though the black servant had not presented a day-to-day account of the events in the commissioner's house. As if she had never existed.

Once upon a morning light, when the dew disappeared and the air was left without a particle of moisture, the modernized regiment of the north moved toward Lauhijaun in all its glory. Reza Shah in full battle regalia, decorated with nacreous buttons and lustrous medals, rode ahead of the artillery on an Arab mare. The regiment moved as quickly as possible and maintained a steady speed without a stopover. By the time the troops reached Lauhijaun, the sun was fast on the descent. The sky was clearing, the weather mild and there was mist in the air.

That night, under the face of the fogged country moon, Reza Shah discussed his plan of action with his senior officers, oversaw synchronization of watches, divided the troops into three columns, and besieged the tiny burg on the outside where the macadam stopped. The surprise attack would begin just before the first beam of sun hit the treetops, when least expected. The night was quiet save for the steady croaking of frogs pouring into the humid air. A perilous immediacy hung over the house at Sheriff's Alley, like the fourteenth moon of the month in the pitch darkness of the sky. The servants sat around their mistress and tried to cheer her now that the defeat of their captors had almost become a surety. God had sent the government to take her revenge, they said. But to their foolish chants Malek Tauj was indifferent. She sat on a cushion on the terrace, dressed in black, dragging on her favorite water pipe. The smoke rose lazily into the air, expanding to invisibility. The servants, having sensed the unusual stir, surrounded her. Firing up samovars and consoling Malek Tauj, they went wild with their speculations. Gorban's head on a golden tray, they predicted, would be delivered at the door in the morning.

The news of the siege and the forthcoming liberation of the town mixed with rumors; prayers and well wishes echoed through the mountains. Gorban withdrew his guerrillas from the main street and posted them on top of the municipality tower, in the vicinity of Sheriff's Alley. He refused to shut his eyes even for a moment lest the attack come under the cover of midnight. His cadaverous shadow was seen by the high walls of the police commissioner's property. Pacing furiously, he puffed his pipe, brooding over the widespread defection among his forces. Dropping one or two at a time, a dozen of his fighters had left their ranks since the first rumors of the town's blockade began to circle—half of those defecting to the enemy. But Reza Shah would not attack at night. He was not a coward. On the contrary, he was braver than the bravest the nation had offered to date, no less than a hero, who had won, for outstanding valor in the service of his country, several coveted medals. Nor with all his faults was he in the final analysis a vicious man, what his enemies thought of him notwithstanding.

That evening was the roughest in Khalou Gorban's entire rebellious career. At two o'clock in the morning he was either consulting with his confidants or accusing them of not giving their best. Having weighed all the other options, his advisors unanimously rejected fleeing to the Bolshevik homeland up north. The emerging decision was to disperse and leave town, one by one while it was still dark out, and meet up later with the Junglee Mirza Kuchek Khan, the rebel of the Geellon Jungles. But how many would truly manage to flee would remain unknown; late in the morning, there would be conflicting reports as to the number of prisoners Reza Shah took back with him to Tehran. Of note was the following: while his guerrillas ran away stealthily, under the cover of darkness, Khalou Gorban was swearing to fight to the end; but the next day, he gave himself up with his closest associates and entered the government's service with the rank of colonel. The state procured him a house in Tehran where he lived the rest of his tame life under the magnanimous shadow of Reza Shah, the onetime General Reza Khan, formerly known as Reza Maxim. Whomp, thunk, whomp.

Forty-Nine

Once upon a morning light there was a warden who, deep down in the bottom of his heart, was convinced of Farzin Rouhani's innocence concerning the outrageous charges of sedition brought against him. Huffing and puffing he had had a hard time going to sleep, and even when the specter of sleep warmed his eyelids, his mind refused to shut down. He rolled this way and that, now on his stomach, now on his back, mulling over the predicament in which he had put an innocent man (well, to the extent a homosexual can be regarded as a man), which was gravely upsetting the balance of his righteous soul. For if the charges had been in any lesser order he would have cared not a straw—*i.e.* buggering another boy or being buggered by one. He did not have time for that. But conspiring to overthrow the reign of Allah on earth? This left him a torn fellow; his conscience carped at him continuously.

Would the prisoner lose his life, wrongfully, as a result of his complacency? And what if he did, is it not one pervert less on the face of the earth? Shouldn't he alert the judges? *And for what? What would he tell them? The truth or just half of it? What should be the basis of any intervention on his part, sheer conviction? But since when was that admissible in the presence of divinity?*

Brother Hamid already knew the essence of the response he would likely get, if he chose to intervene only enough to save Farzin's life. Something along the lines of an age-old maxim: if the accused was guilty, he would merely meet his punishment; if innocent, he would go to the Elysian Fields in the company of seventy-two virgin houris. He reflected on this and what it said about the revolutionary order he had helped create. Was this what his idealism had come down to, a swift and unforgiving justice for all, guilty or not? Fortunately or unfortunately, much depending on how one looked at it, the logic somehow did not cut it with Brother Hamid. He felt an uneasiness creeping under his skin. Martyrs of the revolution would have risen up in horror if they knew the Islamic order they had fought and died for had been sending folks to their graves on shady evidence presented by apathetic prosecutors. No, that was not what he was about. If the gatekeepers of virtue were so nonchalant, what could be expected of the man on the street? Presently, he strove to figure out what it was that he was about. Half of him was debating with the other on the merits of doing the right thing. After all, he was the arresting officer, the warden, and now the examiner of confessions.

He recalled the latest installment of Farzin Rouhani's testimony which, although accurate in facts, was not fooling anyone, Brother Hamid was certain.

Fifty

Morteza Nemat, the Third Division colonel of the infantry unit stationed in Eshratabad, Tehran, had a strong belief in kismet. Growing up in balmy Tehran, in the kind embrace of a lower-middle-class family, he felt bound to fate. It did not matter what name it was given, fate or karma, this thing that led men and women toward their destiny by the nose. One could negate it, oppose it, ignore it, disprove it, rename it, run away from it, complain about it, or justify it. But one could not make sense of it in a dozen lifetimes, nor could one excuse it, define it, or refine it by a long shot. And no matter who you were, misters and sisters, or what you did for a living, you could not grasp it. It stood alone on steel legs, free of man's individual and collective will, making lives, undoing fortunes, and defining moments in the snap of a finger.

That is why Colonel Nemat could not account for the way events had turned out. In the unleashed madness of the Second World War, a Middle Eastern nation such as Iran, despotically governed and left in the backwater of progress, was suddenly deemed important in the regional strategic calculations of the world powers. Foodstuffs and support of other kinds needed to reach the embattled Russian fronts from the Persian Gulf, and oil too, the black gold. The Allies sought to safeguard that route by all means necessary, whereas the Axis powers, naturally, were keen on impeding it. One of history's greatest ironies: the British and the Russians (even though the latter now went by the "Soviet Union," her real motives were not disguised carefully enough), who had left in Iran a bitter legacy of centuries of greed, now designated themselves the "protectors" of the one country that they had, in the past, amicably agreed to pillage. Is it any wonder then that most Iranian political circles hailed the German invasion of the Soviet territory as a good sign and that daily papers carried the news of that attack with gusto?

The prevailing perception was that Iran's historic enemies would soon face defeat in the hands of a powerful friend. However erroneous this view may seem in retrospect, it contributed to a grave illusion on the part of Reza Shah: namely, that the Axis powers were standing on the verge of victory. So when the Allies demanded the expulsion of the Axis nationals, their demands went unheeded. Overnight, the Soviets occupied Azerbaijan, as a consequence of that decision, and were about to move into Geellon; the south of the country was becoming the hippodrome of the British. Accordingly, the Shah abdicated power in favor of the 22-year-old crown prince and fled to Isfahan, while the desperate government of Mr. Furughi entered into negotiations to secure the sovereignty of the nation. The precocious child of these negotiations, the Tripartite Treaty of Alliance of January 1942, left no room for speculation. The occupation was now formal and complete.

At this crucial juncture, the stability of the northern provinces was entrusted to one Colonel Nemat, who was on his way to Geellon for a top secret mission. The prevailing fear in the capital was that the Geelloni division commanders and their civilian leadership did not grasp the precariousness of the situation regarding Iran's northern neighbor. Hence Colonel Morteza Nemat's mission: to explain to Geelloni officialdom the terms of the Tripartite Treaty of Alliance and to bid them to be patient with the Russians at the border, rather than to provoke the Russians into a stronger reaction than anyone could withstand. The trick, as always, involved a bit of diplomacy. And as always, politics turned out to be uncannily complex in the end, so much so that he simply could not make head or tail of it. The task was too awesome, and he was just an inconsequential particle going about his business, a guppy in the narrow stream of life. Presently, he had no idea he would be bringing a wife with him back to Tehran upon the completion of his assignment, let alone a lovely girl of fourteen.

While his motorcar followed the writhing road over the jagged northern mountain range, Colonel Nemat reflected on the events of recent years. The British had already forced Reza Shah's abdication, shipping him in exile to Johannesburg, South Africa, while the crown prince was still too green to fill his father's boots. What kept a minimum of order in the country was a fear of the unknown, a paralysis caused by the contending forces of the dead and the unborn. What the new Shah lacked in experience, his subjects seemed to be compensating with patriotism.

Colonel Nemat had a weak spot for the exiled monarch. Every time he thought about the Shah-in-exile, his eyes welled up. He would reflect on the progress the country had made under Reza Shah's ferrous grip, suddenly metamorphosing from an agrarian society into a bustling modern state. The very road from Tehran to Geellon, on which he was now comfortably riding in his army Jeep, would not have existed a decade earlier had it not been for Reza Shah's staunch drive for modernization. Almost three hundred kilometers of asphalt and tar spiraled up and down the majestic Elburze range with 180-degree turns and wondrous twists and tunnels. He remembered the terrible fate of the engineer who had built the road under the royal decree, then committed suicide for fear of not having met the monarch's high expectations. Such were Reza Shah's standards, and such was the human toll karma took in the name of progress. And that was the defining factor with fate, in Colonel Nemat's view. You could not account for it. Of course there were human sacrifices, and Colonel Nemat was anything but oblivious to the extreme measures that were necessary. As far as he was concerned, nothing was perfect. But in order to make hummus, you had to squash quite a few peas.

Colonel Nemat was born a painter, poet, and violinist, although he indulged in the arts but in his spare time. He knew how much they charged for wheat in the remotest villages of Khorausaun. In his mind, those assaying a political regime had to contrast with the regimes immediately before and after it. The indolence of the Qaujaurs and the present chaos made a good case for the deposed monarch.

If his post with the army had a great many benefits, it had a few drawbacks as well—namely, in the personal department. As he rode northward in the olive green army motorcar, he fumbled with a note in his pocket that bore the address of a matchmaker he was to look up. The ladies at the Officers Club had insisted. If it were not for their sake, being fifty-two and single would not have bothered him a straw. It was they, the officers' spouses, who pressed him to find a "life partner." And as the search took an increasing amount of his time over the years, the ideal woman became ever more elusive. It must be noted here, or else the wrong impression will be given, that looking for a mate on these missions was not his style, and even now as his tired Jeep climbed up and down the alpine track he was uncertain whether he could carry through with it. He did not expect a miracle out of this notepaper, but the nagging voices at the back of his head forced him to oblige, the warnings of the officers' wives—"Time is running out. You must do something." Time was running out all right, as myriad middle-aged afflictions were befalling him.

A mild-mannered gentleman, he was fond of animals, especially birds; he kept a parrot and several bulbuls and canaries. Instead of seeking human company, he preferred staying in his apartment and whistling for his feathered family when he felt lonely or blue. They would whistle back and cheer him with their delight. He had lived with his mother until she died a few years before and left him with a sister dearer to him than his own life. This sister, however, had married a man forever in training to become a radio announcer whom Colonel Nemat did not treasure, agree with, or understand. Houshang was just the opposite of the colonel in every article of every department. Chatty without making much sense, he insisted on singing without a voice to speak of; his off-key renditions of popular tunes were sheer torture to the colonel's musically sensitive ears. What's more, his taste in clothing was always on the fringe of the hippest fashion, for which he squandered a good deal of the colonel's sister's wealth, a quality not exactly endearing to the man who had but one threadbare suit hanging in the closet next to his military uniforms.

Before the 1939 commencement of Radio Iran, Houshang had persuaded Colonel Nemat to buy a receiver, promising that the colonel would be one of the first people in the country to capture the invisible waves. Just to put an end to his insistent prodding, Colonel Nemat had acquiesced and bought the overrated device. This before the programming had even started. His mother had still been alive then. The silent contraption made its way into his home, placed on a shelf in the sitting room where she would throw a questioning glance at it from time to time. Her son did not quite know how to explain it. As superstitious as the old lady was—and she was way out there—she would not have bought his explanations. You could tell her about Judgment Day, Gog and Magog, and visits from angels in the darkness of the tomb all you wanted, but plugging that snake of a black cord into the wall and having both male and female voices come out of the box hardly the size of a suitcase? *Utter nonsense!* He only prayed it would begin working soon and, in doing so, vindicate him.

However, year after year the introduction of radio was delayed due to Reza Shah's lack of faith in it. The autocrat had different reasons from those of Colonel Nemat's mother for dismissing the idea of a disembodied voice coming out of a box with knobs and lights. Ministries and government offices functioned well enough, and trains operated on time. Things were in tight order as they were. No need to introduce a messy thing such as radio, which would blur the lines and introduce unnecessary ideas to the minds of his subjects. Nevertheless, during the final year of his reign, the Germans somehow convinced him that setting up the radio operation would be a wise investment toward progress. Those Germans knew how to make a pitch, and the fact that they had Reza Shah's ear helped tremendously.

Colonel Nemat's first experience with women had come to him rather late in life. His mother was still alive then. For a year or so, he had lived in the southern province of Khuzestaun, where he acquired, through no real effort of his own, the sexual favors of an Arab widow with whom he entered into a temporary marriage. At the end of that year, though, he moved on to points east, following his directives, but even that temporary union had not altered his views on the fair sex. Women remained, as always, intricate creatures swelling with secrets. Even if he were to marry one, he could not expect her to stay with him, for he traveled too far, too long, and too often. Therefore, as he was wont to admit, any possibility of marriage depended on retiring from a career that had already exceeded three decades. And what were the chances of that?

The truth is that it would have devastated him if he were ever to resign his job, a highly unlikely proposition. The army was the provider of his identity, livelihood, and beliefs. Since he had no marketable skill but to relay messages, file records, and conduct policy consultation, and since he was not given to the fancy that he could make a living off his artistic talents, Colonel Nemat had wholeheartedly accepted the army as his lot. Apocryphally titled "Policy Adviser," his job sounded more intriguing than it truly was. In reality he was a go-between. His "lot," as it turned out, had no other use for him.

As far as the material world was concerned, Colonel Nemat was an aesthete, a collector of birds and stamps, an artist, and a social misfit. If it had not been for a boyhood buddy in the upper echelons of the corps who secured him the job in the first place, he would be starving. The very same boyhood friend made sure that he was busy enough to justify his promotions. So in between missions, Colonel Nemat taught music and gave painting lessons to the wives and children of other officers. On occasion, he taught a literacy class to interested petty officers, promoting literature and the arts among his fellow soldiers. After all, the army was his family, and the army had a reputation of looking after its own.

But all that is not to say he was an inept official, not worth the salt. He performed his duties with the utmost care and exhibited supreme loyalty to his superiors. His belief in the army credo ("the Lord, the Shah, the Motherland") was genuine. It was rather in the military brotherhood's interest to embrace him and to develop a fondness for his eccentricities. Colleagues respected him; they let him sit in on their high profile meetings (of course, without a chance to voice his opinions) and attend picnics with their families. He was simple and they liked him for that, even as they teased him for his strange and quiet ways.

At the Officers Club gatherings and picnics, Colonel Nemat enjoyed the distinct status of "oddball," for he had no family of his own. Women especially were sympathetic and engaging, while their husbands gathered elsewhere, exchanging dirty jokes, indulging in opium and card games. But nature's justice enabled Colonel Nemat to compensate for his lack of social skills by building special bonds with children. He related to them as if they were his peers, telling them stories and watching their faces open in smiles or wonder at the mysteries of life. He told them funny yarns about Mullah Nassruddin and horror stories about the fireball-hurling seven-headed dragons. Like a snake charmer, he held their attention with his "Tales of the Desert"—a series of stories he had invented for the occasion. The officers were amazed at how quietly their usually rowdy children sat and listened to him. Indeed a God-sent break for the mothers, too, who had business of their own to attend to at these gatherings. Unanimously they agreed that the eccentric colonel was a well of gentility; happily, they let him take their children off their hands.

For this quality the wives of the officers humored him by alleging that he must have had prior experience with children. They teased him about whether he was certain he had not spawned a few of his own around the country during his travels. After all, he did travel a great deal and did, indeed, have the opportunity to misbehave. To their good-natured ribbing, the colonel humbly offered a stock response: at his age what woman would take him as a mate? It is not known when, but upon detecting a sincere inclination in his confessions, the wives conspired to find him someone, and through mere word of mouth, they received wind of a certain departed schoolmaster in Geellon ("once the wife of a police commissioner who died in battle against an insurgency movement," the rumor said) survived by her daughter and two sons. This time, the ladies did not stop at chatter. Almost immediately they put their heads together like a group of agitated hens and made some fast decisions. Many a growling husband was persuaded to make telephone calls in the middle of the night. Contrary to their better judgment, well-known and disciplined officers allowed their wives to interject their concerns into the affairs of national security, as a result of which hasty meetings were held and ad hoc commissions were adjourned. At length, invisible hands pulled relevant strings to have the over-the-hill bachelor dispatched to Geellon. It is safe to assert that rarely in the history of the Iranian armed forces was a decision executed more efficiently.

The Geelloni military brass was not much to speak of to begin with. The compatriots of Monsieur Yeprim, who had once ridden side by side with the Armenian freedom fighter, now had bloated into round and timorous aged men, not likely to lift a finger even if the Russians invaded their towns and raped their wives and daughters. Long fallen into the delicious habit of accumulating land, they had risen in the ranks by kicking back a percentage of their conquests to the center and by singing sycophantic praises of the former Shah. Even a placid person such as Colonel Nemat could dominate the meeting without facing competition. "Are you kidding?" they responded unanimously. "The government really thinks that standing up to the Soviet Red Army would even enter our minds?"

"Well, gentlemen, the government's position is very sensitive," responded Colonel Nemat. "Dealing with the Allies is a tricky business, please understand."

The bald and bulging middle-aged men with decorated uniforms had rolled their eyes and whispered, "Is this guy for real?"

It did not occur to Colonel Nemat that they might have held a better grip on the situation than they were given credit for. They laughed at his simplicity but he did not take it to heart. Better they had a good time at his expense than give away the motherland on a silver platter, he reasoned to himself in his artist's way. At least he had said what he had come to say, and now he could attend to the other, quite personal business with ease of mind. Then and only then did he reach for the note in his pocket, seeking the matchmaker in the meandering depths of Lauhijaun's narrow back alleys.

Fifty-One

Sophie was as fair a specimen of Persian beauty as one might expect to encounter in Hafiz's odes—as one liked to know existed. Of that rare breed of graceful northern aristocracy that was fast disappearing, she had been only fourteen when her mother died during the opening months of the war, when bread and sugar prices quadrupled, giving rise to mayhem everywhere. The most striking memory Sophie had of her mother belonged to when she had begun the first grade. She remembered a festive celebration at the school: placards and banners, music, colored papers, and sugared candies. For the garish affair, Malek Tauj had ordered, out of her own pocket, new uniforms for all the students—rows of little girls in white shirts under black jumpers stood proudly on school grounds. Touring the province, the Shah had made a point to visit the lady principal and the all-girls school under her supervision. In a letter now framed, adorning the mantelpiece, he had characterized the principal as "The Favorite Daughter of Iran" and "The True Symbol of Persian Womanhood." Praising her crucial role in the defeat of communist uprising, he had written:

Dear Madam: In these trying times during which our great nation is finding her place among nations of the world, every single one of her children should look up to you as a model of matchless courage and supreme dedication. It is my contention that this spirit of self-sacrifice is what has kept our nation together thus far. Madam, we are all proud of you. You are an inspiration to this and many generations of Iranian women to come.

Sophie remembered the deep cerulean blue of the cloudless autumn sky, as she stood in line with her schoolmates, feeling itchy on the soles of her feet. The motorcade was running late, and a murmur of irritability began to percolate on the grassy school grounds, but no one moved from her place. Malek Tauj had warned that even if it took all day they were to stand there, quiet and immobile. Finally, when everyone was exhausted to the core, the Shah's motorcade arrived, engines sputtering. Army personnel surrounded the black convertible on all sides, running around and shouting orders excitedly—all in a grand and festive style. A mobile military band arrived subsequently, playing an off-key rendition of Richard Wagner's *Nibelungen March*. Little hands waved little paper flags in the air or clapped in ecstasy. Separated from her mother, in the jubilant cacophony of the Shah's arrival, Sophie was worried about not remembering the poem she was to recite for the occasion—twelve verses of praise to the king and God and motherland. In the past she had declaimed other poems before the school and the mayor, but never in the presence of such an eminent figure.

The band played on as the monarch took leave of his automobile. The mayor greeted the Shah and bent over to kiss his hand. Next it was the principal's turn to greet him. The whole town witnessed the madam principal walking over to HIM and firmly shaking his hand.

Malek Tauj had personally prepared Sophie to perform before the Shah. Ever so eager to please her mother, to win her approval, Sophie had no other thought than of giving her finest. When the superintendent motioned for her to take the podium, Sophie's firm footsteps resounded unhesitatingly. A fruit crate, tipped upside down, raised her up above the rest of the children. The Shah and his entourage stood where they had met the principal and turned to face the podium. The band stopped, and a little girl began reciting without delay, from memory, the first of the twelve verses with a tingling in her stomach. Her motionless body and raised chin won the Shah's instant approval, and her voice stole his heart. Despite her initial fears, verses came to her one after the other, loops of rhythm tumbled from her tongue. Then a slight turning of the Shah's head to his aides, a praiseful nod, distracted her, the young orator briefly fearing the worst, but as the closing loops turned and rolled, she saw a faint smile return to his lips, and she felt giddy. With the last hemistitch, as she raised her arm indicating the poem's ending, she heard the Shah's loud applause followed by her schoolmates' joyous cheers. Only then did she realize she had done all right. The smile on Reza Shah's lips was as reassuring as a pat on the head. Coming away from the podium, she felt the entire school at her feet.

Years later, a simple phrase would still haunt the adult Sophie. Malek Tauj's stern voice found its way to her conscience and remained there. It was to ring in her head throughout her life. "Now go over and kiss His Imperial Majesty's hand." The words were still with her as she grabbed a basket of flowers, prearranged for the occasion, and contemplated his hands, each big enough to cover her whole face. Tottering steps advanced her to where His Imperial Majesty stood, the Shah tremendously tall. Sophie imagined his head touching the clouds. Was that not where her father was? Maybe His Eminence could speak to him and have him come back to her. He took the flowers from her, patted her head and smiled again, his light touch reassuring her about the performance. His warm hand touching her scalp calmed her racing heart. His lips moved under his funny mustache. He was a funny man, Sophie decided and smiled back. He reminded her of her father. He too had been kind to her, all those far-away days. Only she did not remember much. His Imperial Majesty lowered his head until his face leveled with hers. He looked deep into her eyes and repeated his question.

"What's your name?"

"Sophie."

"That's a beautiful name for a pretty girl. Did you know that you have the blackest Persian eyes?"

Sophie did not understand. She thought His Majesty had mistaken her with someone else. Her questioning, black Persian eyes stared at his funny mustache.

"Are you the principal's daughter?"

She nodded. In that moment she was the proudest little girl in the universe. She wanted to repeat her mother's name for the Shah and say yes, yes, yes, she was the principal's daughter, no one else's. The principal was her mother, the loveliest woman on earth.

The Shah rose to his feet and turned his back to her, walking toward Malek Tauj, his hand unkissed. Sophie had completely forgotten her mother's order. She regarded him for some time while he patiently listened to the principal, one arm supporting an elbow supporting a hand supporting a square jaw. His head bent to one side, listening bemusedly. Sophie still felt his hand where he had patted her carefully combed and parted hair and felt too the weight of the school's stare. Small-town fame was not alien to her. Thanks to her mother's position she was already a popular child in Lauhijaun, but the importance she now felt was beyond anything she had ever known at that young age. She would carry that for the rest of her life like the image of her mother, her German pince-nez, her voice saying, "Now go over and kiss His Imperial Majesty's hand."

With Malek Tauj's passing, Sophie felt the shattering of her dreams and saw only the dark abyss of her future. Who was to blame? Her mother was more than merely the closest person to her; she was a source of warmth, courage, preoccupation. Overwhelmed at the funeral, Sophie felt the familiar world perishing like shadows in late afternoon. At no other time had she felt so horrified, with the exception of when the cavity of her pubescent womb overflowed with warm dirty blood. She had lived in Malek Tauj's shadow and was likely to remain there for the balance of her difficult life.

Fifty-Two

As the elderly lady ushered Colonel Morteza Nemat into the house, he voiced his concern, "At my age, dear lady, who can play house with a schoolgirl?" Whether honest or simpleminded, he often mouthed the first thing that came to his mind.

"Never you mind," the toothless woman snapped back. "Consider, she has never been touched."

"At my age, dear lady, what would people say? Worse, what would they think?"

"Young is fourteen," she admitted, "but ripe enough. Smells like flowers. Take your worries away; knock twenty, thirty years off your age. Then you and her, same age."

"Did you say there are no parents? What happened to them?"

"Father was killed ten years ago in battle with communists. Good man, brave soldier. Mother, a lovely lady. School principal … ppffffeeeew, got sick, become skinny, coughing blood; passed away six months ago she did. Was survived by this girl and two boys, both businessmen in Rasht. They see us just now. Talk with them yourself."

Colonel Nemat prepared himself to meet his future wife's family on the second floor of the manor on Sheriff's Alley, in a large reception room. The elderly lady left him there to seek the girl's siblings. The damp air was stifling despite tall windows left ajar to let in a current. The colonel hadn't felt so tense before. He feared not being able to contain his bursting enthusiasm. To ease his anxiety, he looked around the room at the framed portraits of the madam principal. By the mantelpiece he glanced at the framed letter of the deposed Shah and was vastly impressed by the royal handwriting. All this only heightened his woe as he began to deem himself smaller and smaller by the minute. He turned to walk the fine carpet, weighing the odds against him. What if they rejected him right off? How could he live with the slight? How would he deal with the shame? How dare he pursue a girl from such a noble family? Had he no shame, or had he left it behind in Tehran?

Mansour and Kazim, Sophie's brothers, were handsome and spoke with bucolic courtliness. From the first moment of introduction it was obvious that the colonel had made a lasting impression on them. It was not every day they received an army colonel for company. Their instant approval of him manifested itself in their elaborate show of admiration as they asked the colonel to please brief them on the situation of the Allied forces in Europe and their strategy regarding the war. To Colonel Nemat's great relief, their queries were unspecified, only smothered with the romantic innocence of the rural community. Answering their questions required little military knowledge but a great deal of interest in countryfolk. To justify his olive drab uniform, he recalled some thirdhand war stories and generously shared them with his interviewers. He summoned the gems he casually picked up from office conversations and skillfully mixed them with news items he read in the papers, to dazzling effect. The French defeat in the hands of the Germans, thanks to his skill, had never sounded so grim and final. The fall of Paris and the subsequent withdrawal of hundreds of thousands of British and French soldiers from Dunkirk in small boats were never brought home in so detailed a version. In his words, the embattled French, having abandoned heavy artillery and equipment, sustaining heavy casualties, boarded the small boats meekly murmuring "until victory, until victory."

Colonel Nemat related to his hosts what he thought was happening in a tone laden with melodrama, further impressing them with his emotional candor. Mansour and Kazim nodded their heads throughout and swallowed his stories like the children at the Officers Club did. Pity, he said, that there was not enough time to discuss the Battle of Oran, during which the British forces destroyed the French fleet to prevent its use by Germans. Perhaps he would bring a map of Europe sometime, and they could all study the course of the war. Mansour and Kazim nodded with delight.

The colonel's doubts subsided with the reception from Sophie's brothers: his hosts kept refilling his tea tumbler, held out plates of fruits before him, and hung on every one of his words. To them he appeared a gentleman of distinct character, a disciplinarian and a cosmopolitan. His large head was a thinking man's head with more than traces of white at the temples. It seemed to them that he was quite capable of taking care of their sister. Flattered as they were by his show of civility, his advanced years failed to alarm them, for they were taken—and taken unwittingly—by the kindness of his tone and the honesty of his droopy eyes. How could they object to the man's age when he was so full of knowledge and experience and addressed them with more respect than charm? How could age matter in the life of an orphaned adolescent girl for whom there were no other prospects? They kept their peace and sent for Sophie to come in and speak for herself.

She was a lovely lively filly, dressed in blue calico with white butterflies, confident, plump, rouged. For a moment the colonel imagined she was a phantom in his dream: a belle of medium height and proportionate curves with smooth, radiant skin and the vain walk of a puffed partridge. But it was not a dream of supernal seraphs and luscious houris. Very much awake he was, his lids open, mouth dry, palms sweating, jaw dropping, knees tremulous, heart aflutter, and ears sensitive to the jingle jangle of her silver circumference of bracelets. Fully astir in the presence of a set of large almond eyes in which mischief called capering upon his soul, *come to me, come to me,* yet warned of untold hazards. It was craziness what he read in them. The cupbearer's irresistible eyes right out of Hafiz's odes; the look of Khayyam's lover come alive in the inebriety of a summer night's spree.

As Sophie walked in, the room flamed with a scandalous desire, so much so that her brothers' ears turned beet red and a silence as thick as shame dropped like an anvil. Traipsing to the chair farthest from her suitor, she watched him from the corners of her inky orbs. The bow of her brows pinched in the middle of her fragile face, the empty expression of an inexperienced flirter, the sort that confuses the male into thinking something dear must be going on in her mind. A sweet, vapid, befuddled frown. For a moment the thought of marrying such a pretty girl-child abashed the white-haired man but what to do with the talk and the anticipation that had already whetted his appetite. As those magnets in her face invited him to her, he overcame his modesty and drew near her.

"Would you like to live in Tehran, my dear?"

Fifty-Three

The colonel once again fell in love with his child-wife at the brief ceremony, held in the same house her mother had come to when she had married the police commissioner. Despite the plain affair, a lively spirit beamed from her round face: her teeth glinted under the moonlight, her penciled brows curved slightly to avoid her long lashes. She had the blackest Persian eyes, and Colonel Morteza Nemat was the happiest man alive.

Although he was not much of a drinker, the little wine he had sipped surreptitiously made him dizzy that night, putting his manhood out of commission for the occasion. But as he would admit to the ladies at the Officers Club, it was all worth it—"the Koranic duties, I assure you, were properly fulfilled the following evening."

Sophie's brothers and aunts and uncles were happy too, for the merry occasion and for the lifting of their burden. In the ecstasy of the moment, they even threw in a townhouse in Tehran to sweeten the deal. Only then was the dowry complete, just as Malek Tauj would have wanted.

When the couple arrived in Tehran, they moved into the townhouse listed in her dowry, a small two-bedroom on the Shah Avenue, smack-dab in the middle of the spreading metropolis. It had running water and a roof where clothes could be hung to dry in the sun—adequate for the modest life Colonel Nemat had in mind for Sophie and himself. But for her, it was merely a transient arrangement, a stepping-stone, until bigger and better things came their way. In the early months of their shared life, Sophie played a high-spirited devout young lover with a delicate taste for what is proper and a grand capacity for self-denial.

Although under occupation, her adopted city fascinated Sophie beyond her wildest reveries: Tehran forever crawling upward the slopes of Damauvand, shimmering in the summer heat, sparkling in the wakefulness of the early hours. The magic of electricity had made nightlife possible in the feverish city of sprouting social clubs, she being that constant source of mirth that would give an existential reason to it all. Wide-eyed and open-mouthed at the reception hall of the Officers Club, Sophie basked in the frivolous music, to which couples danced face to face, and became enchanted with their illicit body movements.

Hesitantly but politely, she made the acquaintance of the ladies at the club and arranged to take part in their weekly card games and tea rounds. She exchanged gossip as if she had been born into that kind of carefree indulgence. The ladies at the club in turn found her irresistibly delightful and showered her with their interest. The colonel too enjoyed hearing her unbridled laughter, went out of his way to cater to every item of her fancy. If once a month or two he used to attend the social activities initiated by the corps, now every weekend he was seen enjoying himself in the company of his eye-catching wife. Still tired from a full day's work, with pride and affection, he would take her to the club and show her off to his peers and superiors, letting her live it up to her heart's content. Settling into his middle years, he had found a new life and could not help being at the center of talk at social settings, owing it all to that bundle of grace and laughter that everywhere accompanied him.

At the Officers Club, Hollywood talk preceded the opening of new talkies. Sometimes he took her to see the moving pictures and let her gaze at pictures of actors behind giant glass cases. When a Valentino, Garbo, or Fairbanks flick finally arrived in one of the recently founded theaters downtown, the main star's performance was already a chat item. The colonel would merely hear the talk, whereas Sophie absorbed it through her skin. Predictably, the lure of tinsel soon paled for Colonel Nemat, and he forever remained unimpressed. But Sophie bloomed, her eyes opening to the world, her surging pulse beating in her wishful chest, a pillow to the white-haired colonel of the Third Brigade stationed in Eshratabad, Tehran. Gradually, their peers would notice the sad tone that trickled into Sophie's speech and wonder if the age difference had not caught up with the once seemingly happy duo, if they had not begun trekking along a path that would eventually diverge.

As his innate tendency to love with extreme patience spoiled the inexperienced girl of fourteen, the colonel progressively became dull to the girl-wife of sixteen whose eyes and ears had been opened to life's possibilities by the seasoned womankind of the tea round. She began to sense a craving for something along the line of, say, the spontaneous, unrepentant pouncing of a Latin lover of the Valentino breed. She learned from those movies to long for a lover who would make even simple talk feel as though confiding; a passionate lover who would seize her on an occasion other than Friday mornings, for a vigorous roll on the floor or a new trick on the roof. Much to her chagrin, though, and due to a sudden increase in his responsibilities—or decrease of plain simple verve—the colonel continuously fell short on his duties in that department. Only on Friday mornings would he wake up feeling a sexual stir in his lap, a blip of stiffening, but even then he would not fail to ask her permission to indulge. In fits of embarrassment he would disallow her loving hand to touch him where his manhood used to slowly grow bigger and bigger like Mount Ohod. He deemed it unnatural, and openly said so, and more or less stuck to his Friday morning mechanical ritual of procreation; by year two of their wedlock, when she bore him a daughter, the thrill of their marriage had soared out the window, every ounce of desire for carnal roughhousing having fled her fancy.

Being a devotee of the arts, the colonel had no concept of money. Every morning he would eat, put on his uniform, and catch the bus to Eshratabad, returning home just in time for supper. His avoidance of amorous love besides, he was still a good husband, bringing home a bundle of folded bills every first of the month, handing it to his wife without fuss. And in return, she would peel him off a bill for his bus fare before burying the balance between her breasts. Often he bragged about her having a good head for money on her shoulders while delegating to her the task of managing the household finances. Sophie, keen on living up to those words, ran the ship with an iron hand, becoming the uncompromising captain of the small house on Shah Avenue. And on top of her normal wifely chores of cleaning cooking washing, she decorated the house and went to the market, took care of their daughter and son, all on her own and with the help of an occasional hired hand. She left nothing for the colonel to do but go to his job and bring in the cash.

Days were lengthening for Colonel Nemat as years shortened.

He trusted that she would do right by him, and time proved him right. Inside seven years, she gave him, in addition to a pair of healthy children, another house downtown with a yard in the front and a little fountain pool. Beside themselves with joy, they began to make plans for the new house, painted it inside and out, filled it with furniture, chairs and a long dining table with legs ending in lion paws, and put in a new furnace. Their son, five-year-old Sohrab, was ecstatic about the pool; he kept small orange goldfish in it, and launched flimsy paper boats on the pool's calm surface. It was then the colonel felt the shame of sleeping under his wife's roof for the past seven years. He could now hold his head high and boast about owning a house of his own.

And what an incredible boost it was, this property ownership business, as a result of which a certain sauciness entered his character. For the first time in his life the colonel actually felt adequate. Ever so grateful for the gifts she had brought into his life, his soul filled with her presence and he realized life was impossible without her. He began to draw her in coal, pencil, and oil in sizes large and small. In fits of passion, he picked up his violin and planted soft melodies in her ears. Sophie acknowledged his adoration and tried to love him back.

But love would be the wrong term to describe her feelings for this frumpy aging military man. She tolerated him, his baggy pajamas, and his lack of vigor, his gruff voice, large head, and the wrinkles on his neck. In the new house, in summertime, he had begun the habit of walking around for hours in the afternoon with a flyswatter, chasing loud buzzes, imaginary and real. As the flyswatter thwacked and thumped and whizzed, he expressed extreme satisfaction with deep sighs, disgustingly indistinguishable from his amorous groans. Everything with him had to develop into routine or else he was totally lost in the impromptu activities of daily life. He did not know what to make of things unless he could develop a system, usually a convoluted set of patterns, in which things could be related to one another. All this was a test to her temperament, and it was not uncommon for her to feel the blood simmering inside her veins. To rid herself of her frustration she needed distractions above and beyond what the ladies at the club had to offer.

Yet in those days, no one remembered seeing the colonel happier. Recognizing the change in his lifestyle, his superiors had long stopped sending him out of town on bogus errands. He had somehow elevated in their eyes, as he had in the eyes of his peers. He was sent invitations to exclusive dinner parties and dance programs, out on picnics to which he took his much admired family. Having made every party guest-list at the Officers Club, the pair was invited to receptions by other senior officers, and had them over to the house for supper and tea. The colonel's dream of integration into army life was finally made real.

Fifty-Four

The house the Nemats moved to was on a dead-end alley on which children played small-goal soccer in the summer. Roomier than the one they left behind, it was here that Sophie raised her children for the next three years. After settling in, her house on the Shah Avenue was rented out, the money going straight into a bank account for something as undefined as "the children's future." One never knew what the future held. Especially now that the colonel's white hair was falling out ever faster than before and he complained of chest pains and a worsening case of insomnia. Changing homes, she sensed a quiet dislocation within their relationship as husband and wife. Before the move, she believed maybe letting a bit of control slip from her hand might have a salutary effect. Perhaps a jump in the colonel's self-confidence would bring out the man in him she could adore and respect. Soon she divined the error of her theory. The seed of discontent planted in her heart now grew shoots and boughs.

Even before the Nemats moved out of the house on Shah Avenue, Sophie had begun to get fidgety. At the beginning, having no friends in a strange city had not seemed so bad. Bright lights dazzled, representing what was exciting, but at the same time cast a curious beam at one's self. Sophie was seeing things that she had not suspected there and to which she did not know how to react. She began to suspect there was more to life than her meager experience had allowed her to see. Was something not out there calling her name? Some sort of a destiny she was not allowed to explore? She could not help feeling trapped in a lifestyle that offered her nothing in return for her uprooting experience. She felt like a cricket put in a glass jar for the world's amusement.

Before her world started to crumble around her, those picnics and parties that once were all fun and games had mostly become torturous events. There were also lonely and bitter nights of feeling grossly out of place. She could not help feeling threatened by rootlessness, and yearned for her childhood, the security of her mother's embrace, the incessant Geelloni rain, the fig trees, tea plantations, and pomegranate blossoms. Just as the colonel was relishing his belated assimilation in the military, she was finding herself on the opposite side. In her dreams she heard a distant calling to search for her true self amongst that crowd and to search for a bond with the world, that irritable ceaseless urge to merge. She wanted to be a part of her husband's world, but she also felt that unmistakable distance from her at which his peers put themselves with a curtain of politeness. Even if they were any different from what they were, she would not have been content. Like her mother, the late Malek Tauj, she wanted more out of life than was presently offered.

Fifty-Five

Accent was an immigrant's worst enemy, the kick down the spiral stairs to nowhere. The key to success was in the language. If she could master the dialect, she could wear a crown. To begin with, it was Houshang's idea for Sophie to improve her accent. The radio announcer's main area of expertise was speech training, a claim for which nobody, including his wife, the colonel's sister, could vouch. Almost to a fault, he praised the value of flawless speech and could go on and on about the merits of the crisp Tehrani dialect. He displayed such magnanimity of temper that he even fooled his own wife. Of course, he said, Sophie did not have much of what might have been called an accent, but the little that crept into her speech was distracting, a blemish on her otherwise perfect image.

Sophie had a good voice, a little coaching with her annunciation could indeed help her master the Tehrani tongue. Colonel Nemat's brother-in-law offered to help make a modern woman of her in no time. In his cajoling, he managed to put a name on what she had known all along—she was an immigrant. Harping on that, he sold the idea of Sophie's need for voice training and, of course, he was saying all this for her benefit; he did not expect to be paid for his services. Being constantly "in demand at the radio station," he added he would not have time on the evenings or holidays, understand. But there was no reason for alarm; he would gladly make time during his lunch breaks. "Of course this is no problem for me. What's family for?"

Solid, devoted, dependable Houshang would thus leave his job around lunchtime every day to be with the colonel's wife for a couple of hours. In time, he started wishing their friendship would grow more intimate, fantasizing about the day she would return his affection in kind. His dedication and patience were admirable, considering the total absence of any encouraging signs from his pupil. The problem with him, as with all hopeless romantics, was his tendency to exaggerate his effect on the opposite sex. He might have had a triumph here and there at the radio station where he worked not as the main announcer but as a fill-in. Might have succeeded in wooing a few female apprentices unbeknownst to his wife, the colonel's sister, but mainly his efforts went unrequited. Houshang was handsome and mild, to be sure, with no hint of incivility in his character but this insuppressible urge to brag. Naturally, most of the time his blind obsession with himself caused adverse reactions in his intended subjects. His firm cheeks had become the target for many a smack from jealous husbands, his ears the receivers of quite a few whopping backhanders. All of which failed to steer him toward a different hobby or course of action, or at least to prompt him to strive to know his subjects well before risking another crashing blow.

That he did not know the first thing about Sophie once again would topple his attempts, because an affair was the farthest thing from her mind, let alone carrying on with so close a relative. Houshang should have been able to read the signs—the abrupt moving away of the hand, the courteous silence in response to inappropriate remarks, and, most obvious of all, her sudden flight from the sofa where he liked to pigeonhole her for amatory exercises—which should have been taken as solid evidence of her disinterest. Yet it was hopeless, and he went on wishing the improbable. Nevertheless, she took his intentions lightly and thought well of him for helping her lose the tad bit of Geelloni accent. She never revealed any of his transgressions to anyone. Instead, she patiently dissuaded him, sometimes directly, sometimes by ignoring his pleas. The reward was priceless: he taught her about people and the ways of society, the way a lady carried herself, as he conceived these things in his mind. Thus, little by little, she metamorphosed into his idea of a modern woman—from how she talked to how she walked, from the look of the eyes to the pitch of her sighs. How she made wonders with her hair, and what pose was struck by her nose when she heard the riffraff's whistle. From where the silverware was situated on the dinner table to what was the proper way of addressing a casual acquaintance, male or female.

Slightly plump in the hips, with a stomach that bore no signs of childbearing, Sophie learned how to dress and how to move to make even the least desirable parts of her body work to her advantage. With time she turned her features into graceful indicatives of female maturity and became the object of men's longings wherever she went. Using a feeble Singer, she draped her voluptuous figure in clothing of her own making. Having purchased the used sewing machine with her own money, she had Houshang carry it upstairs as one of the last chores she conferred upon him. That was shortly before the time came when he was to be done away with, or at least to be made to understand that the need for his services had perished. In fact, she had improved and surpassed both his and Colonel Nemat's expectations.

The cat and mouse game with Houshang ended when she ceased to regard any part of her image as undesirable. And the way she managed to stage his departure was a too-subtle indication of her evolving cunning. Suddenly the colonel began to come home for lunch without any explanations. Dallying about for the duration of Houshang's stay, he'd then ask him for a ride back to work, since they shared the same route for part of the way. As they lived close enough to Eshratabad, Houshang truly had no excuse not to oblige. In booting Houshang from her life, the only things Sophie missed were the light and always up-to-date conversations on recent fashion—another area in which the colonel was hopeless.

Sophie's transformation, at the ripened age of twenty-one, could not have come about at a more fortunate time. Vanished was her provincial charm, her raw bashful deportment and her accent, their places taken by an unmistakable Persian of a fluid quality, the seasoned charm of a Tehrani woman, her voice soft and melodious. After a long absence, she reappeared on the social scene with absolute confidence and command of the milieu, a bold aura percolating from her eyes. She moved in circles and those circles moved with her. Officers and their spouses, noticing the change, adjusted their disposition accordingly. More than ever before, men became showy around her and women found themselves vying for her friendship.

Fifty-Six

Gleaming against the darkness was the wall, reflecting the streetlight. Brother Hamid opened his lids. It was still dark out when his eyes fell on the wall clock opposite his bed. As he watched phosphorescent hands glowing, motionless despite the tick-tock music, he thought, *There is still time.* He sat up on the bed, a plain mattress on the floor. There were still a few hours left before the prisoner was to be led down the stairs of the Palace. Save him, he jogged himself. *Save your revolution, save your faith.*

Not far from the clock a color drawing of Imam Ali, Prince of the Faithful, with his *Zulfiqar,* the improbable two-pronged sword, was pinned to the wall. It depicted him in his full majesty of might, a recumbent lion at his feet, handsome, virile. It went through Hamid's head that the image was everywhere: in banks, grocery stores, even in transit buses—the first Shiite Imam sitting three-quarters sideways to the left. His rather feminine hands held an odd looking, curved, two-pronged scabbard comfortably on his lap. Brother Hamid wondered, not for the first time, why the issue of the sword carried by Imam Ali being double-edged and not two-pronged had not been resolved after all these centuries. He remembered his father's claim that the Imam's double-edged sword could chop the heads of the infidel, wham-bam, twice as fast. What purpose would a double-pointed sword serve? And still you saw that impractical sword dangling from that ablest of men.

A heretical thought came to him in the foggy obliviousness of his waking mind: What if the division between right and wrong, instead of in heaven, started on earth? What if men were ill informed, lacking the proper faculties to judge? Wouldn't that make a mockery of their judicious reasoning? What if the minds of men were captives to ill intention? What then? If God is the only being who's all-knowing, which He is, would that not render the rest of us mortals very much lousy arbiters?

Fifty-Seven

Sophie's success wormed its way into the colonel's head, and he began making a fool of himself at social functions. Increasingly he abandoned his shell and mingled with the officers. Sharing their lewd and bawdy jokes, he became a garrulous dolt, inventing fictitious memories and revealing them to whomever cared to listen. He talked incessantly about his dead mother to groups of jovial picnickers, dampening their spirits. He asked his superior officers about his long-lost cousins, who were posted in far-away localities, expecting engaging conversation. Whenever he started to go on with his tales, furious Sophie would nail him with an inimical stare, or deliver a sound kick to his leg under the table. There was no question at this point, and even their most casual acquaintances recognized, that his simplicity and tactlessness embarrassed her. Having mastered the rules of etiquette, Sophie found Colonel Nemat's harmless lack of manners particularly distressing: the shutting of the eye and cocking of the head during conversations, the finger pointing, the scratching of the palm on elbow and knees, the silent belch he muffled in his cheeks and let out with a slow sigh. The loud hiccups and God knew what else. Above all, his nonchalance toward his appearance irritated her to no end, and, let's not forget, his sloppiness when eating before a roomful of eyes—precisely the opposite of what the journals advised—ate at her soul.

A gentle and loving a husband as he still was, but even these endearing qualities had stopped being a solace. At his advanced age, he began to see, God forbid, his very own mother in her. After eight years of marriage, worshipping Sophie as he did in the beginning, he praised her in his poems just as he had his mother when she was still alive. And in the meantime, since she had been smart with money, he went on giving her all his salary. This was his way of showing respect and love, but after eight years, she began to see it as a sign of nothing but repulsive weakness. It was as if the maturing of his wife had had a reverse effect on Colonel Nemat. Everything about him that had once seemed noble and endearing became irksome. What other man who is handsome and confident and intelligent would cast his earnings at his wife's feet? What other man praised his wife so profusely but did not have the facility or whatyoumightcallit to carry on the act of love in the bedroom? At the very least she expected a little disagreement, a touch of cynicism. She craved a little less talk and a bit more roughness under the sheets to calm her on long and dry fidgety summer nights.

Fifty-Eight

No wonder Tehran's inhabitants, come summer, drifted to places like Shemiran, a pleasant village some six miles to the north, where the ridges of Damauvand stood forgivingly in their gargantuan nakedness. May 1951 started off way too hot, even by Tehran's standards, stirring up a dread of mayhem. The young sycamores along Shush and Sepah streets were left dying of thirst, their blossoming interrupted, their spring buds withering prematurely. As if charged by the heightening of political tension, mornings lunged into sizzling afternoons, releasing vapors of frustration into the ether. Spring had not been like this in a long time.

Although there was still some time left before schools let out, the affluent were already making plans to hit their Caspian seaside resorts up north or their cozy villas in the altitudes of the Shemiran suburbs. The shops with their awning sops were closed, and the entire population seemed to have taken refuge in the oases of cool tenebrous basements; everyone that is except the enchanted thousands who had poured into Bahaurestaun Square and the baking sidewalks thereof, demonstrating support for the new prime minister. Nothing could discourage those who had come from schools and hospitals, the bazaar and the university. As the scorching sun made the asphalt ooze like a stream of magma, the demonstrators invariably found themselves in a sticky state of affairs, the soles of their shoes adhering soundly to the street.

In March, Prime Minister Razmaurau had been assassinated. In April, while the flags flew at half-staff, his cabinet absolved itself, and with caution a new one took its place at the helm. Soon it leaked into the gossip flow that the new prime minister had "mortgaged his upstairs." Early in May, in the hubbub of disgust and indignation over the tearing down of governmental institutions, the Majles (as the Parliament was called) passed the oil nationalization bill. The new prime minister, an effective orator by vocation, went on the radio declaring Iranians the masters of their fate. Either he was a genuine article or the whole damn country had gone insane. He shone with his passionate speeches at every public appearance thereafter, and they were all broadcast on the two o'clock news, then later in the evening.

Walking about in his pajamas, Colonel Nemat disproved of all that nationalization business. Neither did he think that Mossadegh was an honest or particularly intelligent man. Then, why were the masses following his lead so blindly? Colonel Nemat attributed the man's popularity to no less a fact than that he was extremely fun to watch, a gifted entertainer. Listen to him on the radio and he sounded like he was about to die of cardiac arrest. The colonel could not help but think that when the prime minister didn't sound ill, he sounded evil. He believed people were just too gullible, capable of being swept off their feet by anyone who proclaimed to be their servant. For the theatrics of his speeches, he called the prime minister a crook. And this he said with the gentlest voice he could muster while feeding his birds.

The colonel characterized his critique of the government as "exercising my right as a citizen." When he cleaned the metal birdcages, he whispered an old tune under his breath and replaced the adjectives with derogatory inferences to "Old Mossey," as the prime minister was known in the West. He carried this on even in Sophie's presence, declaring his opinion as haphazardly as he carried around his flyswatter. Said the old crow should be ashamed of displaying his emotions like that in public, raising his fist and all. It was demagoguery plain and simple. It was a consolation to the colonel that the birds generally agreed with him, unanimously flapping their wings, chirping and twittering. They understood at a time no one else did. Despite his aversion to the nationalists, Colonel Nemat continued to listen to their champion, who had vowed to carry on "the people's wish" to the sour end.

There was no break in the feverish heat of the sky that squeezed the life out of shrubs and weeds. Yet, the early summer heat of that year did not bother Colonel Nemat. His indifference to the unbearable temperatures was such that it drove Sophie around the bend. Not only did hot weather not affect him, he even boasted it was good for his heart. Sun brought vigor to the earth, he said, because it was the preserver of life. If it were not so, God would not have arranged for earth to circle the sun so fastidiously. Large drops of perspiration rolled down his armpits into his lap while he expounded on this, sitting in his pajamas and drawing on a large tablet of drafting paper, prattling on like a mad artist.

The chronic discord between husband and wife had grown to such absurd proportions that any discrepancy in taste could become grounds for new charges; charges that usually she initiated and leveled against him. Presently, the soaring temperature had assumed this unflattering position, and the colonel's resigned posture was of no help. How could he just sit there, unvexed, as she herself saw the sweat running from his white temples to his chin and off his back into the crack of his buttocks? Had he lost his mind? She, in her revealing undershirt, stood in the middle of the kitchen and screamed out her frustrations at him while the children regarded their mother questioningly. In spite of her emotional outbursts he continued sitting put all day, drawing his pictures, which, since his response was not in kind, irritated her further still. "How will you be bothered, husband; what can upset you? Tell me please," she pleaded with him in a tone halfway between feigned anger and gibe. And not that he always absorbed her abuse quietly. Sometimes he would respond, "What nonsense, dear. I'm made for this clime, just as I'm made for you," as if he were saying, "I'm made to serve and adore you, don't you know, and that I shall forever," and "As long as my heart sings, it sings your praise."

Twenty years of traveling in the parched Baluchestaun and Kirmaun provinces had adapted the man to aridity. He was familiar with it through life with the twins, the great salt deserts of Dasht-e Kavir and Dasht-e Lut, where the horizon was a clear line between the golden flats and azure sky, where one had to walk for days before a tree or any sign of life came into sight. He had been on numerous tours of duty to places where the army had no posts. "The desert and I are like this," he liked to brag, locking his middle and index fingers. The desert held no secrets for him, the dried out wasteland, shimmering under the sweltering sun, scattered villages with scattered people living scattered lives. Compared to that, his house in downtown Tehran was an oasis of rest and abundance. His office at the Eshratabad garrison, where he was required to spend more time due to the increasing street unrest thanks to the crisis-loving cabinet of the prime minister, indulged a ceiling fan that worked only erratically. He would open the windows to the rows of soldiers on the training grounds, preparing to confront the street demonstrators, and let the slow current of air dry his moistened shirt. On days he went home early, he would sit in the shade of the only elm in the yard, by the leisure pool, reading the dailies. Summer was just another season that had to be waded through.

Even though the dryness somewhat tamed the heat, still Sophie could not tolerate it. It weighed heavily on her chest, physically wearing her all too quickly, unbalancing her delicate system. She could neither understand nor permit the way in which Colonel Nemat remained unaffected by it. In the early years of her exile in Tehran, she had suffered from the high temperatures but had never complained about the way it cracked the soles of her feet and lightened her hair.

That was Tehran for you. In winters her hands chapped and a big red crack opened on her lower lip, and in summers her swollen feet provided her with an abundance of miserable moments. Add to it the constant perspiration, and her life was a living hell. To remedy her skin problems, she was told to drink plenty of water sprinkled with lemon juice and to avoid exertion. Jars and tins of creams, potions, pomades, and powders found their way into her toiletries, and she spent enormous amounts of time bathing, or sitting in front of her brilliant invention of an air conditioner. To the front shield of all three small rotating fans in the house that blew hot air she tied wickerwork trays holding blocks of ice. The air that pushed through the net of twigs melted the ice and blew a cool current. Only pity was it devoured her supplies of ice with an insatiable appetite. Nevertheless her homemade air conditioner allowed a few hours of rest in the afternoons. And for sleeping arrangements at night, mattresses unfolded outside. She would set up mosquito nets in the yard or on the roof, and they would all crawl under the thin, airy fabric. Meanwhile, searching for a more permanent solution became a hobby she pursued with zeal.

Deeming her efforts superfluous, Colonel Nemat would rather keep himself busy by listening to the radio. He religiously followed the headlines and formed opinions fitting with the opposition's allegations. They charged that Mossadegh's plan was to become the next dictator in the long line of autocrats for whom this land had a huge appetite. Attacking the new cabinet boosted the opposition's appeal; it began to emerge as a formidable foe, publishing papers, and books and underwriting inflammatory propaganda. The colonel flatly rejected the notion that the opposition controlled most newspapers, even though the print media unanimously and constantly jabbed at Mossadegh. Colonel Nemat's biases aside, the press had a love-hate relationship with Mossey. No use in being on the reactionary side of the fence, though most of their money came from the upper crust, who despised the new order. Once they even attacked his enemies. No sooner had the oil nationalization bill passed the Majles, when the papers flayed the British for sending their navy to the Persian Gulf, "supposedly to protect British citizens" but truly "to intimidate the Iranian government, and bully the like-minded liberation movements in the region." All that before any of the dozen or so secret plans for subversive operations were revealed. Even before the disclosure of the British "Operation Buccaneer" to capture the southern city of Abadan, some of the papers published drawings of delicate Mossey combating an ugly hyena cloaked in the English flag.

The propaganda aside, hopes ran high on the oil nationalization bill. The idea out in the sun was that there was nothing a determined nation could not accomplish; only she decided what she wanted to pull off. Papers portrayed Doctor M. as the champion of the independence movement while complaining about his autocratic tendencies. Charges of pan-Americanism were leveled by the leftists, though the Americans counted on the theory that he was a fearless Moslem and therefore a moral anticommunist. After all, he had solicited Uncle Sam's assistance in keeping the British and the Russians at bay. The British suspicion that he pandered to the left and Radio Moscow's assertion that he was a bourgeois lackey notwithstanding, there were very few politicians whose patriotic credentials matched his. With a high-minded aristocratic wave of the hand, Mossadegh would brush aside the opposition's charges, look straight into the eyes of the crowd, and say, "I depend solely on your support" enough to drive the morally hungry masses wild. What did he speak of when he addressed these single-minded, unforgiving crowds? He discussed the great powers, inconceivable conspiracies, grave dangers, and possible spectacular achievements. There was a magical quality about him when he spoke that made the poor feel abundantly rich and the weak, strong. At the end of the road, there would be more wealth to go around, more jobs, and genuine happiness. The working class would enjoy the fruits of its labor. There would be plenty for everybody, if hardships could be borne and monumental obstacles endured.

By August, Colonel Nemat had decided not to read the papers anymore. They all seemed to have bought into this oil nationalization charade. Disgusting they were, he knew … he just knew. They had even fooled the Shah. The young monarch had sent his blessings to the new cabinet and wished it victory over the colonial powers. There was something very seriously wrong with the country.

Fifty-Nine

Connections at the Officers Club revealed to Sophie that certain villas in Shemiran were still available for summer rental. These belonged to the brass of the military, officers who never mixed with the Officers Club crowd, whose spouses did not deign to socialize with them either. The social scene proposed too much similarity of background; it exposed too much of one's life for comfort. These officers of the crème de la crème took their summer vacations in the south of France (in places like Montpellier, Nîmes, and Arles) or Italy (Venice was popular). Her connections, however, were not direct leads that Sophie could promptly pursue. At work was a vast network of contacts and expert hands. Unmentioned were the names, of course, although hints were dropped and locations discussed. She had to be discrete and diligent, patiently developing her leads further. The first time the remote possibility of her actually qualifying for one of these summer homes was hinted at was when her family had settled into their new house, sometime after the summer of 1951. Then she did not hear anything for months, during which time they were all scrutinized, herself in particular. In the end her prayers were answered, and she came across an offer that was decidedly the deal of her lifetime. A certain general needed to rent his place to a quiet family who would vacate the premises before schools reopened in the fall.

Arrangements were unhurriedly made for her to meet with the general's secretary, the general and his wife being tactfully absent from the interview. Putting her best foot forward, she finally managed to secure a large house in a quiet cluster of homes at the base of Mount Damauvand. She smiled inwardly after her triumph. She was grateful for not having to put up with the urban summer heat or her husband's annoying behavior for a few weeks. It gave her immense satisfaction that she had taken positive steps toward a better style of living; a style of which Colonel Nemat did not approve but of which he said nothing to oppose. He stepped aside and let her have her way, with the full understanding that their lives were progressing in two different spheres and there was nothing he could do to reverse it. As schools closed for the summer of 1952, Sophie hired a cab and took off for Shemiran with her children in tow, a routine that would repeat itself for years to come.

The sputtering cab struggled to keep its momentum as it drove up the steep roads. As it climbed to higher altitudes, the clustering neighborhoods became cleaner and more upscale, the trees denser, greener. At the end of their journey, the taxi lurched on top of a breezy arborous hill where a bunch of lavish homes nestled in a depth of poplars. The cab did not stop until it came to the second-to-last home whose window boxes and borders were filled with cascading geraniums. The house, in which Sophie and her children, Nastaran and Sohrab, would find themselves lost for the next three months, was one of the few high-walled residences lined up along a street with a sharp slope—an up-country villa whose owners were gambling their way through Europe, while their children attended summer school in Switzerland.

At the end of the cluster of homes was a narrow hiking trail, winding upward. Somewhere up ahead the trail, lined with cedars and poplars, joined the as yet snowcapped Damauvand. There was a total of five homes—Sohrab counted them twice—all backing on shaded woods that delivered a hill into a glistening brook; it might as well have been the national park itself, with mulberry trees and wildflowers and pines that hosted families of migratory birds. Each edifice was so well hidden in the folds and plies of the Shemiran landscape that no prying eyes could peep from one into another. The unusually cool air, the clear streams, and the abundance of vegetation made it hard to believe that this piece of heaven was but an hour from Tehran.

The villa next door to Sophie's housed no youngsters, as Sohrab discovered in his early expeditions. It was rented to an army doctor with his younger sister, both strangers to Sophie. Nevertheless she saw the young woman every day on her way up the hiking trail. When she phoned her husband next, she also inquired about her neighbors. He did not know them either, but that did not stop him from encouraging her to be the one to break the ice. With Sophie, though, the idea would take some time getting used to. How would she approach the young woman? What would she say? What would be the appropriate setting?

Unlike Sophie, her children had no scruples about choosing their playmates. Always an explorer and a lover of nature, Sohrab found a few friends, the children of other summer renters, to go on lengthy jaunts with into the lush woods, finding small creeks meandering through the thickly rooted trees. They found running, winding water, ice-cold and clear, making small ponds here and there that collected all sorts of life. Their days were spent hiking along the trail up the mountain, climbing mammoth boulders, each day daring to go farther and higher. They discovered tiny lizards and motley butterflies under gigantic rocks, unearthed odd-shaped pebbles in dazzling hues, and swam in the freezing pond formed by melting snow.

An agreeable boy for the most part, Sohrab was lighthearted, adventuresome. Like his father, he had a great propensity for wonder. Even so, when he did nothing but remind her of Colonel Nemat—an irony that she often thought about him in terms of traits he inherited from the colonel—she loved him with all her heart. Whatever Sophie's feelings for her son, her relationship to her daughter was simpler and more direct. Nastaran's attachment to her mother was severe, as she had been brought up according to Sophie's own rigid beliefs. If Sohrab was allowed a fair amount of latitude in his social life, it was because he was a boy, and Sophie knew nothing about raising boys, except boys were raised to become men. Nastaran, however, was a girl, and girls were raised to become ladies, something about which she did know something. Thus, Sophie subjected her daughter to a firm upbringing, even though at the same time she kept her close to her heart. Taught her manners and fretted over her homework; dressed her plainly, and showed her how to sew and cook and tend to her hygiene. She imbued her daughter with pride in the things she accomplished, something Sophie had had to learn on her own and for which she had suffered.

Afternoons saw a group of women roaming up the hiking trail, their laughter echoing off the craggy rocks. In this fatherless, husbandless atmosphere, the wives were trusted to keep one another's company as well as their daughters'. Sophie noticed them on the second day and guessed them to be in their forties and fifties. Previously, she had met two of the women at the Officers Club, and gladly received their acknowledgments. And when they invited her and her next-door neighbor, the doctor's sister, to join them in their strolls up the mountainside she gracefully accepted, not expecting to fall right in with them, what with the generational gap that was so evident. But becoming acquainted with the other women took only a matter of time.

These women had taken to calling themselves the Free-Spirited Women's Society, and held regular weekly meetings. Sophie enjoyed their company and found their meetings to be carefree and fun, with plenty of food and lively gossip. They got along with each other easily, their intimate thoughts and marital problems the subject of numerous free discussions within the group. They even included their young daughters in their activities and thus readily inaugurated the girls in female rituals in all their subtle nuances.

From the outset, Sophie's neighbor, Lily, had set herself apart from the rest of the group by remaining quiet at their meetings. All the members of the Free-Spirited Women's Society knew about her was that she was Dr. Bahman Tofiq's unmarried sister, who taught handicrafts at a public high school in Tehran. Lily struck Sophie as likable because she was not as loud as the other women and did not share their often crude sense of humor. This drew the two young women together, and soon they found themselves lagging behind, hiking alongside each other. As summer raced forward, they shared confidences and spent more time away from their free-spirited sisters.

Lily's combination of a morose air and snobbery had alarmed Sophie well before the two became close. She had heard from one of the other women that Dr. Tofiq was a member of the Communist *Tudeh* Party, which explained Lily's well-informed opinions and bias against the wealthy, but Sophie did not know to what to attribute her lengthy silences and general unhappiness. When the two were alone, Sophie pampered her like a child, told her stories, and made simple overtures of friendship. She spoke of the loss of her father at age five, her mother at fourteen, her life with a man four decades her senior, and her disappointments. Lily listened to her, and her tears dried. Sophie held her head and caressed her long dark hair and spoke of how destiny had brought them together so they could be each other's companion. The young woman softened under Sophie's kindness, and her sorrow swelled in her throat. Finding a gracious friend in Sophie, she could not contain herself any longer.

Hers was a lachrymose tale of love betrayed. One afternoon, Lily's grief poured out of her in one long cry of pain. From between her sobs she said she could no longer resist opening her heart. There and then she confessed to having loved a married man, which was still causing her heart to ache. He had been a teacher too, a coworker of hers who declared so much love she thought he would go mad. Gradually, with trembling knees and a heart full of yearning she had begun with him a surreptitious affair that centered on untethered desires. He was thirty-five with three children and a wife he had said he did not love. In the course of their six-month liaison, he never stopped short of promising her a life of happiness, and she had never stopped believing him. He told her that he loved her, that he would not leave her, that he would not take liberties with her, that they would be happy, and that he would leave his wife; that they'd be together forever and a day. Despite his promises about the future, she found herself deceived one day when he left the warmth of her bed and never returned. His gift to her was the immense heartbreak of abandonment.

"I was seventeen when my parents died," Lily said to Sophie. "My brother looked after me like I was his child. He's all I've got. Pampers me and watches out for me; makes sure I have all the things I need, you know…. He sent me back to the same private school as before, and helped me graduate, just as my parents wanted me to…. I still had everything handed to me like nothing had changed…. How could I be so stupid to disappoint him? God, it's killing me." Here she burst into tears and let Sophie hold her head on her shoulder. It had been a long time since the young woman had wept so freely.

Lily's head felt like a feather ball in Sophie's embrace; Sophie patted her shoulders and said nothing, as Lily poured out her poisoned heart, shedding teardrops like summer rain. Sophie consoled her friend, thanking God out loud that the pain was over and that she, Lily, did not have to deal with a mendacious lover any longer.

"But it's not over," Lily said, lifting her head. And she began to weep all over again.

"Why?" Sophie asked. "What's the matter? Still love that bastard?"

Lily shook her head.

"Then, what is it? Tell me."

"I feel like I'm drowning, and there is nothing I can clutch at to save myself. I'm going deeper every day."

"But what is it?" Sophie's eyes widened.

Lily felt Sophie's eyes searching her face, penetrating her very essence before retiring in quiet comprehension—she knew.

"It's been four months ..."

Sophie closed her eyes and sighed.

As a pragmatist, Sophie knew there was no time to waste. She had taught her daughter self-confidence and now was going to teach it to her friend.

Sophie telephoned one of her acquaintances at the Officers Club and secured the name of a doctor who would, for a fair sum, perform the needed procedure. Four months did not seem too late, although Lily's belly had begun to show. Not that Dr. Tofiq was that attentive; he was hardly around to notice any change at all. Of that they were certain. He worked for a good part of the day and then went to party meetings, or sometimes he had people over with whom he stayed up all night talking politics and party affairs. At the center of Sophie's concern was exactly that which should not have worried her, namely, the Free-Spirited Women's Society. They were not exactly the soul of discretion, and she had, on several occasions, seen them fail to display a free spirit regarding their fellow sisters. She shuddered at what might go on in their minds if they knew, and worse, what they would say.

In the short time since she had known Lily, her heart had found great affection for her. She did not wish Lily to be pitied as a blemished girl, a broken woman. In that small community, although the claims of empathy abounded, one had no personal rights.

Thus the two friends got into a cab the next day and headed toward the clinic, which was not too far from Shemiran.

The stocky physician was a short bespectacled man, educated in France, white-templed and polite. He led the women into his bare facility whose furniture consisted of a table in the middle of the waiting room, glass-topped and heavy, with a sofa and three armchairs around it. Magazines were strewn across the stained table. A ceiling fan rotated indifferently. Foreign-made posters of adorable round babies and bosomy nurses on the walls bore commonsensical messages. "Wash Your Hands *Before* Each Meal," one said, while another one implored, "Please Be Quiet." And a third one simply repeated the mantra "A Healthy Baby Brings Happiness to Your Home."

Lily sat languidly on the examining bed, gripping Sophie's motherly fingers, as the doctor's cold stethoscope searched for the heartbeat of her unborn. He listened for a minute and shook his head. The procedure for the second trimester would be painful, he said. Was she aware of that? Lily nodded her head. Good. The doctor listened some more. Over his bald crown Lily could see the black and white cross section of a vagina on the wall. This was the first time she had been in a clinic to have her privates examined. The gravity of her decision—to purge her body—now dawned on her with all its weight. It was easier to let the doctor do all the talking, even though she could not register a word he said. Through her gloom she watched his lips moving, his apathetic eyes resting on her face. There was no reason to fret now. All she had to do was to change into the robe that he handed her, and lie back.

With that he went to the far end of his office where there sat a gramophone on a solid wooden box. With great care he put on a well-known recording and firmly cranked the handle. It was the immortal voice of Delkash that echoed through the room. *Slowly, slowly, trembling, trembling, I came to your door, you weren't in. A flower-*

stem in my hand, I sat in your path. Music filled the clinic, as the doctor emerged from behind a dingy curtain with a shiny dilator and a curette. He set them on a small table with wheels—sat himself on a stool, at the foot of the examining table—muttering the words of the song under his breath, deliberately greasing his fingers with Vaseline. Momentarily, Lily lay on the cool table, her legs raised in stirrups with the examining fingers of the doctor pushing and probing. The instruments clinked and clanked, as Lily's sobbing merged with the laments of the singer.

All along Sophie resolved to keep her eyes on Lily's face. The woman on the table stared at the ceiling and groaned as the doctor applied his instruments, probing indifferently inside her. In flashes of fear her face contorted, and Sophie could see the terror escalating in her eyes. For a moment, Lily's screams rose above Delkash's voice. Sophie held her friend's face in both her hands and looked in her eyes that were rolling in agony. Lily's face swam through Sophie's tears as her fingers clutched at hers even harder. She pressed so hard, her knuckles turned white, the color of the water-stained walls. For an instant Lily calmed down, but almost at once she was screaming again as the curette was applied once more to her cramping cervix.

Next day, Sophie heard on the radio that a peaceful march before the parliament had ended violently, with the army stepping in and opening fire on the demonstration, killing at least fifty, injuring many more. Doctor Mossadegh came on the air and criticized the actions of the army. "The youths of this land," he complained, "are falling like autumn leaves in the wind." He chastised the army and blamed it for many ghastly deeds. He also reported no improvement in his dialogue with the Americans. He sounded tired, abashed, perplexed. In his familiar aristocratic vernacular he promised to stick by the people, and Sophie believed him because he sounded sincere and humble. Thanking those who stood by him, the grateful man of the people regretted "the blood that had been spilt." Moreover, he vowed to pick the matter up with the Shah and ask for the guilty parties to be punished. Then there was a pause .... The prime minister had run out of things to say. He bid good-bye to his audience, "until the next time," leaving Sophie wondering about the "blood that had been spilt," making her conscious of the sinful purging act she had abetted just the day before.

Sixty

The cruel flight of time. The summer of '52 sped head-on for Sophie, who reveled for weeks in Lily's company. They spent their days in the exclusivity of each other's secret and further disappointed their Free-Spirited Sisters. Comrades in crime, they were now one soul in two bodies. As a result, the memory of their connection to the Free-Spirited Women's Society faded slowly, like a departing train.

Lily met Colonel Nemat twice when he came up for the weekend. Later she expressed astonishment at how Sophie could stay married to that withered, dull man. That was her view and she did not apologize for it; Sophie took no offense.

Colonel Nemat's first visit came on a long weekend in midsummer. One day Lily recognized him coming down the path, panting and sweating, but did not acknowledge him. The single thought that rushed to her mind was the dismal image of him making love to Sophie. At the thought of the two of them sharing the same bed, blood turned her olive cheeks into blushing peaches. That afternoon she went over and formally introduced herself to the colonel. Though he displayed profuse reverence, she did not respond in kind, for she saw no shame in his eyes, only a collected and fatherly demeanor. Further, she was looking for a sign of discord in Sophie's voice but found none. He sat in a straight-backed seat in his uniform while Sophie prepared supper in the kitchen; the odd couple that they were seemed completely at peace with each another. Ever so garrulous, the colonel sat Lily on the opposite chair and told her all about his day. The outside air, he joked, was too good for him. His organs did not respond well. Although he displayed a cordial bearing toward Lily, she remained mute. After supper, he disappeared into the bedroom in haste, and the following day, finding the air too cool for his temperament and the ground underfoot too moist, he returned to the heat of Tehran.

Lily liked confrontations, tangling of the minds, but facts did not interest her; she had a startling ability to ignore them. In her arguments with colleagues of different persuasions she relied heavily on the passion of her belief and the spirit of justice she emitted. Besides, she was fond of verbal fights and drew immense pleasure from disproving theories. If it had not been for the respect she had for Sophie as a friend, there was nothing she would have liked better than getting into a brawl with the colonel. "Since when," she wanted to ask him, "has the army taken up the role of the police? Was its main purpose not to defend the country at the borders? What a spectacle to have them storming the streets and shooting innocent people down!" She wanted to make it known that in the fight between good and evil she defended the prime minister, although, like her brother, she did not think highly of his cabinet.

Politically, Lily was under her brother's influence, but she had more fire in her makeup than that. A man of strong convictions, Tofiq was a creature of science, a doctor, and believed in the power of reason. Anger never got the better of him. He was deeply concerned about the poor and the underfed, and was touched by the plaintive faces of the indigent to whom society had done a grave injustice. With a lieutenant's rank, he worked in the army hospital in the mornings, but his dislike of the military was evident in his disregard for army mandates, such as enlisted doctors not being allowed to venture into private business. He had set up a practice for his afternoons in southern Tehran, through which he offered his services to the poor at minimal operational cost. As long as he did not receive monetary compensation, his activities could not rouse official protest. He devoted most of his energies to this small clinic; in time the insolvent and the impoverished flocked to him by the hundreds. And he saw as many patients as he could, sometimes closing the doors after midnight, which left him tired and ineffectual in the morning. He embraced public work with such diligence you would have thought the end to misery was shortly at hand. The unemployed and the penniless came in carrying their dying mothers, pregnant wives, and asthmatic fathers, suffering, coughing up blood. They brought in their dead children with desperate hopes for a miracle.

Sometime after graduating from medical school, he had gathered a few other like-minded doctors; they held regular meetings and petitioned the government, the wealthy, whomever they could find, for funds and sympathy. This small group of young physicians, mostly from the upper classes, went from being the laughingstock of the medical community to winning the praise of a certain party, and shortly became a front for the communist cause. But all this work did not so much as begin to deflate the monster of poverty. At thirty, Tofiq was experiencing a despairing mental setback. Suddenly, it seemed that what he and his comrades had embarked upon was a drop in the bucket, the number of the needy was forever increasing and depleting the resources. He was always tired, overwhelmed, flustered. Frequently he sank in depression for lack of progress, became angry with the government and the pervasive indifference of society. As a result, his hair turned prematurely white, and deep creases appeared on his calm and compassionate face.

The second time the colonel came up to see his family was right after the army shot into the crowd on the day Prime Minister Mossadegh was holding talks about the oil issue with Mr. Averell Harriman, the foreign policy advisor to President Truman of the United States. A mob of demonstrators had gathered to protest the ostensible reconciliation, and when the crowd seemed to disrupt the negotiations, the soldiers who had been sent to curtail violence became paranoid and opened fire. They were not from the regular regiment stationed at Eshratabad, Nemat reported, as Sophie and Lily devoured the news. Peasants they were, hauled from the countryside to Tehran by the truckload. The colonel was certain. A great flood of hatred went through Lily as she listened to him; her eyes glinting in anger as she leveled charges of manslaughter against the good-natured Colonel Nemat even as he humored her with dignity.

Following the colonel's departure, Lily had Sophie and Nastaran over on the pretense of showing them a new dress she had bought. They'd make an afternoon of it, she said. And they did. She entertained her guests by performing mock speeches and Shakespearean soliloquies. Nastaran enjoyed her theatrics and egged her on, applauding and giggling behind her palms. The girl was an absolute gem, Lily decided, a package of pure delight. Encouraged by the love she felt from Nastaran, Lily refused to let the mother and daughter go home and insisted on having dinner together. Maybe if they stayed, they would meet her brother. "Chances are that he'll be home early tonight."

On Nastaran's insistence, Sophie gave up. So mother and daughter stayed and helped Lily prepare for dinner. And that evening, as Lily roasted the chicken in the backyard—its skin taking on a tawny hue, a heady aroma filling the air—the door opened and a surprised Dr. Tofiq peeked into the kitchen. Sophie had been standing by the sink, putting away the utensils as Tofiq watched. She then picked up the salad bowl and walked to the dining room, not sensing a set of eyes following her every move. In the hall the two strangers found themselves in the bungling position of facing each other, their eyes meeting for a moment. It wasn't like her, but Sophie was dumbstruck. Had he not spoken first she would have kept on gazing at his face, which was now opening into a broad smile.

"And who might you be?" said Dr. Tofiq to Sophie Nemat. "And why are you holding that heavy bowl?"

"Lily's friend," she said, "from next door—Nastaran's mother."

"Oh! Hello …. Congratulations on having such a bright kid. That bowl looks awfully heavy, let me help you." He took the bowl from her and cautiously, as if thousands of eyes were watching him, set it on the table. Sophie's hands were now holding nothing. She didn't know what to do with them, and cursed herself for being so clumsy.

"My husband is in the military too," she said, looking at his epaulets. Didn't know why but she felt she had to say something.

"But the military isn't in me," he was quick to respond. "They paid for my education. As soon as I pay my dues, I'm out of there, no regrets."

"My husband is a colonel." Again she said something she would regret. *Why announce that?* Too late to retract her comment, she was embarrassed, her face betraying her. Thank goodness he was far worse in reading these emotions than she gave him credit for. He turned around and headed for his bedroom.

"Please excuse me," he said while disappearing behind a door. "I have to wash up and get ready for supper. You *are* staying for supper aren't you?"

She watched him dash out of sight and stood there in silence for a moment afterward.

Nastaran came back in from outside. Presently they heard a male voice mildly reproaching Lily for not having alerted him beforehand but did not catch Lily's response. The salad bowl looked out of place on the table. Presently, Tofiq and Lily came into the dining room together, and Lily introduced Sophie to him as her best friend. Now they shook hands formally, with not much else to say.

Suddenly Lily remembered the chicken on the barbecue and again disappeared into the backyard. Once more Dr. Tofiq and Sophie Nemat were facing each other without having anything to say. To overcome the awkward silence, Tofiq began talking to Nastaran. Quick of wit, the polite girl talked back as though they were old friends. This provided Sophie a chance to skip out of sight, following Lily's trail. In the delicate air of the end-of-summer evening, the two friends stood side by side, staring at the still-glowing charcoal embers in silence.

An awkward dinner was had in a soft lemon light while the doctor and the little girl engaged themselves in the liveliest of conversations, a perfect occasion for Sophie to carefully examine, without calling attention to herself, a broad forehead, attractive set of teeth, the longest lashes, and slenderest nose on the gentlest face she had ever seen. All would escape a careless spectator, of course, except for Lily, who registered in her mind's log every glance, gesture, softening of the voice, movement of the brows.

Later in the evening, Lily mulled over the meaning of the looks exchanged between her brother and her friend. She tried to isolate a remark, a look, a smile that would indicate it was not all in her mind; that sparks really were flying. Granted Sophie was married, but so what? Since when had that stopped anyone? Due to her own unfortunate encounter, Lily was beyond respecting the institution of marriage, especially when it involved an unsuitable union such as the one between Sophie and the colonel. Fueled by the aggravating trinity of anger-guilt-remorse, she reasoned that if men could do it and get away with it, why shouldn't women. At the same time her other, wiser half cautioned her to be gentle. Sophie was not just a married woman; she had two children and she was a friend. Lily wondered if what she believed to be nothing more than chains on the feet and wrists of women counted, in the final analysis, for much more .... *Nonsense! Sohrab and Nastaran would learn to love Tofiq like their own father.* Better even. For some unaccountable reason the colonel did not strike her as the kind of father who would take his children to the park or movies, wrestle with his son, or lift up his daughter and press her cheeks against his. Come to think of it, Lily did not remember him even talking to them with much more than a respectful tone, which was both distant and preoccupied. Twice she had met him, and both times he seemed so removed from his surroundings, you would have thought he lived in a different era.

As Lily was planning the next stage of her convoluted design, her subjects remained faultlessly oblivious. Now she had to make them see for themselves that they were attracted to each other. This proved unattainable, however, for the turning of the leaves was a reminder of the dream interrupted. Fall was nearing. Before Lily had another chance, Sophie had turned in her keys and stopped in to say good-bye. Tears rolled unabashedly on soft cheeks, promises to stay in touch were made in haste, telephone numbers were exchanged, but none of that stopped the hurting.

Sixty-One

With the arrival of the winds and turning of the sky, school started. The busy life of Sophie Nemat caught into yet another cycle of endless toil and frustration. She had sheltered slight hope that the summer vacation would dampen her inquietude, that by the time she returned home, change would finally come upon her life. How agonizing it must have felt to find herself in the same house again, tending to the same chores, feeding her children, providing the family with the basics. She heard the same nagging at the back of her head about the future and a life of apathy. The familiar specter of boredom visited her once again.

Colonel Nemat was scarcer these days, which was in itself a relief, though it left her lonelier than before, more desperate. She sought Lily Tofiq, and that proved in vain. Finding her friend seemed more difficult than she had been given to understand, mainly because they lived so far apart. Since Sophie and her children had been back from Shemiran, she had dialed the number Lily had given her, but at no time did anyone answer. Finally she resolved herself to call Dr. Tofiq at the hospital and send Lily a message through him. She knew that in the mornings he worked at the army hospital, so she would call him there. That much she could accomplish on her own.

One fine, early winter morning, Sophie obtained the number from the operator and dialed. After a dreadful scrutiny by an inquisitive nurse and a seemingly endless pause, a distraught male voice came on.

"Hullo?"

"Hello—"

"This is Dr. Bahman Tofiq—"

"Yes .... Hello, I mean, how are you?"

"I am fine. May I ask whom I'm speaking to?"

"Yes .... I'm Sophie ... Sophie Nemat. Lily's friend .... You may not remember me, but—"

"Oh, of course I do." His voice abandoned its initial displeasure and became warm and amicable. "We had dinner together, how could I forget. How's your little daughter?" The warmth coming from him put Sophie somewhat at ease.

"She's fine," said Sophie. "Thank you." God, what else was she supposed to say? *Hurry, hurry, say something. Don't sound like an idiot.* "The reason for bothering you is, I've tried calling Lily at home, but no one answers. Is she all right?"

"No bother at all," said the doctor. He sounded concerned, or perhaps he did not want to talk over the phone. "Yes, she's well ... At least for now. But she became sick after the summer."

"Oh, I didn't know .... What's wrong?"

"I'd rather not talk about it here. She's fine now, believe me."

"But you must tell me, doctor."

"Well, she quit her job and decided to do something different. She was doing fine for a while, but suddenly three weeks ago .... We had to admit her into the hospital, because—"

"Because ...?"

"Look. Why don't we meet somewhere, I'll explain it all then. I must be going now. What do you say?"

"Sure doctor. Where shall we meet?"

"Let me call you back."

An avalanche of conflicting thoughts assaulted Sophie's mind after hanging up the receiver. She felt a part of her had been stolen. What could have possibly happened to Lily? Her first instinct was to feel irritated and angry. For almost three months they had been each other's closest companion, or so she thought. Three months of intense friendship that meant a great deal to Sophie. She wished she had called the hospital sooner and that she had not waited so long to reach her friend, who must have gone through hard times without her. Lily had quit her job; that must have been because it was difficult to run into the father of the child that was no longer.

And what about the doctor? On an inexpressible level, he reminded her how tense she had been that night when they had met. She wondered what lay behind his seemingly warm reception now, his politeness over the phone. He sounded as if he had heard from a long-lost friend. Was Tofiq as uneasy talking to her as she was talking to him? If he was, he managed to contain it well. Over the phone he sounded so, well, casual. But she was too worried about Lily to dwell on this, or to give much more thought to the gentle doctor.

The bringa-linga of the phone broke through the crisp February air, just two weeks later. Sophie recognized Dr. Tofiq's voice on the other end, broken and sad. He was calling from home, about his sister, something about her not being well. A nervous breakdown was what it was, and he was waiting for her to recover a bit before arranging for Sophie to visit her. Not to worry though, he assured her, Lily would be fine. Perhaps it was time for them to meet and talk somewhere? With a torrent of horrible possibilities flashing through her mind, and a dewy sweat breaking out on her upper lip, Sophie agreed to their first rendezvous.

Sixty-Two

Dismissing his earlier doubts, in spite of his strict orders to keep away from the defendant, disregarding his fears and contrary to the common principles that oversee the unity of the faithful in matters concerning the counterrevolution, Brother Hamid leaped out of his bed early that morning and hurried to the Office to Combat Vices. Upon arrival, he went through the motions of registering his name and permitted himself exposure to the questioning stares of the brothers and sisters, who were, that early in the day, standing on their prayer rugs, working their beads. A minor disruption rippled through the rows of devout men as sideway glances were thrown his way. *An innocent man's life is on the line, for God's sake.* He passed by the rows of bearded guards, ignoring them, letting them go back to their beads, climbed up the marble stairs, and stood before the guard on duty outside the ward, panting. Formal salutations endured, he asked to see Farzin Rouhani.

In the interrogation room, there was the usual lack of greeting. Brother Hamid noticed the tired lids drooping over Farzin's bloodshot eyes. Had he, too, been up all night? The positive answer to his inquiry did not surprise him. Seized by a relentless drive to settle scores, Farzin had been crouching earnestly over his papers since their last meeting. Carrying a bundle of them under his arms, he lowered himself into a chair.

"I am sorry for the way you have been treated," Brother Hamid said in a somber tone. "This is the moment of truth."

"Moment of truth, is it?"

"Yes."

"Yes …. Well. I appreciate the irony, but …."

This was no way to warm up to the fellow, Farzin realized. Brother Hamid had stuck his hands in his pockets meanwhile and was smiling. Noticing his helplessness, Farzin forced himself to reciprocate. That seemed to help break the ice. Brother Hamid pushed his rotten-toothed grin very close to Farzin, but his smile dissipated as he said, "What I don't understand is why a smart guy like you insists on wasting everyone's time with trivial matters." He continued after a long pause. "This is it, get it? Have you any idea what's in store for you?"

"Haven't given it much thought," Farzin responded nonchalantly. "Though I have a hunch you're going to fill me in, yes?"

Brother Hamid pointed at the bundle still under Farzin's arm. "What's this? Got more for me?"

Farzin let go, and the sheets of paper scattered and drifted across the floor.

"I know *you've* given up on me," Farzin mumbled, "but you see … I couldn't give up on me." He raised his middle and forefingers before Brother Hamid and went on, "They didn't use to be so crooked, but look at them now." Brother Hamid looked at the two deformed fingers as Farzin Rouhani extended his arm. The tip of his forefinger was pushed in flat, and the other one had a dent that would nicely fit the curve of a pen.

"You don't understand, Hamid," Farzin continued. "I owe it to myself. When was the last time you were candid with yourself? I mean completely and totally honest. When did you last look at yourself in the mirror and confess to something you knew you would have to pay a price for as a result of your confession?"

At this he got up from his chair and went to the door. Brother Hamid didn't quite know how to respond.

"I'm tired, Hamid. I need to get some sleep. Then you can do to me what you will."

After taking Farzin back to the ward, Brother Hamid gathered the strewn sheets from the floor and, with some hesitation, began thumbing through them.

Great Britain had levied sanctions on the Iranian market as a direct challenge to the oil nationalization. In September, Lord Attlee announced the decision to the world; by December the British policy was beginning to bear fruit. The "renegade nation" started to feel the pinch. The cash-strapped government of Doctor Mossadegh struggled to put substance into gesture. Great troubles ahead. Signs of change in the general mood of the country everywhere. Lines that had begun to form in front of grocery stores and even at gas stations became longer and longer as winter closed in with daunting snows. Living conditions became so deplorable, one would have dismissed the remotest possibility of love right off the bat. But love has such a delightful habit of blossoming in the wrong time, in times of crisis.

Tehran in snow had not been a sight to behold that year. Winter dread came upon the city sooner than expected. Heavy black clouds roofed the capital for the entire season, and the sun took retreat for weeks on end. Darkened alleys full of potholes and slush were the unlikeliest sites for Sophie Nemat and Dr. Bahman Tofiq to meet but also the safest. For this reason alone, they had agreed to rendezvous on a steep incline named after the poet Bahaur.

Oncoming cars floundered on the icy street as the couple met on this early afternoon, between the hours of Colonel Nemat's post-lunch departure and the children's return from school. The two of them felt like schoolchildren sneaking out of their parents' sight to satisfy a spontaneous urge that was both delicious and forbidden.

Sixty-Three

Over a glass of scalding tea, in one of Tehran's many basement cafés, Dr. Tofiq, at long last, met with Sophie to discuss his sister's condition. The lights were low and the floor was wet with snow that patrons had unwittingly brought in on the soles of their shoes. A continuous hum of voices droned above their heads—the patrons knocking, rustling, clicking, clucking, laughing and blowing their noses. He spoke of his sister in terms that convinced Sophie he knew absolutely nothing about her medical procedure over the summer. Above them the snow drifted and heaped on the roof and all around in the cold, blustery streets, piling on parked cars and sidewalks. Sophie told him about her friendship to Lily, her daughter's fondness for her. All day long she had felt a tingle in her stomach that put her in a jittery mood. Now she gave it a release, and the words came out of her like the loops of a chain, one dragging the next, as he listened and sipped his hot tea.

He sat in his chair silently, both hands cupping his glass, drawing warmth from it, listening to her and smiling. He wondered at how unpredictably pleasant his day had turned out, sitting in that café with such an astonishing woman, beautiful as she was gregarious, mischievous as a tornado. Leaning back in his chair, he squinted. There she was, a couple feet away from him, an elbow on the table, basking in his attention. Neck muscles showed no sign of stress, her hands were delicate and sublimely petite. Her firm jaws moved tirelessly; he imagined them capable of picking up her children in her teeth, like a lioness carrying her cubs. Strong enough to ward off an enemy, yet gentle enough to love and kiss a lover's most intimate parts.

He listened unhurriedly to her lengthy tales. In her presence he felt void of charm, reticent. Normally that would not have been his defining style around females, even the attractive ones. Strongly built and handsomely groomed, he had had his share of conquests. Women eyed him at parties; widows, virgins, the married, and the divorced. They had been willing to do anything for him at a moment's notice. No novice was he at this sort of thing, but he couldn't account for the change in his bearing now. What was happening to him? What chemical reaction was taking control of his faculties? Lily, on whose behalf they had come together, had not been farther away from his mind in a long time.

From hers either. She could not recall the last time she had been so embarrassingly garrulous, or when she had been in the presence of such a perfect listener, who was attentive, handsome, and supportive of her resolution. She could see the flash of admiration in his eyes that set her head spinning. Every limb in her body became inebriated with the joy of being so desired. Her hands danced above the table, fingers raking the air, her bracelets jingling with each movement of the wrists. The only regret being the afternoon was made up of such short hours, infinity an illusive dream. Suddenly, at five after four, she remembered home and her children and excused herself. With assurances that they would meet again, he acceded to parting. A date was set and a time intimated for her to visit Lily, and he expressed sincere hopes that she would keep her word. Thus in glee she sauntered away, pleased as a pampered puppy, humming a favorite tune.

Sixty-Four

Lily had lost weight; dark halos had appeared around her eyes. She was reserved, somewhat perturbed even, when Sophie showed up at the door a few days later. Even though her brother had notified her of Sophie's coming, she had done nothing to make herself in the least bit presentable. Sitting before the other woman in her pajamas with greasy hair and bad breath, she stared blankly into the air.

"Please don't ask me why."

Sophie had not come to solicit information about Lily's bad choices. That was not why she was there, not even the least of what she was seeking. She looked at her surroundings and did not respond. The Tofiqs lived in an old house with a sprawling garden and a pool whose water had a layer of green on top. The tick-tock of the hallway clock filled the high-ceilinged rooms.

"You know, I thought a lot about you," said Sophie. Lily showed no reaction. She was empty of talk, her head a burden. She felt inadequate and pitiful, not at all like glamorous Sophie to whom everything came so easily, a family, a house, even a secret admirer who was no longer so secret.

Sophie did not press her for conversation. Her approach was to wait and lend an ear.

"How're your children?" asked Lily, finally. "How's my Nastaran?"

"They're fine, and they miss their Aunt Lily. Nastaran is in fifth grade, you know. You ought to come by and see her sometime."

Sophie's sincerity, spoken in simple competent terms, always had this effect on people—it disarmed them. Suddenly, Lily was overcome with something akin to homesickness and reached out for Sophie's hand. She had no explanation for her attempted stupidity and felt deeply ashamed. Once again, shame had become the overriding sense governing her being. Momentarily, she burst into tears and expressed regret for having avoided her friend, her best and only friend. Uncontrollably, she wept amid promises of never ignoring Sophie again. Would Sophie forgive her? Would she think nothing of it? Tears ran down the length of her face as she let herself be held by her friend.

Tofiq noticed the effect Sophie had on Lily immediately and was thankful beyond his means. They had begun to meet in the afternoons between one and five but never went further than holding hands (which had to be broken off intermittently) or exchanging long, meaningful glances. They held each other, she onto his arm, he the slope of her back when leading her through doors, and conducted their whisperings that, regardless of the subject matter, were always laden with undefined sexual yearnings. And what did they discuss strolling along the snow-covered northern parts of town, along streets lined with leafless plane trees and frozen gutters? What was said between them in their billowy breath as they walked through the barren flower gardens? Mostly their talks revolved around his favorite subject: politics.

Then one day, an ominous thing happened: an argument, their first, which would deeply affect the course of their friendship. They had gone to see a Hollywood production, a drama, at the Moulin Rouge. It was called *The Sisters*, casting a dashing Errol Flynn in the role of an unfaithful husband with Bette Davis as his tormented wife. Although the movie was, by all accounts, a success, it did not sit particularly well with Sophie in respect to its adulterous subject matter. It made her all too aware of her dishonesty in leading a double life, even though she had a tendency to push the thought to the back of her mind.

Seeing her in such torturous gears, Tofiq denounced the movie and tried to make her forget its message. From there he launched an attack on all moving pictures, which proved unsound judgment, considering her fascination with movies. They argued, he on the offensive, she trying to see the merits of his argument but ending up defending her idols. The best movies, she begged to differ, were the good novels of the time. They were stories about people with valuable, and sometimes unforgettable, truths to reveal. Caught off guard by her heated response, he switched his position to a more ripened but equally hostile stance. With a disapproving air, he maintained that movies were the stuff of dreams, evanescent, therefore untrustworthy. He was a stern scientist, a realist, believing only in firm facts and the relationship of cause and effect, intention and achievement. The arts he could do without, since the masses could not directly benefit from them.

"There is no use carrying on like this," she said, as they strolled in the crisp, cool winter air. "I belong to my children and also to my husband." Picturing her family, she was filled with a sense of utmost wrongdoing. She felt she had no business whatsoever furtively walking with a stranger into places where only couples with a future dallied.

"Sophie dear, don't be so hard on yourself. The fact is that you're not happy with your marriage. It was a mistake, as you've said yourself. Haven't you mentioned it several times to Lily and me? What am I to make of this?"

"I don't know, I don't know," she said. "I wish I could answer that."

"Listen," he called her to attention, trying to remind her of the facts. "Are you happy with him?"

"What did I think I was doing?" She whispered distressingly. "Exercising a freedom I was not sure I had?" At this, a horrific expression seized her face. "Bahman, please," she said. "Help me. Why am I like this?"

The thought of betraying her family suddenly made her stomach cower with pangs of guilt and dismay.

"There is a name for what I am, isn't there? I'm an adulteress—a traitor."

"Stop torturing yourself."

She could not look into his eyes and articulate the remorse that was going through her like a torrent of electricity. She pulled her hand out of his.

Having used every excuse in the book, and every argument in his arsenal, to reverse her line of thought, Dr. Tofiq found the course of her defeat still unchangeable. He felt he had to do something though, anything to stop her free fall into despair. Having gone through the bitter experience of Lily's breakdown, he could not stomach yet another disaster shaping up right in front of him.

"Marry me, will you?"

After hearing himself say what he said, he knew that he had popped the question more out of conviction than concern, more for his own sake than hers. After all, he had been suppressing the urge to confront his feelings for some time. He had done it now, and it felt good.

"Sorry," she said with a touch of bitter sarcasm, "but I'm already committed." Her sarcasm directed itself inward, as though reminding her of what a woeful life she led.

He in turn decided to press forward; there was no turning back. The result was a blunt tone, bordering on the abrasive. "Get a divorce," he said, rather hurriedly. Definitely not a style he would have admired in himself had he had time to reflect. "Take as much time as you need. I can wait—oh, I can wait."

"And I thought I was crazy."

"I mean it, Sophie. I love you. I've loved you since the first time I saw you. And I love you now more than ever. With everything I am. Please believe me, and please say yes."

"How can I, Doctor? What would I do without my children? They are my lifeblood. I'd die without them."

Such a naked display of emotion caught Dr. Tofiq off guard, giving him a sound shock. He had not prepared himself for what she was saying.

In the months that followed, he engaged in more than a bit of revisionism. He reproached himself for his thoughtless silence at that crucial moment when he should have been more reassuring. In his mind he repeatedly played that scene, and every time he arrived at the part where she spoke so passionately about her children, he would shout, "I don't care. They can be my children, because I want you, all of you, and if that includes your children, then I want them too." But the past had already come and gone, and he could change none of it. The burden of his guilt left Dr. Tofiq with not only a cigarette habit but an acute ulcer as well. He could not forgive himself for his behavior that day, for having uttered exactly nothing after she had spoken to him in such a dire tone. He was shattered, and he had no one to blame but himself. He had been a terrible companion and a lousy, undeserving pursuer. Had he not repeated to himself time and again that a gem like Sophie deserved only the kindest and most tender affection? How could he let the single most promising love of his lifetime slip by him so carelessly?

Sixty-Five

Brother Hamid was pensive. He flipped through the pages, skimming over long descriptive passages, for he was never one to appreciate sentimental prose, which dominated Farzin's latest submission. His own fault, Brother Hamid remained ignorant of the prizes he missed. In his impatient disregard for the details of Sophie's extramarital romance, he skipped over an abundance of facts as well: the silent conspiracy of General Z, a subtle shift in the international politics against Dr. Mossadegh, "the Victor of the Hague," and not too keen a shift in the Tudeh Party disposition toward Old Mossy.

More than a few passages were jumped over. This way, the Shah's appointment of Qavam to replace Mossadegh shuffled under the stack, followed by a summary of street demonstrations for Mossadegh's return and the army's shooting down of demonstrators, killing seventy-six supporters, including some bystanders. Moreover, ending up at the bottom of the pile was the reinstatement of Mossadegh to his premiership with full control of the armed forces, following the bloody uprising of July 21, and a heartening story about the seizure of an Italian oil tanker belonging to a certain Greek millionaire and shipping tycoon for carrying Mossadegh's oil in defiance of the British boycott.

He smirked, Brother Hamid, at these implications and thought how odd someone else's interpretations could be of the same events. In his haste, Brother Hamid inadvertently missed one other item, which should not have been lost in between the pages and pages of harangue, political and otherwise. This regarded a torrent of domestic strife that broke out between the betrayed Colonel Nemat and his disloyal wife, Sophie, who ended up taking her suitcase and hitting the streets against the black of nightfall. Their cataclysmic row had been brewing for some time, slowly simmering under a cloud of pain and mistrust. Since her meeting with Dr. Tofiq had opened her eyes to the possibility of a razzmatazz life with him, Sophie had been behaving as though she was cut from a finer cloth than her aging husband. She seldom deigned even to be seen with the colonel, who, conveniently, was spending increasingly more time away from home, thus clearing the way for Dr. Tofiq to fill her life.

On July 21, 1952, when the army took direct aim at a group of demonstrators, Sophie received a call from Bahman, suggesting she go downtown with him. Lily offered to sit with the children, freeing Sophie to visit her beloved near Zhaleh Square, where Brigadier General Nassiri, commander of the Imperial Bodyguards, had ordered the opening of fire on unarmed civilians. Tanks and armed soldiers kept the demonstrating masses at a thousand feet distance, and the two of them witnessed the most daunting scene of their entire lives as bullets burned the air and ricocheted off the pockmarked walls. In the aftermath of the carnage, Sophie saw with horrified eyes the scores of children, men, and women who were reduced to bloodied corpses.

If you had been indifferent to Mossadegh up to that point, on that day upon seeing the conviction of those people, you would have converted, despite yourself, to an ardent supporter. Such was Dr. Tofiq's change of heart, and with him thousands of the Tudeh sympathizers who became overnight proponents of the government. Dr. Tofiq and his whole intellectual world had such a grip on Sophie's thinking that she converted to his belief, too, just to prove herself worthy of him. Gazing at the paint of blood on innocent faces, she decided there and then to end her sham of a marriage.

That night, strange and inexplicable sounds emanated from the colonel's house. Durable antique china plates crashed on the kitchen tiles with the unstoppable force of pent-up frustration and anger, amid wild shrieks of spite and madness, the clinks and clanks of pots and pans and broken glass too. There were windowpanes crashing, frightened birds flapping, doors slamming, whole chairs thrashing and table legs coming apart. And what came of it all? What did the neighbors hear the colonel do in defense? Did they hear him raise his voice? Did he try to calm his wife's nerve-raking tantrum? Did he make any attempt at all to put a stop to this insanity? What did they decide had happened? What did he do? Pay attention: ignore the cacophony of glass and china and pots and pans. Leave behind the distraction and cries and the sound of slamming doors and windows. What came out was ...wait a minute ...listen ...It was the long single note of a suffering bow they heard, the pain of a violin as its strings were gently stroked, Colonel Nemat's cries of agony through the surrounding dissonance, the solemn ballet of a bow on his sad old instrument.

An urgent question at the end of the day: Where would she go, what would she do? She could not go to her own house, it still being under lease to a tenant. What then? Could she go to Dr. Tofiq and expect him to put her up with her two children? Or pour her heart out to Lily? Considering the weight of her pride, highly unlikely. Not that Lily would not have accommodated her, had Sophie gone to her. But what was wrong was wrong, and what would people say on top of that? No, she would not take her vanity lightly. The gates of a town could be shut; the people's mouths could not. So what did she do, with a suitcase in her hand, in the middle of the night? Was she thinking about going to her sister-in-law's house as she hailed a taxi? Would she have been received warmly there? She must have known Houshang would above all be very understanding. The couple would give her every assurance that she was welcome to stay with them, as long as her domestic quarrel remained unresolved. Well, that was the extent of the facts they would be let in on. Sophie's mind had already been made up not to tell them the particulars. Why should she? Who would have been hurt by a little white lie? Save her time to repossess her house, it would. She could do it. She just knew she could do it.

Sixty-Six

Sophie never considered the impact their separation might have on poor old Colonel Nemat. The day after her flight, suitcase in hand, into the heat of the night, his certainties fell apart, and the last residues of his sanguinity were replaced by vile pessimism. This internal transformation manifested itself in a peculiar physical diminution. His massive presence shriveled to a bony structure with a head the size of a soccer ball; his nose gravitated toward his lips, and his back bent slightly forward. His associates recognized him less and less as the turbulent days of that summer drew to a violent close. Deep creases appeared on his wide forehead, his sunken cheeks, and around the corners of his mouth. White bristles showed up willy-nilly on his emaciated face, and a rancid sour smell began to emanate from him. The stench of a broken heart, distilled in the veins and the pores of his wrinkled skin, merged with the sweat of shame and the vapors of defeat—melancholy in a thick poisonous paste of envy and pain. His voice became coarse and dry, and the patience to play with the birds left him altogether. The parliament of birds, however, sang its heart out at all hours, even in the middle of the night, as if his feathered friends had made a secret pact not to let silence hold sway for long—that, despite his negligence of their upkeep, which resulted in a foul stench hovering above the house. Cages soon filled with their droppings, and one by one the singing inhabitants became ill, fell silent, and died; all sixteen of them.

Mystery works in fateful ways. The man who took note of Colonel Nemat's declining condition was a small-framed, neurotic, humorless, four-star army general, as dark on the inside as on the outside, who, when alone in his office, entertained elaborate dreams of grandeur. At fifty-five this man, a Nazi sympathizer under Reza Shah, imprisoned by the British during the war, a reformed political prisoner after switching his allegiance to the winning side, a winner of his freedom in the hands of the Americans a short while after the war, was hard at work to make a comeback without losing his grand dreams that were now, at long last, beginning to seem not so unattainable after all. In the first few months of 1953 he had been coordinating certain unsavory schemes with Mister Kermit Roosevelt, the grandson of President Theodore Roosevelt and the operative of a certain American agency, but currently could not decide on the exact time on which to make his final assault on Mossadegh's seat.

A good-omened hour; when the mousy four-star general heard the colonel's wife had broken his heart, blood coagulated in his veins, all color took leave of his triangular face, and he leaped out of his chair. What had alerted him? What in that simple story of love betrayed had inspired him to spring up on his toes? What had decisively put an end to his indecision? Well, of course, it was nothing he would readily admit to, but ... he remembered his father always saying, "Each time a woman dares to leave her husband, the world inches a trifle closer to doomsday."

So, General F. Zahedi, rehabilitated by the Americans in order to unseat one Doctor Mossadegh, decided that the hour to act was at hand. An ultimate treachery was begetting another. Since the restoration of his former position, he had had Colonel Nemat's Eshratabad division under his command, but was the colonel let in on the plot? There is plenty of room for conjecture. Who could know what the general was up to? Even his handsome son, Ardeshir, the darling of certain circles, who would go on to reportedly become His Imperial Majesty's favorite poker partner, was kept in the dark as to the nature of the events during the following days. It was for good measure, knowledgeable sources would agree, but then, it might have dismayed the young Ardeshir, being a staunch monarchist all along. The point being, if General Z would not trust his own son, how could anyone accuse Colonel Nemat of collaboration? In all fairness, how could he have known, prior to the completion of the risky mission, that his boss had been put on the path to, among other things, level revenge on the doctor who had stolen his wife?

General Z carried with him at all times a shiny black riding crop, which he would gently tap against his calf. Reminiscent of the old days in the retinue of Reza Shah, he occasionally used it to smack his orderly around, but in the late evening of Tuesday, August 18, he had found a better use for it. The Shah's flight to Rome two days earlier had had a devastating impact on the morale of the soldiers. In his hideout, the basement of the American Embassy, in the company of Mr. Roosevelt, the general pointed at a map of the city with his riding crop and revealed his plan of action to his bespectacled American friend. He explained that a contingency of loyalists from the bazaar were to march to the prime minister's residence on Kaukh Avenue. That morning he had received word that the funds dispersed among the participants of the rally had attracted some quite big names. His voice was vibrant with nostalgia and splendor.

Mr. Roosevelt, Kim to his friends, nodded his head and interjected ideas of his own on the logistics and timing of the event until they were both satisfied with the outcome plan. In Mr. Roosevelt's expert view, what they were about to embark on together was the closest thing to the attack on the Winter Palace during Russia's October Revolution. Though there were questions still in his mind regarding the lower ranks of the army—whether they would, at the least, remain neutral. The general picked up his cigarette, which was consuming itself in the ashtray on the mahogany table, inhaled a chestful of smoke, squinting with ecstasy, opened his eyes, exhaling now the slow billowing smoke from his nostrils. Pointing with the black riding crop at the likeness of the fugitive monarch, he swore to His Majesty to eliminate any and all who blocked his way.

Truth be known, General Z considered the army his turf; he had a blind trust in its core leadership. He did not impress the American spy as being particularly smart. What he lacked in intelligence, though, was compensated tenfold by his thoroughness of resolve and his influence on the armed forces. The mistrust between the two men was accentuated by the fact that the general did not speak English, only a mediocre German, and the two of them thus communicated poorly—he pronounced his R's with a guttural drumroll, unsoftened for American ears. Misterrr Rrrrroosevelt, he had addressed his American collaborator. When their objective was achieved, Mr. Roosevelt would be proud of himself to have done well with not so reliable an ally. But on August 18, 1953, when he articulated his worries about the army, the general did not even let him finish his sentence and dismissed the American's concern right off the bat—"Don't vorry Misterrr Rrrroosvelt. De Arrrmy ees fine, yes."

The formidable problem in the general's mind, at this moment, was the reaction of the Communist Tudeh Party, which had, in recent months, put itself completely at the prime minister's disposal. If anything posed a degree of danger, it was not the army but the Tudeh element, with its trained and armed cadre. "Had the Amerrricans thought vhat to do about dat? *Wurden Vorbeugungsmaßnahmen getroffen um die kommunistische Bedrohung zu verringern?*"

"We'll let Mossey take care of that problem for us," said Mr. Roosevelt with a wide grin.

Mr. Roosevelt did not proceed with the details, but earlier in the afternoon he had counseled Mr. Loy Henderson, the brand-new American ambassador, to call on Doctor Mossadegh, ostensibly to complain about the safety of American citizens residing in the country, but in reality to feign ignorance of the menacing coup underway.

In that meeting, which took place on a heated afternoon at the very home of the prime minister, the two men stood in ceremony with each other. The prime minister did not seem such a pajama-clad weeper as the ambassador had been given to understand. It didn't seem such a struggle for him to overcome his natural modesty and state his concerns.

"What is the world coming to, my good man?" Doctor M had asked the ambassador. "Vows are no more to be respected? What are your compatriots saying about my country? That we've become atheists, communists, or whatnot? Our nation has a long memory, Mr. Ambassador, and will remember its friends and foes for years to come. In the meantime, it's most unfortunate that a great democracy, such as yours, is voicing its support for a tyrant who has fled to foreign lands. We find this most improper. What gives your country the right to pressure us on behalf of a man who is no more than a rebel?"

The ambassador, who had troubled himself with the visit to alarm the prime minister of the rising mob violence, was quick to hand out a lesson in Islamic tradition.

"As a Christian," said Mr. Henderson, "may I remind a Moslem, such as yourself, of the tradition of *higra*, started by the Prophet Mohammad (after whom you are named) in his famous flight from Mecca? Isn't that the starting point of the Islamic calendar? I presume, if I may be allowed, that the Prophet fled not from fear but to dramatize a point. The *higra* marked the rise of Islam as a world force. His Majesty's *higra* may mark *his* rise also!"

The American ambassador was probably shocked hearing himself comparing His Imperial Majesty to the prophet of Islam. However, having said that, he changed the course of talks to more pragmatic issues, namely, his mission to divert the old gentleman's attention. He contended that the Communist Tudeh agitators were behind a series of mob attacks against American citizens. Stories about anonymous phone calls answered by innocent children who were then subjected to the most appalling language were concocted on the spot and dished out to the discomfited prime minister. The ambassador's deception did not stop there. In addition to the threatening phone calls, he also reported violations of automobiles belonging to Americans, their tires deflated when left unattended, shouts of "Yankee Go Home" ringing out in the middle of the night.

On hearing the American's concerns, Doctor M was puzzled. His long face transformed into a disfigured mess. When he pointed to the rumor that the American Embassy had become a sanctuary for General Zahedi and Co., out of which all sorts of evil were assembled against his cabinet, Mr. Henderson tore down the curtain of shame and swore to God and the angels that the rumor had no base in reality, that the American Embassy was hiding no one. He pretended to be offended even at the mention of the rumor. Then he brought up the matter of the safety of American citizens again and cunningly watched as his host's bashful face turned hot crimson.

Presently, the prime minister picked up the receiver of the black telephone beside his chair and began to speak with his chief of police. Given the tone of Mossadegh's voice and the content of the part of the conversation he could make out, the ambassador assured himself, he had succeeded in his mission. His objective established, he rushed out to catch the next flight to Europe. He did not wish to stay in the country when the coup took place, so that just in case it failed he could palm off his innocence.

As a result of that telephone call, though, the Eshratabad Garrison was unleashed like a pack of mad dogs to attack with rifle butts and bayonets the demonstrators supporting Doctor M.

Back in the basement of the American Embassy, Mr. Roosevelt was averse to divulge his whole plan to everyone involved. If his special training and long experience in covert operations had taught him anything, it was the importance of keeping all operatives ignorant of each other's missions and of imparting information on an as-needed basis. His confidence was detectable in his whistling of "Luck Be a Lady Tonight," which had become the theme song for the operation. He stared at the map and whistled the entire piece without interruption. We'll-let-Mossey-take-care-of-that-problem-for-us seemed both a sufficient answer and a succinct one, as close to truth as any answer could be under the circumstances. And he was right. General Zahedi, a subscriber to the same principle, did not show further curiosity in the matter, and let it drop at that, for a long day was ahead of him.

Sixty-Seven

The plot congealed on Wednesday morning, August 19. It was the third day following the Shah's flight, the city was left in a state of prolonged anxiety. The shops had pulled down their sliding corrugated iron gates, and Tehran looked not unlike a ghost town. Government agencies and offices were shut, as if in protest, and even gas stations were without attendants. There was not a soul anywhere to be seen. The streets were suspiciously empty and silent; a silence that within itself carried a tumultuous promise.

At eleven, a mob began to veer its way northward, roaring itself into lather. At the helm were shadowy characters with names like Golaum Nafti the Kerosene Seller, Ramezoon Yakhi the Ice Seller, Asghar Gauvkosh the Cow Killer and such. They led an assortment of mercenaries armed with switchblades and brass knuckles, prostitutes in chadors, pimps in squash-heeled shoes, and *Zoorkhaneh* giants with sticks and clubs.

In the meantime, out of Eshratabad Garrison came a surly M4 Sherman tank, its caterpillar tracks plowing the sun-softened asphalt. Crawling on top of the tank were a number of General Z devotees and loyal subordinates, some in undershirts and baggy pants, unshaven, raging. Wielding World War II Mausers and pronged clubs they joined the rally and replaced Nafti-Yakhi-Gauvkosh at the front, leading the club-wielding mob to its final destination, shouting "Long live the Shah" and "Death to Mossadegh." The tank also carried images of His Imperial Majesty, who had fled to Rome in order to be able to wash his hands of the mess in case the coup attempt backfired—a precautionary underestimation. Not once did the mob encounter a serious challenge by Mossadegh followers, the National Front supporters, the Tudeh members. They were all presently sitting at home waiting and waiting to be called into action by their defeatist leaders, who had chosen at this particular moment to stand outside history and observe their hero crumble under the forces of reaction. Somewhere along the way, the tank stopped and a photographer snapped a picture of the history makers. The voices of the protesters merged and grew stronger, mixing religious hymns with chants of "Long Live the Shah."

At noon, the mob burgeoned; it moved cantankerously on account of growing in size and vehemence. As it attracted the unemployed, the disaffected, the old chadori women excited by having something to do, the idle illiterate peasants brought to the city by busloads to protect the sanctity of the monarchy, the adventurous construction workers long snubbed by the clean-cut bureaucrats and government employees, it whipped itself into an anti-Mossadegh frenzy. The instigators of the mayhem, the bazaar *lutis*, became bolder as the crowd ballooned. They allowed increasingly more misbehavior among the ranks, intimidating the passersby into joining the crowd or attacking anyone on the sidewalk wearing glasses.

It was two o'clock, and the sun was at its most cruel, shooting arrows of fire down at the throng amassing in front of Mossadegh's residence. By Doctor M's estimation there were enough of them—almost two thousand—to make him feel disheartened, not to mention defeated. At this time, precisely at the moment all resolve had left him, on the other side of town, General Z put on his battledress and crawled out of his darkened hole, rushing to the limelight to claim his long-awaited victory. He arrived at the scene of his wickedness and stood on top of the tank, looked at his watch, and waved his shiny black riding crop uncontrollably. High on power, he dared Mossadegh, history, and the nation to stop him now. After less than twenty minutes of this, the word spread through the crowd that the prime minister had, in his striped pajamas, fled through the back of the building to his doom.

Sixty-Eight

That night there was a major celebration at the Officers Club, where the new cabinet formed as soon as the news of Mossadegh's disappearance was broadcast over the radio. Packed with conspirators of all shades, it rang with squalls of laughter and jubilant howls. From outside, the festive crackle of rifles could be heard. At one point Mr. Roosevelt rose to his feet and delivered an upbeat speech, which inspired the crowd's jubilant applause and hurray hurrays. He was then hugged and kissed by more sweaty men with bloodshot eyes than a cheap harlot. Much later he went on his merry way to become vice-president of one of the Seven Sisters with immense holdings in Iran, the Gulf Oil Company.

The army vehicle carrying Colonel Nemat on the back seat made a quick stop in front of the Officers Club to drop off its important passenger. At this point Colonel Nemat had yet to understand the reason for which he was summoned to the festivities. Under General Z's direct orders he had been picked up from his house in a Jeep and brought here to symbolize yet another wronged man's honor restored. The general, intoxicated with his success, slapped the colonel on the back upon seeing him and hugged him, as hugging had become the order of the day.

"Colonel, let me congratulate you on this fine day."

"General, it is I who should congratulate *you*," Colonel Nemat retorted, displaying he knew how to return a compliment. "You're the hope and the role model for our youth. Long live His Imperial Majesty."

"Long live His Imperial Majesty," the general responded. They drank their vodkas. Sweat was pouring down the general's face, his back and armpits drenched.

"Colonel, I'll be direct with you. The new cabinet is in need of a Minister of Information to oversee the rounding up and prosecution of communist infiltrators and traitors to the Shah. I'm not going to order you to fill the position if you're not ready for it, but .... I want you to think about it and get back to me first thing in the morning."

"Is that why I was brought out here, sir?"

"That is, Colonel."

"Sir, with all due respect, I have no *information*. My job has always been to carry messages for the army. I don't see myself—"

"Nonsense, Colonel. Long live His Imperial Majesty."

"Long live His Imperial Majesty."

They gulped down their second shots. The general continued. "What is it? The alcohol has already impaired your judgment? The reason I want you for the job is not because you have professional experience."

"Sir?"

"I want you for your *personal* experience. I want someone with a personal ax to grind."

"I don't understand, sir."

"You don't have to, Colonel."

"But, with all due respect, sir, you said it's not an order—"

"Ah, don't be a shit; report to me first thing in the morning."

Colonel Nemat began his job immediately. Thousands of Mossadegh supporters and Tudeh sympathizers were rounded up within the next few months and treated to the cruelest bone-breaking, skull-smashing, muscle-ripping, fingernail-pulling, anal-raping tortures imaginable. The excuses for these tortures were, as always, matters of national security and the hypothetical public danger that the Tudeh sympathizers had come to symbolize. That and a wisdom according to which physical pain can produce the truth became the operating mode of the regime. In the capable hands of the wronged colonel from the Eshratabad Garrison, torture found a new definition for itself. Just as General Z had foreseen, the colonel proved an excellent choice for the job. Consequently, having demonstrated his devotion to the crown, he was included in the general's close circle of confidants—a highly sought-after inclusion. That's how His Imperial Majesty came back to reclaim his crown amid widespread arrests and detainment, praising the superb performance of both the general and the colonel. He then went to Saadabad Palace and had photographers take his picture squatting in prayer. The papers carried those pictures on the front pages of their morning and afternoon editions.

Suddenly, photography became a national hobby; it was certainly in tune with the spirit of the time. What are pictures, if not testaments to history, immortalizers of great men and their daring deeds? Dictators would go to any extreme to see their larger-than-life blowups all over towns and villages, at major throughways and intersections, the larger the better, affirming their aggrandized sense of themselves. After the coup, everyone claimed to have ridden on the Sherman to Mossadegh's house. General Z, now proudly substituting for Mossadegh as the prime minister, mounted a picture of the clunky tank on the wall of his office with the names of all those who were in the picture affixed to it. He became omnipotent, the ultimate definer of heroism, the Bestower of the Crown, the Liberator of the Motherland. His decrees were wired to the remotest posts, establishing the rules of the darkest military junta in the history of the nation. Moreover, he disposed to name the heroes of August 19 and naturally secured the top place for himself. His transformation was complete.

Sixty-Nine

In the second phase of this macabre regime, under Colonel Nemat's direction, orders went out for the arrest of those suspected of unpatriotic tendencies, anyone with a record of having criticized His Imperial Majesty. Fears of a massive reprisal enveloped the nation. Guns and revolvers, even hunting rifles, were slathered with grease, buried three feet underground in backyards all across the country. Many a home was looted in the middle of the night by the heavily armed soldiers, their rifles glinting in the dark. Many a door was kicked open, arms were twisted out of joints, bones cracking, to produce submission. Anyone with a personal enemy could effortlessly find himself pointed out, then beaten to a pulp, blood discharging from every orifice. Those suspected of supporting Mossadegh at some time or other were pulled into the street in their sleeping garb, beaten half-dead, and left in the gutter. Having surrendered a few days after his disappearance, in a noble move meant to shame his victorious enemies, Doctor M awaited his trial in jail, naively expecting it would be a just and fair one. His deputy premier and Foreign Minister, Hossein Fatemi, was summarily tried and executed by firing squad. The regime of junkyard dogs and Chaleh Maidan thugs was bent on teaching much needed lessons on loyalty to a few wayward intellectuals and their soft-brained followers. In the weeks that followed, an expansive Tudeh Party network within the army went belly up as officers were demoted, sentenced, or even executed.

The news had an unexpected, surreal aspect. It startled Sophie as thunder used to shock her father; her eyes wished to spring out of their sockets. She was keen on hiding or, better yet, escaping from under her skin. One day, in the dead of winter, Lily's voice came over the phone in short gasps. Bahman had been arrested. In the semitransparent pearl gray of the winter night, there had been an intense, successive pounding at the front door. Boom boom boom boom boom! Lily had been having a dream about being surrounded by ill children in a hospital. Boom boom boom boom boom, pangs of conscience and fists of little children on her temples. Boom boom boom boom boom, her frontal lobe imploding under the strikes, pressing inward like a squeezed lemon. Boom boom boom boom boom, her lids opening hesitantly, heart beating in her head—she was not in a hospital. Boom boom boom boom boom, she was home, and the front door was being forced out of its frame. Boom boom boom boom boom! Half awake, she put on her pajama top, and thought she saw shadows crawling from the walls, leaping to life in the murky yard.

Before long, a hand came out of the break in the clouds and grabbed her from behind. Before she could open her mouth in protest, she saw soldiers marching into the house from every entrance. Soldiers in full battle gear stormed in and began to smash things. Bam! Down went a china cabinet, sending thousands of tiny pieces of gleaming broken dishes scattering on the floor. Smash! A lamp flew into the air, hitting the wall and collapsing on a sofa. Whomp, Whomp! Bahman Tofiq's door was kicked in, and it fell with a heavy thwack. A pair of hands pulled a sack over Lily's head and tied her to the bed with clothesline, and she felt gruff hands grabbing her thighs under her gown; poor devices to muffle sound, gunnysacks. She heard pshaw-ing and pish-ing from the hall and a final thwack of a heavy blow against a soft target. She tried to struggle but that proved useless. Meanwhile, without a pause, she could hear the destruction going on in the background: Wham! Scrrrunchhh. Thud.

Marching, marching, soldiers marching …. They did not leave her until just before sunrise. It took her the rest of the morning to free herself, only to find the house in war-torn shape: furniture thrown into the yard, sofas and mirror-worked cushions gutted, walls and curtains poked with bayonets. Most important, there was no sign of Doctor Tofiq anywhere. Dropping the phone into its cradle, Lily left a powerless Sophie bracing herself, weeping.

Seventy

As the district attorney in Tehran's central court, Nozar Rouhani was finally recovering from a long bout with malaria when he met a young woman who would unsettle his life forever. He would remember the day, the hour; what he was wearing, what she smelled like. She had come to him over a dispute with a tenant of hers who refused to evacuate her townhouse. The very day that she stepped into his dusty office, he had awoken in the morning feeling refreshed and free, risen out of bed sensing the last residue of his long-lasting fever trickling out of his frail body. His hair, long neglected, had allowed a cowlick to form in the back and therefore had to be subdued with the aid of a hat. A complicated man, he wore simple but always clean and immaculately pressed suits. The only extravagant articles he allowed himself were a pair of gold cufflinks that gave him the aura of an old-money gentleman, which in truth he was not. When he had finished dressing up to report to work that morning, he'd been feeling ready to take on the world.

Despite having had five children with Golsha, he saw his life as an unfinished saga whose decisive chapters are yet to be written. Often having to work twelve hours a day, he had missed his children's growing up; they seemed alien to him, as though they were someone else's flesh and blood. And for what—a job that brought him no satisfaction? Increasingly there was evidence of the emerging system, following the coup of August 19, being rigged to benefit the new money. There had been too many rumors circulating in the pistachio orchards against the army for its excesses, against the Shah for his new found autocratic style and lack of regard for the law, and against the land-grabbing practices of the royal siblings that made the previous monarch, Reza Shah, look like a novice. These rumors were stifled in the bud, or the sources were identified and picked up at the last minute on the pretense of safeguarding national security, never to be heard from again. Justices and attorneys not connected to the arising elite could hardly help but notice that another justice system had been set up by the army, parallel to the official ministry, that dealt strictly with the pro-Mossadegh and Tudeh activists with whom Nozar had no personal affiliation, but for whom he expected nothing short of impartiality from the law.

That Nozar did not consider himself from an old-money family had a role in his decision not to support Mossadegh in his challenge against the Shah. In the years prior to the coup, he had been approached a number of times by colleagues who had joined with Mossadegh followers, but every time he flatly refused their offers. Neither was he of the new breed of intellectuals who had found themselves at home within the Tudeh ranks. Add to this a score of Nozar's close friends, even, who went so far as to introduce him to a member of the Central Committee of the Tudeh Communist Party. At one time in 1951, it seemed as though everyone Nozar knew on a personal level was a member of the pro-Moscow organization. There were not only lawyers and judges and doctors but the greengrocer from whom Golsha purchased her tomatoes and fenugreek, the bus-driver who took his children to school, the city garbage collectors, shopkeepers, engineers, and teachers. The whole world seemed to be overt or covert card-carrying members of that atheist party, all urging him in vain to knot his fate to theirs. Every time Nozar Rouhani turned them down, he imagined the credulity of his great ancestor who had unleashed enormous rage on the arrogant invaders of his home, his single-mindedness that had saved Damkan, until death took him out of circulation, wrapped him up and put him under an ancient pistachio tree for good.

Nozar refused to join the Tudeh, not out of ideological differences, for he was unsure that they mattered, but because he saw himself, vainly, as above politics. He was just not party material. Refusing to apply for membership became easier after the party was outlawed following an unsuccessful assassination attempt that put the Shah in the hospital, and the assassin (ironically, a photographer) six feet under; whereupon, for the first time ever, Nozar felt the consequences of terror in the society. Not unlike his father before him, Nozar considered himself a man of logic and ideas, a lawyer, and a bureaucrat trained to preserve the status quo through legal means, which included prosecuting those who violated the laws. And who was violating the laws most in the aftermath of Mossadegh's fall? The Tudeh Party had an answer: "The unholy alliance of the army, the new money, and the flesh-peddling community." With minor changes in the wording, Nozar tended to agree with them. And for that matter, he was now glad he had refrained from joining the organized opposition. For personal and selfish reasons, he congratulated himself for having made such a wise choice. Otherwise he would likely have wound up in undesirable circumstances, like the many who were lost and disappeared for months on end. These unfortunates, it was said, were locked up under the most merciless conditions. There were unofficial reports of innovative tortures being administered to the National Front sympathizers. Gang rapes, fingertip burning, leg breaking, and in one case force-feeding a live cat to a prisoner—piece by piece plucking its flesh with a pair of pliers and shoving it down the poor slob's gullet. All without officially disclosing the horror of the Zahedi-Nemat regime to the Justice Ministry, a body that should have, at least in Nozar's naive estimation, guaranteed due process of law. But even in the ministry, an unprecedented fear had spread, and the justices were respectfully reminded to keep their noses out of affairs of the state. Nozar Rouhani had his eyes set on a promotion up the proverbial ladder.

Therefore, he who had not thought twice about standing up to the occupying Russians suppressed his instincts.

Perhaps that was what stalled him at the midsection of the ladder. One would have supposed there was something in his life that would give him a degree of contentment. Nozar had moved up within the ranks of the ministry, and his name was mentioned periodically as a choice for the bench. But there had been a delay in the promotion, and he was tired of waiting. Furthermore, his domestic life was such that, at the end of the day, he did not look forward to going home, where there was not a soul to whom he could spout his uncertainties.

After a long period of rest, that morning he had the strength to see his life's shortcomings and still go to his job with relative habitual ease. He went to work whistling, disregarding the grayness of post-coup inertia, and sat behind his desk, which was covered by court subpoenas, police reports, and files of diverse content, all having waited there patiently for his return. Marital disputes, business disputes, neighborly disputes, spouse beatings, sibling murders, crimes of greed, crimes of passion, crimes of men against women, crimes of men against little boys, formal petitions, divorce petitions, petitions to annul former petitions, petitions to repeal former court decisions, and petitions to disinherit insubordinate offspring. The pile requiring his immediate attention was high enough to hide behind. He was working off that particular heap when the young woman entered his dismal office, pretending not to notice the dinginess of the walls or the dust on the crummy furniture while taking her seat in front of him.

"What can we do for you, ma'am?"

"Are you Mr. Rouhani?" she said, her voice fresh, in stark contrast to the archaic atmosphere of the building. He just had to emerge from behind his paperwork to see who had emitted that fine utterance, which reminded him of his first love and cool rains and patient afternoons all at the same time. She was fairer skinned than anyone Nozar knew, barely twenty-five, with mannerisms that could best be described as carefree. Wearing a green V-necked sweater over a black skirt, she appeared shaplier than she was, especially her cleavage, which enticed the austere bureaucrat beyond his vilest reveries. Staring at her lips mouthing a mundane story of a tenant-landlord dispute, he lost himself in the sea of the full-fleshed, dimpled beauty of the young woman, his head swimming in the smell of her freshly washed, short brown hair. For the first time in his marriage of a dozen years, Nozar Rouhani was recklessly given to indecent fantasies about a woman other than his wife.

This woman had been separated from her husband, who happened to occupy a high position at the moment and who, she suspected, was causing her hardship. She had not supposed him capable of revenge—he was not the vindictive type—but now that she had left him, her children in tow, he was trying everything under the sun to force her back. Where were she and the children staying for the time being? She was staying at her sister-in-law's but could clearly see his hand behind her tenants' refusal to vacate her house. Her by-now should have been ex-husband knew that she had no place to stay for an extended period except her own house at Shah Avenue. And he was denying her that to make her go back to him. How did she find him behind it?

"Who else could it be, Mr. Rouhani?" she asked by way of assuring him, slightly challenged. "You don't know me. I'm not an incompetent woman, and besides, it's not in my tenant's nature to stand up to me." Aglow with confidence, she came across as a woman who could move a mountain. Nozar Rouhani could not imagine anyone who would even dream of opposing her wish.

"He's a timid little fellow with three children, my tenant," she went on. "Not much meat on his bones, working at a petty government job. His wife is even less forcefull than he is. But come and see them now. They're talking of not evacuating the premises that legally belong to me. Not only that, but he's stopped paying his rent also. What's a woman to do, Mr. Rouhani, what?"

"Failing to pay rent is disingenuous," Nozar conceded. At this point his curiosity piqued. Who was her husband who could command such authority and fear? When she told him, his eyes widened—"The eminent Colonel Morteza Nemat?"

"Yes, the very and the same," came the reply. "But please do take my petition. There are two innocent children involved and myself who are counting on you. He's not as scary as people think he is. I know him; I lived with him for ten years—not an insignificant amount of time."

"Tell me …. Just out of curiosity …. Why *did* you leave your husband?"

Noticing that the district attorney's inquiry was not triggered out of professional concerns, she hesitated.

"Maybe I'll tell you, sometime, Mr. Rouhani." At this, he shuffled the papers on his desk to conceal that he was, unwittingly, intrigued beyond the limits he normally allowed himself.

He produced a Vacating Request form for her to fill out and drew up a formal petition on her behalf, which she then signed and dated. From the outset, she decided to trust this man and placed her fate completely in his hands. Elevated to the position of her legal advisor, as such, he advised her to submit a divorce petition as soon as possible, so that legally her husband could not have a hold on her anymore. That, too, was urgently signed and dated.

The months following Dr. Bahman Tofiq's arrest had not been without stress for Sophie. Counting, perhaps too sanguinely, on marrying the doctor and starting a new life under his roof, she had taken the gamble that now seemed to be cashing in on her bad luck. Overnight, her long hopes had flown with the winds, and she had nothing to fill their place; not with Dr. Tofiq having a life sentence stamped on his fate. Was it a freak occurrence that let these dark equations into her calculations? Or was it her destiny to be so miserable always? The response she received from within her would ferment, somewhere in the deep recess of her subconscious, to become the spindle around which she spun a gamut of explanations—it would become her leitmotif, the defining rhetoric of her existence.

"My luck of the draw; my very bad luck."

Amazing that with such a negative outlook she still commanded a duteous zeal for life. What else was she to do? Life, with all its crushing betrayals and despairing turning points, had to go on, if only to give rise to new hopes and optimism (if only to crush them on their own sweet turn). She was determined to pull her assets together and, at least, provide a decent enough living for her children. She still had a house, which she was fighting to get back, and with the income from her estate in Geellon and the small alimony Colonel Nemat would grant her, she could begin her independent life.

Seventy-One

In the following weeks, as she went in for further evidence-collecting interviews, Sophie began to feel a degree of security in Nozar's office, which helped her open up to the district attorney. She expected the full support of the law, she said, but failed to add she hoped to gain his personal sympathy as well. The district attorney's sad eyes touched Sophie's motherly instincts, and she felt somehow drawn to this bashful man. And who after one botched marriage still does not appreciate that sympathy, and even love, is like a wind instrument, it ought to have two ends? That's how Sophie began to see her position regarding the district attorney. As of yet she knew nothing of his personal life, whether he was married, had any children, his likes, dislikes. Inasmuch as she knew, he was a rational man with a boundless knowledge of the law, and above all he seemed more than willing to help. But the details started to trickle in the way details do, in moments of weakness when a man with huge responsibilities is just looking for a friend to unload. And these details did't seem too important, not the way he put them to her, the fact that he was a married man with children, and that he saw no future in that marriage.

So what if she accepted his lunch offers, offers to go see movies together, invitations for innocent afterwork strolls in the park, his offers for rides, a cup of tea, a decent heart-to-heart? Was the poor slob not pouring his heart out during those excursions? Was she not performing a service for the community by listening to his life story of an unrewarding career and children whom he regarded as aliens, and who regarded him as one in return? Was she not saving a sad man from drowning in his sorrows, giving him an ear to talk into, to ease his pains, to give him hope? Was it a crime that she offered the man a bit of her courage? If there is blame to distribute, should Nozar not be at least partially responsible for his share of the guilt? After all, was he not the one who initiated those rendezvous, which continued throughout the case's proceedings and continued even after he successfully evacuated her tenants? Was he not the one who bought her flowers for the occasion of her birthday in 1954 and 1955 and 1956? Was he not the one who pursued her tirelessly for three years and promised her he was going to divorce his wife soon, very soon? Did he not tell her that his wife meant nothing to him, that she was a watchdog—"to look after my children"—in a house he would soon get rid of? Was he not the one who, when she occasionally declined his offers, stalked her, with one good leg and a bad one, limping in the shadows after her, a man of his stature? Did he not call on her numerous times to make sure she had not been seeing someone else? Was he not the one who threw caution to the wind in 1956, at last overcoming his insecurity, and professed his love—yes, love—to her, and promised to take care of her for the rest of his life and beyond? Could he not legally marry her without divorcing his first wife, since the laws against polygamy had not yet been written into the civil codes and would not go into effect until 1961? Why not put some of the blame on him?

And what was she supposed to do?

"My luck of the draw," she was fond of saying. "My very bad luck."

With her husband's death in 1955 (finally, the anguish of losing his family catching up with him) were people not spreading untruthful stories behind her back? Where from came the canard that she had been selling her body to support her children? To the ladies at the Officers Club who inquired about the colonel's wife, had not her sister-in-law said, "It's not like she has a job or anything"? Why were people so wicked? Did Sophie's sister-in-law not know very well that for one, she had a house of her own; that for two, she had an income from her Geellon property; that for three, Colonel Nemat had made good on his financial responsibilities as a father while he was alive and had willed his pension, upon his death, to go to his estranged wife? Was she not privy to all that? And the ladies at the Officers Club, they had to chime in with their two pennies' worth, didn't they? Where was the sense of justice and fairness in all this? Did they not care that, perhaps, they were pushing her toward making an unwise decision?

"My luck of the draw; my very bad luck."

At twenty-eight, Sophie found white strands in her hair as it dawned on her that the world she lived in was unkind to single women who chose not to marry. She was tired of women's heartless judgments, men's lewd comments, and the future's foggy outlook. On the eve of the first anniversary of her husband's death, she was tired of fighting with the world. With Dr. Tofiq still behind bars, Sophie saw no end to her loneliness and misery. Reluctantly, she had come to the conclusion that, to stop the rumors, she had to remarry. It was not a pleasant admission on her part, but this much was certain, without having the shadow of a man above her head, the gossip would never cease on its own. However, one look at the pool of her suitors was enough to make anyone sad. She loved none of the men who fervently pursued her, her sole love remaining the imprisoned Bahman Tofiq.

It so happened that only one out of that lot stood a neck and shoulder above the rest, and what was going to stop her from marrying the man who would later become Farzin's father? Helpless Sophie, Sophie of dreams betrayed, Sophie of immaterialized hopes.

After all she *did* resist Nozar for three years. The day Nozar Rouhani ascended to the bench he was so happy that he proposed to her for the umpteenth time, and she just could not help making his day complete. When she finally agreed to marry him, of course, there were conditions, prenuptials—the works. At the top of her list was her stern emphasis on his need to divorce the other woman, to which he swore, "I will; I promise you I will."

They married a fortnight before the New Year, Noeruze of 1957. Just before the brief ceremony at the notary public's office, Nozar bought a house with a full view of Damauvand pasted to its northern horizon. She had seen it and fallen in love with it. If she was not meant to have love in her life, at least her children could enjoy a semblance of comfort. Then, there was no excuse to delay; what do we say, Marry in haste; repent at leisure? Of Sophie's friends, no one bothered to show for the occasion. Of the Rouhanis only Nozar's brothers, Pirooz and Oscar, attended, but even they disappeared soon thereafter.

Seventy-Two

It was obvious that in the rift between Nozar and Golsha, the entire Rouhani clan had sided with her, the innocent victim of an indecent arrangement. Golsha beat herself night and day—the common lot of co-wives—ululating all over the place and beyond. For the magnitude of the pain bestowed on her, the clan was not to forgive him or ever to call on him again.

Nevertheless, those were the happiest two weeks of his life. He could count a number of reasons for his happiness, namely, achieving at least two of his goals in life: obtaining a seat on the bench and marrying the most beautiful woman he had ever laid eyes upon. For that he was grateful and resolved to keep his promises to Sophie. Little did he know that his happiness was to be short-lived, and that his second bride would hit the roof on the first day of the New Year, at exactly 2:17 p.m.

Here's how it went. Nozar is recuperating from a common case of honeymoon burnout. He is possibly kicking himself for having overworked his member, now sore pink. With his one bad leg, he is playfully and contentedly tending his garden in the backyard of his new house. Sophie is in the kitchen in a state of seminakedness, brewing her husband's afternoon tea. The radio, tuned in to the government-controlled station, the only station on the dial, is on the kitchen table next to the steaming copper samovar with a pompous air, demanding attention .... The news program begins at two o'clock. The announcer is welcoming his compatriots into the New Year and wishes everyone a happy, prosperous one. His voice comes crisply .... At the top of the news is an announcement. There are 367 prisoners to be freed as a gesture of goodwill by His Imperial Majesty, the undisputed leader of the coup regime. Sophie pauses; the steam from the samovar makes generous gestures of its own before vanishing. She holds her breath; she turns up the volume. She stares at the radio as though it's something to be feared and becomes a statue of tender nerves. The announcer is taking his time, making certain his voice maintains an even pitch throughout the alphabetically arranged list. She feels the muscles in her legs stiffening, the acid in her stomach forming puddles of fire. "Taraghi, Tavaunau, Tohid …." Sophie feels her lungs freeze like organs of ice. The next name is thrown at her mercilessly. Tofiq.

Bahman Tofiq's name crashes in the middle of her forehead. A pain sharp as an icepick pierces her skull. She cannot trust her ears. There is only one phrase on her lips; if we pay close attention we can hear it:

"—My luck of the draw; my very bad luck."

Seventy-Three

March 21, 1957, the first day of the year in the Persian calendar, marked a turning point in Nozar and Sophie's relationship. Nozar was to discover what Colonel Nemat had learned half a dozen years ago, that Sophie was an unhappy soul and there wasn't much anyone could do about it. That with the smallest provocation, there was hell to pay. Unleashing a barrage of cursing, she showed him plenty of what she felt about her marriage. And there was highly charged talk—of divorce, threats, suicide, running away; outrageous threats to be sure—until a fetus that would become Farzin announced its presence in her womb by blocking her monthly flow. When Sophie missed it the first time, every bird and mammal within a half mile radius of their unhappy house knew better than to show its rear. In a scenario repeated from her previous marriage, flying china and dancing glasses charged the air even before little Farzin was born. The slamming of doors and hysterical screams were heard throughout the neighborhood, until it dawned on Sophie there was no escaping her fate. "My luck of the draw; my very bad luck" became a self-fulfilling prophecy, the mantra that continued to pass her lips. From then on, she made a silent vow to make life hell for both Nozar and herself, and when Farzin was born, for the three of them. Meanwhile, Nozar Rouhani's shunning by his family outlasted his happiness. He felt like the loneliest man in the world all over again, decent but bitter. What to do with a second wife who had brought more misery to his life than the first one? That was probably when he unilaterally reneged on his promise to Sophie and decided against all rules of decency not to divorce Golsha.

The marriage of Nozar Rouhani and his second wife, Sophie, formerly known as Sophie Nemat, now became a tempestuous business, filled with violent fights, morning, noon, evening, with such metronomic regularity, the neighborhood stray dogs knew exactly what time of day to avoid their alley. Farzin often wondered why he had not gotten used to their violence over the years. To be sure, the circumstances of the fights differed from time to time in temperament, the frequency and pitch of her screams, the low tone of resignation with which she denounced her destiny. When Farzin was little, he used to get caught up in her moods like his father did, but as he grew older he learned to deal with them. He devised his own technique to block her anger from poisoning him. He ignored her completely, or left the house to put a comfortable distance between himself and his neurotic mother.

In response to Brother Hamid's question, What had he been doing in the streets, on June 20? he now had prepared the background for the answer. That morning they'd gone at it again, his parents, the mother of all fights, which had driven him out of the house. He was dodging the verbal bullets, a mere self-preservation tactic—*survival of the keenest.*

On June 20, he went to seek refuge in the arms of his lover, a refuge he badly needed but that didn't come about. He was casually walking southward on the pavements, hands in pockets. Coming to a newsstand, he stopped to scan the headlines. His interest in the news was as casual as his stroll in the heat. He did not intend to make a purchase. The contempt with which the newsstand owner stared at him indicated he was on to him. The man had but a threadbare undershirt on his back. Lumpy, blue veins streaked his thin arms.

There was a row of magazines staggered to the right of the stand. The fanciest of all was *Zan-e Rouz,* a women's magazine that reminded Farzin of the simpler days of his childhood. His mother subscribed to Zan-e Rouz for a long time, which was another source of turbulence at home. A quasi-feminist weekly, it contained articles on women who took lovers and a series entitled "At the Junction." These long pieces often had a protagonist who somehow complicated her life by giving in to passion; then readers were asked to advise her what to do. It was these stories that drove Nozar around the bend. The Rouhanis often pitched into each other as a general rule, the least important of all reasons being the coyly feminist publication with its sleazy stories. Hence, Sophie gave up her subscription in a dramatic bout of martyr syndrome, just so she could feel better about herself.

The fact that giving up her magazine did not discourage their fights made Farzin wonder, since the age of eleven, if, perversely, his parents cherished these bouts, which got progressively worse as they advanced in years. After all, their quarreling earlier on the day of his arrest was a small piece of an ongoing argument spanning the 25-year marriage, it had endured despite physical bullying, shameful divorce threats, wicked schemes, and stupid plots. That's why Farzin had to get out of the house at ten, even though his date with Bijan was not until noon. While on the subject, on the very same day Farzin wondered if his parents did not fight with each other for the sake of breaking the yawning silence that was even less bearable. It was not even a fight anymore, just a slow scraping of the soul, a gnawing of the nerves that drove Farzin mad with the desire to flee. At any rate, he was glad to be out of the house.

SEVENTY-FOUR

In the middle of the afternoon, the speakers at the Office to Combat Vices were turned on to carry an announcement. "The following individual should prepare for an investigative hearing."

Then his name was mentioned, spoken plainly and out of rage, Farzin Rouhani. He raised his head from his papers and looked in Mohammad's direction.

"Hey, *baba*," said the Marlboro Man. "Can't be that bad. Keep up your spirit." Farzin heard the words, swimming in empathy, but they did not register. Things certainly could not have been any worse. *Keep up what spirit?* An image of Jamal with his tea-making accoutrements flashed through his mind. Listlessly, Farzin put on his shoes. There were voices rising all around him, which he blocked with his own mélange of thoughts.

Hold on to tomorrow, who knows about spirit? Can't be bad. Who said it's bad? What does he know about how it is? What's in the air besides the heat? There's the door, and the pile of foot odor guarding it.

Brother Hamid, in his Revolutionary Guard uniform, was waiting for him outside. His boots reflected the light from the windows and sounded crisp against the floor. He lifted the logbook from the duty officer's desk and signed his name under the receiver column. "Follow me," he ordered sternly.

On the way down the white-marbled steps Brother Hamid was smoking. Throwing sideways glances at Farzin, he resisted the urge to say what had been on his mind all along that morning. A wish to show empathy craved to be expressed and Brother Hamid went to extremes to subdue it, the whole while thinking, *Something, anything, is better than silence.* His sense of duty shut him up, except when he looked at the bundle of paper Farzin carried under his arm.

"I see you've got more stories. What is it this time, flying carpets?" His sense of humor seemed out of place, even to Brother Hamid.

One more flight of steps.

Down in the basement of the Palace, in a wide area the size of a basketball court, there were four desks on four sides facing the center. Behind each desk sat a bearded man, shirt buttoned up, with not a hint of a smile or an air of casualness on his visage. Small men, these were, quietly laboring on the nuts and bolts of the grand faith; instruments of justice, solemn and dry as blocks of wood. They sat there playing with their Mohammad-beads and their there-is-no-God-except-Allah beads, twisting and turning, tumbling and spinning. In front of each desk was a rickety chair, of which two were occupied at the moment by male inmates. One was empty and on the fourth sat a female inmate clad in an unsteady chador. Black mane, locked in a constant battle, challenging the forces of shame to peek out. From her appearance, the woman had been flogged. As Farzin and Brother Hamid descended the stairs and passed the guards, the lash marks on her back called for their attention; black lines from her shoulders to the soft curve of her calves. Her inquisitor was calmly sifting through a manila folder. The other two officers were questioning their subjects loudly and with ire. The prisoners were silent while obscene insults and wads of spit were hurled at them; voices echoed across the vault.

Brother Hamid guided his charge by the sleeve to the desk with an empty chair in front of it. Farzin filled the chair quietly and greeted the bearded man behind the desk with a nod, while Brother Hamid located another chair by the wall, pulled it up, and sat down. The interrogator pretended to be busy reading a report out of a file that was open on his desk, did not even return Farzin's greeting. Sheets of reports were strewn across his desk. Farzin even recognized his own handwriting on some of them.

"This is Brother Daudyaur," Hamid said. "State your name and address."

"Farzin Rouhani, number 87 Vozarau Street, Tehran."

Brother Daudyaur's thinning hair receded on two sides of his forehead, leaving a peninsula of thin fuzz in the middle, combed upward just so. Patches of white on his brown temples and in his beard animated his dull facade. Finally, he raised his head and looked disdainfully at Farzin; Brother Hamid leaned over.

"Your case has been reviewed by Brother Daudyaur. Do you have anything else to add?"

Farzin offered him the stack of papers he had been carrying. Brother Hamid put the paper heap in front of Daudyaur, who looked at it casually and resumed his scornful stare. Out to the right, the voices of two men, arguing, rose above the clamor. A portly, bald examiner was yelling at the top of his lungs, while his subject sat defiantly on his chair. In a brief moment the man had reached over the desk and given his prisoner a backhander across the earlobe, the sound of which cut the air icily. A guard rushed forward, and the examiner whispered in his ear. Garbled whispers echoed against the walls. The guard raised the prisoner and escorted him behind the desk, where, Farzin noticed for the first time, there was a door.

As his eyes were getting used to the semidarkness of the basement, Farzin noticed there was a number tacked up on the door. And there were two other closed doors like the first one farther along the wall. A square cardboard sign, with numbers hand-lettered on it with a heavy black marker, was nailed to each one. Presently, the sound of lashing came from behind door number one, followed by a long shriek of pain. While Hamid shook his head a faint smile spread across Brother Daudyaur's thin lips as if to admire the effects the sounds were having on Farzin

Pointing at door number one, Brother Hamid cast a meaningful stare at Farzin and arched his eyebrows. As the lashing continued, the screams changed to loud moans. Brother Hamid kept silent for having run out of things to say. What he wanted to stop was already taking place, and there wasn't much he could do. Revolutionary justice he had fought and risked his life for was unfolding before him, and for the first time in his revolutionary career he was not enjoying it. The Palace somehow no longer seemed like an exalted place.

Brother Daudyaur, however, remained silent through the agony to give the moaning they were hearing time to register with Farzin. As far as he was concerned, everything in his environment was solid evidence of revolutionary justice working efficiently. Then the moaning too stopped. It was just the sound of leather now that could be heard smacking bare skin.

"Yours is a serious case," Daudyaur finally said, straightening the stack of papers in front of him. "My advice is not to take lightly the charges against you. Attempts to instigate rebellion and sedition are high treason, punishable severely by our law. Do you understand what I'm saying to you?"

Farzin gave a nod. With all the free advice he had been receiving, he felt like a rich fool.

"*Ahsant,* bravo," said Brother Daudyaur. "You can lose your head easily for this one. However, Brother Hamid, who's been conducting investigations regarding your case, and who's written an extensive report on your character, is convinced that you're totally reformed. He has assured me you are ready for a full-fledged confession and a first rate repentance. *Ahsant* to both of you."

Brother Hamid turned his head away from Farzin and said nothing. Brother Daudyaur went on. "I will take that into consideration. Well done. Our faith is one of peace and forgiveness. And kindness. I have the authority to propose a light sentence—"

The woman with the lash marks on her back stood up and went ahead of her officer up the stairs and out of sight. It took the physical motion of the woman and her officer for Farzin to notice that the flogging had stopped. Only then did Brother Hamid let out a deep sigh and lean back in his chair. Daudyaur was perturbed. Ignoring the disruption, he resumed.

"The Agha has recommended leniency on your behalf, providing that you show goodwill and make a clean breast of it. This is where your stories are concerned—"

"I've told everything I know—" Farzin managed, unwisely, to blurt before Brother Hamid interrupted him with his own assertion.

"I've already informed the prisoner that it's all irrelevant, Brother Daudyaur. There is not a single useful thread in the whole darn thing." He was prepared to go on, but Daudyaur stopped him with an intense gaze. He then turned to Farzin.

"Listen to me; we deal only with facts here. Your reports, as extensive as they are, contain very little of them. Besides, they don't tell us what you were doing in the middle of an antigovernment rally." Daudyaur was a no-nonsense kind of a guy. He said, "What am I to make of the fact that, on the very same day, in the vicinity of where you were arrested, two of our Hezbollahi brothers were beaten to a pulp? You were right in the middle of the whole damn demonstration. How are we to interpret the proof, huh? The evidence against your goodwill is all over the place. Even now I'm not sure what you could tell us that would turn things around and disprove it."

"I think you'll find the answer to your question in the last installment of my report. Please, read it. It's all there."

Brother Daudyaur stared at Farzin with disbelief. He said, "If you weren't fortunate enough to have the Agha on your side, your fate would have been decided by the Evin officials, if you know what I mean. Not that anything un-Islamic is administered there, absolutely not. But it would have been tough, had you been sent there."

Even to Farzin it was obvious that Daudyaur, with his claptrap effected empathy, had failed to allege a specific crime. He appeared tough, noncompromising, in control, but appearances aside, he had failed. This was a good time for Farzin to ask for clarifications; in truth he *was* tempted to make some objections, but shame overtook his better judgment.

"I repent. I've confessed everything. If you read my reports, I've revealed everything I know. Beyond this I know nothing. But I do repent anything that you think I have done that I shouldn't have." Brother Daudyaur and Brother Hamid exchanged victorious glances.

"Nah," said Brother Daudyaur. "Your heart isn't in it." He seemed to be attempting one last bluff. "Come on. Who're you kidding?" He lit a cigarette and took a long drag. He was a master at knowing the perfect moment to say nothing. Time and silence were both on his side, and he used them like his words to crush the last vestiges of defiance in his subject.

"I don't think you really mean it. On the one hand you refute the charges of sedition, and on the other, you say you repent. Repent what? May I conclude that you finally accept the charges?"

"No, you may not, Brother." Heat rose in Farzin's ears. "No, no. I deny the big charges, but I said I repent anyway, because that seems to be what you want to hear from me in order *to believe me*. And please don't read more into it than what's intended."

Daudyaur, as the inquisitor, sat back patiently. He regarded Farzin with suspicion at first but soon, in that bubble of silence that shaped around them, uncertainty eased the knot in his brows. He stretched forward and stabbed his cigarette out in the ashtray, as his face lit up with a grin. He looked at Brother Hamid and raised his eyebrows, uttering, "*Ahsant*, bravo. To believe." He smiled like one graced with superior knowledge.

"He's finally catching on," Brother Hamid asserted, beside himself.

"To believe," Brother Daudyaur emphasized. Brother Hamid took his cue from Brother Daudyaur and repeated, "To believe."

"To believe," Brother Daudyaur reemphasized. "That's all that it boils down to, isn't it? Belief. Do I believe you now?" He lowered the corners of his mouth, shaking his head. "Can't say I do. Do I *want* to believe you?"

Farzin was lost in the game of semantics Hamid and Daudyaur were playing. They were agents of a belief system that claimed an order of logic he had yet to divine. With mouth slightly agape, he waited.

The inquisitor rose from his chair.

"You say you repent. Let's test your innocence, Brother Farzin." Grinding his teeth, he pretended to be mulling over an idea. He turned to Brother Hamid and said, "You may go back to your post. This fellow and I are going to really get acquainted with each other." Brother Hamid uttered the Lord's name under his breath and stood up. He shook hands with Brother Daudyaur and headed toward the stairs. At the foot of the staircase he turned around and, through watery orbs, watched Farzin walking toward door number two with Daudyaur one step behind him.

Door number two opened with a slight push of Brother Daudyaur's hairy hands, and first Farzin, then Daudyaur, entered a corridor barely the width of the two men. The corridor was a long, straight tube with cement walls echoing sounds coming from a room at its end, where they were heading, and where the slapping and beatings meshed with the cries of a man. An angry voice could be heard above all the other sounds and Farzin had a lasting notion. *Blood isn't just blood; it's more than blood. The gaudy unambiguity of blood, its thinness, has a certain remarkable character that gives life purpose, something extraordinary, indispensable, if not for this life, at any rate for the hereafter. It is so, because it emanates valor, transferring a sense of importance to things that otherwise seem trivial, vapid. More than that, blood interprets inscrutable events, examines souls, and tests innocence with its indisputable authority.*

Seventy-Five

Farzin grew up with a sense of reverence for heroes for exactly that reason: their blood. All boys are reared in that fashion in this part of the world. Heroes are men whose blood had been shed for the motherland or the holy faith. The phantom of the martyred grandson of Prophet Mohammed, Hossein—also the third Shiite Imam—who symbolizes the oppression of the meek in Shiite mythology, had always stuck in a sacred corner of his mind, separate from his darker secrets. It did not give him an identity, like it did to many other boys of his age and class, but it did give him a sense of reverence. And guilt. And shame. Above all, shame. And another thought: Hand in hand with blood goes martyrdom. The faithful follow Imam Hossein, emulating him in piety and courage. One follows his footsteps even though one knows one will never be quite as selfless and compassionate as he was. So what to do? Sacrifice one's self and become a martyr. One pays in blood; it's the only thing that washes away the sin committed: the sin of living. And what life required of a gay man, in a cruel land of shame and bloodletting, was to hide in layers, much like an onion. So, if anything, blood saves one. When one follows the chief of martyrs, he becomes eternal. Listen, *baba*: it's a PR gold mine, win or lose. You win either way: If you die, you will be expressed directly to heaven, to join the angels and naked houris. If you kill, on the other hand, you will survive as a hero, and you will be treated like one. Not a bad deal, ask anyone. This is promised in the Holy Book. Read it in the name of the Lord.

Seventy-Six

The door at the end of the narrow passage opened into a twenty-by-twenty poorly lit room. Led in by Brother Daudyaur, Farzin stepped inside with a sense of cold apprehension. The walls were bare, furniture scarce. Moments after entering the room, Farzin noticed a barely moving body that seemed like a young man tied to a wooden chair, his head numbed under a succession of blows, a stream of blood running down his nostrils. Farzin tried to appear innocuous. A tremendous bulk of muscle and sweat was standing by the young man, motionless, gently breathing and observing the newcomer. The first things noticeable about him were his hairy hands and knotty knuckles.

Brother Daudyaur carried himself as he would at home; ownership of the room and everybody and everything in it oozed out of him like the summer heat. He went over to a corner of the room, leaned against the wall, and looked at Farzin like he was trying to read his mind.

Everyone was quiet as Farzin stared at the beaten young man, *a bloodied youth, truly,* whom, with a little difficulty, Farzin came to recognize. Though he was gaunt and pale, his hair greasy and matted, Farzin recalled seeing him on the day of his arrest. In flashes of memory, he remembered the world slowing down the first time, interrupting his stroll to Bijan's, and the tall figure that had emerged from the crowd. No mistaking his bony structure and Adam's apple, this was the guy at the march who had carried the butchered woman off the scene à la Vivien Leigh in *Gone with the Wind*, now tied to a chair. Clothes torn, he seemed a good deal scrawnier. Farzin peered at the caked blood on his scalp, forehead, down one side of the neck, and tried to keep his lower lip from trembling. He stared longer than he should have.

"You know this guy?" Brother Daudyaur asked suspiciously.

"No. No, I don't."

Brother Daudyaur walked to the youth, grabbed his hair in a fist, and pulled his head back. "Look at this mess," said Brother Daudyaur, his eyes lifeless, as if he were disgusted by the sight of blood. The youth was unconscious.

"This animal," Brother Daudyaur began to explain, "was one of the organizers of an antigovernment rally. In fact, it was the same march you took part in. Remember?"

"I remember the day," said Farzin. "But I was part of no march. And I don't remember this guy either. You're trying to make a case by linking me to this—animal?"

Brother Daudyaur seemed to like the answer. He smiled bitterly.

"And you've never been a part of any opposition group or organization?"

"No. Absolutely not."

"Ever participated in a rally or march declared illegal by the government?"

"No, never. I have never."

"Ever been affiliated with or had friends associated with the enemies of Islam?"

"No," said Farzin.

"Tell me something. What is your opinion of the counterrevolutionary elements such as this worm?" Brother Daudyaur was pointing at the unconscious man with the two fingers holding the cigarette, which was now at its end. From the looks of it he could have been about to put it out on some part of the barely conscious youth.

"They are exactly that," said Farzin without a flinch. "Worms." And for good measure, he added, "They deserve everything that comes their way." He felt his knees quivering.

"Very well then," Brother Daudyaur said, walking backward to the far corner of the room, where Farzin now saw a frail brown desk with a cracked glass top. Without taking his eyes off his prisoners, Brother Daudyaur opened the desk drawer and produced a shiny, black handgun. "Do you know what this is?" he asked.

Farzin could only nod his head. The bulky man, who until now had not uttered a word, let out a grunt.

"Are you innocent?" Brother Daudyaur asked. "Haven't you committed any sins?"

"Well ... I wouldn't say that. I mean .... What *am* I supposed to say?"

"Say I repent for all the wrongs I've committed in my life. So help me God."

Farzin followed the order. "I repent for all the wrongs I've committed in my life."

"So help me God."

"So help me God."

"Take this," Brother Daudyaur commanded, thrusting the pistol in the air toward Farzin, handle first.

"See this scum? He won't repent. Waste him."

Farzin took the gun from Brother Daudyaur with pure dread. He did not expect the piece of iron to be so heavy. Cold and unfriendly, it felt unwieldy as it sat in his sweaty palm.

He looked at the bloodied youth and tried to process the order just given by Brother Daudyaur. His mind felt slow; he was not sure he understood. He nodded with his head, more than once, and was taken aback when he could not stop nodding. He looked about the room and found it darker than moments ago. Had he been drugged? He had not taken anything and did not recall seeing a needle administered to his flesh. He wondered if the other two knew what was going on with him, then remembered experiencing the same uncertainty before, the same inability to control his limbs. The room became blurry, and the two men seemed frozen in their shoes.

A gurgle of blood spewed from the youth's throat. "Ghaaaghaa ghurrrghaa." Farzin turned to him and wondered if the world was slowing down around him again. The young man was coming to; there was movement under his closed lids. Farzin examined the pistol in his right hand and lightly touched the trigger. It was solid steel, hard and heavy. Unyielding. *Am I able to pull it?* His eyes froze on the piece, then slid once again to the youth who was opening his lids tremulously, staring back at Farzin. Somewhere in the background he heard voices, as if coming from a well. "Waste him! NOW! Do it!" Brother Dauyaur was prodding him, his mouth issuing orders while the rest of him blended in the haze.

As Brother Daudyaur shouted his instructions, Farzin noticed his arm raising, and his hand placing the pistol between his own teeth. At that moment the dark background came alive and he saw two figures springing toward him, out of the dimness, in a nebulous arch. They seemed to be moving underwater, their voices garbled and distant. The single thought going through Farzin's mind was the farce in holding the phallic piece of steel in his mouth, ready to shoot its love load. He tapped the trigger gently with his finger, in a gesture of foreplay, before pulling it completely. Sluggishly, the shadows caught up with him but not before the crescendo that felt like a final release. In lieu of a searing bullet delivering him at last, the cold click of an empty chamber echoed in his mouth. And it clicked twice. Farzin felt the cold barrel against his palate, tasted the remnants of industrial lubricant on his tongue. Brother Daudyaur was by his side now, shouting profanity as he wrestled the firearm out of Farzin's clenched and moist fingers. He had regained his speed and normal dimensions once again.

Seventy-Seven

An interruption may be thought of as an event as much as a profound absence thereof. There always comes in the course of a human life, or of a nation's evolution in history, a moment at which an unexpected affair appears to derail the natural progression of the state of being. The greater the forces of the purported progression, the larger the impact of the interruption. Natural consequences of undesirable interruptions on a personal scale could be disappointment, indolence, and sadness, whereas the desirable ones may allow relief, jubilance, and zeal. The evolutionary process of survival of the fittest has endowed humans with effective emotional tools to cope with inevitable adverse interruptions that occur in their personal lives. In consoling each other, we have learned to undermine the significance of any interruption, or to belittle it into oblivion. Some stick their paws into the belly of an unwelcome interruption, in despair, and pull out its grisly innards in an attempt to transform it into a pleasing shape. Some balance it out against the past desired interruptions and compartmentalize it like a report card—such are the gifts of subliminal awareness; veiled, subtle, and constructive—in effect baptizing it into normalcy, the holy grail of the pragmatic mind.

On a national level, the consequences of uninvited interruptions are overt, ungraceful, and destructive, at least in the short run, until amnesia takes over the collective psyche and wipes out its memory. The ensuing reaction is as emotionally overpowering, messy, and unruly as the interrupting incident. In the final analysis, if there ever was a general pattern to decipher, it is the supremacy of the collective emotions to historic wisdom that reigns. At first, nations are thunderstruck and paralyzed, unbelieving of the unfolding conspiracies, blaming themselves and each other, the neighbors, that other who had always displayed a lack of common sense. Consequently and understandably, nations fold unto themselves and, for the longest time, lose all ability to probe the events leading up to an interruption in order to weigh in with the appropriate response.

The most common human reaction to an interruption is forming a judgment and fervently attaching a value to it. This urge to make judgments about any interruption is so strong, absolute, and overwhelming that it often takes a life of its own, roaming in the dark recesses of the interrupted (and insecure) nation's psyche. Befuddled and lackadaisical, with a film of ancient glories glazing over their eyes, nations stare into their pasts to find answers to present dilemmas and complex modern questions, while the thing that has taken the life of its own feeds off their anxieties. Often the search goes deep into the labyrinth of history to feed the monster's bottomless appetite, nurturing it, prodding it until the mesmerizing ghoul swallows the history of the nation in whole and foists its identity unto it, acting as its surrogate. From this point on, the deeds of the monster are seen as the actions of the nation, and the true character of a people is buried with its soul. The nation and the monster become one and the same, and the search ends there, its place taken by lackluster, monotonous, and long-winded sermons.

As Farzin was led through the double doors and then the main gate of the Palace, a faint smile appeared on his lips. At the gate, his name was crossed off a list; his belongings were handed to him in a brown paper bag. He looked at the bag carefully. *Enough paper there to record yet another yarn?* He stepped out into the world, once again a free man, well, at least as free as he had been before this whole mess of an interruption began. He was fully alive, glad that he wasn't going to be sent to the bughouse, thanks to Brother Hamid's winning ways with the Agha. Now all he had to mind was make his way homeward. He crossed the street before him and headed west, toward a popular short-cut into the city. As he approached the alley he wanted to take he noticed it had been sealed off for construction. Once again, Farzin was heading off in a fresh direction.

Birds sat on the wires that dissected the urban sky, their droppings falling indiscriminately on everything. Tehran's byways certainly deserved more attention. They always did. Head tilted to one side, the bag under his arm, Farzin shoved his hands in his pockets and followed the trail of the wall. It was nighttime, patches of cotton staining the sky, stars shining, one here, one there. A cool breeze rushed through his hair. Autumn was underway.

THE END

Author's Note

Everyone was helpful in this endeavor. I would like to express my gratitude to all who read and commented on earlier versions of the manuscript, particularly Mastee Badii, Alexandra Alemi and Said Izadi. I am forever in debt to Ali, who's been above all an invaluable friend and a steadfast source of inspiration.

This is a purely fanciful yarn. Damkan, which does not exist, gets its name from the city of Daumghaun, which exists between the northern latitudes of 35 and 36 degrees, and between the eastern longitudes of 54 and 55 degrees. Other geographical names and towns referred to in this novel are real. Historical references and personalities are also real—insofar as they could be verified—however, immense liberties have been taken with them. The conversation between Loy Henderson and Mohammad Mossadegh is inspired by one as reported by Kermit Roosevelt. Fictitious characters are not real ones in disguise. As the inimitable Saadi once said, "A lie concocted for good is better than a truth that brings on strife."

The text of this book was set in Bembo, an old style serif typeface based on a face cut by Francesco Griffo, first used in 1495 in the setting of a short text, entitled De Aetna, about a journey to Mount Aetna written by Italian Cardinal Pietro Bembo. The typeface Bembo we see today is a revived version designed by Stanley Morison in 1929, carefully redrawn to capture the spirit and intention of the original.